He wished he could do more for the boys...

But he'd failed them, and his nephew Miller wasn't the only one who would never forgive him for that.

Fortunately, the rest of his family didn't look at him the way Miller did. They didn't blame him, but he blamed himself.

"I'm glad we all agreed to meet tonight," Jake began.

Baker could have argued that he hadn't really agreed; he hadn't felt like he had much choice. But that had more to do with wanting to help the boys than his big brother's coercion.

His brother Ben voiced that thought when he said, "We all want to do what's best for the boys."

Baker glanced at his grandmother, expecting her to chime in with her usual comment that what was best for them was for all the family to be at the ranch. Heck, he expected her to take it even further and tell him that what was best for the boys was marrying Taye Cooper. But Sadie remained silent. And so very pale...

He cleared the emotion from his throat and asked Emily, who worked with the school psychologist, "Does she think that I should stay away from him?"

"No!" Emily said quickly. "She thinks that you might be the one person who can really reach him."

Dear Reader,

Welcome back to Willow Creek, Wyoming! At Ranch Haven, Sadie Haven has been basking in the recent success of her matchmaking scheme to pair off her grandsons with the women she's hired to help take care of her orphaned great grandsons.

Sadie just has one grandson left to match up: the youngest, firefighter/EMT Baker Haven. But Baker's determined to resist her efforts...despite how attractive he finds the ranch cook, Taye Cooper. Baker doesn't think he has anything to offer anyone but the guilt he feels over not being able to save his brother and sister-in-law after being the first on the scene of their accident. But in helping his young nephews, Baker just might find a way to help himself. Before he can share his epiphany with his family or Taye, he uncovers a secret he didn't know his grandmother had been keeping. And as everyone else learns the truth, the Haven family will never be the same.

Coming from a big family myself, I love writing about family relationships and dynamics. Sadie is very much a manifestation of the strong-women role models I had growing up in my mom and grandmother and aunts and older sisters.

I hope you've enjoyed reading about the Haven family and will continue following their adventures because the Bachelor Cowboys series doesn't end with Baker—there are four more stories to tell.

Happy reading!

Lisa Childs

HEARTWARMING

The Cowboy's Ranch Rescue

———

Lisa Childs

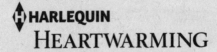

HARLEQUIN
HEARTWARMING

HARLEQUIN®
HEARTWARMING™

Recycling programs
for this product may
not exist in your area.

ISBN-13: 978-1-335-58478-6

The Cowboy's Ranch Rescue

Copyright © 2022 by Lisa Childs

For questions and comments about the quality of this book,
please contact us at CustomerService@Harlequin.com.

Harlequin Enterprises ULC
22 Adelaide St. West, 41st Floor
Toronto, Ontario M5H 4E3, Canada
www.Harlequin.com

Printed in U.S.A.

Ever since **Lisa Childs** read her first romance novel (a Harlequin story, of course) at age eleven, all she wanted was to be a romance writer. With over seventy novels published with Harlequin, Lisa is living her dream. She is an award-winning, bestselling romance author. She loves to hear from readers, who can contact her on Facebook or through her website, lisachilds.com.

Books by Lisa Childs

Harlequin Heartwarming

Bachelor Cowboys

A Rancher's Promise
The Cowboy's Unlikely Match
The Bronc Rider's Twin Surprise

Harlequin Romantic Suspense

Hotshot Heroes

Hotshot Hero Under Fire
Hotshot Hero on the Edge
Hotshot Heroes Under Threat

Love Inspired Cold Case

Buried Ranch Secrets

Visit the Author Profile page
at Harlequin.com for more titles.

For my editor, Katie Gowrie. It has been so much fun working with and learning from you!

CHAPTER ONE

As HE HAD so many times before, Baker Haven stepped out of the automatic doors of the Willow Creek Memorial Hospital emergency room. The late June sun burned brightly even as it began to slide from the sky, making him squint and reach for the brim of his hat. He pulled it lower over his eyes. It had to be the sun that was making him tear up. Not being here.

As a paramedic and firefighter, Baker was often at the hospital, so the place shouldn't upset him. And it probably wouldn't have if not for how it reminded him of the tragedy nearly four months ago, when he'd come here with his wounded nephews and the bodies of the two people he hadn't been able to save: his brother and sister-in-law. At least he'd kept their hearts beating so they could be donated.

Pain struck him, like it had then, and a slight gasp slipped past his lips. He looked around the parking lot and noticed that it was beginning to empty of vehicles. His oldest brother, Jake, was leaving with his wife and stepson, Caleb. Their nephew Ian was no doubt in their truck. He was the same age as five-year-old Caleb; the two boys were best friends as well as cousins. He spotted his brother Ben strapping the youngest of Baker's nephews into the car seat in Ben's Lincoln SUV. Ben's fiancée, Emily, sat in the front passenger seat. She was turned around, peering over at the toddler, Little Jake, as Ben buckled him up. The oldest of Baker's nephews, seven-year-old Miller, sat beside Little Jake. The three Haven brothers were orphans now. They'd lost their parents, Dale and Jenny, and while Baker and his brothers had tried to step in to help, nothing would ever be the same. Despite the tint on the back windows, Baker could feel Miller's glare as they drove away.

Leaving Baker alone in the lot.

He shouldn't have been surprised that his brothers had forgotten about him. When his pregnant sister-in-law, Melanie, had been rushed here, he'd ridden in the ambulance. They'd forgotten he would need a ride back to the ranch. That was how it had always been growing up. As the youngest of five boys, he'd often felt overlooked. While he was only a year younger than the twins, Dale and Dusty, they'd always been so close to each other that they'd paid him no attention. And his older brothers, Jake and Ben, had been too busy, one chasing his dream of running the family ranch someday and the other of running their hometown of Willow Creek, Wyoming. Even his mother had forgotten about him after their father died.

She'd taken off and left them, and while Baker's brothers had managed fine without her, he'd been so young and had needed her the most. But that was all for the best because Baker had learned early on to rely on no one but himself, to need no one but himself. He drew in a deep breath and raised his head. The firehouse wasn't far from the hospital; he could walk there and…

Do what?

He didn't want to ask any of his fellow firefighters to drive him nearly an hour away to the ranch so he could grab his truck. If they were on duty, they wouldn't be able to anyway. So he'd probably have to call an Uber.

He had to acknowledge then that the lot wasn't completely empty. Grandma's truck was there. But Baker knew that if he rode back with her, he'd regret it. With all his brothers coupled up now, she had only him to focus her matchmaking games on…him and the cook she'd hired for the ranch a few months ago: Taye Cooper.

His pulse quickened at just the thought of the golden-haired beauty. She was tall and curvy and had a smile that lit up her whole face—the whole room. But she had more than her physical attributes. She was smart and funny and…

His attraction to her only complicated the situation since there was no way they were ever getting together. While his other brothers had said the same—that they'd never get married—Baker sincerely meant it because he was the only one who had a *real* reason for never marrying. He wasn't just afraid of getting hurt himself; he was afraid of hurting—

"Looks like you need a ride," a woman remarked.

He recognized that husky voice, and his pulse quickened even more until it was racing. Or maybe that had more to do with what they'd all just been through—why they'd come to the hospital. How close Baker thought he'd come to letting down his family again, to not saving them.

But Melanie, his brother Dusty's wife, and their unborn babies were going to be fine. Baker couldn't take any of the credit for that, though. Dusty was waiting for Melanie to be discharged after her blood sugar and blood pressure were under control, so they might be here a while yet. While Melanie needed to be careful, she wasn't in danger of losing her life or her babies. Baker expelled a shaky sigh of relief over that.

"Are you okay?" Taye asked as she approached him. Her long legs made short work of the distance between them. Despite the warmth of the day and the sun, she wore jeans and a long-sleeve blouse, but her long gold hair was bound back in a thick braid. Unlike everyone else who'd been driving away from the hospital, she was walking up to it. But she'd been inside the waiting room earlier, so it wasn't as if she'd just arrived. She must have noticed him standing outside by himself and walked over from her parked vehicle to check on him.

His heart beat even harder with her consideration.

He knew not to take it personally; Taye just had a nurturing personality. She was always taking care of everyone and not just with her delicious cooking. She had an empathy and a wisdom far beyond her age, which had to be even younger than his twenty-eight.

Not that he'd spent that much time around her.

In fact he'd made it a point to stay away from the house, away from her, whenever he was at the ranch, which, unfortunately, had been a lot over the past few weeks. He'd been covering ranch duties for Jake while he'd been on his honeymoon and had continued helping out since he'd returned.

It'd been hard being at the ranch, being with the boys.

A hard jab of guilt struck him, and he felt dizzy for a moment.

"Baker, are you okay?" she asked again, and she reached out, just briefly, her hand sliding over his forearm, steadying him. But he jerked away from her as tension gripped him. Her face flushed with color while her pale blue eyes darkened.

He hadn't meant to hurt her feelings, but right now he couldn't deal with *his* feelings, especially not with his attraction to her. His throat thick with all the emotions assailing him, he could only nod in reply to her question. She, with all her intuition, could probably tell he was lying. He wasn't okay. He didn't think he ever would be okay.

"I'm sorry," she said. "I didn't mean to bother you. I just noticed you standing here while I was about to drive away, but you're probably waiting for your grandmother." She turned away from him then, and he was the one who reached for her, grasping her arm to stop her from leaving without him.

"No!" He really couldn't deal with Sadie's matchmaking right now. She'd had a winning streak lately, pairing up her grandsons. After Dale and Jenny's funeral, she'd hired Jake's ex, Katie O'Brien, to balance the ranch books, pushing them together. Then Ben had got with Emily Trent, who'd been hired as a nanny to the boys. Melanie had come to the ranch as a physical therapist to Miller, who'd sustained injuries in the crash—unbeknownst to all of them, she and Dusty were already married. And Grandma had also hired Taye… "If you don't mind, I really would like a ride back to the ranch." Although with as rude as he'd probably seemed to her, he wouldn't blame her if she rescinded her earlier offer.

She shrugged, which dislodged his hand from her arm. "Sure, I'm heading there anyway."

And suddenly he wasn't all that eager to return to the ranch. "You don't have to stop in town anywhere?" he asked.

Her brow furrowed, and she shook her head. "No, I don't. But... Did you want to stop somewhere?" she asked.

If he could go anywhere, he'd want it to be the past, back all those months ago when he had been the first one on the scene of that accident.

But he was already frozen there, unable to move beyond it, just like his nephews. Little Jake woke up with nightmares. While it seemed Ian had recovered from the concussion that affected his short-term memory, he still kept "forgetting" that his parents were dead. And Miller...

He was so angry.

Baker's brothers, all happily coupled up now, had moved beyond the crash that had taken their brother. But then they hadn't been there...not like Baker and the boys had been.

HE WAS STUCK...as if glued to that spot on the sidewalk outside the hospital. Taye would have reached for him again, but her pride still smarted from the way he'd jerked away from her just now. She'd only meant to comfort him because he'd looked so lost, so abandoned, standing outside alone while everyone else had driven off without him.

Her heart had ached for him. So much that she had to close her eyes for a moment in order to regroup. That was the problem with being empathetic, with feeling the emotions of others, especially when someone was hurting as much as Baker was: it was overwhelming.

His pain wasn't the only overwhelming thing about Baker Haven. His good looks were the other reason Taye needed to regroup, to shut out his handsome face for a moment. He had the classic chiseled features, rigid jaw, sharp cheekbones and those eyes… They weren't brown or green but an eerie topaz color. Closing her eyes for a moment didn't erase his image from her mind. It was burned there thanks to a firemen charity calendar he'd posed for that had been pinned up in the kitchen of the diner she used to work at.

It had been kept on his page all through January, February, March and the beginning of April, before she'd left the place. It might still be stuck on his page, which was July, even though it was June. But she hadn't been back to the diner since Sadie Haven had asked her to come work at the ranch. And she didn't want to look at the calendar.

She didn't really even want to look at the man himself, not when she could feel how much he was hurting, and she knew that she was helpless to comfort him. She hated feeling that way, hated the way he made her feel. What he reminded her of.

Not the calendar—though maybe that was why he'd jerked away from her, because he didn't want any more women flirting with him.

Taye could commiserate with him on being judged by appearance. She had never fit the standards for size and beauty, at least not her stepmother's standards. Fortunately the world was coming to appreciate that beauty came in all shapes and sizes and that true beauty came from within. She wasn't certain what Baker had inside him...except pain.

She drew in a breath and opened her eyes to focus on him again. While she couldn't help him, she could at least get him back to the ranch even though he certainly didn't seem in any hurry to get there. "Are you sure you don't want to wait for your grandmother?" she asked again.

He shuddered. "No!"

She knew why. And she forced herself to chuckle and tease him instead of taking offense. "Ah, that's right. You're the last bachelor cowboy standing. You must be afraid that she's going to focus all of her matchmaking energy on you now that all your brothers are paired up."

He tipped back his hat and stared down at her, which was an odd sensation for Taye. Not many people were taller than her, at least as much taller as the Haven men.

"Aren't *you* worried?" he asked.

She laughed at the thought of anyone—even Sadie Haven—manipulating her into doing what she didn't want to do. She'd learned at a young age how to handle people who wanted to make her into something she wasn't. "What? Because you and I are the last singles at the ranch? Don't worry," she told him. "I'm not expecting you to propose." And she certainly wouldn't accept if he did. Then she grinned as a thought occurred to her. "Although that would probably be the only way to get your grandmother off your back. Maybe we should stop off at a jeweler's and the church on our way back to the ranch. Get them to save a date for our wedding…"

She laughed again and turned to walk back to her car.

But she didn't hear any footsteps behind her. Either Baker still couldn't move away from his spot on the sidewalk, or she'd scared him too badly with her comments. She turned back and, sure enough, he was frozen in place, his long, lean body rigid with tension. She uttered a weary sigh and assured him, "I was just kidding. I'm not fishing for a ring."

She'd determined long ago to never get married, to never risk that kind of heartbreak, the kind her mother hadn't been able to survive.

"Seriously," she said. "You're going to be safe getting into the car with me. I'm not stopping anywhere but the ranch."

She was already getting a little edgy that everyone else had returned before her. Despite having eaten dinner earlier, they might be hungry again after the trip to town, and while she always had food prepared or left over for the ranch residents to eat, she liked to be the one who heated it up for them. That way she could make sure that everyone ate enough and that they all stayed healthy and happy.

She hadn't been doing a very good job of

that with Melanie, though, or they probably wouldn't have had to come here today. Taye hadn't been doing all she could to ensure that her pregnant friend's blood sugar didn't drop as low as it had. She would do better; she would find out from Melanie's mother what her favorite foods were and prepare all of them. But she needed to get back to the ranch to do that.

"I'm leaving now," she said. And she was sticking to that no matter how sad he looked standing there alone.

Footsteps echoed hers this time as she started across the lot again. And before she could reach for the handle of the driver's door of her compact SUV, another hand—a big hand—was on it, trying to pull it open. As Baker tugged on it, the car alarm sounded. She gasped at the noise and at his closeness, before clicking off her key fob.

"What are you doing?" she asked. With the way he'd reached around her to grab the door handle, she was caught between the vehicle and him. He stood so close to her that she could feel the heat from his body, and with every breath she drew in, she inhaled his unique scent, some rain-fresh aftershave mixed with hay and horses.

"I'm trying to open your door for you," he said.

"Why?" she asked with suspicion.

Men never opened doors for her; they believed—rightfully so—that she could open her own doors. They also never saw her as that super-feminine girl who needed their protection or help. And Taye preferred it that way, which was good since it was all she knew.

"Because my grandmother taught me to be a gentleman," he said.

She snorted. "If you did everything Sadie wanted you to do, we *would* be stopping at the jeweler's and the church on the way back to the ranch." She'd expected him to jump back then, like he'd jerked away from her touch earlier.

But he leaned just a little closer, so that she could see the glimmer in his topaz eyes when he remarked, "Maybe we should…"

She furrowed her brow. "Should…what?" she asked in confusion. She'd lost the thread of their conversation. He was so close. He was standing right in front of her, his arm still wrapped around her as he held on to the door handle. Her pulse had quickened until it was racing. And she wasn't just edgy to get back to the ranch. She was edgy to get away from him, or maybe to get closer...

She shook her head and with it, she tried shaking off all thoughts of where that would lead—to heartbreak for both of them. "What are you talking about?"

"Stopping at the jeweler's, at the church," he said, and then he leaned closer and added, "Maybe we should..."

"What are you doing?" she asked in shock, jerking back.

"Proposing..."

CHAPTER TWO

BAKER NEARLY CHUCKLED at the look of shock on Taye Cooper's beautiful face. Her lips parted with a soft gasp, and he was tempted to lean just a little closer and brush his mouth across hers. But before he could close that short distance, a voice called out.

"Baker! Baker!"

He suppressed a groan of regret and frustration. He'd heard his grandmother and Old Man Lemmon talking earlier when the doors to the hospital lobby had automatically opened for their exit. That was why he'd rushed after Taye because he hadn't wanted *them* to catch him.

But even though Grandma and Lem were closer to a hundred than fifty, they'd easily caught up with him. He braced himself before turning toward his grandmother and her... What was Old Man Lemmon to her?

They used to be enemies, or so Grandma

had claimed. But now they were friends. Maybe more…

He nearly grimaced at the thought of his grandmother's love life. Ben had set up the deputy mayor with their grandmother to give her a dose of her own matchmaking medicine with the hope that she'd be too busy to mess with their lives anymore. He should have realized how much Grandma was able to handle since she'd been taking care of all of them for so long. Ever since their dad had died and their mom had left shortly after. And then all by herself after Grandpa Jake had passed while Baker was still in high school.

Now when he focused on her, he noticed the slight stoop to her wide shoulders, the new lines in her face and the dark circles beneath her dark eyes. She'd always been tall and fierce and for as long as he could remember, her hair had been long and thick and white, like it was now. But she was beginning to show her eighty years more now than she ever had. Lemar "Lem" Lemmon looked the same as he had since as far back as Baker's memory went. Albeit the former mayor, current deputy to Ben, who was the mayor of Willow Creek, was a little neater looking now. His white beard was trimmed, his clothes more tailored and not as wrinkly as they used to be, but he still looked like a short, rotund, red-cheeked Santa Claus, which was the role he assumed every holiday season in the town square.

Lem was the one who'd called his name. But now that Baker had turned around, the old man looked nonplussed, as if he'd forgotten why he'd called out to him. Maybe he'd only been doing Sadie's bidding because she was the one who spoke now.

"Baker, I need you to drive my truck back to the ranch for me," she said. "I'm getting a ride with Lem."

He should have been relieved. His grandmother wasn't trying to manipulate him into driving her back, nor was he going to have to ride with Taye. But the last thought actually elicited a twinge of disappointment. He'd wanted to ride back with her.

But that was just because he wanted to clarify what he meant about proposing. He had no intention of marrying her. Or anyone else.

His proposition had been about something else, but he didn't get the chance to explain before Taye was opening her car door and muttering, "I better get back to the ranch, then." She jumped inside the small SUV and slammed her door. Without giving him a chance to say anything, she started the engine and reversed out of her parking spot, leaving him standing alone in the space with Lem and his grandmother.

Did she think he'd been serious? Was that how horrified she'd been at the thought of marrying him that she nearly peeled out of the lot in her haste to escape him?

Sadie handed him the keys to her truck. "Thanks, honey. And thank you for taking such good care of Melanie for us."

He shook his head, refusing to accept her appreciation. "I didn't do anything. She was never in any danger." At least not from her pregnancy, but his sister-in-law had collapsed in front of the open stall door of that wild bronco her husband had won in a bet and then shipped to the ranch. Melanie was lucky that thing hadn't trampled her to death. Baker had no doubt that if he had been lying there instead of Melanie, Midnight would have stomped all over him. The thing reared up whenever Baker was in the barn, which over the past few weeks had been quite often.

Baker wasn't as fascinated with that beast as the rest of his family was, especially Jake's stepson, Caleb. Baker didn't think it was beautiful or special, just very dangerous. But he did understand the feeling of being trapped, like that wild horse probably felt, being cooped up in the ranch barn.

He'd had enough of the ranch by the time he'd finished high school. He'd used the army as an excuse to leave. He could have gone off to college, but that wouldn't have been as much of a commitment as enlisting. Nor probably as much of an education. He'd learned to be a medic in the army, and he'd served as one during his deployments with them. But he hadn't learned enough to save his brother and sister-in-law.

"You still helped," his grandmother insisted. "And having you at the ranch is the greatest help of all."

A smile tugged at his lips at her blatant manipulation. She wanted him at the ranch. She wanted all of them living at the ranch. But after losing Dale and Jenny, and her son and husband before them, he couldn't really blame her for wanting to keep her family close. That was how she dealt with her loss.

He dealt by maintaining his distance. But that wasn't easy to do at the ranch. It wasn't easy to do with his family.

Or with Taye Cooper.

As close as he'd been to her moments ago, he'd wanted to be closer. And if he gave in to that longing, they were both going to get hurt. He hadn't been able to protect his nephews from the anguish of losing their parents, but he could protect Taye. He could stay away from her.

"WHAT WAS THAT ABOUT?" Lem asked, as he rushed ahead of Sadie to open the passenger door of his vintage Cadillac for her.

As if she couldn't open her own door…

She should have been irritated with him, but somehow she was charmed, which was unbelievable. Just like his question. She furrowed her brow. "I need Baker to bring my truck back to the ranch, so that you can drive me to that other ranch…" The one Dusty had just told her she could find her daughter-in-law at. When she'd gone in to check on Dusty and Melanie before leaving, he'd told her about the ranch and that he hoped to buy it. It was just an hour from Ranch Haven. Had Darlene been that close all this time? To her family? To her children?

That wasn't all that Dusty had told her; he'd shared what his father-in-law had told him earlier today, that Darlene had permanently retired from the rodeo to help raise her brother-in-law's kids. Had he been talking about Jessup? Was Sadie's other son still alive?

Her stomach fluttered with hope, but she stopped herself from going there, knowing where it had led before whenever she'd looked for her oldest son, who'd run away when he was a teenager. To disappointment.

And really, what would Darlene have been doing with Jessup? Jessup had left long before she'd married his younger brother; they'd never met. But apparently Michael had told her about Jessup and after Michael died, Darlene had gone looking for him.

How had she found him when Sadie had never been able?

"I'm not talking about you," Lem said as she eased into the big leather seat of his car. He closed the door on her before coming around to the driver's side. Once he slid behind the wheel, he elaborated, "I meant Baker and the Cooper girl. What was going on with them?"

"What do you mean?" she asked. "She was probably just giving him a ride back to the ranch since he rode in the ambulance."

Lem chuckled. "Really? That's all that was?"

"All what was?" Sadie asked. What had she missed?

"You didn't see how close they were standing to each other? How they were looking at each other?" Lem asked, and he sounded almost disappointed in her.

Usually she was more observant than he was, or she wouldn't have known the exact matches to pick for her grandsons. Well... Dusty had found Melanie on his own. He'd done so well that Sadie had decided maybe it was easier for her grandsons to arrive at the same conclusions she had without her involvement. They seemed to fight harder when they thought she was pushing. So she'd decided she would step back with Baker. Had that approach already begun to work?

"How were they looking at each other?" she asked curiously.

Lem looked across the console at her, and his blue eyes were unusually alert and intense, so much so that Sadie shivered. "Like that..."

Refusing to admit how that look had affected her, she played dumb and asked, "What?"

"Like you used to look at Big Jake," he said, referring to her husband. "And like how I used to look at Mary…"

She smiled at the mention of his wife; she'd been such a beautiful soul, inside and out. Sadie's late granddaughter-in-law, Jenny, had reminded her of Mary. She sighed. "I can't think about them right now…" And she wasn't referring to Baker and Taye. She was referring to her husband and how he'd betrayed her. And she couldn't help but think that she was betraying her friend Mary with the thoughts she'd recently been having about Lem.

But they were just friends. That was all they were. Despite their rivalry, that was all they had ever been. Even when they used to compete against each other and snipe at each other from the first day of kindergarten up until a few weeks ago, they'd still always been there for each other. And she hoped that they always would be. Because she had a feeling that she was going to need Lem if this latest search for her missing son led to where she feared it was going—to more than disappointment, to devastation…if she found out he was dead. Why else would Darlene have had to help raise his kids? Because he couldn't…

Sadie had already had more than enough of that kind of grief and loss in her lifetime.

WHY IN THE world would Baker Haven propose to her? He couldn't have been serious. He had to have just been joking, like she'd been kidding with him when she'd suggested making those stops in town. A joke: that was all his proposal was.

She laughed, but the sound echoed hollowly inside her SUV. She hadn't realized he even possessed a sense of humor. He always looked so serious and uptight and unhappy. Unlike his brothers, who joked around and laughed and smiled.

But his brothers had all found love.

She doubted that Baker would ever let himself fall in love. He was too uptight for that, too unhappy to reach for happiness. She'd once known someone else like that, someone whose unhappiness had destroyed her and had nearly destroyed Taye as well. She couldn't put herself through that again.

For anyone.

She'd opened herself up to the little Haven boys, but that was because she could identify with them, having survived her own tragedy when she was not yet an adult herself. She could relate to what the boys were feeling, and she could help them deal with it. She also knew that children were resilient, like she'd been. They could heal, like she had, and find happiness.

She wasn't sure that Baker could heal and find happiness. She wasn't even sure what was weighing so heavily on him. If not for that firemen calendar, she might have thought it was the recent tragedy—the loss of his brother and sister-in-law. While everyone else had been drooling over his body on the page of that calendar for months now, Taye had focused on his eyes instead. Those eerie topaz eyes and the depth of sadness in them. He'd been unhappy even before the accident.

Why?

She released a shaky breath now and tried to release her curiosity about Baker along with it. That curiosity was going to have to go unsatisfied for a couple of reasons. One: she doubted he would ever open up to her. And two: she wasn't even going to try.

He'd done a good job of avoiding her since she'd started working for his grandmother a little over three months ago, and she had no reason to think that would change. With Dusty returned from the rodeo and Ben spending more time at the ranch, Baker didn't have to come around as often as he had lately. He could focus on his job in town.

On being a firefighter and paramedic.

Somehow she didn't think those roles made him very happy. Or maybe he'd just looked sad in that calendar photo because he hadn't wanted to participate in the shoot. With the way his brothers teased him about it, she couldn't blame him. Between his brothers' quips and his grandmother's meddling in his dating life, it was no wonder he kept his distance from the main house while he'd been staying on the ranch these past few weeks.

But he hadn't avoided Sadie at the hospital. And instead of staying to help him out of a potentially sticky situation, Taye had taken off. She *had* to get back to the ranch. That was why she'd left as quickly as she had.

It wasn't as if he'd unsettled her with how close he'd been standing to her, with how intently he'd been staring at her...

With how he'd leaned just a little closer, as if he'd intended to kiss her.

At the thought of that, her heart did a little flippy thing in her chest. Of course, he hadn't really intended to kiss her any more than he'd really intended to propose.

She glanced into the rearview mirror, checking to see if he'd caught up with her yet. But she was driving fast, anxious to return to the ranch and make sure everyone had found enough to eat. And to talk to Juliet, Melanie's mother, about her favorite foods. She had to make sure she did everything she could to help the Havens.

And maybe, if she knew she'd done that, Taye could accept and finally let go of her regrets over not being able to help the person she'd loved most in the world...and lost.

CHAPTER THREE

RELUCTANT TO RETURN to the ranch, Baker drove slowly—so slowly that Grandma's truck probably wasn't used to operating in the lower gear and speed. For an octogenarian, Sadie Haven drove fast and confidently— the same way she'd plotted her matchmaking schemes to manipulate her family.

And she had reason for that confidence. Jake and Dusty were married, and Ben was as good as married. As soon as the boys were able to handle a separation from Ben's fiancée, who was also their teacher, they would be getting hitched.

Just like Taye had teased him about… He was the "last bachelor cowboy standing."

He shuddered, and his suddenly damp palms nearly slipped off the steering wheel. All of his brothers, except for Dale, had sworn to never get married. But Dale was gone now…along with his sweet Jenny.

Leaving their sons behind to mourn them and to blame Baker.

That was fine, though. He blamed himself, too. He should have done more, should have tried harder, and while he'd kept Dale's and Jenny's hearts beating until they'd made it to the hospital, he hadn't been able to do enough to save them.

Tears stung his eyes, but he quickly blinked them away to focus on his driving. He almost missed the turn onto the ranch driveway. It was more of a road than a driveway, and the ranch more of a small town than a ranch. There was so much work to do on it, so much that needed to be taken care of every day. How could Jake do it alone now that Dale was gone? He'd been the ranch foreman for over a decade while Jake was general manager. They'd run the family business together for years. With Jake having a wife and stepson, and maybe even a child on the way, he was about to get a lot busier.

He needed help. He needed Dale. But nobody could bring Dale back, and as his twin, Dusty, had pointed out, he couldn't be replaced either. Not in the hearts of his sons and not with his brothers.

Ever since their deaths, Baker had had an

achy, hollow feeling in his chest…where his heart was. He knew that ache well; he'd had it after his dad died and his mom took off and after Grandpa Jake had passed.

He'd had so many other losses while he'd served. So many other people he hadn't been able to save, just as he hadn't been able to save Dale and Jenny.

That ache intensified for a moment until the ranch building and pastures came into view, and then a calm settled over Baker. It wasn't peace. He doubted he would ever experience that again. But for some reason over the past few weeks, this place where he'd felt like he never fit in, where he'd never felt like he belonged, had brought a comfort he hadn't known since his mom had left.

Why here?

It made no sense. No more sense than Sadie trying to marry them all off for some reason. What did she think—that being coupled up would somehow erase their grief? He had to admit that his brothers seemed happier but then he'd caught them in quiet moments, seen tears in their eyes, and he knew that some memory of Dale had come back to them. Or maybe they'd been thinking about their dad or Grandpa Jake.

He had to blink again to clear his vision and focus on finding a spot to park Sadie's truck in the driveway crowded with vehicles. Taye's small SUV, empty now, was parked farther down the drive, as if she'd left a spot open for Sadie. Of course she would have; she was thoughtful like that, like getting up early to make Jake breakfast and pack his lunch before he went to work. She'd done the same for Ben when he'd been staying at the ranch while Jake was on his honeymoon.

She might have done the same for Baker if he'd stayed in the house, but that was impossible for him to do for a few reasons.

Three of them were his nephews.

Then he had another reason that was all his own. A reason he had no intention of sharing with anyone, though he suspected Dusty might have guessed.

Baker parked the truck and turned off the ignition, but before he reached for the handle, someone jerked open the door. Had Taye been waiting for him? His heart raced at the thought, but then his brother Jake leaned down and peered inside at him. And disappointment slowed his pulse.

"Why are you driving Grandma's truck?

Is she all right?" Jake asked, his voice gruff with concern.

And Baker felt dizzy with his own fear. He hadn't realized that might have been why she hadn't wanted to drive herself home, that she might not have been feeling well. While Melanie's blood pressure had been too low since her husband's reappearance at the ranch, Baker's grandmother's had been too high. Dusty had done something, said something, that had upset her. But surely he wouldn't have done that at the hospital…

"She—she asked me to drive it back because she's riding with Old Man Lemmon," he explained.

Jake expelled a sigh of relief.

But Baker wasn't relieved. It wasn't like his grandmother to let someone else take the driver's seat, so why hadn't she insisted on driving Lem back? And if they were coming to the ranch, where were they? Baker glanced anxiously down the driveway toward the street. He'd driven back as slowly as he could, and Lem didn't drive his classic Cadillac any more sedately than Sadie drove her truck. In fact, he drove faster. If they'd been heading here, the elderly couple should have passed him and beaten him back.

As a Willow Creek paramedic firefighter, even off duty he would have received a notice on his phone if there had been an accident. While the town was relatively small—although thanks to Ben's efforts ever-expanding—the Willow Creek fire department also served as backup for the entire county, which was far-reaching in this area of Wyoming. He pulled his cell from his pocket and glanced at the screen, just to make sure he hadn't missed the telltale chime of a notice. But he had no notifications.

Sadie and Lem had probably just stopped off somewhere, but it wouldn't have been to eat. Everyone seemed to prefer Taye's cooking to anyone else's. Baker did, too, even though he'd only eaten at the main house for mandatory parties and family dinners. When he stayed at the ranch, like he'd had to during Jake's honeymoon, he used the foreman cottage that was a good distance from the sprawling ranch house.

Grandma had kept adding on to the main house over the years. Even then she must have been planning to get them all to move back in and raise their families on the ranch. While that was happening for everyone else, it wasn't going to happen for Baker. Telling her that would just be a waste of breath because she figured he would eventually change his mind like his brothers had.

Should he try to beat her at her own game? It hadn't worked for Ben, but maybe that was because she'd been expecting *him* to try something. He was the one most like her. But Baker...

Could he pull off what he'd briefly considered in the hospital parking lot? What he'd intended to propose to Taye before Grandma and Lem had interrupted him? Taye was the one who'd actually given him the idea, but when he'd brought up proposing, she'd looked so horrified.

He chuckled as he remembered the expression on her beautiful face, the way her mouth had fallen open...the way he'd wanted to kiss her.

And he sucked in a breath.

"What's going on with you?" Jake asked. He'd nearly forgotten his brother was there.

"What do you mean?" Baker asked.

"Well, I could have sworn I just heard you laugh, and here I was worrying about you..."

He'd thought Jake had been waiting for their grandmother, but now he wondered if there was another reason Jake had been standing in the driveway. "Why were you worried?" Baker asked. "Afraid I might not find my way back after you all drove off and left me at the hospital?"

Jake's face flushed. "Yeah, sorry about that. With the boys chattering in the back seat I totally forgot that you'd ridden in the ambulance."

Baker shrugged off the apology and the hurt he'd felt that they'd all left him there.

"And I, maybe more than anyone else, want you to find your way back to the ranch," Jake said, and there was a strange solemnity in his voice and to his words, like he was talking about something other than Baker just getting a ride back from town. He stood so close to the open driver's door that Baker was trapped inside Grandma's truck.

Despite the heat of the late June day, a strange chill slithered down his spine. "Then step back so I can get out," he said.

"If I do that, I have a feeling you're going to beeline to your truck and rush off like you always do," Jake said.

His oldest brother knew him better than Baker had realized. But no one knew him as well as they thought they did.

"There's no reason for me to stick around

now," Baker pointed out. "Dusty's back to help you with the ranch—"

"No, he's not—"

"Well, he will be once Melanie is released from the hospital," Baker said. "And she's going to be fine, so they should be back soon." He glanced out the back window again, but he was still looking for Grandma and Lem.

Where would they have stopped? And why?

"Dusty's going to be busy with Melanie and getting ready for the twins," Jake said. "And with Midnight…"

Baker grimaced at the mention of the bronco. "Yeah, he never should have sent that bronco here to begin with. This ranch is about working cattle and horses—not rodeo stock."

Jake grinned.

Baker wasn't surprised that was how his big brother felt, too. Jake and Ben blamed the rodeo for their mother leaving. Because of Dusty's career as a rodeo rider, they'd always thought of him as reckless—the most like Darlene. But Baker didn't fault him for his career choice, which was no more dangerous than any of the jobs Baker had had, in the army or as a firefighting paramedic. Unlike his other brothers, Baker didn't think the rodeo was evil just because that was where their mother had gone after deserting them.

She'd returned to the life she'd loved before she'd gotten married, before she'd had children. She must have always loved that life more than she'd loved her sons. Maybe that was why Jake and Ben resented the rodeo so much. Why Jake wanted nothing to do with it on the ranch. Baker knew the institution wasn't to blame. If not the rodeo, Baker suspected their mother would have found some other reason to leave them.

"I don't have anything against raising rodeo stock," he insisted. While he didn't like Midnight, the bronco seemed to have more of a problem with him for some reason. "I just think it's smarter to focus on the cattle and the working horses—the things Ranch Haven is known and respected for raising."

"I agree," Jake said. "And I want to talk to you more about that, but there are a couple of other things we need to talk about, too. A few actually."

Baker's brow furrowed with confusion. "What? Did something happen?"

Jake nodded. "Yeah, it did. We didn't have a chance to talk about the boys meeting with that psychologist earlier today."

Baker groaned. "Let me guess… Someone's called another *family* meeting." He glanced at the sky where the sun was sliding even lower; it would disappear completely in just an hour or so. "It's a little late, don't you think?" And if he wanted to get back to his apartment in town, he needed to leave soon.

But he had wanted to talk to Taye tonight, to explain what his proposal had really been about—to get people to stop manipulating or pressuring him into making a real proposal.

"Yeah, it's a little late for the meeting," Jake agreed with a heavy sigh. "And a lot late for us to have gotten the boys this kind of help, the help they've probably needed most since the accident. But they'll be going to bed soon, so this is actually the best time to talk about them." He finally stepped back, giving Baker room to get out.

Just like Jake had said, Baker was tempted to run to his truck and speed away from the ranch. While he definitely wanted to help the boys, he suspected he could help them the most by staying away from them, by staying out of their lives. But before he could do anything other than step out of Sadie's truck, Lem's Cadillac headed down the drive, followed closely by Dusty's truck.

"This is perfect," Jake said when the others exited their vehicles. "Everybody's home."

Baker glanced at his grandmother, expecting her to be smiling a smug, self-satisfied smile. But instead her mouth was pulled into a frown, and she seemed even a little more stooped than she'd been, a little more tired, and her face was pale.

Concern gripped Baker. Was she not feeling well? But then she focused on him, and she stood a little straighter and forced a smile. And he had an uneasy feeling that she was now focusing solely on him, on carrying out the last phase of her scheme...on making sure that there were no Haven bachelors left.

A FAMILY MEETING...

Taye had once thought it was sweet that they'd included her in the meetings. Katie, Emily and Melanie had been included as well when they'd started working at the ranch, so it hadn't been awkward. But now as they were becoming real family, it was more bittersweet than sweet, especially because the Haven family meetings were the only ones in which she'd ever been included. There had been none with her mom and dad before the divorce, and even after she'd gone to live permanently with her dad and stepmom, she'd never been included, maybe because her stepmom had never really considered her family. Just an inconvenient reminder that her husband had had a life before her and her daughters. Her dad hadn't minded reminders of his new wife's life before him; he'd been more of a father to Taye's stepsisters than he'd ever been to her. He had attended their school events and beauty pageants while he'd always been too busy for Taye entirely.

Taye closed her eyes a moment, shutting out the memories and refusing to give in to any self-pity. Any *more* self-pity. But in that brief moment of blindness, she stumbled over a rock on the stretch of driveway between the ranch house and the business office in an old schoolhouse Sadie had had moved to the property years ago. Taye probably wouldn't have fallen, but before she could do more than stagger a step, someone gripped her arm and steadied her.

Baker.

He'd only touched her briefly before, back in the hospital parking lot, to stop her from leaving without him. Despite the brief contact, she recognized his touch, the size and strength of his hand wrapped around her forearm. And then the deep rumble of his voice as he whispered, "Are you all right?"

She nodded. "Yes, yes, fine." She opened her eyes and pulled her arm free of his grasp. "Just tired," she added, and it was true. "It's been a long day."

Baker nodded. "Too long for another meeting…"

She agreed, but she felt compelled to defend the reason for it being called. "But none of us really had a chance to discuss how the boys interacted with the school psychologist who came for dinner today." What felt like hours ago. No, it actually *had* been hours ago because the days were longer now that summer was here.

"Still, the meeting could have waited until tomorrow," Baker said. "Until Melanie had a chance to rest."

Taye glanced ahead of them to where the physical therapist walked hand in hand with her handsome, rodeo-riding husband. As close as Dusty and Melanie were now, it was hard to believe that they'd allowed misunderstandings and miscommunications to separate them for months. They looked good now; both of them glowed with happiness and with health.

She exhaled in relief. "Melanie is the one who insisted," she said with a smile and a flood of respect for her. "She heard about how upset Miller got when she was rushed to the hospital." Melanie and Miller had become particularly close in the months since Melanie had been working with him to regain mobility of his leg, which had been broken in the crash. She glanced back at Baker just in time to catch him flinch. Baker was the one the little boy had attacked when he'd been so distraught over Melanie having passed out.

"Yeah, that was my fault," Baker said with a heavy sigh.

Taye reached out and grasped his arm now. "No, it wasn't. You were trying to help Melanie."

"That's not what I meant…" But he trailed off before elaborating any more, just like he had in the parking lot. As if the same thing had occurred to him, he added, "Kind of like when I was talking about proposing to you earlier…"

She chuckled. "Were you afraid that I took you seriously? That I've been poring over bridal magazines since we talked?"

He snorted. "I think you prefer to pore over the stove," he said.

She felt a flash of longing to go back to the kitchen. Juliet had shared a few of Melanie's favorite dishes with her, and she wanted to check the pantry to make sure she had everything she needed. "I love what I do," she admitted. "You must, too." She glanced over at him, but his body was tense. "Being a paramedic, a firefighter..."

A slight shudder seemed to come over him, but it couldn't have been because it was cold. At least Taye didn't feel cold, standing as close as they were in the shadows of the night on that gravel drive. She hadn't realized they'd stopped walking until she noticed that everyone else had continued on toward the old schoolhouse.

They hadn't gone inside, though. His family, his entire family, stood on the steps of the schoolhouse's small porch and stared back at them. And a shudder passed through Taye now. "Uh-oh..." She could almost feel the speculation in them. "They're all watching us."

With the distance and the shadows between them, she couldn't see their expressions. But she could guess what they were thinking...

That she and Baker would be next.

Baker turned toward his family, too, but

instead of shuddering again, he chuckled. "That's what I wanted to talk to you about," he said. "What I wanted to propose…"

"What?"

"Tricking them into leaving us alone," he said.

"How?" she asked.

But before he could answer her, Jake called out, "Are you two coming? It's late and we need to get this meeting started."

"I think our little brother was about to get something else started," Ben said with a chuckle. "Grandma's going to be mad that you're messing with her scheme, Jake."

"The only thing I'm going to be mad about is losing my beauty sleep," Sadie spoke up from the shadows. "But this meeting is important, so let's all get inside now."

When everybody turned away from her and Baker, Taye relaxed. "That's good. They're going to focus on the boys and not us."

But Baker didn't look relieved. His brow creased as he stared after his grandmother. "She's up to something…" he muttered speculatively.

Taye chuckled. "She's always up to something," she agreed. Sadie had shared some of her schemes with Taye when Taye checked in on her before bed.

"Maybe it's time she wasn't the only one," Baker suggested in an almost ominous-sounding tone.

She shivered a little with concern that he intended to involve her in whatever he intended to get up to. When they reached the bottom of the steps, she stopped to ask him, "What are you talking about?"

"I'll explain later," he said, and his arm brushed hers as he passed her on the steps.

Even that slight contact affected her, made her more aware of him, and she'd already been too aware.

"We better get inside to that meeting now," he said, with what sounded like dread in his voice. His body was still tense as well. He obviously felt as uncomfortable about this family meeting as she did.

But he was family...

Taye would never be a Haven, no matter how much Sadie schemed or plotted.

CHAPTER FOUR

BAKER WOULD HAVE rather kept talking to Taye out in the dark than enter the business office for a family meeting. And it wasn't just because all of them turned toward him when he walked into the building.

That was the opposite of what usually happened. They usually ignored or forgot about him like they had at the hospital. That was why he might as well have been left out of this meeting like the little boys had been. If Miller didn't hate him so much, Baker would have rather played games with his nephews and Old Man Lemmon at the house than listen to his brothers and his grandmother make decisions without his input. It was probably too late for games, though, and not just for the boys who'd already gone to bed at this hour.

Weariness hung heavily on him, too, bowing his shoulders so that he felt a little like Grandma looked. A little older… He was getting older, probably too old to play the game he'd been tempted to with Taye's help. And he was too tired.

But he didn't sleep well even when he went to bed. So he might as well be here now; it was the least he could do for the boys. He wished he could do much more; he wished that he *had* done so much more. But he'd failed them, and Miller wasn't the only one who would never forgive him for that.

Fortunately, the rest of his family didn't look at him the way Miller did. They didn't blame him.

But he blamed himself.

"I'm glad we all agreed to meet tonight," Jake began.

Baker could have argued that he hadn't really agreed; he hadn't felt like he had much choice. But that had more to do with wanting to help the boys than his big brother's coercion.

Ben voiced that thought when he said, "We all want to do what's best for the boys."

Baker glanced at his grandmother, expecting her to chime in with her usual comment that what was best for them was for all the family to be at the ranch. Heck, he expected her to take it even further and tell him that what was best for the boys was his marrying

Taye Cooper. But Sadie remained silent. And so very pale…

Concern coursed through him, and he edged a little closer to his grandmother. Maybe he should check her blood pressure again. He'd been checking it more frequently since Dusty's return. As if he'd been adding to her stress.

Maybe it was just seeing him… Every time Baker looked at him, a twinge struck his heart. Dusty was Dale's identical twin in appearance. In personality… They were different. Even Dusty's voice had a slight twang from all his years traveling with the rodeo.

Baker reached for his grandmother's wrist, sliding his fingers around it to check her pulse. She gave him the side-eye before tugging free of his loose grasp.

"I'm fine," she told him. "I would like to hear more about what Mrs. Lancaster had to say."

Emily, who worked with the school psychologist at the elementary building in Willow Creek, spoke up then. "I talked to her again after we got back from the hospital, and I told her about how Miller reacted to Baker taking Melanie away in the ambulance."

Baker would probably have some bruises

on his shins from the little boy kicking him. Miller might have done more damage had Dusty not pulled him back so that Baker could leave with Melanie. His legs didn't hurt as much as his heart did over how upset the little boy had been, how upset he always was with him. He cleared the emotion from his throat and asked, "Does she think that I should stay away from him?"

That was what he'd been thinking all these weeks, that his presence alone brought back horrible memories for the boys of the immediate aftermath of the crash. He knew that seeing the boys brought back horrible memories for him.

"No!" Emily said quickly. "Just the opposite. She thinks that you might be the one person who can really reach him."

"But Melanie is much closer to him," Dusty said. "I'm even closer to him than Baker is."

Emily smiled at the rodeo rider who stood with his arm around his pregnant wife. Melanie leaned back against him, totally trusting of him now that they were reunited.

Baker was happy for them, happy that they'd found their way back to each other. With a little help from Sadie, of course.

"You two *are* comforting to him," Emily

said. "I think we all are but…" With a furtive glance at Baker, she trailed off.

He knew what she'd left unsaid. He cleared the emotion from his throat that was threatening to choke him. "But for me…"

He wasn't comforting to them at all.

Emily offered him a sympathetic smile even as she nodded. "No, you remind them of the crash."

The heaviness that had been on his shoulders and on his chest since the accident intensified, making it hard for Baker to draw a deep breath. "That's why I should stay away from them. Give them a chance to recover…"

"No!" Emily said. "Mrs. Lancaster thinks you need to do exactly the opposite."

His brow furrowed with confusion and suspicion. "Why?"

"Because they can't deal with their loss if they aren't able to face it," Emily said. "Mrs. Lancaster would like to meet with you and the boys together. She thinks that all four of you need to talk about what happened that day."

The heavy guilt turned to panic that had his pulse racing. "No…" He shook his head. "*She* didn't say that."

"Emily isn't lying," Ben said, leaping to his fiancée's defense.

Baker ignored them both to turn toward his grandmother. He knew she was up to something. But this…

"How could you?" he asked her. "What purpose do you think this will serve?"

Sadie's dark eyes went wide with surprise. That he'd figured it out? Or that he would think she was responsible?

She had to be.

Dusty stepped forward now, as if to protect their grandmother from him, and Baker nearly chuckled at the irony of that since she'd been upset since Dusty's return.

"Grandma had nothing to do with this," Dusty said. "And I don't get why you're so against the idea. A week or so ago you mentioned talking to Mrs. Lancaster yourself."

Baker's face heated with embarrassment. Dusty had caught him in a weak moment when a nightmare had awakened him. His brother had been walking past the foreman's cottage and had heard him. He was probably lucky that they hadn't heard him up at the main house that night since he'd awakened the next morning with a raspy throat from yelling out in his sleep. He shook his head now. "I was joking. I wasn't serious."

"This is no joke," Dusty said. "The boys need help."

Baker shook his head again. "Not like this..." And not from him. "They're just little kids. They don't need to relive the accident over and over again." *He* didn't need to relive it over and over again. But he did, almost every night, unless he was too exhausted for the dreams to come.

And he only got that exhausted when he worked hard here, at the ranch. Maybe that was why that strange calm came over him when he drove up to the place...until he saw his nephews or the rest of his family.

Sadie uttered a ragged sigh. "I want to protect them, too," she said, her voice quavering with either weariness or emotion. "But sometimes...when you try too hard to protect someone...you hurt them more."

Baker studied her face closely, then he turned toward the others. Everyone was staring at him. "Is this about the boys or about me?" he wondered. "What is this? Some kind of intervention? Tough love?"

Had Dusty told them about what he'd heard

that night? Did they all know what he'd been going through?

He couldn't tell if they'd already been worried about him, or if his reaction to their urging him to go into therapy had raised their concerns. They just stared at him until Jake cleared his throat. But before his big brother could speak, Baker shook his head. "Forget it," he said. "I don't want to hear it. I don't want to hear anything."

Least of all the screams...

Miller crying out in pain...

Little Jake in fear...

And when Ian had regained consciousness for just a moment, he'd cried, too.

Baker wasn't going to make the boys relive that. Not again. Never again.

He shook his head. "No. That isn't happening. You're not going to make me put them through that!" He turned then and rushed out of the old schoolhouse.

He wanted no part of this meeting anymore. And if they pushed this harmful agenda, he wanted no part of this family.

LIKE THE REST of Baker's family, Taye had been frozen with shock over how vehemently he'd reacted to Mrs. Lancaster's suggestion.

But the minute he stalked out of the schoolhouse, she thawed…from the rush of anger coursing through her. "You shouldn't have blindsided him like that," she admonished no one in particular.

He'd already been exhausted from working the ranch and his job as the paramedic firefighter. And then today… Today had been interminably long for all of them. But it had to have been the longest and most emotionally draining for Baker. He'd had to take care of Melanie and deal with being the target for all of Miller's fear and anger.

And now it was late and he was probably going to try to drive back to town. Thinking of him out on the road, upset and tired as he was, at risk of having a crash like the one that had taken Jenny and Dale, had her racing out of the schoolhouse to find him. She had to stop him before he left, had to calm him down.

She wasn't sure why she thought she could. She wasn't family. They barely knew each other. But maybe that was why she was the only one who could soothe him, the only one not part of whatever he thought the meeting was.

She wasn't sure herself. Maybe Mrs. Lancaster had actually told Emily that Baker needed to talk to her with his orphaned nephews, but was she right? Would any good come of making the boys relive that horrible day? Or would it only intensify the loss they already felt?

And what about Baker?

Had anyone realized how much the crash had affected him? He'd been the first on the scene, after all. She didn't know what he'd been like before the accident; she had only seen him in that calendar and the handful of times he'd come into the diner when she'd worked in town. Because she'd been in the kitchen, she'd only caught glimpses of him through the window where she set the prepared dishes under heat lamps for the waitstaff to deliver to the customers. And, unlike some other customers, who'd peeked through the window to compliment her cooking, he'd never said a word to her.

She doubted that he'd noticed her at all.

And now she couldn't see him either. While some yard lights illuminated small circles of the darkness around her, the shadows were so thick that Taye couldn't catch sight of him anywhere. She checked his truck first, but it was dark and empty.

Then she heard it...that bronco.

The loud whinnies and pounding of hooves against wood had to be coming from that horse. The other animals were well-trained and docile. While for some of the family, the bronco was behaving better, she'd seen from when Dusty had ridden it earlier this week that it was still wild. It had seemed to delight in tossing the bronc rider off its back.

Was it tossing Baker around now?

Wouldn't he have known better than to go anywhere near it?

She ran toward the barn then with such speed and force that she sent some gravel flinging around the drive. She had to push open one of the big doors to get inside it, and she found Baker, just as she'd feared, standing in front of the stall of that horse.

It was rearing up, its hooves pawing the air dangerously close to Baker's head. She ran forward and grabbed his arm, jerking him back from the stall. "What are you doing?"

He shook his head. "I don't know..." He stepped farther away from the bronco, which then settled down again. "I shouldn't have stayed. I should have just taken off."

"No," she said. "You're too upset to drive right now."

"I meant earlier," he said. "Before the ambush..."

"Do you really believe that's what it was?" she asked. She'd already berated his family for blindsiding him, but surely they'd done that inadvertently.

"You don't?" he asked. "I don't understand why in the world they're trying to get me to be the one to force the boys to go through that all over again." He shuddered, making Taye realize she had a hand on his arm still. She let go and gave him some space.

But she was tempted to touch him again, to hold him because he looked so distraught. Clearly it wasn't just the boys he didn't want to relive the accident.

"I'm sorry," she said.

He turned toward her then, his topaz eyes intently assessing her face. "Did you know that's what they were going to say? That that was what this meeting was about?" He looked so betrayed. "And you didn't warn me?"

She shook her head. "No. I didn't know. But even if I did, I'm not sure it would have been my place to warn you."

He sighed unsteadily and nodded. "You're right. I'm sorry. I know you barely know me."

"Whose fault is that?" she asked, the words

slipping out unbidden. Heat rushed to her face with embarrassment that she'd sounded like it mattered to her, like she was offended over how hard he seemed to avoid her. But when his eyes widened with surprise, anger replaced her embarrassment. "It's like you think I'm part of your grandmother's plot, like I'm going to try to trap you into a relationship, and I have no more interest in you than you do in me." Then the embarrassment kicked back in as she realized how defensive she sounded, like she was protesting too much.

Like she actually cared that he had no interest in her...

"I haven't been avoiding you," Baker said earnestly. "I've been avoiding the boys."

She gasped, offended now for the boys. The rest of his family had been rallying around Dale and Jenny's orphaned children, and while she'd noticed that Baker hadn't, she'd figured it was because he was just too busy with his job in town and trying to help Jake with the ranch.

"You have to see why I don't come around them," Baker said. "Just the sight of me upsets them."

She softened toward him a little then. "Maybe Miller," she conceded, "but Ian and

Little Jake don't react like he does." In fact, Ian had recently professed his desire to become a firefighter like his uncle Baker.

He shrugged. "That doesn't mean they don't feel like their brother does, that they don't blame me, too."

"Blame you?" she asked. "For the accident? How could they blame you for that?"

"Not for the accident," Baker said. "But they blame me for their parents dying."

She shook her head. "No, I don't think so…" But then she remembered how Miller had previously accused Baker of lying to him when the paramedic had told the little boy that Melanie was going to be all right. "Why do you think that any of them would?"

Baker squeezed his eyes shut but not before she noticed a glimmer of tears in them. Then he grimaced and turned away from her.

And she realized Miller wasn't the only one who blamed Baker. "You blame yourself…" she said in wonder.

And he nodded.

"Why would you do that?" she asked, appalled that he would torture himself like that. "I'm sure you did everything you could to save them."

He shrugged. "I don't know if I did. I just know that I didn't save them…"

"I'm sure that you couldn't," she said. Because surely if he'd been able, Dale and Jenny would be here now. And she wouldn't be.

"I'm not sure," he admitted. "I don't know…"

"Tell me," she said. Maybe if he talked it out, he would realize that there was nothing he could have done that would have changed the tragic outcome. "What happened that day?"

She knew about the accident, that Dale and Jenny and their boys had been leaving that morning for spring break. But then a freak storm hit, and the roads were covered in ice—black ice that Dale must not have noticed until it was too late. Until their vehicle hit it and spun out of control, rolling over and over again before coming to rest in one of the deep ditches on the side of the road.

"I knew Dale and Jenny and the boys were leaving for spring break," Baker said, his voice oddly hollow sounding, as if he was empty inside. "And I was on my way to the ranch to help Jake out while they were gone. I saw the vehicle lying upside down…"

"That's how you were the first on the scene..." she murmured.

"I just had my first aid bag with me," he said. "I didn't have..." His voice trailed off, sounding strangled with emotion. He cleared his throat and continued, "I didn't have what I needed to save them all, and even though I called it in, the ambulance was so far away... too far away..."

Tears stung her eyes at the predicament he'd been in, at how difficult that must have been to be at the crash on his own, the only one able to help and not being equipped to do enough to save all five victims.

"Oh, Baker..." She slid her arms around him, hugging him to offer whatever comfort she could as her heart ached for what he'd been through.

She couldn't help but think that Mrs. Lancaster was right, that if anyone was able to relate to the boys, to help them heal, it was Baker, because he was hurting probably as badly as they were.

THE MINUTE SHE'D gotten back to the house, Sadie had collapsed into her favorite easy chair in the sitting area of her main-floor suite. Feisty, her longhaired Chihuahua, leaped onto her lap, but she must have been tired, too. Instead of pressing tiny doggy kisses to Sadie's face like she usually did, she settled down with a weary-sounding doggy sigh. "It's been a long day, girl," Sadie told her furry companion and then released a weary sigh of her own and closed her eyes.

She hadn't had them closed long when a soft knock rattled the door in the frame. It was probably Lem. He'd been upstairs watching over the sleeping boys in case Little Jake woke up with one of his nightmares or the other kids needed something.

He was so good with the little kids, always had been. A smile curved her lips, and she called out, "You don't have to knock. Come on in..."

When once she would have slammed the door in his face after he'd knocked, now she wanted him to feel comfortable enough to walk right in. She wanted him to know that they were friends.

No matter what...

Even when she got mad when he told her something she didn't want to hear.

Like the day he'd told her that her husband, Big Jake, had been sending money to Jessup without her knowledge, that he'd been keeping secrets from her about something other than his forbidden cigars. Getting mad about that, especially at Lem, had been hypocritical of her.

She'd been keeping Jessup a secret from her grandsons; she hadn't told any of them about him. But one of them knew...

He was the one who walked into her suite now, with his wife. "Are you okay, Grandma?" Dusty asked, the slight twang in his voice a little more pronounced with weariness and with concern.

She nodded. "I'm fine." And she nearly cringed that once again she was keeping things from her family, like how upset she really was—but more so with herself than anyone or anything else. She turned to Melanie. "How are you feeling? Shouldn't you be in bed?"

"I am really good now," Melanie said, and her smile widened. "And we're going up to bed, but we wanted to check on you first."

"I'm fine," she insisted.

"Are you really?" Dusty asked, and he was clearly skeptical despite her insisting that she was. "I thought you were going to see my mother after you left the hospital, but you weren't gone long enough to get out to that ranch and back here when you did."

She shook her head. "I couldn't bring myself to…" Her voice trailed off, and tears stung her eyes.

"Why not?" Dusty asked.

She released a shaky sigh. "Because I'm afraid of what she'll tell me about Jessup…"

Dusty narrowed his eyes. "What do you mean?"

And she realized he didn't know everything. Although Darlene had told him about his uncle running away all those years ago, she must not have told him *why* he had. "I'm afraid that it might be too late…"

"Too late for what, Grandma?" Dusty asked.

She shook her head. "Too late for this discussion."

"You have to tell everyone else about our uncle," Dusty said, his shoulders bowing as if he was tired of carrying the burden of her secret. "And I need to tell them about Mom." He uttered a weary sigh. "Even though I wanted her to do that herself…"

"Give her time," Sadie suggested, knowing that it was what she needed herself. "We need to focus on the boys right now." But the little boys weren't the only ones she was worried about. "And Baker…"

Dusty groaned. "Give up your matchmaking scheme where Baker's concerned," he advised. "He clearly has bigger things he needs to deal with than falling in love."

His reaction tonight had certainly proved that to her. She released another shaky sigh. "I know. He's been hurting far more than I realized…"

"Than any of us realized," Melanie added, and she blinked her long lashes as if fighting back tears of empathy.

Sadie might have cried, too, if she wasn't already cried out from all the losses in her life. And not just the recent ones.

"He needs to talk to Mrs. Lancaster as much as Miller and Ian do," Dusty said. "Maybe he needs to talk to her more than they do, but he's even more determined than Miller to not talk to anyone."

"Miller opened up to you," Sadie said. And maybe Baker was opening up to someone now. Taye had run out of the office after him. Hopefully she'd caught up with him. Maybe Dusty was wrong. Maybe falling in love was exactly what Baker needed to heal.

But if not… If he wasn't too stubborn to

let anyone help him, then he would wind up hurting Taye. And that poor girl had already been through so much.

Even though Sadie had the best of intentions for all of them, she might have made another mistake. One that was going to cause even more heartbreak.

CHAPTER FIVE

BAKER STOOD STIFFLY within Taye's embrace. He wanted to wrap his arms around her, wanted to hold her close, but he didn't feel like he deserved her sympathy and her comfort.

She must have taken his reaction as a rejection because she quickly released him and stepped back, wrapping her arms around herself now as her face flushed. "I'm sorry…"

He didn't know if she was referring to the hug or if she was sorry about what he'd told her. He wished he could take it back, that he hadn't shared what had happened that horrific day with her or anyone else. "I'm sorry," he said. "I know that what I went through… it's nothing compared to what the boys lost… and what Dale and Jenny lost…" Their lives. They'd lost everything. Heat rushed into his face. "I probably sound like I'm full of self-pity…" And he hated that he'd sounded that way to her—for some reason—of all people.

"No," she said, and she shook her head. "You didn't sound that way at all."

Some of the tension eased from him with relief that she didn't think less of him. He wasn't sure why it mattered to him what she thought of him, but it did.

And it wasn't just because she was such a beautiful woman. It was because of that insight and shrewdness she had that belied her years. She reminded him of Sadie in a way. When she looked at a person, it was like she could see right through him. He wanted her to like what she saw.

Even though he didn't like it.

"I don't want to make this horrible tragedy about me," he said. "That's why I think it would be wrong for me to talk to Mrs. Lancaster with the boys. The focus needs to be on them and their feelings."

"Maybe Mrs. Lancaster thinks you can help them because you know what they went through during the accident better than anyone else does," she said.

He shook his head. "I wasn't there when their SUV crashed. I was there after..." He shuddered.

"When no one else was," she persisted.

"For the boys or for you. It was just you and them, and maybe that's why…"

"Stop," he implored her. "Please, stop. I don't want to talk about this anymore." He didn't want to think about it, dream about it…but he did.

"I'm sorry," she said again. "I didn't mean to push."

He groaned. "You're the only one. The rest of them *will* push." Just like Jake and Sadie and Ben had pushed Dusty to come home the past several weeks. So had he…a few times. He felt a twinge of regret for that because he had a feeling he was going to find out exactly how it felt to be pressured like that, pressured to do something he didn't want to do.

But Dusty hadn't necessarily not wanted to come back to the ranch; he'd just wanted to find his runaway wife first. He'd had no idea that Grandma had already found her and moved her to the ranch.

Baker was sick of secrets and schemes; or at least, he was sick of being unaware of the secrets and a target of the schemer. It was time that he turned the tables on his grandmother.

"I want to push back," he said.

"About the boys?"

"No, of course not," he said. "I want to help them. I just don't believe that I can do anything but hurt them more." And a sharp jab of pain stabbed his heart with the admission. It was true, though. He was the last person who could help the boys; he'd already proved that the day of the crash when he hadn't saved their parents for them.

"I don't think you'd hurt them, especially not with Mrs. Lancaster there to help."

"No," he said with quick shake of his head. "What I want to push back about is all Grandma's matchmaking."

Her eyes, that beautiful pale blue, narrowed then. "This is what you were talking about at the hospital..."

He nodded. "You gave me the idea when you said we should stop at the jewelers and the church, that that's probably the only way to get Grandma off my back."

She smiled and shook her head. "I was just kidding. I wasn't serious."

"What if we got serious?" he asked.

Her smile slipped away, and she stepped back as if appalled at the thought of being serious about him. He felt a twinge of hurt, but maybe it was just wounded pride that she obviously wasn't into him at all while he thought she was so beautiful and kind. She had followed him out of the schoolhouse to the barn and offered him the comfort his family hadn't. Apparently she hadn't done that because she was attracted to him. She'd done it just because she was a genuinely nice person. And because she was, she deserved to wind up with someone who didn't have all the issues Baker was well aware that he had.

"I don't mean that we actually date for real," he assured her. "But if Grandma and my brothers thought we were already seeing each other, they'd back off and stop trying to throw us together."

Her brow furrowed again. "But in order to fool them, we'd have to actually be seeing each other. Isn't that falling in with Sadie's plan?"

He shook his head. "No. We could claim we're going out together, that we're going to town to see a movie or something, but when we got into town, we would go our separate ways. We wouldn't actually have to spend that much time together. Just make everyone else think that we are." Heat flushed his face as he realized how ridiculous and juvenile he sounded.

She slowly shook her head as her mouth

downturned into a frown. "I don't think I would be comfortable doing that."

"Why not?" he wondered aloud. Maybe she didn't want anyone to believe that she might actually be interested in him.

"I don't like lying or keeping things from people," she replied. "Especially people I care about."

"You care about my family?" He wasn't sure why he'd asked. Even though he hadn't been around Taye that often, every time he had been he'd seen how sweet and nurturing she was with everyone from Little Jake to Sadie. And even though she was just innately kind, taking care of his family was obviously more than a job to her.

"Yes," she replied. "I care very much. And Katie and Emily and Melanie are very important to me. I can't lie to them and…"

"And if you don't, they would tell my brothers the truth anyways," he finished when she trailed off.

"You can't expect them to keep anything from their partners," she pointed out.

He nodded. "I understand."

"I'm sorry."

"You're sorry for turning down my fake

proposal?" A smile tugged at his mouth at the irony of it.

She smiled, too, and the teasing tone was back in her voice when she replied, "I hope you don't take the rejection too hard."

He chuckled. "Thank you."

"For turning you down?" she asked, and she arched a dark blond brow over one of her eyes.

"For making me feel better," he said. He'd been so upset when he'd come out here, so upset that he'd even upset Midnight. But she'd calmed Baker down and somehow calmed down the bronco as well.

The horse was quiet in its stall. And Baker was a little quieter inside.

"I'm glad that I did," she said. "Are you going to stay tonight or drive back to town?"

It was late. And he was tired, probably too tired to make that long drive back to town. But he also didn't want to stay here where his family could apply more pressure. "I don't know how much rest I'd get here," he said. Not that he ever slept all that well or all that long.

"Were you going to stay in the house?" she asked, her blue eyes widening with surprise.

"Are you worried about Little Jake's nightmares?"

It wasn't Little Jake's nightmares he was worried about; it was his own. He shook his head. "No. I would stay in the foreman's cottage if I didn't think that I'd wake up to another intervention of my family trying to get me into counseling with the boys."

Did they really think that kind of counseling, with him present, would benefit the boys? Or were they just trying to trick Baker into getting counseling for himself? Were they worried about him for some reason?

Taye didn't seem to be as she began backing toward the open barn door. "I should get back to the house," she said. "Everyone else is probably already asleep."

So he could stay the night, then, without any of them harassing him. And he would just have to make certain to wake up early and leave before anyone had the chance to talk to him again.

"Good night," Taye whispered before she turned and walked away from him.

And as she did, he felt a strange feeling in his chest, something almost like yearning. He wanted to call her back, to talk to her some more. But that was a bad idea, just like his irrational proposal to pretend that they were dating.

Once she'd disappeared through the open barn doors into the night, he wondered aloud, "What's wrong with me?" He couldn't believe he'd come up with such a crazy idea, let alone that he'd shared it with her and asked her to be part of it. His stomach twisted with embarrassment, and he leaned back against the stall door behind him. Inside it, Midnight uttered a strange noise. It wasn't the guttural sound he generally made around Baker, the almost warning he gave before he reared up.

This was different, more like a nicker, and then the horse's head poked over the stall door, dangerously close to Baker's head. He jumped away, rattled that he'd let the wild animal get so close to him—twice that night.

The first time Taye had rescued him.

Now… The horse just stared at him. And Baker realized he might not need rescuing from it this time. "Why didn't you stop me?" he asked it. "Why didn't you stop me before I made such a fool of myself?"

The horse made that sound again, the new one…almost as if he was laughing at Baker.

Baker chuckled along with him, but then he shook his head. "I better get some sleep. I think I'm starting to get loopy, out here talking to you like you can actually understand me."

Baker couldn't even understand himself half the time, so he doubted a horse could. Yet he'd rather talk to the horse than to Mrs. Lancaster. No. He'd rather talk to Taye Cooper. And that was probably even stupider than having a conversation with a horse.

He'd already told her too much, more than he should have. And after he had, she'd wanted no part of his scheme, probably because she wanted no part of him—even for pretend.

SHOULD SHE HAVE gone along with his plan? Should she have pretended to be in a relationship with Baker Haven? Taye had been afraid that if she'd agreed to that, she might start hoping they weren't just pretending.

That fear had kept her awake most of the night after she'd returned to the house. She'd tossed and turned before finally giving up on sleeping. She got up early, got dressed and headed down the back stairwell to the kitchen. With each step she descended, she felt a little less restless, a little more at home. She'd fallen in love with the ranch kitchen the minute she'd seen it. The room was enormous, far bigger than any commercial kitchen she'd worked in before. It had a long stainless steel island, top-of-the-line appliances, an enormous walk-in pantry, and with its warm green cabinets and brick floor that matched the fireplace, it was as beautiful as it was functional. Usually sunshine poured in through the patio doors on the other side of the big dining table. But it was too early for much more than dawn's faint thinning of the darkness of the night.

Taye rubbed her eyes, which were gritty and strained from her having lain awake for so much of the night. Then she opened a cabinet and reached inside for the coffee canister. As she pulled it down, she felt how light it was, and she remembered using the last of it the day before. There would be some in the pantry; she always kept extra bags of coffee on hand.

But when she started toward the pantry door, she noticed the light beneath it, and then something crashed inside the space. Was an intruder in the house?

Had her coming down to the kitchen made him dart into the pantry to hide? But why hide? Why not go out the patio doors and escape?

Realizing she was jumping to too many conclusions, she shook her head. She doubted anyone had broken into the ranch—any more than Baker's family had really intended to ambush him last night. They only wanted to help him.

However, she was all too well aware that some people weren't willing to accept help from anyone, even their family. Sometimes especially their family. Like her mother…

She hadn't let Taye help her; instead she'd wallowed in her pain until it had destroyed her. That was why Taye couldn't risk the kind of heartbreak that had broken her mother. She'd rather stay single the rest of her life than ever experience that kind of pain and loss. Again.

She expelled a shaky sigh that her "intruder" must have heard because a gasp spilled out with the light beneath the pantry door. She smiled as she realized who it probably was. She pulled open the door to find Caleb Morris-Haven balanced precariously on the top of a small stepladder, his arms extended toward the top shelf. Apparently he'd figured out where she'd hidden the cookie jar. Before he could fall, she caught the little blond-haired boy around his waist and lifted him down.

"What are you doing up so early?" she asked him. She didn't have to ask what he was doing in the pantry; she knew...

Caleb was addicted to her chocolate chip cookies. She wasn't sure now if it was good or bad that she'd hidden them on such a high shelf. She certainly didn't want him getting hurt, but if he had easy access to the jar, he would eat all the cookies and make himself as sick as Melanie had been in the early days of pregnancy.

Though at the time Taye and Emily hadn't realized what the physical therapist was really going through. Emily had thought she'd had a flu bug, and Taye had worried that she might have had an eating disorder like one of her stepsisters had struggled with during their teen years.

"I couldn't sleep," Caleb said.

So she hadn't been the only one.

"Why not?" she asked. "I didn't hear Little Jake." And she would have if he'd awakened. Everyone in the house and probably a few-miles radius heard him screaming when one of his nightmares woke him up.

Caleb shook his head. "No. It wasn't Little Jake. Ian was hogging the bed." Ian had taken to slipping into his friend's room during the night. Or sometimes he refused to be tucked into his own bed because he wanted to sleep with his new cousin instead. Caleb had never complained before, but from the dark circles beneath his eyes, maybe it was time that somebody addressed the situation or at least got them bunk beds.

"And you were going to use cookies to get him out of your room?" she asked.

Caleb's face flushed a bright pink. "Uh, no... I was looking for carrots for Midnight. He deserves some extra ones after letting everybody know that Aunt Melanie fell in the barn yesterday."

She wasn't sure that Midnight had actually been pulling a Lassie and trying to alert anyone to Melanie's plight. But he hadn't harmed her when she'd fallen in front of his stall and inadvertently opened the door to it. "He does deserve extra carrots," she agreed. But then she pointedly reminded the little boy, "Those are in the refrigerator, not in the pantry."

His face turned a deeper shade of pink as he stammered, "I—I forgot..." Then he yawned and added, "Prolly cuz I'm so tired."

She wished being tired could make her forgetful, so that she could forget the conversations she'd had with Baker the day before. But the more tired she'd gotten over not sleeping last night, the more she had replayed every word of those conversations as well as every look and every touch...

She'd definitely touched him more than he had her. And remembering how stiffly he'd stood within her awkward embrace last night, her face got hot.

He probably thought she was as obsessed with him as most of the single women in Willow Creek seemed to be. Actually the women at the diner who'd refused to turn the calendar to any page but his hadn't been single. They'd just objectified him solely on his appearance.

She didn't want to act like the other women in town, especially now that she knew how much he was hurting. He clearly blamed himself for his brother and sister-in-law dying.

And her heart ached for his misplaced guilt and his pain.

He needed to talk to someone, even if not Mrs. Lancaster. But because he'd talked to Taye last night, she hadn't wanted to push him; she hadn't wanted him to get as upset with her as he'd been with his family.

Had he stayed on the ranch overnight? Or had he left after all because he hadn't trusted his family to not try to pressure him either into counseling or into dating her.

"Are you okay, Miss Taye?" Caleb asked.

His question startled her into realizing she'd zoned out, thinking about Baker again—still—and she'd forgotten she was holding the little boy in her arms. He reached out and touched her cheek with one of his small hands.

"You look tired, too, Miss Taye," he said.

She smiled. Someday she'd have to clue him in that some women didn't like being told they looked tired. It didn't bother her, though. In fact she appreciated his endearing honesty.

Being open and honest was very important to her; that was why she'd turned down Baker's proposal, that and her fear that she might want to really date if they started "pretend" dating. And after what she'd gone through with her mom, after her parents' divorce, she didn't think love was worth the risk, not when it could lead to so much pain.

"I am tired," she admitted.

"Then why are you up so early?" he asked.

"I couldn't sleep either," she said. "So I decided I'd get up early and do some baking.

Seems like the cookies I make just keep disappearing..."

Caleb smiled. "I don't know where they could be going..." And he snuck a sidelong glance at the top shelf where she'd hidden the jar.

She smiled, too. Then she gently poked his tummy. "I think I have some idea..." She set him on his feet and moved toward the shelf.

And his eyes widened with hope and anticipation.

But she reached for the coffee canister instead. "This is why I came in here," she told him. "I thought you were looking for carrots..."

He pressed his hand to his forehead. "Midnight! I better get those carrots out to him." He turned then and rushed out of the pantry and straight to the fridge.

Taye followed him out. "You can't go out to the barn by yourself," she reminded him. That was the rule—one Caleb seemed to ignore more than not. But after seeing how that horse had reacted to Baker's presence yesterday, she really didn't want the five-year-old being anywhere near it ever, especially not when he was alone.

Caleb sighed. "But nobody else is up."

The sky was a little lighter, but it was probably going to be a least an hour before anyone else—even Jake—headed out to the barn. "Caleb, I'm sure Midnight can wait."

"But he was a hero yesterday," Caleb persisted. "He needs a reward for saving Aunt Melanie."

"I'm not sure he saved her." But he definitely could have hurt her if he hadn't somehow stepped over her. "Uncle Baker is the one who really helped her."

"Should we bring him carrots, too?" Caleb asked.

Taye snorted. "I'm not sure if he likes them as much as Midnight does." While she always made a point of finding out everyone's favorite foods, she hadn't had the chance to get to know Baker's. Until yesterday they hadn't exchanged more than a few words. He had probably only shared so much with her last night because he'd been tired and vulnerable. She was glad, though, that she'd been there for him, and she hoped she'd given him some comfort…even though being that close to him had unsettled her. Learning how troubled he was had just reinforced all her reasons for not dating him…for pretend and especially for real.

"I'm sure he likes cookies," Caleb said. "If only we knew where some were—" he glanced back at the closed door to the pantry "—we could bring them to Uncle Baker."

"I think Uncle Baker probably already left for town," she said.

"To fight a fire?" he asked, his blue eyes bright with excitement. "I should go wake up Ian and tell him. He wants to be a firefighter, too."

Baker thought all his nephews hated him, but Ian actually idolized him. And Little Jake always seemed to perk up when his youngest uncle walked into a room. Miller was the only one who was angry with him. Miller was the one who needed Mrs. Lancaster the most and had refused to talk to her—just like his uncle Baker. Maybe their issue was that they were too much alike.

"Let Ian sleep," she said. "It's really early yet."

"So Uncle Baker is probably still here," Caleb said. "I can take a bag of cookies to him when I bring Midnight his carrots."

A smile tugged at her lips. "And what will you do with that bag if Uncle Baker is already gone?"

A smile tugged up his lips. "Well… I wouldn't want them to go to waste."

She chuckled. "I doubt that ever happens around here."

"I make sure it doesn't," he admitted with that sweet honesty she loved so much about him.

She laughed. "Oh, so you're the one who's been making sure the cookies don't go stale."

He gave her a solemn nod as if it was a tough job but he'd taken on the responsibility.

She reached out and tousled his silky blond hair. "You're a special kid, Caleb Morris."

"Caleb Morris-*Haven*." He reminded her that he was taking his stepfather's name as well as keeping his late father's. That obviously meant a lot to him, to be an official Haven.

The Haven family had always been well respected in Willow Creek, or in Sadie's case, perhaps feared. She was a fierce woman, but not nearly as intimidating to Taye as others found her. She understood that Sadie's family was everything to her and that she couldn't lose any more of them to death or to unhappiness. They'd talked about it before…at night when Taye checked on the older woman before she headed off to bed herself. They'd talked then about Sadie's family and about Taye's. Sadie was one of the few who knew how Taye's mother had died and how her stepmother had treated her. Taye was pretty sure the older woman had known even before she'd told her, though. Probably before she'd hired her...

And maybe that was why she'd hired her, because she'd known that Taye would be able to commiserate and understand the orphaned Haven boys. Not that Taye was an orphan...

"So Caleb Morris-Haven, you can't go out to that barn alone..." And since Taye suspected that he would slip away the minute she turned her back, she continued, "So I will go with you."

"To the barn?" he asked with surprise, as if her being anywhere but the kitchen was a shock.

Maybe she needed to get out of it more. Melanie's mom was staying at the ranch now, and Juliet Shepard loved to cook and take care of people as much as Taye did. So Taye could have agreed to Baker's plan. She could have pretended that they were dating.

And maybe she should...face her fear. She was strong, strong enough to be close to Baker Haven without falling for him. She was smart, too, too smart to risk her heart on a man like him.

CHAPTER SIX

BAKER HAD SWORN not to fall victim to it like his brothers had, to remain immune to love. But he found himself falling...

If not into love then certainly at least infatuation...

With that dang horse.

That had to be the reason he was standing outside its stall at the crack of dawn. He'd intended to get in his truck and head to town. But the barn was between the foreman's cottage and where his truck was parked by the main house, and he'd found himself pushing open the stable doors he'd shut the night before and coming inside.

To Midnight. The bronco had greeted Baker the minute he'd stepped inside the barn and not with that usual guttural warning he used to give him. Instead he nickered softly again, as if the horse was still laughing at Baker.

"So you don't want to stomp all over me

anymore?" Baker asked. That was the way it had seemed to him, that the horse didn't like him for some reason. If he'd fallen in front of his open stall like Melanie had, he was pretty sure that the horse wouldn't have been as careful not to step on him. Or would he have been?

Baker pondered the animal. With his sleek black coat stretched taut over muscled flesh, the beast was a beauty. Baker understood why Dusty wanted to use Midnight to breed rodeo stock broncos. But he agreed with Jake that it shouldn't be done here where there were kids, especially when one of those little boys was intent on becoming a rodeo rider someday. As if just thinking of him had conjured him up, Caleb ran into the barn, a bunch of carrots dangling from one hand and a baggie of something else in his other hand. The little boy saw Baker and stopped short with his forehead creasing slightly as if he was disappointed.

Maybe at getting caught…

Baker stepped between him and the stall and leaned down to his new nephew's eye level. "Good morning, little man. What are you doing out here all by yourself?"

"He's not all by himself," Taye said between pants for breath. "He's just faster than I am."

Baker found himself struggling to breathe for a moment at the sight of her. For once her golden hair wasn't bound in a braid but shimmering in long waves around her shoulders, and her face glowed.

"You're not fighting a fire," Caleb murmured, and there was that disappointment again.

"No..." Baker acknowledged. "Not yet." But he did have to report to the fire station today. Or he might risk losing his job. The thought of that didn't bother him like it once would have. "Did you want me to be fighting a fire?" he asked the boy.

Taye chuckled. "He wanted you to be gone already, so he didn't have to give you your reward."

"Reward?" Baker asked, and dread churned in his stomach at the reminder of the military awards he'd received and the reasons why he'd earned them. He shook his head. "I don't deserve a reward for anything I've done."

Caleb's brow furrowed more, but this time with confusion. "Yes, you do. You and Midnight saved Aunt Melanie."

Unable to refuse the little boy's generous offer, Baker broke off a piece of the mound and popped it into his mouth. Then as the sweet dough and rich chocolate melted on his tongue, making his taste buds dance with pleasure, he moaned and nodded. Now he understood Caleb's well-known obsession.

"They're good, huh?" Caleb asked.

And Baker nodded again.

"Sure you don't want more?" Caleb asked.

He did, but Baker shook his head. And with apparent delight that he got to keep the rest of the treats, Caleb skipped out of the barn with his baggie, leaving Baker and Taye alone together.

"Where's he going?" he wondered aloud.

Taye shrugged. "I think he's just getting out of here before you change your mind," she said.

"He's smart." He chuckled then and admitted, "I was tempted."

Taye's lips curved into a slight almost shy smile. "You really liked them?"

He gave her a vigorous nod. "They're amazing."

She shrugged. "They're just cookies. I'm going to make more this morning."

He had no intention of going anywhere

near the house to get any more, though. And as if she knew it, she continued speaking, "Caleb's the one who's amazing."

So was she. But Baker nodded again and said, "He's a sweet kid. Really special…"

"He survived losing his father," she said. "And he's often talked about how close they were."

He narrowed his eyes and studied her face. "What are you saying?" That he should have survived losing his? He had. He was still here. But then he realized she was talking about his other nephews. "Little Jake and Ian and Miller lost both their dad and their mom."

"From what I've heard, so did you," she said gently.

He tensed and shook his head. "My mom's alive…" Or so he assumed despite not having heard from her in years. But Dusty claimed he'd spoken to her, that he'd told her that Dale and Jenny had died. And yet she hadn't come to the funeral; she hadn't reached out to express sympathy to any of them. Not even her grandsons.

He refused to waste any more time thinking about her and focused instead on Taye. Her pale blue eyes glinted with a faint sheen, almost as if she was near tears. "Are you okay?" he asked with concern.

She nodded. "Fine."

"I'm sorry," he said.

Her shoulders straightened, and she raised her chin with either tension or pride. "For what?"

He sighed. "For proposing."

She tensed even more. "You make that sound as if you're serious…"

He shook his head. "No. No chance of that."

She sucked in a breath, as if she was shocked or offended.

And he reached out to grasp her shoulders, assuring her, "I didn't mean that I don't find you attractive…" Because he did, and that was part of his problem—he found her *too* attractive.

She shrugged. "I'm not insulted if you don't…"

Because she obviously didn't care what he thought, and he didn't blame her. "I'm sorry that I brought up that idiotic idea to you about pretending to be involved," he said. "I know it was immature."

And if his actions put some distance be-tween, so much the better. It was as much for his benefit as for hers, "I know I just need to make it clear to my family that no matter how much meddling any of them do, I'm never getting married," he stated resolutely.

A deep laugh echoed inside the barn, startling both of them and the horse in the stall behind them. Midnight reared up for a moment while Taye moved closer to Baker, her hand against his chest, as if she was bracing herself. His heart leaped beneath her palm.

But that had to be because of Jake's sudden appearance in the barn. Baker hadn't noticed his oldest brother was there. Jake laughed again and said, "I've heard that before. From Dusty, from Ben... Heck, I've even said it myself."

"But I mean it," Baker insisted.

Jake chuckled again. "I don't know. I bet Taye could get you to change your mind..."

Taye jerked her hand away from his chest, and her face flushed a deep crimson color. "I—I don't want to do that," she stammered, and then like Caleb had moments ago, she turned and hurried out of the barn.

Baker cursed his older brother. "Don't pick on Taye," he warned him. "She wants nothing to do with Sadie's scheme." Or his, or with him...and he felt a flash of disappointment over that. But as attractive as he found her, he didn't want to hurt her, and he was pretty sure that was all that he would do... given how he had already let down too many people he loved.

"I wasn't picking on Taye," Jake assured him. "I think the world of her. And I don't think I'm the only one..." From Jake's smug grin, it was clear that he wasn't referring to just the kids' or the rest of the family's thoughts about Taye.

Baker glared. "What are you talking about?"

Jake shrugged. "Just that you seem awfully protective of her," he replied. "Maybe you're already starting to care about her."

"I don't even know her," he said, and disappointment flashed through him again, a little more intensely. Did he want to know her better?

"That's your fault," Jake remarked. "If you'd come up to the house more since Grandma hired her, you would have gotten to know her."

He glared harder at his oldest brother. "Grandma?" he asked. "Is that you in disguise?"

Jake chuckled and held up his hands. "I'm not playing matchmaker."

Skeptical of his brother's claim, Baker snorted. "Yeah, right."

"I'm not. Not between you and Taye, anyway. But between you and the ranch…" Jake said.

Baker scoffed. "It would make more sense to play matchmaker between me and Taye."

Jake's dark eyes widened with surprise. "You're interested?"

He was more interested in her than he had any right to be. "I'm tired," Baker said, "and I need to get to town for a meeting with my boss. Or I might not have a job much longer."

"You have a job," Jake said.

Baker might have believed it if Ben told him that, since the fire chief essentially worked for the mayor of Willow Creek. "You don't know that…" Jake hardly ever went into town. Except for his honeymoon a couple of weeks ago, he'd rarely left the ranch since their grandfather had died and he'd taken charge of it.

"I know that you have a job *here*," Jake said. "At the ranch."

Baker's brow furrowed with confusion. "I'm a firefighter, not a rancher."

Jake snorted now. "Yeah, right…"

Baker flinched at the sting to his pride. His big brother obviously didn't think much of his firefighting skills. Not that he got much opportunity to use them in Willow Creek. Fortunately. There weren't many fires. But as a paramedic as well…

He'd failed.

"I'm sure you're good at it," Jake said quickly, as if he'd realized he'd offended Baker. "Heck, over the past couple of weeks I've seen for myself how good an emergency responder you are, but it's not *who* you are."

His brothers didn't know him any better than he knew Taye. "So who am I, Jake?"

"You're a rancher."

Baker chuckled. "Dusty must have turned you down for the ranch foreman position, and now you're getting desperate."

"I didn't want Dusty as the ranch foreman," Jake said.

Skeptical, Baker shook his head. "That's why you were hounding him to come back after the funeral?"

Jake sighed sheepishly and nodded. "Okay, maybe I thought he could take the job, but when I was gone, you were the one who did it, Baker. You were the one who handled everything on the ranch when Katie and I were on our honeymoon."

"For two weeks with Ben's help."

Jake laughed. "Yeah, and I can imagine how much help the mayor was with the ranch. You handled that on your own."

The praise unsettled Baker; he wasn't used to his brothers doing anything but teasing him and each other. He studied Jake's face. "Well, you're back now and Dusty is, too, so you don't need me."

"But I do," Jake insisted. "And so do the boys."

Baker groaned. "That's what this is all about, getting me to hang around so you can ambush me again—what, with Mrs. Lancaster?" He shook his head. "I don't have time for this. I have to get to the fire station." His vacation time was up, and he needed to report back to his real job. His real life. Staying at the ranch had only been temporary and now it'd come to an end.

Like Caleb and Taye had, Baker rushed out of the barn. And as he passed through the doors, he heard Midnight nicker again, like he was laughing at him. Like Jake had earlier when he'd heard Baker state that he was never getting married.

Heck, he was more likely to get married than become a rancher. When he was a kid, he couldn't wait to leave the ranch—to live his own life instead of the one he'd been born into, the life of people leaving you.

TAYE SHOULD HAVE been relieved that Baker had changed his mind about their pretend relationship. But since she'd started warming up to the idea, she was actually a little disappointed. It might have been fun to pull a fast one on shrewd Sadie Haven.

And to spend more time with Baker...

But just being in the barn with him had apparently given Jake the wrong idea, the idea that she might actually try to change Baker's mind about marriage, that *she* might change her own mind about it. Just the thought of risking her heart, of being that vulnerable to someone else, made her shudder with revulsion.

"Are you cold?" Emily asked, her voice full of concern as she joined Taye in the kitchen.

Heat wafted from the griddle on the stove over which Taye stood, flipping blueberry pancakes. The sun was up now, and soon everyone else would be, too.

"I'm fine," Taye said, but she felt a twinge

of guilt over not being entirely truthful with her friend. She'd initially turned down Baker's fake proposal because she'd thought she wouldn't be able to lie to her friends. But there were things she hadn't shared with them.

Things she hadn't wanted to bring up, hadn't wanted to think about anymore herself. But Sadie knew, just as Sadie knew everything. There probably would have been no fooling her with a pretend relationship; she would have known the truth.

Sadie walked into the kitchen then with Feisty bouncing around her feet. The little dog was always full of energy, and usually Sadie was, too. But she moved slowly today, and there were dark circles beneath her eyes. Apparently Taye wasn't the only one who'd had trouble sleeping the night before.

With her hand that was not holding the spatula, she poured coffee into one of the empty mugs sitting on the counter and handed it to her employer. "Looks like you can use this," she said with a smile.

Sadie studied her face for a moment and nodded. "Looks like you could use some, too."

Taye smiled. Sadie didn't miss anything,

which would have made it challenging and maybe even more fun to try to fool her.

"Caleb said you went out to the barn with him," Katie said as she stepped off the last tread of the back stairwell.

Taye smiled. Obviously she hadn't talked to Jake yet, but he was probably still out in the barn or already in the pastures. "Checking to make sure he's telling the truth?"

Katie sighed. "He knows he's not supposed to go out to the barn alone."

"He wasn't," Taye assured her. "I went out with him."

Katie's green eyes widened with surprise. "Really?"

"I was up earlier than usual," she said.

"You're always up early," Katie said. "But you rarely go out to the barn."

She shrugged. "I didn't want him sneaking off by himself. He was determined to give Midnight his carrots."

"As a reward," Caleb said as he bounded down the back stairs. "And Uncle Baker got one, too." Only the little boy would consider a small bite of a cookie a reward.

Taye smiled.

"Baker's still here?" Sadie asked.

"I doubt it." He couldn't have been happy

that Jake had caught him in the barn since he'd been so determined to get away from the ranch before anyone had a chance to have another go at getting him into therapy. "He had to meet his boss in town."

"How was he?" Sadie asked.

Taye assessed the older woman. Was she really concerned or just prying to see how much he and Taye had talked? She shrugged. "I don't really know him, so I don't know... but he seemed the same."

Sadie sighed as if disappointed.

"He was really upset last night," Emily said, her brow furrowing with worry. "I didn't mean for that to happen."

"He doesn't blame you," Taye assured her.

Sadie sighed again. "No, he probably blames me."

Taye didn't think it was that concern that had kept Sadie awake last night, though. There was something else going on with her. Something that she was keeping to herself, like she seemed to keep everything else, just as she wanted to keep everyone at the ranch.

Taye doubted that Baker would permanently move back, no matter how much Sadie schemed. And she felt that flash of disappointment again when she should have been relieved. The last thing she should want was to spend any more time with Baker Haven… because she suspected it would lead to nothing but unhappiness for her. Just as love and marriage had for her mother…

CHAPTER SEVEN

I LOVE WHAT I do. You must too...

Taye's words resonated in Baker's head when he walked into the firehouse. Where was the love? Or at least the excitement he'd once felt over being a firefighter? A paramedic?

Had it died the day Dale and Jenny had? Or had he fallen out of love with it even before then? He remembered the day he'd fallen in love with it; when there'd been a fire in his elementary school's cafeteria and the firefighters, clad in all their gear, had shown up to put it out. The hats and coats, the boots, the equipment...hoses and axes and the engine itself...had all fascinated him so much. Then the firefighters had stayed to address the student body, answering questions in the parking lot about their gear and telling them about their career.

All Baker had known before that was cowboy hats and boots, horses and cattle...but a whole new world had opened up to him that day. A world where a firefighting paramedic could rescue and save people instead of losing them. And Baker had wanted to be part of that world, one of that profession of rescuers. To get that training and get away from the ranch, he'd joined the army out of high school, and when he'd finished his military commitment, there had been an opening with the Willow Creek fire department, probably thanks to Sadie. It hadn't taken him long to learn that not every rescue was successful. If he'd only known how many times…

But he'd wanted to find his own career, his own world, because he'd never felt like he'd been part of the ranch. So for Jake to say what he had that morning…

Baker shook his head to clear it of those thoughts. He was not a rancher. But he wasn't sure he was a firefighter anymore either. He was worried that his boss had the same doubts about him.

When Baker stepped through the open door to the man's office, he cleared his throat and said, "Sorry I'm late." He'd gotten stuck behind a tractor on the main road to town, and with several sharp curves in it, he hadn't been able to pass without risking a head-on collision.

The gray-haired chief looked up from his desk and focused on Baker's face. "I wasn't sure that you were going to show up at all," Chet Maynard said. "You've been pretty scarce around here lately."

"I'm sorry, sir," Baker said. "I know I've needed a lot of time off—"

"Understandably," the chief interjected. "I know your family suffered a great loss."

Baker flinched at the sharp jab of pain at the reminder of that loss. "And I appreciate how much time off you've given me."

Chief Maynard nodded. "I know family comes first," he said. "But with you being single, you've been the one who's always picked up the extra shifts since you joined the department five years ago. So you being off hasn't been easy."

"I'm sorry, sir," Baker said again.

The guy waved away his apology. "It couldn't be helped. But now that your brother Dusty is back from the rodeo, I'm sure he'll take his twin's spot, and you'll be back to covering all those shifts."

Irritation crept up on Baker now. Why was it that everyone assumed Dusty could take

Dale's place? Just because they looked alike? Exactly alike, but that was just their outer appearance. They'd had different personalities, different interests.

Dusty's had always been the rodeo while Dale's had been Jenny and the ranch. Getting married might have changed Dusty's priorities a bit as he put Melanie and their babies-to-be above the rodeo, but Ranch Haven wasn't up there on his list.

Not that it was on Baker's. But he couldn't stop himself from thinking constantly about what needed to be done, the calves that needed to be moved to new pastures, the foals that needed vaccinations and training… There was always so much to do. While at the firehouse, Baker often just sat around, waiting for something to happen. Something terrible… At the ranch, he was always busy. Always occupied and sometimes he even got tired enough to sleep without the nightmares. But here…

He wasn't sure he would get any rest if he signed back up for the twenty-four shifts he used to work. Because firefighters needed to be available and alert, they were expected to sleep at the firehouse during those shifts. But Baker would be afraid to fall asleep because he was afraid that he might wake the rest of the team, like Little Jake often woke the rest of the Haven household. That was why he never stayed in the main house when he was at the ranch; he didn't want anyone to know that Little Jake wasn't the only one who had nightmares.

"Dusty isn't taking Dale's job at the ranch," he told his boss. "And I'm not sure how much he's even going to be helping Jake."

The chief shoved a hand through his gray hair, mussing up the thin strands. "What does that mean for you? For your job here?"

"I want to stay on," he said, yet even he heard the lack of enthusiasm in his voice. But what was the alternative? Trying to take Dale's place at the ranch?

Baker had sworn that Ranch Haven was never going to consume his life, or take it, like it had the lives of other people he'd loved. Like his dad and Grandpa Big Jake. And in a way it must have taken his mom because she hadn't wanted to stay there. And neither had he. He'd sworn that once he left he was never coming back. But after serving out his four-year contract and two deployments with the army, he hadn't reenlisted. He'd found himself moving back to Willow Creek. He'd resisted moving back to the ranch like Grandma had wanted, though. Like she still wanted… Baker had pursued the career he'd wanted since elementary school when he'd joined the fire department. He couldn't just abandon that dream. But he couldn't abandon his family either. Not like his mother had.

He drew in a deep breath, bracing himself before admitting, "I just don't want to leave my family in the lurch."

While he'd felt ambushed the night before, after talking to Taye and thinking about it, he had to accept that his family's hearts had probably been in the right places. With the boys…and with him.

He still didn't think his meeting with Mrs. Lancaster and the boys would help anyone, though. It would only hurt them more, and they were already hurting too much.

"I understand that," the chief said but then uttered a weary-sounding sigh. "I just wish…"

"Just give me tonight off," Baker said. And he would try to get some sleep. "And I'll report for duty tomorrow night."

The chief grinned. "Great. That's great."

For some reason Baker didn't feel the same way. He couldn't summon any enthusiasm for his job; all he could summon was curiosity about whether Jake had been serious that morning, if he really wanted Baker as his ranch foreman. He was curious about more than the job; he was curious about Taye Cooper. As he'd told his brother that morning, he didn't even know her. And he wanted to. If only she would have agreed to pretend dating him…that was the only dating that would have been safe for either of them.

"WILL YOU TEACH me how to cook?"

The question startled Taye because it came from an unexpected source. Seven-year-old Miller sidled up beside her at the kitchen island where she and Little Jake were making cookies. The dark-haired toddler sat atop the stainless steel counter, his pudgy fingers coated in cookie dough. As much of it probably made it into his mouth as made it onto the baking sheet, but to give Emily a break, Taye had first started enlisting Little Jake's help a few weeks ago. Now he insisted on "helping"—by tugging on her until she lifted him onto the counter—every time she baked.

She'd asked Miller before, but he'd turned her down. While Caleb loved eating what she baked, he would rather be outside, trailing one of the cowboys around the ranch. And Ian would rather be trailing Caleb.

"You really want to learn to cook?" she asked. Maybe with school done for the summer, he was bored. Really bored.

He nodded. "Yeah, Miss—Aunt Melanie— needs to eat a lot so she doesn't pass out. And I want to learn to cook for her." He still wasn't used to calling his physical therapist *aunt* since he'd only just recently discovered that she was. Melanie had kept it secret from them out of embarrassment over her whirlwind wedding. Taye couldn't fault her for that; she kept secrets of her own out of embarrassment. And hurt…

She felt nothing but affection right now for Miller. "I would love to teach you to cook," she assured him. He was so sweet to want to help take care of Melanie. He'd bonded with his physical therapist even before they'd returned to the ranch, probably from the minute she'd arrived at the hospital where he'd been recovering from surgery to his leg.

"Thanks, Miss Taye," he said, and a smile curved his lips.

He so rarely smiled, and Taye was so moved that she wrapped her arm around him and hugged him close to her side. Usually he would stand stiffly in anyone's embrace except Melanie's, but this time he slid his arm around Taye's waist and hugged her back.

Warmth flooded her chest.

Little Jake must have been moved too because he reached out; with one hand he gripped his brother's head and with his other Taye's side.

"Ew..." Miller groaned and jerked away, but his brother's fingers stuck to his sandy-brown hair with globs of raw cookie dough. His other hand was stuck to Taye's knit shirt, but she was used to the mess that resulted in baking with Little Jake.

"It'll wash right out," she assured him as she grabbed a wet dishcloth to dislodge the toddler's sticky fingers without pulling Miller's hair any more than his little brother already had.

"But I don't wanna take a shower now," Miller said. "I want to learn to cook."

"You can take the shower later." Chances were that he was going to get messier cooking with her, especially if Little Jake stayed around to help out.

"You can learn to cook a little later," a deep voice with a slight Texas drawl said as Dusty joined them in the kitchen. "I've been looking for you to have that conversation I told you we needed to have."

Miller's face flushed a deep red. "I don't wanna talk about it."

Taye looked over the little boy's head and focused on his uncle. "Do you guys need to be alone?" she asked, not wanting to intrude.

Dusty sighed and shook his head. "No. I think I'm going to need the reinforcement," he said.

"Reinforcement?" Taye didn't like the sound of that, especially when she wasn't sure that it was really her place to get involved in family drama. But that hadn't stopped her from running after Baker last night to make sure he was all right. After doing that, she probably wouldn't have had to work hard at pretending to have a relationship with Baker. She cautiously asked Dusty, "About what?"

"About the fact that Miller needs to apologize for the way he treated Uncle Baker yesterday," Dusty said.

The little boy had physically attacked his uncle when Baker had been getting into the ambulance with an unconscious Melanie. Taye understood that the boy had been scared that he was about to lose his aunt like he had his parents.

Dusty must have realized that as well because he spoke gently to his nephew. "I know you were worried about Aunt Melanie," he said. "But Uncle Baker was helping her, not hurting her. And you hurt him, so you need to apologize to him."

The little boy's body stiffened with what looked like rebellion, and he vehemently shook his head. "No!"

"You can't hurt people like that and not apologize," Dusty persisted.

"I wanted to hurt him," Miller defiantly said. "But I don't think he even felt it."

Baker was a muscular man. He might not have physically felt the blows, but Taye knew that he had emotionally. And she found herself speaking up. "Miller, Uncle Baker thinks you don't like him—"

"I don't!" Miller said. "I hate him!" Then he jerked away from her, dodged around Dusty and ran up the stairs.

While she was upset now that he'd confirmed Baker's fear, she was also happy to see the little boy run again. He'd had a heavy cast on for so long. And even now there was metal rod in his leg holding the bone together. But in the weeks Melanie had been working with him, he'd regained mobility.

She sighed. "Guess he changed his mind about those cooking lessons…"

"He's not mad at you," Dusty assured her.

She nodded. "I know. He's not mad at you either. Just like Baker said, he's mad at him."

Dusty groaned. "Poor kid…"

"Which one of them?" Taye asked with a teasing smile because she couldn't imagine anyone calling Baker a kid.

"Both of them," Dusty replied.

Baker couldn't have been much younger than Dusty, and he was taller and broader than him. But apparently to his older brother, he was still a kid. Taye would have laughed if she didn't feel sorry for Baker all over again. No wonder he'd been so furious last night; his family really didn't understand him.

"Are you going to go after him?" she asked.

Dusty grinned slightly and repeated her question back to her, "Which one of them?"

She narrowed her eyes slightly. "Miller."

Dusty shook his head. "He's probably up with Melanie now. She'll have better luck reasoning with him than I will."

"He's become really attached to you, too," Taye assured him. Maybe that was because Dusty looked exactly like Miller's dad—and like Miller himself. He had the light sandy-brown hair and hazel eyes that Dale had had, which Miller and Ian had. Little Jake looked like his uncles Jake and Ben with his dark hair and big, dark eyes.

"Mi-Mi," Little Jake murmured as he tried to squirm down from the countertop.

Taye moved the toddler farther down the island to the sink and washed his hands before helping him down onto the brick-tiled floor. The minute he was on his feet, he rushed off toward the stairwell, babbling "Mi-Mi" as he climbed up the steps on all fours.

"Maybe Miller will listen to Little Jake," Dusty said with a smile as he watched his youngest nephew on the stairs.

"Everybody listens to Little Jake," she said. Even though he was only a toddler, he'd apparently babbled and giggled and chattered away nonstop until the accident. Then after that, the child had made no sounds but the screams from his nightmares. Recently he'd started talking again. His first word had been *Cab* for Caleb, but he'd added more names to his repertoire. And he giggled now, too. He'd started doing that again even before he'd spoken any words, also because of Caleb.

Caleb had brought laughter back to the ranch. Back to his friends who were now his family. Children were resilient. Adults not so much…

If only she could help Baker, could help relieve that unhappiness that seemed to hang so heavily and darkly over him like a persistent storm cloud.

"I should have stayed," Dusty said softly, pulling Taye out of her thoughts. Dusty had stayed at the ranch in the couple of weeks between his twin's death and the funeral. Then he'd taken off to find his missing bride just as Taye, Emily, Katie and Dusty's bride had moved into the ranch house.

Everybody understood now why he'd left. "You were looking for Melanie," she said. Dusty wasn't like his mother, like his brothers had accused him of being. Their mother had taken off after their father's funeral because she'd wanted to return to the rodeo; Taye suspected that she hadn't been able to handle her grief.

Some people couldn't. Just as her mom hadn't been able to handle the dissolution of her marriage, of the love of her life falling in love with someone else. She hadn't been able to cope, but Taye had always wondered how hard she'd tried…and wished she would have tried harder…for Taye's sake as much as her own.

"I should have known Grandma would have found out about our marriage and brought Melanie here," he said.

She smiled. "She doesn't miss much." Sadie had somehow also known that Jake was still in love with Katie, and that Ben and Emily would fall for each other.

Dusty sighed. "I'm not so sure about that…" And his brow furrowed as if something was weighing on his mind.

Like something seemed to be weighing on Sadie. Taye's smile slipped away as she asked, "What's going on with her?" If anyone would know, it was Dusty. Since his return to the ranch, Sadie hadn't been herself; she wasn't as feisty. She seemed older now than even her eighty years.

"You don't miss much either," Dusty mumbled.

"No, I don't," she said.

"You remind me of her," he said. "No offense."

She smiled again. "No offense taken. It's a compliment being compared to a woman as strong as Sadie Haven." She just wished that it was true, but she worried that if she was tested, like her mother had been tested, she would find out she wasn't as strong as she wanted to be. That she was more like her mother than Sadie. That was why she didn't dare risk her heart on falling deeply, irrevocably in love.

"She is strong," Dusty said, and he drew in a deep breath as if he'd reassured himself with that statement.

"I'm worried about her," Taye said. "I know it's not any of my business, but if there's something I can do to help, please let me know."

Dusty gave her a solemn nod.

And Taye felt reassured for a moment.

Until he chuckled dryly and said, "You *should* be worried about her. You know she's going to focus on matching you up with Baker now."

"The last bachelor cowboy…" A smile twitched at her lips. "I'm not worried about that." She knew that she was in no danger of falling for anyone, let alone someone as troubled as Baker was. "Although I suspect it might be giving your younger brother nightmares."

Baker had certainly been concerned enough about his grandmother's meddling to consider faking a relationship with Taye. She felt that flash of regret that she'd initially turned down his proposal. A fake relationship might have been fun, certainly more fun and less threatening than a real one…unless the lines between fake and real had become blurred.

Dusty uttered a ragged sigh. "I don't think that's what's giving Baker nightmares."

Taye tensed. "Baker actually does have nightmares?" she asked with surprise. "How do you know?" Had Baker opened up to Dusty like Miller was starting to?

Dusty shrugged. "I don't know for sure, but my first night back, I was walking around the ranch, and when I was outside the foreman cottage, I heard something…" He shuddered as if the memory was that troubling.

"What?" she prodded when he trailed off.

He studied her for a moment as if wondering if he should confide in her. He didn't know her as well as Ben and Jake did, but he must have been starting to trust her because he replied, "I don't know for certain. Baker wouldn't admit to anything, but I don't think Little Jake is the only one who wakes up screaming at night."

"Why?" she wondered aloud. "Because of

the accident?" That was certainly troubling Baker more than he would admit…until last night, until he'd confided in her. Then he'd immediately appeared guilty for being upset about it, under the misapprehension that he didn't have that right—that only his nephews had a right to the crushing sadness. But she wasn't about to share that with Dusty, or Baker's family might push him even harder to go into therapy with the boys. Taye knew all too well that pushing someone to do something they weren't ready for only made them more determined to deny that they needed help. Like her mom had refused to talk to anyone, even Taye…

Dusty sighed. "I don't know if it's over the accident or over whatever he might have seen before that as a paramedic or even in the army when he was a medic on his deployments."

That would explain the sadness in his eyes in the calendar picture; he was already carrying around some guilt or regret or trauma from what had happened before the accident.

She doubted he would open up about that any easier than he had about the accident. And while he'd briefly opened up with her, he'd shut himself up very quickly.

He was obviously determined to deal with

his troubles on his own, or worse yet, not deal with them at all. And Taye knew all too well where that would lead him...deeper and deeper into the darkness.

And his own destruction.

She couldn't watch someone self-destruct like that. Not again.

Never again.

SHE DOESN'T MISS *MUCH*...

That was what Sadie had overheard Taye and Dusty saying about her in the kitchen moments ago. But they were wrong. She'd missed a lot. She'd missed how troubled Baker was.

Having nightmares?

Her youngest grandson was apparently struggling as hard as her great-grandsons, and she hadn't noticed. Poor Baker. She knew he'd grown up feeling unseen in the shadow of his older brothers. She knew that was why he'd been so determined to get away from the ranch and away from Willow Creek. And even though he'd come back a few years ago, he wasn't entirely here. He'd lost a piece of himself somewhere.

Or maybe he'd lost that piece of himself all those years ago when his father had died and his mother had taken off. Maybe bringing Darlene back to the ranch would help him.

Silently cursing herself for chickening out of talking to Darlene the day before, Sadie slipped back into her suite, where she'd left Feisty and Lem asleep in one of the recliners in the sitting area. Despite being over late last night, Lem had gone into the mayor's office early, finished up some work for Ben, and then come back out to the ranch to check on her.

Then he'd fallen asleep while they'd been watching the news. A politician to the core, Lem was usually much more interested in world events than she was now. As the daughter of the longest-running mayor of Willow Creek, Sadie had once been interested herself. But now she was concerned with just her small corner of the world, with the ranch and with her family. She had enough trouble keeping tabs on all of them.

So much trouble that she'd lost track of a few of them.

Darlene.

And Jessup.

And maybe even Baker...

While he'd once wanted to be seen as more than a shadow of his brothers, he'd clearly changed his mind about that. He hadn't liked his family focusing on him last night, on them pressuring him to help the boys.

He didn't think he could. And maybe he was right.

Because in order to help them, he would have to help himself first.

CHAPTER EIGHT

COMING BACK TO the ranch was the right thing to do. Baker knew that, but he'd expected to dread it even though it was just for the night and not—like his grandmother wanted—forever. His visit tonight to Ranch Haven was all about making it clear to Jake that he wasn't taking the foreman job, that he had to find someone else. He also intended to make it clear to the rest of his family that he wasn't going to put the boys through the trauma of reliving the accident with Mrs. Lancaster or with anyone else.

Baker should have dreaded coming back for those reasons, for the arguments that he was certain to have. But instead of dread, his pulse quickened with excitement when he pulled his truck up outside the sprawling main house. He wasn't excited about seeing his family; he was excited about seeing the one person in this house who wasn't family.

When he opened the driver's door and

stepped out, he chuckled at the sight of Old Man Lemmon's vintage Cadillac. But that wasn't whom he'd been thinking about... whom he couldn't seem to stop thinking about...

He could have come back earlier and caught Jake out in the pastures or in one of the barns. But he'd chosen to return at dinnertime. For her...

Not that anything could ever come of his attraction to her. Just the little he knew about her, how sweet she was with the boys and his grandmother, and how warm and kind she'd been to him, he liked her too much. She was a nice person, and she deserved someone who didn't have the issues he had.

So tonight he would savor the food and her presence—because it wasn't just the ranch and his family that he was going to be around less. He needed to stay away from her, too. For her sake as much as for his...

He climbed the steps of the porch but instead of heading toward the front door, he slipped around the side of the house to the back, to the patio and the French doors that opened onto the kitchen. Through the glass, he could see his family already gathered around the table. Melanie's mother was here, and he felt a twinge of guilt that he'd forgotten about her. But as his sister-in-law's mom, she was family, too. Old Man Lemmon was beginning to feel like one of the family as well, just like all the women his grandmother had hired. But they were already family or about to become family...except for Taye. While the rest of the family was gathered around the long dining table, she stood at the island, her golden hair aglow in the sunshine streaming through those patio doors.

Something clamped around his heart, and he sucked in a breath. Then he drew in another one, a deeper one, bracing himself before he opened the French doors to step inside the house. Conversation at the table ceased as everyone turned toward him, and he understood how Dusty had felt a couple of weeks ago when he'd shown up unexpectedly at Jake and Katie's "welcome back from the honeymoon" party.

But this wasn't a party—it was just an ordinary dinner. And nobody should have been all that shocked that Baker was here. It wasn't like he'd been gone for weeks like Dusty had after the funeral. Actually, the rodeo rider had been gone for years before his twin died. Baker hadn't even been gone twenty-four hours. Yet, after how he'd reacted at the family meeting the evening before, they probably hadn't expected to see him again, at least not so soon.

Self-conscious at being the center of attention, he quickly closed the doors and moved around the table to an empty chair next to Emily.

"I'm so glad you're here," the blonde schoolteacher told him. "I'm so sorry about last night. I didn't mean to upset you."

Heat rushed to his face with embarrassment over how he'd reacted. "I know," he assured her. "I don't blame you..." He glanced at the head of the table, where his grandmother sat.

Sadie didn't sit as tall and straight as she normally did; her shoulders were slumped, and she slouched forward a bit. Maybe with guilt.

"She didn't put me up to it," Emily said. "I really was just relaying what Mrs. Lancaster told me."

He shrugged. "It doesn't matter..." Because he had no intention of talking to the school psychologist now any more than he'd wanted to talk to her all those years ago when his dad had died and his mom had left. The principal had sent him to her office then, but he'd just shaken his head when she'd asked if he wanted to share his feelings with her.

"Emily isn't the one who should be apologizing to you," Dusty said from across the table.

Baker whipped his head around with surprise that any of his brothers would offer him an apology. And of all of them, Dusty probably had the least to do with what had happened last night since he was more concerned about his wife and their unborn babies. "You don't owe me one either," Baker assured his brother.

Dusty chuckled. "I know." He sat on the long bench, wedged between Caleb and Miller. He had his hand on Miller's shoulder and appeared to squeeze it lightly.

Miller leaned away from him, pressing up against Melanie's side. He peered up at her with a pleading look in his hazel eyes.

Melanie shook her head. "We talked about this earlier," she said. "You know you owe your uncle Baker an apology for how you treated him yesterday."

"But I thought..." the boy began.

"You were wrong," Melanie interjected before he could continue. "I know you were worried about me, but that still doesn't give you a reason or a right to lash out at your uncle like that, especially when he was actually helping me."

Miller's face flushed a deep crimson, and his bottom lip trembled slightly.

A jab struck Baker. He knew how the little boy felt, how upset and embarrassed he was with everyone staring at him. "He doesn't need to do this," he said. "And everybody's dinner is getting cold. Just finish eating..." And once they were done, he would talk to Jake.

Now a hand touched his shoulder lightly, and a plate of food appeared in front of him. Steam rose from the dish, bringing with it the delicious aroma of savory spices and baked chicken. His stomach growled like a chained dog smelling a wild animal. He glanced up at Taye, who was starting to straighten from her position leaning over him, but she froze mid-motion with her face so near his that he could see her incredible pale blue irises close up.

"Thank you," he said, and he was surprised at the gruffness of his own voice.

The sound of it must've surprised her, too, because she jerked upright and pulled her hand away from his shoulder. He could still feel the imprint and warmth of her palm even as she backed away toward the island, where steam wafted from another plate. She picked it up and carried it to an open chair at the table, next to his grandmother and across from where Old Man Lemmon sat on the bench next to Ian.

Ian waved his hand as if he wanted to be called on in the classroom. But he wasn't trying to get his teacher's attention. He was waving his hand in Baker's direction.

His stomach grumbled again, but this time he suspected it was dread rather than hunger churning inside it. He hoped his nephew wasn't going to ask him the question he'd been asking everyone since he'd sustained a concussion in the crash.

Where are Mommy and Daddy?

If Emily and Mrs. Lancaster were right and the little boy's memory had returned, why did he keep asking? Why did he keep putting himself and everyone else through that?

"Uncle Baker!" Ian called out.

He couldn't ignore him, so he forced a smile and asked, "What is it?"

"Were you putting out a fire today?" Ian's question bubbled out of him with excitement. "Is that why you had to go to town?"

He had been putting out a fire, of sorts, because he wasn't sure how much longer his job in town would be held for him if he didn't start picking up more shifts. He shook his head. "No fires today."

Ian sighed with disappointment before turning his attention back to his plate. Baker focused on his, spearing a piece of chicken with his fork and bringing it to his mouth. Unlike the chicken some of the guys made at the firehouse, this wasn't dry and rubbery. It fell apart in his mouth, moist and full of savory flavors. He swallowed a moan with the delicious bite and stabbed his fork into a roasted chunk of potato next. It was expertly seasoned with a crispy skin.

He wanted to praise Taye for her cooking, but he was worried how the others might construe his compliment, especially after that moment they'd just had. He doubted any of his family had missed that. If only she'd agreed to his pretend relationship…

"You know it's the right thing to do," Dusty murmured.

And Baker tensed because he knew his brother was right. But before he could express his appreciation to Taye for the meal, a child's voice, with a slight quaver, said, "I'm sorry, Uncle Baker…"

He turned toward Miller. The little boy's face was down as he stared into his plate. Even though Miller wasn't looking at him, Baker knew he'd spoken to him. Not freely. Dusty's hand was still on the seven-year-old's shoulder, but this time he patted it with what was probably approval because Dusty said, "Good job."

Miller glanced up at Dusty with a slight smile. But when he turned back toward Baker, the smile was gone. A coerced apology was rarely ever sincere; Baker remembered that from all the times his grandmother had made him or one of his brothers apologize for something they'd done growing up. Miller's apology hadn't been given freely, but it had been given, and Baker knew how hard that must have been for the kid to do.

Baker held the little boy's hostile gaze and replied, "I understand…" And he probably did better than anyone else. He cleared his throat and glanced around the table at his family. "And I'm sorry, too, for last night…" he said. That was something else he'd realized he needed to do, no matter how difficult. "I overreacted."

Ian's little brow creased with lines of confusion and he asked, "What did you do? What happened?" And there was a trace of panic making his voice rise, as if he was worried that his memory was going away again.

Baker offered him a reassuring smile. "Nothing for you to worry about," he said, and he would make certain that the kid didn't worry, at least not like he had that day…that horrible day…

He turned back to Miller, who was staring at him speculatively. "What did *you* do?" the boy asked.

Baker sighed. "I got mad at people who were only trying to do the right thing." Or at least, what they thought was the right thing.

Miller's face flushed before he stared down at his plate again. And Baker felt a twinge of regret. He hadn't been talking about his nephew but about himself.

"For both of you overreacting yesterday, you should have kitchen cleanup detail after dinner," Jake said.

Miller groaned.

And while Baker was tempted to groan as well, he suppressed it. He would have expected his grandmother to suggest such a punishment to get him to spend more time around Taye Cooper. But what was Jake up to? His grandmother's dirty work? Or was he just trying to avoid having a conversation of his own with Baker?

He had to know that there was no way Baker was taking Dale's job as ranch foreman. That was a position no one would ever be able to adequately fill. Nobody would ever measure up to Dale, as a foreman or as a father. The boys didn't need him or Mrs. Lancaster; they needed their dad. But Dale wasn't ever coming back…like too many others who'd left before him. Their dad. Grandpa Jake. Their mom.

"I can handle cleanup on my own," Baker said. "There's no reason for Miller to have to help me."

Miller glanced at him then, his hazel eyes wide with surprise and something that looked almost like appreciation no matter how begrudging.

"No," Dusty said. "Miller helped Miss Taye make the mess, so he should help clean it up."

"It wasn't just me," Miller said. "Little Jake helped make the cookies."

"What?" Baker asked. He was definitely missing something.

Taye spoke up then, her voice full of praise.

"Miller helped me make tonight's dinner. He's already quite the chef."

"Wow," Baker said. "It's really good." And he wondered how she'd managed that with the distractions she must have had with both a seven-year-old and a toddler in her kitchen.

Miller's mouth curved into a slight smile of pride, and warmth flooded Baker's chest. He hadn't seen the little boy look that happy in a long time. But his nephew's mouth turned down again quickly, as if he felt guilty over that moment of happiness. That was something else Baker understood all too well. The survivor's guilt.

The kid really did need to talk to someone. But that someone wasn't him.

He wished it was. He wished he could help the boy, but he also knew his limitations all too well. He couldn't help him emotionally, so the least he could do was his cleanup duty. "Since Miller helped make this meal, he's already worked today," Baker said. "So I can handle KP duty on my own."

"What's KP duty?" Caleb asked with curiosity.

"Kitchen patrol," Baker said. "It's one of the duties that army recruits get assigned. I thought I'd be done with that when I left the army, but I still pull it at the firehouse."

"What do you patrol the kitchen for?" Ian asked with confusion.

"Mostly dirty dishes," he admitted. But there had been thieves at some of the bases, people desperate for food. He didn't share that with his nephews, though. They were already growing up much too fast; they didn't need to lose any other illusions of childhood yet.

"What about fires?" Ian asked. "Do you patrol the kitchens for that?"

"I have had to put out a kitchen fire or two," he admitted. "One of the guys tried to deep-fry a frozen turkey last Thanksgiving, and that didn't go well." He shuddered in remembrance while his family chuckled with amusement. The sound warmed him just like Miller's smile had. He didn't often make people laugh. "And there was the time that Smitty left a chicken in the oven when we got called out to an accident…"

As he said that word, the room fell silent. Their thoughts had probably gone where his had, to the accident that had caused them all so much pain. He wished he could take back the word. No, he wished he could take back that day.

"Guess what we have for dessert?" Taye asked loudly, her voice full of enthusiasm.

He shot her a grateful glance for smoothing over his gaffe and asked, "Peanut butter cookies? Those are my favorite."

She shook her head and smiled back. "No. And you can't have any until you clean that plate, Uncle Baker," she chided, but her smile widened.

"That *is* the rule," Caleb informed him with a regretful sigh. He'd probably been reminded of that rule more than anyone else. Then the little blond boy turned back to Taye and held up his plate. "Mine's empty. So what's for dessert?"

Even from down the table, Baker could see the uneaten vegetables hiding beneath a crumpled-up napkin. But he didn't rat out the little boy.

Taye tilted her head as she studied his plate, but instead of busting him, she smiled. And more warmth flooded Baker. She was incredibly beautiful, the kind of beauty that radiated from the inside out. "We are having Mississippi mud pie."

Caleb grimaced. "I don't wanna eat mud."

Everybody laughed except for Caleb and Ian. "I don't want to eat mud either," Ian said.

"It's not real mud," Miller said. "I helped Miss Taye make it, and it's mostly chocolate pudding."

"It's my favorite dessert," Melanie said, and her brown eyes glistened as she smiled at the cook. "Thank you for making it."

"Thank your mom," Taye said. "She shared her recipe with me and Miller and helped us make it."

Juliet Shepard shook her head. "It looks better than anything I've ever made, just like this meal. You're incredible, Taye."

Now Taye's eyes glistened with tears, but she blinked them away as she jumped up from the table. "It probably doesn't look that pretty now. Miller and I had some fun with it."

"We put gummy worms and ground-up Oreos on it, so it looks like a real mud pie," he shared, his voice vibrating with excitement as he grinned.

She'd done this. Taye Cooper had made his nephew smile again. And now emotion rushed up on Baker, threatening to choke him. He quietly cleared his throat and hoped nobody noticed how affected he was by her generosity and goodness.

"Gummy worms!" Caleb exclaimed, and he jumped up from the table to rush over to where Taye was taking the dessert from the refrigerator. Ian rushed after him, and both boys jumped up and down as Taye put a big pan on the counter.

"I wanted to put real worms on it," Miller said, "but Miss Taye wouldn't let me." He sneaked a telling glance at Baker, who had a pretty good idea of whom the little boy had intended as the recipient of the slice with the real worms.

Maybe Baker would skip dessert and just eat a second helping of the chicken and potatoes instead. Even the cooked veggies were good…just soft enough that they weren't mushy with a sweet buttery coating on them. Maybe Old Man Lemmon really was just coming out to the ranch so much for the cooking, like he and Sadie liked to claim. But when Baker glanced down the table, he noticed that Lem was more focused on Grandma than on his meal. Her former nemesis stared at her with concern, and that concern quickened Baker's pulse.

Was she all right?

She'd been having some issues with high blood pressure. Too high. But she was too stubborn to let him take her to the ER or to even check with her own doctor.

"Grandma?" he called out to her.

She raised her head and met his gaze, and she seemed to summon a smile as she shook her head. "You're not getting out of cleaning that plate or your KP duty," she informed him, as if he would have ever tried to get her to bend the rules for him.

But she had.

He realized that now, how she'd always gone a little easier on him than she had his brothers. They must have been aware of it because Ben snorted derisively while Jake remarked, "Like he couldn't sweet-talk you into letting him out of it."

Sadie chuckled. "Ben's the sweet talker."

"And Baker's the baby. He never had to talk to get you to give him what he wanted," Dusty said.

"That's not true," Sadie said before Baker could even open his mouth to protest. Then she met his gaze.

And he knew she'd been thinking exactly what he was: that she hadn't been able to give him what he really wanted…his dad and mom back. Just like he couldn't give back what his nephews really wanted, what they really needed. Their mom and dad.

JUST IN CASE his family had been playing matchmaker by assigning Baker cleanup duty, Taye hadn't stayed in the kitchen to help out like she normally would have. After dishing up the dessert, she'd headed out to the patio and had contented herself with catching just glimpses of Baker through the glass doors. Jake or Dusty must have insisted that Miller stay to help out, and while he and Baker worked together, they didn't exchange any words.

Miller was stubborn. And Baker must have instinctively known not to push. During dinner she'd thought he'd made progress with his nephew. That Miller was beginning to soften a little in his resentment and anger toward his uncle.

But as well as glimpses of Baker, she caught some of the glances Miller sent his uncle. And the resentment and anger were still there. She uttered a heavy sigh.

"Why don't you go up to bed?" Melanie was the one who asked, startling Taye, who'd thought she was alone on the patio. Melanie smiled at her. "I'm sorry. I have a habit of sneaking out here for some fresh air. I thought you knew I was here."

Taye shook her head. "No, I'm a little out of it today. I didn't get much sleep last night."

Because of him. Because of his ridiculous proposal.

Was that why he'd returned tonight? For dinner? Had he changed his mind again about trying to fool his family? He'd fooled her for a moment when he'd turned to thank her for the plate she'd put in front of him. Or had she been fooling herself when she'd touched him…when she'd thought she could be that close to him and not react as so many other women did to how attractive he was?

"That's why you should go up to bed now," Melanie said. "You always get up so early in the morning. You're always taking care of everyone else." She stepped closer and reached for Taye's hand, squeezing it. "Thank you for today, for making all of my favorite foods."

Taye shrugged. "My job is to cook," she said. "That's all I'm doing, and I like making things that I know will get eaten."

Melanie patted her slightly protruding belly. "The babies and I did our part tonight to make sure there were no leftovers for Miller and Baker to clean up."

Clean up…

"That's what you're doing out here," Taye

guessed. "You're making sure that Miller doesn't go at his uncle again."

Melanie sighed but nodded. "He's just so angry with him. I really think that Mrs. Lancaster is right, that Baker and Miller need to speak to her together, at least to work out this issue between them."

"You know what the issue is," Taye said. Baker was right. "Miller blames him for his parents dying."

Melanie sighed again. "Poor Miller..."

"Poor Baker," Taye said.

Melanie squeezed her hand again. "You like him."

Taye shook her head. "I don't know him."

"You could change that," Melanie suggested.

Taye turned toward her. "Are you playing matchmaker for Sadie now?"

Melanie smiled. "She's not been wrong."

Taye shuddered and shook her head. "I am not getting matched up with anyone." Ever. "Let alone Baker Haven."

"Why not?" Melanie asked, and now she sounded offended. She'd recently come to her husband's defense against his brothers, and now she seemed about to come to her brother-in-law's.

Taye didn't want to explain her feelings because then she'd have to talk about her mother and explain how she didn't want to make any of the mistakes her mother had, like falling deeply in love and wallowing in the past. In the what-might-have-been... So she uttered a sigh, which became a yawn. "I am tired," she said. "I'm going up to bed."

She managed to slip through the kitchen unnoticed since Jake had joined Baker and they were deep in conversation. Once she was upstairs in her bedroom, she even managed to fall asleep relatively quickly.

But she awoke some hours later, wide awake and restless. So restless that she knew she wouldn't fall back to sleep. She dressed and headed downstairs to the kitchen. But instead of reaching for bowls or pans, she passed the island and the long dining table and headed to the patio doors.

Maybe the fresh air would make her tired again like it had earlier. But once she stepped outside, the restlessness increased, making her edgy. Or maybe that was the fault of the full moon. It was so big and bright that it felt more like day than night.

In the distance she could hear howling...

Coyotes maybe.

She shivered despite the warmth of the summer night. But she wasn't worried about the coyotes. She was worried about herself, about the restlessness.

And for the first time since its arrival at the ranch, she understood the bronco. How caged he must feel after being allowed to go so wild during a rodeo.

She smiled and found herself heading toward the barn. She was just about to open the doors when she heard more howling. It wasn't as far away as the sounds she'd heard earlier.

And it wasn't coyotes.

It wasn't quite howling either. It was something even more primal than that. It was pain.

CHAPTER NINE

BAKER HADN'T INTENDED to spend the night again. But after dinner and KP duty, he'd dreaded heading back to his apartment in town. And not just because of the long drive but because it had sounded so empty. So much like he often felt inside.

He'd stayed in the foreman's cottage as usual. While it was empty, it was close enough to the main house and the barn that it didn't feel quite as lonely as his apartment.

Of course, his apartment had other units in the building, but those people were strangers. Maybe thankfully so, in case they ever overheard his nightmares. Like the one he'd just had, which had had him jerking awake. He could never remember what he saw in them—only that they left him feeling terrified and helpless and his throat raw from the sounds he'd been making.

He shivered, his body slick with sweat, fought off the tangled sheets and rolled out of bed. He wasn't going to go back to sleep. He couldn't trust that the dream, whichever dream it had been, would not return if he closed his eyes again. So he stepped into some jeans, pulled on a shirt and headed out the door of the foreman's cottage. It was close to the barn, close to Midnight.

And he found himself getting closer to Midnight as well.

Something about that wild horse made him feel a little less wild himself. Made him a little less restless.

That was what churned inside him now: restlessness. There was definitely no way he was going back to sleep anytime soon. Not with the energy coursing through him, fraying his nerves.

He had no idea what time it even was. Well past midnight, he imagined. Or maybe that was just the full moon that was making it seem like it was close to daybreak. He would just slip inside the barn, clean Midnight's stall and then head into town. He had that shift at the firehouse tonight.

His stomach dropped, heavy with dread, at the thought of reporting for work at the job he'd once thought was all he wanted. Now he wasn't sure he wanted it at all.

But he'd already told Jake that he didn't want the foreman job. He'd told him twice actually. Once yesterday morning and again last night in the kitchen after he and Miller had finished cleaning up. But Jake hadn't seemed to listen either time.

Or maybe he'd listened, but he'd just refused to believe Baker. Like he was lying or something.

He never lied. Not anymore.

Not since the accident when he'd lied to Miller, when he'd promised him that they would all be all right. That his parents would be fine.

He sucked in a breath at a sudden stabbing sensation in his heart. He shouldn't have lied, but Miller had been so distraught and in so much pain. Baker had just wanted to calm him down so he could treat him, so he could help him.

But that hadn't helped at all. Lying never helped. And Baker couldn't help but wonder if he was lying to himself. But he wasn't ready yet to face the truth. He wasn't ready.

He pressed his hand against his chest, trying to ease that ache. The regret. The loss.

"Are you all right?"

He gasped and jumped, stumbling backward on the gravel drive. She stepped out of the shadows of the barn and reached for him, catching his arm and steadying him. "Taye?" he murmured, and he wondered if he was still dreaming.

But meeting Taye Cooper in the moonlight wouldn't have been like his usual dreams. He wouldn't have woken up yelling if he'd been dreaming about her.

"Yes, it's me," she confirmed. "What? Did you think Midnight started talking?"

He chuckled. "I wouldn't put it past that horse."

"Me neither," she agreed.

"I didn't realize you were such a fan of Midnight," he said.

She lifted her face toward the moonlight and uttered a blissful-sounding sigh. "I am tonight."

He laughed again. "So we're not talking about the horse…"

"I didn't think you were a fan of his either," she said.

He shrugged. "I wasn't…" Until recently, anyway. "What are you doing here?" he asked.

She shrugged now. "I woke up and just knew I wouldn't be able to get back to sleep."

He nodded. "So you decided to come out to see him?"

She glanced at the barn behind her. The doors were closed. Either she hadn't opened them yet, or she'd already seen the horse and was on her way back to the house.

"Have you finished your visit?" he asked.

She shook her head, and her long hair moved in waves around her shoulders. It was loose and so incredibly soft and silky looking that his fingers twitched with the yearning to slide through it, to feel it…

"Did you realize you forgot his carrots?"

She glanced down at her empty hands and smiled. "I guess I did." Then she looked up at him, and as her gaze locked with his, her smile slipped away. "I was distracted. I heard something."

Emotion rushed up on him, choking him, so that he had to swallow. Hard.

"*Someone* maybe…" she hedged.

And he knew that she knew. He clenched his jaw so tightly that he felt a muscle twitch along it.

She gazed at him steadily. "It was you," she said. "Dusty was right. Little Jake isn't the only one who has nightmares."

He released a ragged sigh. "I thought he heard me that night…"

"What is it?" she asked. "What keeps you from sleeping?"

A smile tugged at his lips as he stared at her, into those pale blue eyes that glistened with sympathy and concern. She was so kind. And so very beautiful. "Tonight? You…"

She smiled then, too, but it didn't reach those beautiful eyes. "That's why you were yelling? Dreaming about me was a nightmare?"

He shook his head. "No. I'm the nightmare, Taye." But he suspected she already knew that; that was why she'd slipped past him and Jake tonight without a word, why she'd fled first outside and then upstairs, because she hadn't wanted to be near him.

He stepped back. He had to let her go. More for her sake than for his…

TAYE COULD HEAR Midnight inside the barn, pawing at the ground, kicking at his stall as he made noises. And in that moment, she felt like him. She wanted to run.

She wanted to get as far away from Ranch Haven as she could. No. She just wanted to

she remembered it, remembered how frightened she'd been, how helpless she'd felt. "I tried to make things that she would like. That's when I started watching TV cooking shows and poring over cookbooks."

"Oh, Taye..." he whispered. "I'm so sorry. That must have been so scary for you. Wasn't there anyone else who could help?"

"I tried to find someone," she said. "But my mom was estranged from her parents, and my dad just thought she was doing it for his attention, to get him back, or at least that's what my stepmother convinced him my mother was doing."

"But she must have been clinically depressed," Baker said. "She needed medical help."

She smiled faintly at the irony of the EMT thinking of that first. But he was right. "She did, but she refused to go to the doctor. And then I refused to go to my dad's. I was worried that she wouldn't eat at all if I wasn't there. I was worried that she might hurt herself..." She'd often skipped school for that same reason, for fear that she would come home to find that her mother was gone. Her heart pounded hard with the fear she'd felt back then.

Baker placed a hand gently on her shoulder, and then he wrapped his arms around her, pulling her close...offering her the comfort he refused to accept for himself. "Oh, Taye... and you were only ten..."

She leaned against him for a moment, savoring the warmth and strength of his muscular body. "You were younger when you lost your dad and mom," she said, and she wrapped her arms loosely around his waist. *Just for a moment.* She wasn't any more inclined to accept comfort than he was. "The boys are younger than I was."

"You were still just a child," he said. "And you did lose her?"

"To the depression before she died," she said, and her heart felt so incredibly heavy in her chest like it always did whenever she talked about or thought about her mother. "But she did die...when I was fourteen. Her body just eventually shut down. She basically died of a broken heart." That was why Taye would never risk hers. "And then I went to live with my dad and stepmother and stepsisters." Tension gripped her as she remembered how uncomfortable that had been.

She must have stiffened in his embrace because he smoothed his hand down her back, like he was trying to soothe her in the same way he might rub his hand along Midnight's back to soothe him. And his deep voice was soft when he asked, "I take it that wasn't a good experience…?"

She sighed. "No. I was clearly unwelcome."

"In your own dad's house?"

"I didn't fit in," she said. She pulled back from him and forced a slight smile. "But I didn't even try." She hadn't cared about the same things that her stepmother and stepsisters cared about…like the latest fashions and fad diets and social status.

"I find that hard to believe," he said. "You do so much around here."

"I cooked there, too," she admitted. "I helped out."

"And you still weren't welcome. Sounds like you were Cinderella."

She jerked back, completely out of his arms, and shook her head. "Oh, no…" A laugh slipped out, and she winced at the slightly hysterical sound of it. But the comparison offended her on so many levels. "I'm no Cinderella. I have no interest in finding a prince."

He smiled. "Don't you like fairy tales?" he asked.

She laughed naturally now. "No. I don't. I much prefer the self-help books. They're more realistic about what you need for happily-ever-after."

"What is that?" he asked as if he really wanted to know.

"The first thing. The most important thing—the ability to admit when you need help."

His lips curved into a slight smile now. "I walked into that one, huh?"

"There's no shame in admitting it," she said. "In reaching out for it."

He reached out for her then, with his fingers on her chin. He tipped up her face as he began to lower his. "I'd rather reach for this…" he murmured.

He was deflecting again. Changing the subject. She should pull back, pull away. But she needed to know what it would feel like to kiss him. So she rose up on her toes, closed the distance between them and touched her mouth to his.

He kissed her back, sliding his lips across hers…making her mouth tingle, making her entire body tingle with awareness. She'd never felt anything so intense.

And that intensity scared her so much that

she jolted away from him and backed up a couple of steps.

Baker caught her shoulders, steadying her. "I'm sorry."

She shook her head, rejecting his apology. She was the one who'd kissed him first. "Let's just blame the moonlight," she suggested. "I better get back to the house..." And she started backing away from him, away from the barn.

"I do dream about the crash," he said.

And that admission stopped her.

"And other things," he admitted. "I dream about my last deployment. When we came under fire...and the soldiers I couldn't save, just like I couldn't save my brother and sister-in-law."

Her heart wrenched for him. "Baker..."

"And talking about any of that isn't going to make me forget about it," he said. "It's only going to make me think about it more."

"Have you tried?" she asked. "Have you talked to anyone about it before?"

He nodded. "After that deployment, I had to. It was protocol."

"So you only did it because you had no other choice," she surmised.

He nodded again.

"So did you talk to them? Or did you just keep changing the subject like you have with me tonight?" she asked.

His mouth curved into a slight smile. "You're tougher than that military shrink, and I've talked more to you than I did to him."

"You didn't tell me anything about the deployment," she said. "Not until now…"

"I've told you more about the accident," he said. "And that's what got me thinking about other times I couldn't save people."

"I understand that," she said. "I felt that way about my mom, that it was my fault. That if only I'd tried a little harder, I would have been able to save her."

"Oh, Taye." And he reached for her again.

But she held up her hand, warding him off. She wanted more than comfort from him now, and she suspected that would only cause her more heartache.

He kept his distance. But he added, "You were just a child. You did all you could."

"And I believe that you did, too," she said. "You need to find a way to believe that yourself, so you can make your peace with the past."

"Have you?" he asked.

"Yes. I know that I couldn't have done anything else for my mother. She needed to want to help herself. And she didn't want to." She hadn't wanted to live after Taye's father left. She'd been so hung up on him, on the romantic ideal that he was her soul mate and there was no one else for her. Her mother must have read too many fairy tales when she'd been growing up since she'd believed she couldn't be happy without her husband.

Taye believed she would be happier without one, without ever caring that much about a man. But when she'd kissed Baker… She'd understood a little how much a kiss could awaken inside a person. An intensity she'd never felt before…but she couldn't feel that for Baker.

She was afraid that he was too much like her mother, that he didn't want help. And she couldn't watch someone else she cared about succumb to the darkness. So she forced herself to turn away from him and head toward the house. And she only glanced back once.

He was no longer standing in the moonlight. He must have slipped into the shadows of the barn. And she had a feeling that was where he would stay.

CHAPTER TEN

BAKER HAD TO force himself to stay where he was…where he'd been for the past week. In town, mostly at the firehouse, except for the few calls he'd responded to with the crew. A couple of out-of-control bonfires. A few, fortunately minor, car accidents.

Nothing catastrophic had happened. He hadn't even had another nightmare since that night. And maybe that was because he couldn't stop thinking about that night. About Taye… About their intense talk and their even more intense kiss. That was why he had to force himself to stay in town…because he wanted too badly to see her again. To talk to her.

To kiss her.

And knowing now what he knew about her, what she'd gone through, he was even more certain that she deserved better than him. Someone who wouldn't remind her of that unhappiness of her childhood, and while she hadn't outright accused him of being like her mother, it was clearly what she thought.

That he didn't want to get help. But that wasn't the reason that he'd refused to meet with Mrs. Lancaster and the boys. He really didn't believe he could help the boys, especially when they didn't even want him around the ranch. And so he'd forced himself to stay away for them, too.

He missed them, which was weird since every time he'd seen them since the crash, they'd only made him think of it again. Of Dale and Jenny.

But now he was thinking only of the boys, of Little Jake's return to babbling and giggling, and of Ian's and Caleb's incessant chatter. He even missed Miller's scowls.

He missed them so much that as he lay in one of the bunks at the firehouse, trying to take an afternoon nap after a late-night call, he imagined he could hear that little giggle of Jake's, the chatter of Ian and Caleb…and when he opened his eyes, he saw them. Even scowling Miller.

And he saw her standing behind his nephew with Little Jake perched on her hip, one of his chubby hands wrapped tightly around her thick golden braid. Wondering if he was still asleep, he rubbed his hand across his eyes, but when he pulled his hand away, they were still there.

"Is this where all the firemen sleep?" Ian asked as he jumped onto the bunk beside him. "We saw the big truck in the garage. But I didn't see a dog. Do you have a dog?"

"One of those spotted ones," Caleb added as he climbed the ladder at the end of the bunk. "Aren't all firemen supposed to have a spotted dog?"

"Doggie…" Little Jake said, as his neck swiveled around looking for one.

"I don't have a dog," Baker said.

"We know *you* don't," Miller said. "But doesn't one just live at the firehouse and ride on the truck?"

His interest surprised Baker, and he sat up and focused on him. "We used to have one," he said.

"Let me guess? It died," Miller said with his usual resentment.

"No," Baker said. "Dottie was really attached to one of the guys who retired, so now they're both living in Florida." Or at least that was the story he'd heard.

"Do you live here?" Ian asked, and he pressed up against Baker's side.

He couldn't really believe that he was awake. That they were here.

"Uh, I live here when I'm pulling a double shift like I am today," he said. He'd pulled a lot of them in the past week to make up for all the time he'd taken off, and to get his mind off her…and them.

But here they are.

"I hope we didn't wake you up," Taye said. "Emily asked me to bring the boys here to meet Ben, but we must have beaten him…" From the speculative tone of her voice, she'd already realized what Baker just did: Ben was scheming just like he'd done when he'd set up Sadie and his deputy mayor. "Then the fire chief saw us and told the boys that it was all right for them to explore the firehouse."

Baker swallowed a groan. Had Ben recruited Baker's boss to help out with his matchmaking scheme, too? Since technically the mayor was the fire chief's boss, Baker wouldn't put it past his brother to pull rank on Chet Maynard.

"I take it you didn't know anything about this meeting…" Taye mused.

Baker shook his head. "Nope."

"I'm sorry," she said. "I should have checked with you, especially when Emily disappeared this morning and then called from town asking me to bring the boys."

He tensed then and glanced around Taye toward the open door to the bunkroom. Was Mrs. Lancaster going to show up with Emily and Ben? "This isn't another ambush, is it?"

"Ambush?" Ian asked, clearly with no clue what the word meant.

But Miller stared at him like he knew, and like the same thing had occurred to him. He glanced toward that open door, too, before turning back to Baker. "So who else is supposed to be here?" he asked, and he cast a distrustful glower at Baker.

Baker held up his hands. "Hey, I swear I didn't know anything about any of this either."

Miller's head bobbed up and down in a quick nod. "I know. You wouldn't want us here."

"You don't want us here?" Ian asked, his voice cracking as tears suddenly started pooling in his hazel eyes.

Baker wrapped his arm around the little boy and squeezed him close. "No, I am very happy that you're all here," he assured his nephew.

Miller didn't look convinced, his scowl

twisting into more of a grimace. "Yeah, right," he scoffed. "If that's true, why didn't you ever bring us here before?"

Baker stilled as he realized he hadn't. "I don't know," he admitted. "I guess I didn't realize you'd be interested in seeing the firehouse."

"I'm not," Miller said quickly.

"I am!" Ian exclaimed. "I want to be a firefighter just like you!"

Baker's heart twisted in his chest. "I'm sure you'll be even better," he told the boy.

Miller snorted derisively and Baker wasn't sure if it was meant for him or Ian. "You gotta be able to remember stuff better than you do now," Miller said, making it clear of whom he was derisive. "Or you'll forget where the fire is and show up at the wrong house."

"No, I won't!" Ian said, and he jumped up and shoved Miller, who stumbled back into Taye and Little Jake.

"His memory is almost all better now," Caleb said in defense of his best friend.

"Then why does he keep asking stupid stuff?" Miller asked, and tears shimmered in his eyes now. Clearly, he didn't think the question Ian kept asking was stupid but painful. Then his face flushed as his temper snapped, and he shoved Ian again.

"Hey, hey," Baker said. "There's no fighting in a firehouse." And surprisingly the boys stopped and turned to him.

"What are the firehouse rules?" Caleb asked from where he dangled off the top bunk.

Baker reached up and snagged him off before he could fall. Caleb wrapped his arms around his neck and hung from him like he had the bunk.

"And who gets to drive the truck?" Ian asked. "Can I?"

At the mention of the truck, Caleb scrambled off Baker. "Can I?"

Baker chuckled. "I don't believe any of you have your driver's license yet."

"Do you get to drive it?" Miller asked, begrudgingly, but still he asked. He was interested. More interested than he'd ever been in Baker even before the crash.

Baker nodded. "I have. But usually I drive the paramedic van…" If only he'd been driving it the day of the crash, if only he hadn't been alone.

The color left Miller's face. Anxious to change the subject, Baker said, "I'll show you guys around." A twinge of regret jabbed at him that he hadn't thought to do it before. But he'd had no idea that any of his nephews were interested in his job.

"Unc Bak!" Little Jake exclaimed, holding out his arms toward him. Stunned, he reached for the little boy. Even before the accident, Little Jake hadn't ever called out for him. And since... He hadn't said anyone's name until Caleb's. Or *Cab*, as the toddler called him.

As he took him from Taye's arms, he touched her. And that tingling sensation he'd felt during their kiss spread throughout him again. She was so beautiful. And while he knew he should be mad at Ben for meddling and manipulating like Grandma, he couldn't summon any anger right now.

In fact, he was happy...and he couldn't remember the last time he'd felt that...

"I AM NOT happy about this," Taye whispered into her cell phone, so that the boys wouldn't hear her. Not that they were listening to her. They were bouncing around Baker, firing questions at him as he showed them the fire truck and all the equipment on it.

They were so excited and so loud that she barely heard Emily utter an apology. "I'm sorry," the schoolteacher said. "Ben totally intended to meet you there and take the boys from you, but Old Man Lemmon didn't show up today and he had to take a meeting with some architects and real estate developers."

"What about you?" Taye asked. "Why couldn't you bring them again?"

"I have to meet with the principal at the school."

"In town," Taye pointed out. "So you could have brought them since you were coming here anyway." But instead, Emily had taken off without the boys. She'd disappeared, leaving the kids anxious for the firehouse trip that Ben had promised them at dinner the night before.

"I couldn't be late," Emily said, "and you know how hard it is to get them ready. It's like herding cats."

Baker was finding that out as he tried to give each of them a turn to sit behind the steering wheel of the fire truck. Despite Taye's irritation with Ben and Emily, she couldn't help but smile at the sight of the boys wearing the little plastic hats that the fire department handed out to kids as part of their community outreach. Even Miller was wearing the one he'd begrudgingly accepted from the uncle he treated so coldly.

"I can come and pick them up on my way back to the ranch," Emily offered. "I'm nearly through with my meeting. Mrs. Lancaster is here, too. I can bring her with…"

"No!" Taye said. At the sound of her shout, all the boys—even Baker—froze before turning toward her. She shook her head and pointed toward the cell phone she held.

"Don't you want a turn in the fire truck, Miss Taye?" Ian asked her.

She smiled at him and shook her head again. Then she turned away from them to whisper urgently into the phone. "Please, don't do that," she told Emily. "Baker has been pulling double shifts."

When the fire chief had seen them sitting in Taye's SUV waiting for Ben, he'd tapped on her window and invited them to wait inside, and as he'd walked them in, he'd praised the boys' uncle as being his best, hardest-working firefighter.

She regretted that she and the boys had woken him up; she suspected he didn't get much sleep. Not with the double shifts and not with the nightmares he'd admitted to having. Which she'd heard him having the other night. Ever since that night *she'd* been having nightmares…over what she'd shared with him, over how vulnerable she'd been and over how stupid she'd been to kiss him. Because she hadn't been able to stop thinking about that kiss, about him.

"You're right," Emily said. "Now is not the right time, and the firehouse is not the right place."

Taye exhaled in relief. "No, it's not."

"I'll invite Mrs. Lancaster to dinner again," Emily continued. "Tomorrow night. I'll have Ben make sure that Baker has it off, and you can get him to come out to dinner, too."

"Emily…"

"Taye, you know he's the one who can help them the most," she said. "You saw him with Miller that night. As angry as Miller is with Baker, he knows that Baker is the only one who understands what he's really going through. And Ian idolizes him. He'll be truthful with Baker."

Taye turned back to where Baker had resumed showing the boys the fire truck. No. He wasn't just showing it to them. He was playing with them. He lifted Little Jake into the driver's seat of the rig. And the sudden

that he just liked feeling less helpless than he must have been feeling? That was why she'd started cooking…because it had given her something to do, something she could control.

He rushed off with the keys and returned moments later, struggling with the heavy cooler. It had wheels on it, but Miller wasn't rolling it. Baker started toward him, but Taye rushed forward and intercepted him with a shake of her head. Miller was too proud to accept anyone's help, least of all Baker's. The two of them really were the most alike.

"The kitchen's upstairs," Baker said—more to her than to him.

"You all need to wash your hands," Taye said. "So if Uncle Baker will show you where the bathroom is, I'll bring up the cooler."

Miller dropped it and for once was eager to follow Baker. Little Jake was getting sleepy, though, and instead of wriggling down from her, he held out his arms to Baker like he had earlier. And like earlier, when they exchanged him, their hands and arms brushed, and that sensation raced through Taye again—that awareness.

She stepped back and reached for the cooler.

"Do you need help with that?" Baker asked her.

She chuckled and Caleb said, "Miss Taye is really strong. She lifts a lot of stuff."

Miss Taye was strong physically. But she wasn't sure how strong she was emotionally. She suspected it wasn't strong enough to risk getting involved with a man like Baker Haven. She wasn't sure she was strong enough to get involved with any man.

Even these little males were making her lose sleep, worrying about them. And if Baker could help them, she had to convince him to try. She just had to find the right moment to talk to him, and since she was concerned that he might react the way he had when his family had suggested he meet with Mrs. Lancaster and his nephews, she couldn't do it in front of the boys. But she didn't know how they would find a minute to talk without them.

She'd just carried the cooler into the kitchen when Miller, Caleb and Ian ran in to join her. Miller, despite his limp, had beaten the two younger boys.

"Miss Taye, did the sandwiches and potato salad stay cold enough?" Miller asked with concern.

She handed him one of the containers. "Perfectly cold enough," she assured him. "And perfectly delicious."

"We're having salad?" Caleb asked, his little face twisting into a grimace of distaste.

"Potato salad," Miller said. "With bacon bits and shredded cheese, it's so good."

"Sounds good," Baker remarked as he carried Little Jake into the kitchen. Small, wet handprints covered Baker's shirt.

"Guess I don't have to ask if he washed up," she said with a smile.

"Are there any cookies?" Caleb hopefully asked.

Her mouth stretched into a wider smile. "Yes, Miller and I made peanut butter ones."

"Yum," Baker said. "Those are my favorite."

He'd mentioned it that night he'd come to dinner. She always made a point of learning everyone's preferences, but Baker hadn't been around enough to learn what else he liked.

"They're my favorite, too!" Ian proclaimed.

Miller snorted. "No, they're not."

"Yes, they are!" Ian insisted.

"Like you remember..."

Taye stepped between them before they

could start shoving again. "Hey, let's get the cooler unpacked. I'm starving."

"Yes, Miss Taye," Miller replied. Then he softly whispered, "The peanut butter cookies are my favorite."

And Baker sucked in a breath as if surprised that his oldest nephew would admit to having anything in common with him. Taye was surprised, too, because Miller had grumbled about coming to the firehouse. But he'd been happy to help her cook, as he always was.

"Miller helped me cut up everything for the potato salad and the fruit salad," she said, praising him.

"You used a knife?" Caleb asked, clearly in awe.

Miller nodded. "A really sharp one."

Baker leaned close to Taye and whispered, "Probably good I wasn't around then…"

She smiled and shook her head. "He was very careful. He's going to be quite the chef. Might take over my job and leave me unemployed and homeless."

"Taaa…" Little Jake called out to her, his voice a little sharp, as if he was worried she might leave the ranch. He clutched at her shirt, and she took him from Baker, settling him onto her hip.

"Miss Taye is the best cook in the whole world," Caleb said.

"Did you really teach yourself?" Miller asked with awe.

She nodded. "I read a lot of books too and watched a lot of cooking shows."

"I don't like reading that much," Miller said. "And the shows are boring. I'm lucky I have you to teach me."

Taye reached out and squeezed his shoulder. She was the lucky one…lucky that these sweet boys had come into her life…even though she was so sorry for the tragedy that had brought her to them, to the ranch. They were doing better now, but they needed more help. They weren't the only ones…

Baker made certain to praise all the food with every bite he took. But she knew that he wasn't flattering her…or just her… He was trying to get closer to Miller. She couldn't tell if it was working or not, but the boy didn't glare at him as many times as he usually did.

Little Jake's head settled onto her shoulder. "Somebody needs a nap…" she murmured.

"You can put him down in my bunk," Baker offered.

"Can we sleep in the bunkroom, too?" Ian asked.

"Are you tired?" Baker asked.

"I wanna sleep like the firemen do," he said.

"Me, too!" Caleb agreed.

She chuckled. Usually those two insisted that at five they were too old for naps. And while Miller had taken them in the early days of recovering from the accident, he rarely ever rested now. But surprisingly he chimed in, "Me, too…"

"I think you all just want to get out of KP duty," Baker said with a laugh.

But with the biodegradable containers Taye had packed, cleanup took just a few minutes. Then she and Baker tucked up all the boys in the bunkroom, where they were pretending to be firefighters sleeping while they waited for a fire. After she and Baker closed the door to the room, she had no more excuses to putting off that conversation with him, so she turned toward him in the hall and said, "There's something I'd like to talk to you about…"

No. That was a lie. She wasn't going to like this at all because he was going to like it even less.

But before she could continue, he asked, "You're thinking what I am?"

She furrowed her brow with doubt. "About…?"

"That the only way we're going to prevent more of these matchmaking attempts by my family is to reconsider that proposal I made to you a while ago…"

"You think this was a matchmaking attempt?" she asked.

He chuckled. "You don't? First Jake insists on me doing KP duty with Miller, probably thinking that you'd stay in the kitchen with us. Now Emily and Ben set *you* up to bring *the boys* to visit me."

She sighed. "Yes, and I stupidly fell for it. But the boys were super excited."

"Really?" he asked. "I had no idea they were that interested in firefighting."

"Don't all little boys want to be firefighters?" she asked.

He chuckled. "Not Caleb. While he told me all the equipment and the trucks were cool, he said he still wants to be a rodeo rider like Uncle Dusty and somebody called Shorty."

She laughed. Caleb must be referring to Melanie's father, who was a rodeo champ before he became an announcer. "I missed that."

"You were on the phone," he said. "Emily?"

She nodded. "I'm sorry I fell for their trick. I thought you were aware that the boys were coming." But she should have known better.

"No. Remember how my family likes to ambush me…"

"Speaking of ambushes," she began with a grimace.

He groaned. "What?"

"Emily was going to bring Mrs. Lancaster here, but I put her off."

"Thank you," he said.

"Just until tomorrow night," she said. "She invited her to dinner and wants me to convince you to come, too."

"Sounds like they already think we're together," he said.

She shrugged. "I don't know. But I agree that maybe we should pretend that we are…"

He widened his eyes in surprise. "You changed your mind about lying to them?" he asked.

"After they lied to get me to come here," she said, "I have far fewer qualms about it."

"And Sadie?"

She smiled. "I doubt we'll fool her, but it might be fun to try."

He grinned. "Yeah, I think it could be fun."

"And tomorrow night?" she asked albeit hesitantly.

He sighed. "Thanks for being straight with me about that, about Mrs. Lancaster."

"So you're not coming," she surmised. "Not even if it could help the boys?"

"Emily and Ben really got to you," he said.

She pointed toward the closed door but noticed it wasn't closed all that tightly anymore. "They're the ones who've gotten to me." In the past week she'd gotten closer to them than she had since moving into the ranch. With Melanie's pregnancy progressing, and Emily and Ben driving into town for work and wedding planning, she'd gotten more time with the boys and often watched them. Which only proved to her how much she'd already fallen for them. "I would do anything to help them. Would you?"

He stepped closer again and smiled at her, a flirty smile, as he lowered his head until it was close to hers, until she could see only his handsome face, his gorgeous topaz eyes. "What would you do?"

"I already accepted your proposal," she reminded him…although she suspected she was going to regret that and not just because she wouldn't be entirely truthful with her friends anymore. But because she wasn't being entirely truthful with herself…

But it was just pretend. She could handle that. Surely, she could handle that…

"Maybe we should seal this arrangement with something," he suggested.

And she knew that he wanted her to kiss him again. And she wanted to…so badly… that she rose up on tiptoe. Her lips had just touched his when she heard fumbling by the door and then a voice as Caleb asked, "Are they kissing?"

"I dunno…" Ian stage-whispered. "I can't see anything…" As the door opened farther, Taye stepped back, away from Baker.

Away from the invitation of another kiss.

It wasn't until later, until after she'd bundled the boys back into her SUV, that she realized he hadn't answered her. And she had no idea if he was showing up for dinner.

I CAN'T JUST show up there without knowing.

That was the excuse Sadie had given herself for putting off a trip to that ranch, the one Dusty wanted to buy. The one where Darlene was staying…where she may have been helping Jessup raise his children.

Could Sadie really have more grandchildren? Maybe even more great-grandchildren?

Her heart beat faster with hope and anticipation that she might have more family than she'd known about after having lost so many of them—too soon, too painfully. Like Big Jake and Michael and Dale and Jenny… And Jessup. Jessup had been lost to her so long ago when he'd run away. Where? To a ranch just an hour away from Ranch Haven?

Dusty was there now; he was touring the place before extending his offer to purchase it. He'd asked if she'd wanted to join him, but she wasn't ready. Not yet. Not until she knew…

So, instead, she was pacing her suite, anxiously awaiting Dusty's return. He hadn't gone alone; Melanie had made the trip with him. And they hadn't wanted Sadie to be alone while they were gone, so Dusty had summoned Lem to the ranch to sit with her while they were away.

Not that he was much company at the moment as he and Feisty snoozed together in one of the easy chairs in her suite. "Sit down, woman, before you wear out the floors," Lem instructed. So maybe he wasn't as sound asleep as she'd thought he was.

His deep breathing had been the only sound in the eerily quiet house because the little boys were gone, too. Taye had taken them to meet *Ben* at the firehouse, though he'd actually had no intention of showing up there. The kids had been so excited to go that Taye, with her big heart, hadn't been able to refuse to take them. A smile tugged at her lips; Ben really was the most like her when it came to meddling. Hopefully his match-making attempt would prove as successful as hers had been.

"It's good to see you smile again," Lem said as he stared up at her. Even if he wasn't sitting down, he had to stare up at her. She was that much taller than him.

Not that it bothered either of them.

"I was just thinking of the little boys," she admitted.

Lem smiled, too. The kids meant as much to him as if they were his own great-grand-kids. Not that he had any great-grandkids, yet, just grandkids who were too busy with their careers to settle down. At least one of them was moving back to Willow Creek, so that was good. "They've been gone a while," he said.

"They aren't the only ones," she said, and

that heaviness settled onto her chest again. "What could be taking Dusty so long?"

But she had a feeling that she knew...

A knock rattled the door to the hall, startling a gasp out of her. She'd closed it earlier when she'd thought Lem was sleeping because she hadn't wanted the kids' return to the ranch waking him up. Even though she was on her feet, Lem and Feisty jumped up and beat her to opening the door.

He seemed to exchange a long silent look with whoever had knocked before stepping back to let the visitor inside her suite. Her nerves intensified so much when she saw it was Dusty that she dropped heavily into the chair behind her. He rushed toward her and fell to his knees in front of her. "Grandma, are you all right?"

Lem hovered over Dusty, his face creased with lines of worry. "Are you okay? Should I call Baker?"

"Baker's in town," she reminded them both. But he belonged here at the ranch; hopefully he would realize that soon. "But I don't need medical help. I need answers. What did you find out?"

Dusty sighed and shook his head.

And her heart plummeted. She'd accepted

long ago that Jessup was probably dead; with all the medical issues lupus had caused him, they'd been warned that he was going to have ongoing organ issues his entire life, for however long that lasted.

It hadn't lasted long enough. He hadn't lasted long enough. Her breath caught, burning in her lungs, and a tear escaped from one eye and trailed down her cheek.

"No, Grandma," Dusty said. "Don't think the worst."

"He's not dead?"

"I don't know," Dusty said. "A Realtor was the only person Melanie and I met at the ranch. My mom wasn't there, and neither was…"

"Your uncle," she said.

He shook his head again. "I don't know if he's ever been there. The Realtor said the ranch owner is a trust. It might be an estate-type situation now."

Sadie took an unsteady breath. An estate meant that someone had died…

"Uncle Jessup isn't listed on the deed or property records or even as a trustee," Dusty said.

"He never was listed either," Lem said

softly, as if regretfully. "I checked property records earlier this week."

"And you didn't tell me?" Sadie asked, and another pang struck her heart. "You promised not to keep anything from me." Like her husband had, not sharing with her that he'd been sending money to Jessup and to Darlene after they'd both left the ranch.

"I thought maybe he changed his name, like Dusty here did," Lem explained. "So I wasn't sure…"

"The only way we're going to know for sure is to talk to my mother," Dusty said. "To get her to tell us what she knows about Uncle Jessup."

And those kids she'd been rumored to have helped him raise. More grandkids.

Sadie nodded. "We will talk to her," she said. "But let's make sure that the boys can handle more upheaval in this house first."

"The boys?" Dusty asked. "What about you?"

"I'm used to upheaval," she said. "I just don't want to confuse and upset Miller, Ian and Little Jake any more than they already are."

And Baker…

He was as fragile as they were. She realized that now, and regret filled her that she hadn't been more aware of how hard he'd taken Dale's and Jenny's deaths. If he would come back to the ranch, to work, to live, he might fully heal. But she worried that he might never come back if they pushed him too hard.

CHAPTER ELEVEN

BAKER HAD HAD no idea that he was going to show up for dinner. Not when he knew Mrs. Lancaster was going to be there. And he only knew that because of Taye. While his brothers had each called and asked him to dinner, none of them had been honest with him. Jake had used the excuse that he had to ask Baker about some ranch business. And Ben had claimed that he was so worried about Sadie that he wanted Baker to check her blood pressure. Dusty had also used the Sadie excuse, but when he'd used it, there had been some sincerity along with the slight twang in his voice.

Dusty was genuinely worried about her. So was Baker. But she wasn't the reason he drove out to the ranch that afternoon. And despite how attracted he was to Taye, he wasn't even here because of her. He was here because of what she'd said, though, about doing whatever she could to help the boys.

He wanted to do that, too. And he wasn't so stubborn or vain to think that he was right and everyone else was wrong. He just had a feeling that he was probably going to prove that they were. But in case he was the one who was wrong, he had to do what he could. Anything he could to help them…even if he had to relive that crash again. What he hated more than that was making the boys relive it again.

Dread had wound a tight knot in his stomach, so tight that he had no desire to eat. Until he stepped inside the house. Even though he used the front door this time, he could smell the aroma of cinnamon and vanilla. There was probably an apple pie in the oven or maybe a cobbler. Under that fresher scent was the heavy richness of meat loaf and roasted vegetables. And the dread in his stomach uncurled as hunger growled, like Feisty when she was tugging on the leg of Jake's jeans. She never tugged on Baker's jeans like that, probably because he never tried to ignore her like Jake did. When the longhaired Chihuahua ran up to him now, he stooped and patted her little head and back. She wagged her tail in greeting and then pranced off down the hall toward the kitchen.

you did Ian?" Jake asked, and now all Baker's brothers surrounded him.

Ian tightly held on to his hand still, even though Baker couldn't see him around his brothers. He glared at Ben. "I wasn't the one who lured them to the firehouse."

Ben just laughed again. Then with a pointed glance down at Ian, he asked, "Are you really upset about that?"

"No," Baker admitted, feeling that twinge of regret again that he hadn't brought them for a tour sooner.

"Even Miller wanted to go," Emily said, as she joined them, sliding under Ben's arm, which curled naturally around her shoulders.

"And I understand you were supposed to bring them," Baker added, and while he was usually cordial to his soon-to-be-sister-in-law, he gave her a slight glare, too. "Sadie, you really are shrinking," he teased her. Sadie often complained that she was shrinking as she aged.

Emily shook her head. "I'm not the one most like Sadie."

"No, your fiancé is."

"I was talking about Taye," Emily said.

Baker shook his head. "She's tall. That's about all they have in common."

"She's very wise, too," Emily insisted. "Wise beyond her years. I expect that's why you're here tonight."

He sighed. "She does make a lot of sense."

"She's pretty special," Emily said. "She used to call me the kid whisperer, but she's certainly taken over that role. She's taken Little Jake from me and Miller from Melanie without even trying."

And maybe that was why it had happened—she hadn't forced herself on the kids. She'd just quietly been there, taking care of all of them. And now they went to her.

Baker's arm jerked as Ian tugged harder on him. "Uncle Baker, sit beside me!"

"And you've taken Ian," Emily said, but instead of regret, tears glistened in her eyes. "I'm so glad you came here tonight. I know that Taye told you Mrs. Lancaster is coming, too. It's wonderful that you're willing to talk to her."

"For them," Baker said. "Only for them…"

"Not a little bit for her?" Emily asked softly with a twinkle in her eyes.

Remembering that Taye had finally accepted his proposal, he grinned and chuckled. "Well…"

Emily and his brothers all gasped. "Well?

What does that mean? Are you and Taye seeing each other?"

"They're kissing," Caleb chimed in with a sigh of disgust.

"They are?" Emily asked. But instead of addressing Caleb, she was looking at Baker. He felt his face getting hot, but he didn't have to say anything because the doorbell saved him. "She's here," Emily said as she rushed off toward the front door.

Only visitors rang the bell. Not family. Not Old Man Lemmon…

Everybody knew that and the room fell silent. Miller must have shut off the electric mixer. He'd obviously been warned about the visit because, in a very loud voice into the sudden quiet, he announced, "I'm not talking to her!"

"You said you…" Dusty began.

"No!" Miller shouted. "You can't make me talk to her! You know you can't!" And he turned and ran up the back stairwell.

Dusty started after him, but Baker called out, "Wait! Let me go after him." He turned toward Ian, who was still holding his hand, and said, "I'll come back and sit by you. Save me the seat, okay?"

Ian nodded.

Baker crossed the kitchen and headed toward the stairs. And as he did, he had to pass Taye, who stood at the island yet with Little Jake. She turned slightly toward him and mouthed the words, *Thank you...*

Baker shook his head, unwilling to accept her gratitude. He shouldn't have to be thanked to do the right thing, and being here for his nephews was the right thing. Lying to his family about having a relationship with Taye probably was not the right thing, but for their meddling, they deserved it. Taye deserved better, though, but he couldn't stop himself from leaning close and brushing a kiss across her cheek.

While Taye sucked in a breath, nobody else reacted; they were probably all concerned about Miller. And so was he.

He forced himself to move away from Taye and continue to the back stairwell, where Dusty waited. His older brother narrowed his eyes and studied his face. "Are you sure you're the right one to talk to him when you don't want to talk to her either?" Then Dusty's face flushed, and Baker didn't have to turn back to realize that Mrs. Lancaster must have walked into the kitchen with Emily.

He hurried up the steps, anxious to catch

Miller before the kid either escaped the house down the front stairwell or locked himself into his room. When Baker rushed down the hall, he found the boy's bedroom door closed, but when he twisted the knob, it turned easily. Before he pushed open the door, though, he knocked.

Miller didn't say anything. Since Baker didn't hear a "keep out," he pushed the door open and stepped inside. The little boy was sprawled across his bed, and when he glanced up, his tear-filled eyes widened in surprise. Normally Baker wouldn't check up on him, figuring that he was the last one Miller would accept comfort from. But in this case, he didn't need comfort so much as comprehension. "They want me to talk to *her*, too," Baker admitted. He didn't have to specify to Miller which *her* he was talking about—the little boy would know.

Miller's watery eyes widened even more. "Why? Only the screwed-up kids talk to her at school. You're not a kid."

"No, no, I'm not," Baker agreed. "And it's not people who get screwed up, it's life. And it can get too hard to deal with sometimes, even for me..."

Miller's brow lowered in a scowl, one of suspicion. "You're just saying that."

Baker shook his head. "No. It's the truth. But that's not why they want me to be at the meeting. They want me to be there for you and Ian and Little Jake."

"Why you?" Miller asked.

"Because I was *there*," Baker said. Not just on that day, but so many times in his nightmares he went back to that day...

Miller shuddered. "So they do want us to talk about *that*?"

Baker nodded and made another frank admission. "I don't want to do it either."

"Then why are you here?"

"Because if they're right, if it will help Ian and Little Jake and...you...if I talk to Mrs. Lancaster with you all, then I want to help," he said. And that was all that mattered; *they* were all that mattered. "I want to help you more than I don't want to talk to her."

Miller swiped at his tears and sat up on his bed, staring at Baker so intently, as if debating whether or not he believed him. "Why don't you want to do it?" he asked.

Baker released a shaky sigh and admitted, "Because I don't like to think about it, let alone talk about it. But maybe that's why I'm like Little Jake."

Miller's brow furrowed with confusion. "How are *you* like him?"

"I have nightmares, too," he said.

"You do?"

Baker nodded.

And Miller whispered. "So do I..."

"Then let's talk to her," he urged the boy. "Maybe it will help."

Or maybe it would hurt. A lot.

HE SHOWED UP...

Taye's pulse hadn't slowed since he'd walked into the kitchen. She wasn't even sure why he was here. Had he changed his mind about talking to Mrs. Lancaster? Did he intend to help out the boys like they'd talked about, or was he just here to put their plan into motion about pretending to be involved? Her skin tingled where his lips had brushed her cheek, and her face was hot. Not that anyone was paying attention to her.

They were all worried about Miller. Maybe Baker was right that forcing this meeting with Mrs. Lancaster was a bad idea, at least for Miller. The seven-year-old had finally seemed better, less angry, less attached to just Melanie. He'd shown an interest in cooking and a talent for it. Taye didn't want him to go back to the sullen little boy he'd been for so long. But it was already too late.

He descended the back steps with a slow speed that had nothing to do with his injury and everything to do with his obvious dread to come back down to the kitchen. When he hit the bottom step, his small body tensed, probably with dread, and his lower lip protruded in a not-so-subtle pout. He'd been so happy earlier, so excited to showcase his cooking talents to the rest of the family. Regret struck her that she'd thought it was a good idea that Mrs. Lancaster come to dinner. She'd agreed with the others, and now she wondered if she should have agreed with Baker instead. He came down the stairs behind his nephew, his pace every bit as slow, as if he was going to the guillotine.

Her pulse quickened even more with nerves. Were they both going to refuse and run away? Or would they participate…and regret it?

"Is everyone here now?" Jake asked. "Shall we start dinner?"

Miller shook his head. "No…"

"You must be hungry," Melanie said as she

rushed up to the little boy. He shook his head again. "No, I can't eat. I just wanna get this over with."

"What?" Jake asked.

Miller tipped his head back and stared up at Baker. "*We* want to get this over with... talking to Mrs. Lancaster."

"Yes," Baker agreed. "We do." And then he reached down, holding out his hand for Miller.

The seven-year-old hesitated for a long moment before he slowly but resolutely put his hand in his uncle's. Baker wrapped his long fingers around that small hand, holding it close.

Tears stung Taye's eyes. She hadn't thought she would ever see Miller willingly hold Baker's hand, let alone clutch it like he was now.

"Okay," Emily said. "Beth, would you mind waiting to eat for a bit?"

The older woman stood up from where she'd been sitting near Sadie at the table. She had pretty white hair and pale skin with faint lines around her mouth and eyes. She wasn't much younger than Sadie and probably could have retired years ago. She must love what she did to keep working. "Of course, I can wait," Mrs. Lancaster assured her.

"I'll keep everything warm," Taye assured them, but there was a slight break in her voice. "I'll make sure the meal Miller made stays fresh and delicious."

"The rest of you can eat," Baker said. "Don't wait for us."

"Yes, please," Mrs. Lancaster said. "I didn't come out here just for dinner."

"But I want Uncle Baker to sit next to me at dinner," Ian said as he jumped up from the table and headed toward the firefighter he'd come to idolize.

"You can sit next to me when we talk to Mrs. Lancaster," Baker said, holding out his left hand toward the five-year-old. It was clear that Miller wasn't going to let go of his right hand.

"Uncle Bak," Little Jake called out as he tried to wriggle down from the island where he was sitting next to Taye. She caught him and helped him to the floor. He was hardly on his feet before he rushed toward his uncle and clutched Baker's jeans, as if he was going to use them to climb up his uncle. But Ian released his hand so that Baker could lift Little Jake. Like his younger brother had clutched Baker's jeans, Ian clutched his uncle's sleeve, hanging on to him yet.

Taye blinked hard to fight back the threatening tears. When she'd been tricked into bringing the boys to the firehouse, she'd been irritated, but seeing now how much the boys had bonded with Baker during that outing, she was happy that she'd been part of it.

And she wished she could go with them now as they all headed, so slowly, upstairs. When Caleb started after them, Katie caught her son around the shoulders and held him back. "No, honey, you need to stay here," she told him.

"But I want to go, too," he said.

"This doesn't have anything to do with you," Katie told him.

"What are they going to do?" Caleb asked. He always wanted to be in the middle of everything, part of the big family he'd come to love so much.

Taye could identify with that; she felt more a part of the Haven family than she'd ever felt of her own.

Until now.

Until she knew she could be no part of this. And because she understood, she crouched down in front of Caleb and told him, "They're going to talk about the accident."

Caleb's brow furrowed. "What accident?"

"*The* accident," Katie said, as if that was all that needed to be said.

And maybe it was because Caleb nodded and stepped back. "Okay...but if we're waiting to eat dinner, can I have a cookie or two now?" And he widened his blue eyes as he stared imploringly up at Taye.

She chuckled. "That's up to your mama about the cookies," she said, "but I think we probably should hold dinner."

Katie nodded in agreement and smiled at Taye over her son's head. "Yes, let's wait on dinner, but you can have just one cookie," she said.

"I'll get it," Taye offered.

But Katie caught her arm and held her back. "I'll get it. You have enough to do with holding dinner."

"I'll show you where the cookie jar is," Caleb said as he tugged his mom toward the pantry.

"I'm not sure you can reach the shelf," Taye warned her.

"Then I'll have Jake grab it for him," Katie said.

Melanie's mom was already helping with the food, putting the containers into the warming drawer of the oven. So Taye didn't have much to do but worry. With the eerie silence in the crowded kitchen, she clearly wasn't the only one.

She wasn't just concerned about the children; she was worried about Baker, too. His family might be as well, but she doubted that many of them, with the exception of Dusty, knew how much the accident had been haunting him, how he blamed himself for the deaths of Dale and Jenny.

Her stomach churned with nerves over how difficult it was going to be for him to talk about that day. She shouldn't have pushed him so hard to be here tonight for the boys. Maybe she'd done it to push him away because he was getting too close, way too close to her heart.

CHAPTER TWELVE

BAKER WAS GLAD that Miller had wanted to get this over with before eating. Because if Baker had had any food in him, he probably would have lost it with the way his stomach was churning with dread and nerves. He didn't want to do this, probably almost as much as Miller didn't want to do this.

The little boy had hesitated before taking Baker's hand, but now he clutched it so tightly that it was beginning to go a little numb. Ian had let him go, so that he could lift up Little Jake. The toddler's arm was slung around his neck, his chubby fingers clutched in Baker's shirt. And Ian leaned against his side.

They'd decided to meet with Mrs. Lancaster in their playroom, in which Emily had also been teaching them while they'd been recovering from their injuries from the crash. So amid the toys were tables set up like a classroom.

Mrs. Lancaster gravitated toward the table,

taking a seat in the one adult-sized chair in the room. Baker wasn't about to try to fold himself into one of the little plastic chairs. Since the playroom also doubled as the movie room, there was a big sectional couch in one corner of it, so Baker led the boys there, trusting that Mrs. Lancaster would follow them. She did, but instead of joining them on the couch, she pushed over Emily's wheeled office chair and took a seat in it, in front of them. As if she wanted to make it clear that this was a counseling session.

Miller must have picked up on the same thing because he said, "I don't know why we gotta talk about this..."

"Talk about what?" Ian asked.

Miller groaned, and Little Jake, as if he sensed the tension, too, clutched Baker's shirt so tightly that the collar was beginning to feel like a noose. That might not have been just the shirt that was making Baker feel like he was being strangled, though, but the emotions already rushing up to overwhelm him.

"We're going to talk about the accident," Mrs. Lancaster said.

"What accident?"

"Stop it!" Miller yelled. "Stop pretending you don't remember!"

"Don't remember what?" Ian asked, and he sounded genuinely confused.

Baker suspected the five-year-old might need more counseling than a school psychologist was equipped to provide.

"You *know*!" Miller shouted at him. "You know about the crash. You know Mom and Dad died." He tugged his hand free of Baker's as if he'd just realized how tightly he'd been holding on to it, and his face screwed up into a grimace of disgust as if he'd been holding a snake. "He let them die!"

And all that progress Baker had been making with his oldest nephew receded back to that day, that horrible day.

"I'm sure your uncle didn't let them die," Mrs. Lancaster said.

"You weren't there!" Miller turned toward her, turned *on* her as he shouted, "You don't know what happened!"

"Tell me," she said evenly. "Tell me what happened."

Tears trailed down Miller's face, and his body shook almost uncontrollably. Baker tried to slide his arm around the boy, but he jerked away from him.

"What happened?" Ian repeated.

"You know what happened!" Miller shouted at him. "It was your fault!"

"No, it wasn't," Baker said. "Don't blame him."

Tears trailed down Ian's face now. He had to remember the accident despite his frequent claims that he didn't.

"You took my seat—behind Mom's. That's my seat because I'm bigger and need more room. But you wouldn't give it up and I was arguing with you and Dad was looking back in the mirror and telling us to stop...and then he hit the ice and everything..." Miller's body shook even more. "It was my fault... It was my fault..."

Baker wrapped his arms around him and pulled his trembling body close. "No. No, it wasn't. The roads were too slippery. It didn't matter what you and Ian were doing. There was no way for your dad to control the vehicle, not on that ice."

"You didn't crash," Miller murmured into Baker's shirt, which was getting damp with his tears. "You stopped your truck."

"My truck has four-wheel drive," Baker said. "Their vehicle didn't. It didn't have the tire traction, the ability to stop on ice like that. Your dad did everything he could."

Miller jerked back then and said, "You didn't!"

"Your uncle wasn't in the vehicle with you," Mrs. Lancaster reminded him. "He didn't arrive until later. What was that like, Baker?"

But Miller didn't give him a chance to answer—even if he could have with all the feelings clawing at his chest.

"You didn't get them out. You kept working on my leg," Miller said. "You should have helped them."

"It was too late for your mom," Baker admitted. While Ian was able to recover from his concussion, Jenny's head injury had been too severe. Her heart had kept beating for a while, but there had been no hope for her survival. "There was nothing I could do for her. And your dad..." His breath caught, making his lungs ache like his heart already was.

"I heard him," Ian said, his voice soft but oddly stoic.

And Baker's skin chilled at the little boy's admission. "I heard him say that you needed to take care of us," he said. "He didn't want you to worry about him. That he wanted *you* to take us..." And finally his voice cracked.

Baker shivered. "I tried, though," he promised Miller. "I tried to keep them alive…" Tears flowed down his face now. "I didn't want to lie to you, but I knew…" His own voice cracked as all that guilt and frustration rushed over him again, threatening to consume him. "I knew they weren't going to survive. I didn't have my equipment. I didn't have the rig, and the ambulance was so far away…" Too far away to get there in time…

"You lied," Miller said, but it was without the accusation this time. It was almost with acceptance.

"I wanted to keep you calm," Baker said. "You were going into shock. And then you…" He focused on Ian. "You passed out, and I didn't know… Miller was in so much pain. And Little Jake just kept screaming…" Like he did in his nightmares. Like Baker did in his nightmares.

And he knew this…session…or whatever it was with Mrs. Lancaster wasn't going to help him. It wasn't going to end his nightmares. He knew then that this had been a mistake. Because he was right.

It hurt.

It hurt too much…

TAYE HATED THE silence that hung in the kitchen and elsewhere in the house. That eerie silence had fallen a while ago, leaving them all wondering.

Worrying…

Dusty released a shaky sigh. "Well, even though he said he wouldn't, Miller talked to her."

He'd yelled. While nobody had heard his words, they'd heard his shouts from upstairs. His pain…

So much pain.

Dusty held his wife, his arms wrapped around her. Tears rolled down Melanie's face, so she must have been thinking the same thing Taye was. Worrying about Miller like Taye was worrying about him, worrying about all of them.

Baker…

She hadn't heard his words either, just a deep rumble that must have been his voice. He also hadn't wanted to talk to Mrs. Lancaster, but he had. For the boys.

How was he doing?

Was he okay?

"It's been quiet for a while," Ben mused. "Do you think they're done?"

Emily, who leaned against him, peered up

at him. Her beautiful face was tight with concern. "Should I go up and check?"

Taye apparently wasn't the only one hesitant to intrude.

"I can!" Caleb volunteered with no hesitation at all. But when he started for the stairs again, Katie held him back.

"We should wait," she said. "Give them time..."

"Time to do what?" Caleb asked. "What are they doing up there?"

They could still be talking, without raised voices. But for some reason Taye doubted that. And then Mrs. Lancaster appeared on the back stairwell, and Taye had confirmation that she was right.

Everyone rushed forward, trapping the older woman at the bottom of the stairs. Everyone except Sadie, who bellowed from her end of the long dining table, "Let the woman breathe."

Mrs. Lancaster emitted a nervous laugh as everyone gave her room. "I understand you've all been worrying about what was going on up there," she said.

"What are they doing now?" Caleb asked. "Do you have them coloring like you had me color when I used to come see you to talk about my dad?"

She smiled at the little boy. "Yep, that's what they're doing."

"Even Uncle Baker?" Caleb asked with the same surprise that was on everybody else's faces.

But Taye wasn't surprised. She'd seen him playing with the boys in the fire truck, running them through make-believe emergency scenarios, which had ended with their *nap* in the bunkroom.

"No, Baker didn't stay," Mrs. Lancaster said.

"Did he leave the session early?" Jake asked the question, and he sounded annoyed.

"Oh, no, he stayed despite how difficult it was for him, but when the boys started coloring, he had to leave," she said.

How difficult it was for him... The words struck Taye's heart like blows. She shouldn't have made him do this; he wasn't ready. She'd pushed too hard.

"Did he have a fire to put out?" Caleb asked with curiosity and a quaver of excitement.

"I don't think so," Mrs. Lancaster replied. "I think he just needed a little time alone."

"Is that wise?" Dusty was the one who asked that question. "Will he be okay?"

From the sudden tightness in Mrs. Lancaster's slightly wrinkled face, it was clear that she wasn't certain. And she admitted as much when she confided, "I don't know. It was difficult for him."

That wasn't good enough for Taye. She had to know. "I'll go look for him," she said.

"I can go," Dusty offered.

She shook her head. "You stay here in case Miller needs you," she suggested.

"How is Miller?" Melanie asked.

The tension left Mrs. Lancaster's face as she released a heavy sigh. "I think he made a lot of progress today. They all did…"

But for Baker. Taye heard what she left unsaid. And she began to head toward the patio doors, but Jake caught her arm, holding her back.

"You don't have to do this," he said. "He's my brother. I'll go talk to him. You have dinner to put on the table."

She sucked in a breath, deeply hurt that she'd been put in her place. Jake must have seen her reaction because he shook his head.

"That's not what I meant," he said. "I know you're seeing each other now, but this could be a lot to deal with if he's really upset. And maybe he won't want you to see him like that…"

"He's already talked to me about the accident," she said. "I know how badly it affected him. And even knowing how upset and guilty he feels about it, I talked him into coming tonight. I told him this would be good for the boys." And she hadn't worried about him like she should have; she hadn't considered how great a toll this might take on him.

"Oh, Taye, I'm sorry," Jake began.

She didn't know what he was sorry about, and she didn't particularly care right now. "Let me go," she said as she pulled free of Jake's light grasp. Then she pushed open the patio doors, rushing out of them before anyone else could try to stop her. Could try to keep her from Baker…

She wasn't certain she would find him. He might have already left. He might have driven away, off the ranch, to someplace she wouldn't think to look for him. Like wherever he lived.

She didn't even know where his place in town was. They could have been neighbors for all she knew. But she'd given up her small apartment when Sadie had hired her. The rental had come furnished, so she hadn't had any furniture to worry about, just clothes and other personal items. She didn't have much.

Unlike her stepmother, Taye had never cared about having many possessions. People had always mattered more to her. Like her mother.

And now the Havens.

While she wanted to hear more about the progress the boys had made, she needed to know how Baker was. She needed to know how much the boys' progress had cost him.

SADIE COULDN'T REACH out to hold Jake back when he started out the patio doors after Taye. He was too far away. So she shouted, "Stop!"

And he did, but so did everyone else. And in the eerie silence that followed her shout, she added, "Jake, let Taye go after him."

"But…" Jake sputtered. "I want to make sure he's all right, too." And his broad shoulders slumped with the heavy burden of responsibility he'd assumed way before he'd needed to.

"He's not going to tell you if he is or isn't," Sadie pointed out. "But he'll tell her. He'll talk to Taye."

Jake shook his head, and he grimaced with

disgust. "You must be happy with yourself that another one of your matchmaking attempts seems to be working out. But I think Baker needs his family right now, too."

Sadie suspected that little kiss Baker had given Taye earlier might have been for show, that they were going to try to fool everyone into backing off. But Sadie had a feeling that it was already too late for them. Taye was much more to Baker than either of them was probably ready to acknowledge or admit it. "He needs to talk to someone who understands," she persisted, and she glanced over at Lem with gratitude. Nobody understood her like he did. "And that's not always family. Sometimes that's family last."

Jake released a ragged sigh. "I had no idea he felt so guilty about the accident."

Nobody had realized how much Baker had been suffering since that family meeting when he'd gotten so upset and defensive. How had she missed it?

Taye hadn't missed it; it was probably why she'd initially not connected with him like she had everyone else in the family...because he'd reminded her too much of someone else who'd suffered like that, someone whose suffering had made Taye suffer. Even before

Taye had confided in her one night, Sadie had heard all about the young woman's troubled past from the small-town gossip mill. Her chest ached with sympathy over what she'd gone through with her mother, and with regret that Sadie might be putting her through more heartbreak. Baker wouldn't purposely hurt her, but Sadie knew that sometimes it was easier to lash out than admit to weakness and accept help.

She'd recently done that with Lem. And maybe that was what Jessup had done with her all those years ago when he'd run away. After he was diagnosed with lupus, she'd wanted to wrap him in cotton and keep him safe and healthy. She'd tried to put restrictions on his activities so that he wouldn't get hurt, so that he wouldn't wind up in the hospital where he'd already spent so much time. But his health wasn't something she could control no matter how much she had tried, how hard she would have continued to try if Jessup had let her.

He'd chosen to run away instead—from her smothering and rules and fear.

Was that what Baker had done? Had he run away instead of seeking help? Maybe she should have let Jake go after him, too.

But she had a feeling that Taye would have more success at finding Baker than his big brother would. And she hoped that the young woman had more success comforting him... and that he accepted the comfort instead of lashing out.

Taye was a strong woman, but there was only so much rejection and pain that a person, even one as tough as Taye, could handle.

CHAPTER THIRTEEN

BAKER HAD NEVER understood Midnight more than he had during that long session he'd been trapped inside the playroom with the boys, reliving that horrific day. He'd identified with all the times Midnight had tried to kick his way out of his stall because Baker had felt like that then, like he'd needed to escape no matter the physical *pain*.

But he'd waited. He'd controlled all that hurt until the boys had started coloring and then he'd fled from the room, down the front stairwell and out of the house.

Knowing he wasn't in any condition to drive back to town, he'd headed out to the barn. To Midnight...

As if the bronco identified with him, he kicked at his stall door now and reared up. Was he so empathetic that he was experiencing the same agitation that was inside Baker? The turmoil that had battered him during those long minutes he'd been trapped in that playroom, listening to the boys tell their memories of that day.

Miller...

Tears rolled down Baker's face as he relived those moments when Miller had revealed his guilt. He'd been blaming himself for the accident, blaming himself and Ian for it happening.

He could empathize with Miller. With the guilt, the incredible crushing weight of it bowed his body, and he slumped against the stall door. And Midnight stopped kicking and rearing up. He calmed down and arched his neck over the stall door until his head bumped against Baker's.

That weight eased off Baker, and he let out a laugh. "Gee, Midnight, if Dusty doesn't bring you back to the rodeo, you could start a new career as a service animal."

The horse had given him more comfort than Mrs. Lancaster had. She'd gotten them all talking, fighting, crying and hurting, and she'd done nothing to help them.

Coloring...

He snorted, and Midnight echoed the sound.

Like coloring pictures was going to help

three little boys who missed their parents, who blamed themselves for their deaths.

"You can help them most," she'd said again when Baker had started backing toward the door once the boys had settled around that table. "They need you."

"Need me for what?" he murmured to himself. "Need me to remind them? To make them hurt more?"

He hadn't asked her then because his need to get away had been too great. He'd just shaken his head, turned and fled out of that playroom and out of that house.

He needed to leave the ranch entirely before anyone tracked him down out here, before anyone thought it was a good idea to make him talk some more. His throat was raw already, from the talking and from the sobs that had clawed at the back of it, making his voice as raspy as it was when he awakened from one of those horrendous nightmares.

He reached up and ran his hand along Midnight's long neck, over his silky mane, and then he sighed. "I need to get out of here, buddy..." But as he eased away from the door and stepped away from the stall, he realized it was already too late...when Taye stepped out of the shadows.

How long had she been there?

Watching him?

Listening?

"You don't want to be around me now," he warned her. He was too raw, his emotions too overwhelming for him not to overwhelm her, too. He didn't want to hurt her. Too many people at the ranch were already hurting.

"I'm sorry." She stepped closer to him. "I was so focused on the boys, and making sure that they got all the help they needed, that I wasn't as worried about you as I should have been."

Despite her claim, there was a deep crease between her eyebrows, and tension in her beautiful face. She was obviously concerned about him.

"You shouldn't be worried about me," he said. "The focus should be on the boys. They opened up a lot. They talked a lot." Emotion rising up the back of his throat choked him for a moment, until he cleared it and added, "Cried a lot."

Tears brimmed, filling her blue eyes before falling down her face. "That's terrible."

"They seemed better when I left them," he admitted. "They were fighting over crayons. But it wasn't like their usual fighting…

It was like the old way, the way my brothers used to fight."

"Your brothers are worried about you," she said. "Especially Jake."

A smile tugged at his lips. "Of course." Jake took responsibility for everything and everyone. He really needed a ranch foreman, someone to help ease his load.

"How are you?" she asked.

He released a ragged sigh. "I'm not better..."

"I'm sorry," she said again.

And he realized how much like Jake she was, that she always took responsibility for everyone else, for taking care of them. "That's not your fault," he assured her.

"But I talked you into coming here tonight, to meet with Mrs. Lancaster and the boys," she said, and tears glistened still in her pretty blue eyes.

He reached out then and cupped her cheek in his hand. Her skin was so silky, so warm, that his palm tingled. "Stop apologizing," he said. "As Jake will tell you, you can't talk me into something I don't want to do. He's been trying hard to get me to take that foreman job."

"And you don't want it?"

He froze at the question as he realized he'd never asked himself that. He'd only focused on the fact that it was Dale's job, but Dale wasn't coming back...despite Baker's efforts that day. Tears rushed up on him again, but he'd already cried too many. He closed his eyes to hold them back.

Then her fingers touched his face, stroking lightly across his jaw. And he sucked in a breath before opening his eyes and staring directly into hers. She must have been on her tiptoes because as tall as she was, she couldn't look him straight in the eye. Few people could.

It felt as if she was looking not only into his eyes but into his soul, like she could see things he didn't even know were there. All his secrets, the ones he kept even from himself. He didn't want her to see them because maybe she would tell him what they were— what he really wanted. He was well aware of one thing he wanted: to kiss her again. He shut his eyes and leaned forward, closing the distance between them.

And he brushed his lips across the silkiness of hers.

She emitted a soft gasp, her breath whispering across his skin. And he deepened the kiss. As he did, he felt himself slipping deeper…

Falling… For her. But this wasn't supposed to be real; they'd only agreed to pretend…

ONE MINUTE BAKER Haven was kissing her, and the next… Taye was falling. Because suddenly he was gone. The chest she'd been leaning against, to steady herself while she'd stood on tiptoe, was gone. She opened her eyes, reached out and caught herself, her hands pressing against the door of Midnight's stall. The horse shifted inside, hooves scraping against the ground as if he was about to rear up.

She turned around and found Baker standing just a few feet away from her. He was physically present but emotionally gone. The tears that had shimmered in his topaz eyes had dried. And his handsome face, with its chiseled features, was unreadable. He'd closed down, shut her out.

A sudden chill raced down her spine. "What are you going to do?" she wondered aloud. She didn't really expect him to answer her. Not now.

"I have to go back to town," he said.

She nodded. She'd already figured he

wasn't going to stay. She'd probably been lucky to catch him in the barn before he'd taken off. But had she been lucky? Because she was doing something she'd promised herself she would never do: she was risking her heart...

"I have a shift tomorrow," he said, and he sounded slightly defensive, as if he felt the need to explain.

"Are you going to come back?" she asked.

"What do you mean?" he asked. "Are you talking about our pretend dating? You could tell the family you're meeting me in town, like we talked about..."

It felt so long ago now that he'd proposed his fake relationship. And even though she'd agreed to do it now, she wasn't very concerned about fooling his family. She just didn't want to fool herself. She wanted to focus instead on what was most important. The boys. And him... "Are you going to meet with Mrs. Lancaster and your nephews again?"

He looked away from her, toward the open doors of the barn, and he shifted restlessly, scraping his boots against the ground. "I—I don't think I'll need to be with them when they talk to her again," he said. "I think we worked through what was really bothering

Miller—that he felt guilty over the accident. He was fighting with Ian in the back seat and thought he caused it."

A sharp pang of what the little boy must have felt struck Taye's heart. "And he doesn't feel that way now?" she asked.

"I told him how bad the roads were, that their vehicle didn't have four-wheel drive, and that there was no way his dad could have prevented the crash," he said.

And despite knowing that she shouldn't, she felt herself falling for him because of what he'd done for his nephew.

"He seemed better," Baker said. "Like a weight was lifted, and Ian remembered that... He remembered things I didn't think he could remember from the crash."

"Maybe he blamed himself for the crash, too, and that was why he kept *forgetting* about it," she mused.

Baker nodded. "I think so."

Relief eased some of the guilt she'd felt over pressuring Baker to help the boys. "It sounds like they had a major breakthrough."

"I hope so," he said. "Then it was worth it."

"What about you?" she asked. "Did you have a major breakthrough?"

He shrugged. "I don't know if Miller will

forgive me yet for not saving his parents and for lying to him right after the crash, for telling him that they would be all right."

Even after everything Baker had shared with her about the accident, she couldn't imagine how horrific it must have been. Her heart ached for all of them. "I think he's already beginning to forgive you," she said. "He took your hand and he held on tight when you headed up to the playroom."

His lips curved slightly. "When you're drowning, you'll grab anything to keep your head above water."

"Is that why you kissed me?" she asked.

"I kissed you because you're beautiful and you're kind…and you scare me more than anything ever has."

His sweet words soothed the sting she'd felt from his rejection, from how abruptly he'd ended that kiss. "Is that why you jerked away like you did?" she asked.

"If I drown, I don't want to pull you down with me," he said. "That wouldn't be fair. You've already been through too much…"

"That's what scares me, too," she admitted. "That's why you scare me, too."

"Good," he said, nodding in acknowledgment. "We both know that whatever this is between us can only ever be fake. You deserve someone better than me. Someone who doesn't wake up with nightmares. Who doesn't live with all the guilt and regret that I live with."

"You don't have to," she said. "You could keep talking to Mrs. Lancaster. Or someone else…someone who could help you free yourself of that guilt and regret."

"Are you free of yours?" he asked.

She tensed and eased away from the stall door, and Midnight shifted behind her. It was probably her tension that the horse was feeling now. "I don't know what you mean."

"You still blame yourself for your mom dying," he said. "And you were just a kid, Taye. There was nothing you could have done."

Most of the time she believed that, but a doubt or two lingered and sometimes nagged her at night. Even though she didn't have them, she understood Baker's nightmares. At the end of a long day, sometimes she was just too tired to fight back those doubts. "And you did everything you could to save your brother and his wife and whoever else you lost that haunts you, Baker."

"How do you know?"

"Because I know you," she said. "I know that you put everyone else before yourself."

He shook his head, and she didn't know what he was denying—that she knew him or that he put everyone else first.

"You did it just now," she pointed out, "talking to Mrs. Lancaster with the boys when that was the last thing you wanted to do."

He smiled. "You do the same thing. You take care of everyone else. Who takes care of you?"

She shrugged. "I don't need anyone to take care of me."

"That's right," he said. "You're not looking for your Prince Charming. You're not interested in a fairy-tale ending."

"No," she said. "I don't want to drown either." She'd nearly done that with her mother. Had barely survived...when her mother hadn't.

"There are a lot of guys out there who can swim just fine," Baker said.

She smiled, too, but just slightly. "I'm not interested..."

"See, I'm not the only one who can't let go of the past."

"What do you mean?"

"Because of your mom, because of what happened with your mom, you're determined to be independent, to never need anyone."

She shivered as she realized he knew her just as well as she knew him.

"What you don't know is it's already too late." Then he turned on the heel of his boot and walked out of the barn.

And she remained behind, in the shadows near Midnight's stall, wondering what he meant...

Did he think she needed him?

That she'd become dependent on him?

He was the last person she would ever let herself fall for...if she could control it. But she wasn't sure that she could anymore.

DUSTY COULDN'T BELIEVE the difference just that one session with Mrs. Lancaster had made with the boys. Miller actually seemed happy again. And Ian hadn't asked once where his parents were. Even Little Jake had stopped having nightmares. Mrs. Lancaster would meet with them again, would continue to counsel them, but she couldn't help them with the one thing that was bothering the little boys now.

Uncle Baker.

He hadn't come back in the house that night for dinner, breaking his promise to sit beside Ian. The little boy had been disappointed, and he hadn't been the only one. Even Miller had kept glancing around, as if he was looking for the youngest of his uncles. But Dusty's younger brother had hopped in his truck and taken off, and in the week since that session, Baker hadn't come back.

And to think that for years, everybody had thought Dusty was the most like their mom. Of course, nobody knew what she was really like.

He'd wanted her to tell them herself when she came to visit, but she wasn't taking his calls now. He'd left her a few voice mails over the past week asking her to come tonight for the family meeting that was about to start. He'd left the same voice mail for Baker. But as he gazed around the old schoolhouse at the people who'd shown up for the family meeting, those two were the only faces he didn't see. Besides the younger boys. They were in the house with Lem, playing games and watching movies. He envied them. He would rather be there, too.

But he'd put this off too long.

Too long to wait for his mother to explain

herself. And too long to wait for Baker to come around again. There was one person present who would have to explain herself during this meeting. She was another reason he wished Baker had shown up.

"Are you sure about this, Grandma?" he asked her. Concerned, he assessed her carefully. Her skin, which was usually tanned from all the time she spent in the saddle, was almost ghostly pale but for the dark circles beneath her dark eyes. "We don't have to do this."

"You've put in an offer on that ranch. If anyone wants to go see it and finds her there…"

He nodded in acknowledgment of the discussion that he and his wife had already had. Melanie didn't want to keep any more secrets from the family like she had when she'd lived here for weeks without telling anyone she was his wife. That had been his fault, though, for keeping so much from her. She squeezed his hand now; she'd been holding it since they'd walked out to the schoolhouse from the main house. He loved her so much that it scared him sometimes.

He had never been as happy as he was now, but he suspected he was going to be even happier when their twins were born. Twins like he and Dale had been…

His chest tightened with thoughts of that loss. He would never get over losing his brother. None of them would get over Dale and Jenny being taken from them much too soon. But they were all doing better. Except for one.

"What about Baker?" he asked. "Should we have this discussion without him?"

"It was his choice not to come," his grandmother pointed out. "Somebody else will just have to fill him in." Sadie tilted her neck so her head pointed toward the tall, golden-haired woman who'd become so much more than the cook. She was family, too, and had been even before she and Baker had started dating.

At least everyone thought they were dating. She had been to town a couple of times over the past week, but she'd come back with groceries and produce from the farmers' market. Would Baker have gone shopping with her? While Dusty narrowed his eyes with suspicion as he studied her face, her blue eyes widened. "I don't think *I* should be here…" She'd protested taking part in the family meeting when he'd first announced it, but Sadie had insisted. And few people rarely stood up to Sadie. Though if anyone could, he suspected Taye Cooper could hold her own. But she hadn't been quite herself lately, probably since that night Mrs. Lancaster had come to dinner. She'd been quieter, except with the boys. She played with them and cooked with them and joked and laughed with them. They seemed to gravitate toward her much more than they ever had. She'd somehow replaced Emily as their favorite person at the ranch.

Although Lem was probably giving her a challenge to that title right now...

"Yeah, let's get this meeting going," Ben urged. "Emily and I want to announce the date we've set for the wedding."

"Took you long enough," Dusty teased. He knew why they'd waited to set the date; they'd wanted to make sure that the boys would be all right with sharing Emily with their uncle. And with her possibly moving back to town and returning to her teaching position at the school.

"Not everybody gets married on the first date," Melanie said, poking fun at him and herself since that was exactly what they had done. And yet it felt like he'd loved her forever, even before he really knew her.

He grinned and leaned down to press a kiss to her cheek. "That's too bad…because when you know it's right…"

"It's right," she agreed.

And everything was…but for some secrets that hadn't yet come to light.

"Make your announcement," he told Ben. Because he had a feeling that when he shared what their mother had told him, there wouldn't be a chance for Ben to share his news. Everyone would have too many questions.

Dusty really didn't want to do this without Baker. But he'd already put it off too long. And it wasn't as if Baker was going to run into their mother before anyone had a chance to fill him in. If he hadn't crossed paths with her in all the years she'd been just an hour from Ranch Haven, he wasn't likely to run into her anytime soon.

CHAPTER FOURTEEN

How could his idiot brother have called a family meeting already? A week wasn't long enough for Baker to process everything from that session and what had happened afterward in the barn with Taye. She'd just been trying to comfort him, and he'd turned it all around on her, pointing out the hang-ups she had because of her past.

The understandable hang-ups.

What she didn't realize was that she'd already fallen for his nephews just as hard as the little boys were falling for her. She wouldn't be able to just walk away from them. From any of them. Like he'd forced himself to walk away from her. But it really was for the best. She deserved someone a whole lot less complicated than he was.

Surprisingly, in the past week, he hadn't had any nightmares. Maybe because every time he'd managed to sleep, he'd dreamed of her. Of the warmth of her smile and the wisdom in her blue eyes and the heat of her kisses… While he might have been trying to get the focus off his problems by bringing up her past, he wasn't wrong. She deserved to have a happily-ever-after with someone who could make her as happy as she deserved to be.

The thought of her with anyone else had his stomach muscles tightening to the point that he lost his breath for a moment. And he shifted on the narrow bunk, turning onto his side from his back. He needed to be sleeping now, any moment that he could with the double shifts he'd been pulling. When he'd played the message Dusty had left him a few days ago about this meeting, he'd picked up this shift. Not that he needed an excuse not to attend…

But he'd hoped that maybe he would feel a little less guilty if he was distracted with work. There hadn't been many calls, though, and those had been minor. A fender bender with no real injuries and a grass fire. He would have been busier at the ranch; there was always something to do there, something to keep him busy. At the firehouse, with the other guys staying at their nearby homes, he had nothing to distract him from his thoughts about Taye and the boys.

Was Mrs. Lancaster right? Was he the one they needed the most? And instead of going back to the ranch, to them, he'd been staying away. Was he letting down the people who needed him most? Like his mom—he'd needed her after his dad had died.

At eight he'd been older than Miller. It must be so hard on his nephews to have lost both their parents so young. He'd had Sadie and his grandpa, too. The boys had all of Baker's brothers and now their wives and fiancée and Taye. The thought of her brought out that yearning in his chest, intensifying the hollow ache that had been there for far too long.

Maybe since his mom had left.

It didn't matter how many other people were in the boys' lives when their parents weren't. When they couldn't be.

They had to be hurting yet. And if he could help that somehow...

He needed to go back. Just as he rolled off the bunk and his feet hit the floor, the alarm sounded. And he heard the echo of other sirens as the rest of the crew drove to the firehouse. As the one on duty, he had to get the engine ready. He rushed around, doing the job he'd done so long and so many times that it was automatic for him.

"Thank God," the chief said as he rushed in, already in his gear. He jumped behind the wheel of the rig. "We gotta get going."

"Where's the call?" Baker asked.

"Cassidy Ranch outside Willow Creek, just on the limits of the county."

"Is that even our jurisdiction?" Baker asked. "It's going to take us too long to get there to be much help."

"It's a firefighter's family ranch," the chief said. "So all hands on deck. We gotta back him up, do what we can..."

A chill chased down Baker's spine. Was that what the chief's order had been when Baker had called in for help? When he'd used his cell to report the accident he'd stumbled across on the way to Ranch Haven?

"Hurry!" he urged his boss. Because he knew that feeling, that helplessness. More than anyone else, he could identify with what his fellow firefighter was going through. A crew had turned up from another fire department within the county that day to help him, too.

He wasn't sure he'd ever thanked them; he'd been in such a fog since that day...like he'd never fully awakened from the night-mare of it no matter how loudly he'd yelled.

Screams were the first thing he heard when they arrived at Cassidy Ranch just a little less than an hour later. Once the doors to the rig opened, and he jumped out, he could hear a woman crying, and another woman held her, as if holding her back from the black-ened skeleton of a house that barely stood on a crumbling stone foundation.

Smoke rose from it, but the fire had died down to faint flickering flames throughout what little remained of the structure. A fire-fighter, clad in all his gear, emerged from the smoke. And the crying woman broke free of the other one to rush up to him.

He shook his head.

And she dropped in front of him, as if her legs had given out. The other woman rushed up to her, trying to help her up.

The man dragged off his helmet and mask and said, "No, there's nobody inside. He's not in there."

"We'll find him," the older woman said.

Baker rushed up to the other firefighter. "Where do you need us?" And when the guy turned toward him, he felt a jolt of recogni-tion. It was almost as if he was looking at

Jake or Ben. The same dark hair, the same brown eyes, the same chiseled features...

"If you guys can finish up here, get the flames out, make sure it doesn't spread to the barn, I'm going to get my idiot brothers and my stubborn dad to the hospital." And he started off in the direction of the ambulance that was parked near the other rigs, the back doors standing open.

Even as the rest of his crew headed past him toward the smoldering house, Baker was compelled to follow the other man. "I'm a paramedic, too," he said. "Maybe I can help."

The guy's head bobbed in a quick nod. "Do you have idiot brothers, too?"

"Four..." Not anymore. Not since Dale died. "... Three of them," he amended.

The guy peered behind Baker at the women. The younger one was sniffling now, still upset but less distraught. "We'll find him," he called to her. "Her son is missing," he explained to Baker. "I'm betting he's in the barn. He likes the mare."

"Sounds like my nephew," Baker mused, thinking of Caleb and his obsession with Midnight.

Then the guy spoke to the older woman. "Did you check the barn, Darlene?"

Baker froze between the ambulance and the women. That name. Could it be? No...

He turned back, and even though nearly twenty years had passed, he recognized her sandy-brown hair, her hazel eyes and the delicate features of the face he'd thought he'd probably forgotten. His mother...

He hadn't really looked at the woman until now, and recognition slammed through him, hard and cold. She didn't even glance at him as she and the other woman rushed off toward the barn.

"I'm sure he's fine," the man said again. But he was speaking into the ambulance now. "He'd rather be in the barn than the house anyways. He probably was nowhere near the fire. Unlike you idiots..."

Snapping himself back into paramedic mode, Baker stepped around the open door and peered into the ambulance. If these men needed to be treated...

He froze again at the sight of the three of them. They all looked like Jake. Big. Broad. Chiseled features. Dark eyes, dark hair...but for the older one, who had an oxygen mask over his face. Looking at him was like looking at an age-progression photo of the others, or of Baker's dad.

And like that crying woman's, his legs began to shake, and he worried that they might crumple beneath them.

"We need to help her search," one of the younger men said, then he dissolved into a coughing fit.

The other younger guy reached for the oxygen mask, but his hands were so heavily bandaged that he fumbled with it.

So the firefighter stepped in. "I got this," he told Baker. "You can close the doors. I'll have my partner drive us to the ER." He was like Baker, a firefighter and an EMT.

But that wasn't the only way he was like Baker. They looked alike, so much alike...all of them did. Knowing they needed treatment, he pushed the doors closed. But it wasn't gone and forgotten, even once the ambulance disappeared down the long drive, lights flashing.

He would never forget what he'd found here.

His mother?

And other family?

But those guys all had to be older than he was, so they couldn't be Darlene's children. Where had she gone?

To the barn?

Before he could start toward it, the chief

called out to him for help. And he was forced to revert to firefighter mode. He had to deal with the situation at hand, make sure the fire was completely out and the threat was gone.

But there was another threat out there...the threat of the truth. And how much it might hurt him and the rest of his family...all of his family.

TAYE WISHED THAT family meeting had been after dinner, not after lunch, because she wasn't sure she could focus enough on cooking not to mess up the evening meal. Fortunately Miller was helping her, as he usually did while she guided him through the necessary steps. But Juliet Shepard was picking up her slack now, helping Miller help her as she reeled yet from the revelations of that family meeting.

Baker's mother was alive and living somewhere near them. But she hadn't reached out to any of them. Not even after Dale and Jenny died...

Finding that out, knowing that, would probably devastate Baker. Somebody had to tell him. But when Sadie had asked her to do it, she'd shaken her head. "It really isn't my place," she'd insisted.

"But you're dating, right?" Sadie had asked, with enough of an inflection that Taye realized fooling the older woman was going to be as hard as she'd thought it would be.

"Yes…but this is a huge family secret that I think one of the family should tell him," she'd explained, and that had been no lie.

And so Jake had offered to make the drive to town. His mother wasn't the only news that had been shared at the family meeting; she wasn't the only family that was out there. Somewhere… Sadie had had another son before the one she'd lost. Another son she'd lost, when he'd run away, and she didn't know whether he was dead or alive. Tears stung Taye's eyes over how emotional the usually strong, stoic Sadie had been when she'd spoken about Jessup, how she'd been haunted all these years not knowing what had happened to him, never hearing from him.

Sadie had left the meeting then, needing a moment to regroup. Lem was with her now, but Taye wanted to check on her, too, make sure she was all right.

"Are you okay?" Melanie asked, her voice soft as she nearly whispered the question.

Taye glanced across the island at her. Melanie had taken a seat at one of the stools at the insistence of her husband, who hovered nearby, as he usually did over his pregnant wife. He was holding Little Jake, probably knowing that Taye was too distracted to watch him as she'd done so much lately. Ben and Emily had slipped off somewhere, probably to talk about Sadie's and Dusty's revelations. And Katie, Caleb and Ian were in the barn with the bronco. Melanie had had to take time to process the news like everyone else at the meeting.

"You knew…" Taye mused softly.

She nodded, and her wavy brown hair shifted around her shoulders. "Yes. Dusty told me, but it wasn't my secret to share."

"What secret?" Miller asked.

"Nothing you need to worry about," Melanie assured him.

But a deep crease formed between his sandy eyebrows as he stared across the island at his aunt. "That means I probably need to worry." The little boy was wise far beyond his years. "Is Mrs. Lancaster coming out again?" he asked. But he didn't tense up like he had the last couple of times he'd known she was coming. Then he looked hopefully up at Taye and asked, "Does that mean Uncle Baker's coming back?"

And a pang struck Taye's heart so sharply she had to rub her chest. Baker was wrong; Miller *had* forgiven him for not saving his parents. He needed to know that. She wished now that she'd gone to town to talk to him. She shouldn't have refused and made Jake take on more responsibility than he already had. If only Baker would accept the foreman position at the ranch...

She suspected he wanted it, but for some reason he wouldn't let himself admit it. Because of Dale and the guilt he felt over his death?

"I don't know when Uncle Baker's coming back," Taye said.

"Uncle Jake went to get him," Dusty chimed in. Little Jake had moved up to his shoulders now, and Dusty bounced him up and down. He was going to be a wonderful father. Then he suddenly stilled and reached into his pocket, pulling out his vibrating cell phone. "Hello..."

As he listened to the caller, the color left his face, leaving him nearly as pale as Sadie had looked earlier. And he clenched his jaw so tightly that a muscle twitched in his cheek.

Melanie slid off the stool and moved toward him, lifting Little Jake down from his shoulders. The toddler scampered around the island to Taye, clutching her jeans in his hands.

"Up, Taye, up," he demanded.

A smile tugged at her lips and she lifted him into her arms. But her focus remained on Dusty and the grim expression on his face.

"Thanks for letting me know," he said, and then he disconnected the cell, his hand shaking slightly as he slid it back into his pocket.

"Was that Jake?" Taye asked, anxiety making her pulse race. "Did he tell Baker?" And now she wished she'd gone with him. She wished she'd told him. That she'd been there to hold him.

Dusty shook his head. "No, it wasn't Jake."

"Who was it?" Melanie asked now, and she sounded as anxious as Taye was.

"That was the Realtor calling about the Cassidy Ranch," Dusty said.

"Didn't we get it?" Melanie asked. "Did someone else outbid us?"

He shook his head. "No. It burned down."

Melanie gasped. "Is everyone all right?"

He shrugged, his shoulders slumped down as if with a heavy burden. "I don't know. The Realtor had a meeting with the owner to sign the acceptance of our offer, and as she drove up, an ambulance was pulling away. The lights were flashing. Someone needed medical treatment."

Taye clutched Little Jake a bit closer, taking comfort in the warmth of his small, wriggling body. If something had happened to Darlene Haven before her sons were able to reconnect with her...

How cruel that would be for all of them, but for some reason the one she worried about the most was Baker. She wished she was with him right now, to comfort him...like Melanie comforted her husband as she wrapped her arms around him and held him close.

"What's going on?" Miller asked Taye.

She couldn't tell him that he might have lost a grandmother he hadn't even known he had. She couldn't tell him about Darlene; it wasn't her place. She could only slide an arm around him and hug him against her side and say, "We'll find out..."

"Find out what?" Big Jake asked as he sauntered into the kitchen, Feisty tugging at the bottom of his jeans. He scooped up the growling Chihuahua in one big hand, and she yipped with joy as she licked his chin.

"Did you talk to Baker?" she asked urgently.

He shook his head. "Just missed him. They got called out to some fire in a neighboring area of the county. Not their jurisdiction but I guess it was a big fire at a ranch. That's what one of the guys who stayed behind at the fire-house told me."

"Oh, no..." Dread gripped Taye. It was unlikely that there would be two ranch fires at the same time. It had to be the same place, and Baker would find out what he'd missed at the family meeting. He would be totally blindsided if he saw his mother and recognized her. And if he had to treat her like he'd had to treat his family at the crash site...

She shuddered as she considered what he might be going through...and with everything he'd already endured, she wasn't sure how much more he could handle.

HER LEGS TREMBLING, Sadie leaned back against the door to her suite, which she'd just closed. She'd been standing in the hallway outside the kitchen when Dusty had taken that call, when he'd shared with the others what had happened. A fire at the Cassidy Ranch. Where Darlene was staying. Where she might have been helping raise Jessup's kids...

Where Jessup might have been…if he was still alive.

Was he still alive?

Her whole body shook now, and sweat beaded on her brow and slithered down her back as her heart raced. And raced…with fear.

Lem had left just a short time ago. She'd insisted he go back to town. His granddaughter had arrived in Willow Creek today, and Lem hadn't seen her for a while. Sadie had told him she would be fine without him.

But she wasn't fine.

Something was very wrong. And not just at the Cassidy Ranch…

As she continued to shake and sweat, her legs gave out entirely and she slid down the door onto the carpet. She opened her mouth to call out, but she could barely draw a breath… let alone the strength to yell.

She had never felt more alone or more afraid. Lem was gone, and Feisty was in the kitchen with the others. Nobody could hear her. Nobody could help her.

And Sadie knew that she needed help. Or she might not make it.

CHAPTER FIFTEEN

SHE WAS GONE.

Just like she had all those years ago, his mom had disappeared again. After putting out the last of the hot spots, Baker had looked around the ranch, but only the fire crew remained. Both women were gone. They must have found the child in the barn, which had been deserted but for one horse. A mare with a sleek brown coat.

But what about Darlene? Where had she gone?

Had she recognized him? Had she realized who he was and didn't want to talk to him?

Dusty had said he'd spoken with her, that he'd let her know about Dale's and Jenny's deaths. But she hadn't come for the funeral. And she'd been so close...

Had Dusty known how close she was?

Anger began to churn inside him that he'd been left out of the loop, just like he had since they were kids. His older brothers seemed to still consider him a kid. He rushed out of the barn and approached one of the volunteer fire crew who'd driven separately from the rig. "Can I borrow your truck?" he asked. "I need to go check on my family."

And find out if he had more…like that firefighter and those guys in the ambulance. But how was that possible? The guys hadn't looked like Darlene; they'd looked like his dad. And his dad was gone. And too young to have had any kids older than Jake. But the other man, the older man…

No. Baker didn't need to talk to Dusty; he needed to talk to his grandmother.

"Yeah, I can ride back in the rig," the guy offered. Everybody involved with the fire department knew about Baker's family's recent tragedy. They'd been supportive.

"Where are you going, Haven?" the chief called out, stopping him just as he reached for the door handle. "You signed up for a double."

Baker drew in a breath that burned his lungs, like the lungs of those men might have been. Like his mom's could have been. Had she been inside the house, too? "One of those women was my mother," he told his boss. "I have to find out where she is."

His brows arched. "I thought your mom

took off years ago," Chief Maynard remarked, then his face flushed—probably with embarrassment for his bluntness.

Baker didn't care. "She did." Or so he'd always thought. But had she been this close the entire time? Not at the rodeo like they'd thought? "I need to find out what's going on."

"It can't wait until you're off?" the chief asked.

Irritation built in Baker again. He'd spent his entire childhood waiting for his mother to come back and being disappointed on every birthday, every holiday... Maybe that was why he'd been so determined to leave the ranch and never come back. He'd gotten sick of waiting around, sick of that disappointment, sick of loss...

"No, sir," he said. "It can't." But it wasn't just his grandmother he wanted to see; he wanted to see Taye, too. To talk to her with the hopes that she could help him make sense of it all.

When his boss begrudgingly nodded in acceptance of his leaving, Baker hopped in the truck and headed toward Ranch Haven. In just a little less than an hour, he was there. Except for the cities, everything was a distance apart in a state the size of Wyoming, so an hour's drive wasn't far.

Not so far that Darlene couldn't have traveled it, that she couldn't have come to see them, to check on them, or at least attend her son and daughter-in-law's funeral.

His irritation built to a fury now, so much so that when he arrived at Ranch Haven, he'd barely shut off the engine before he thrust open the door and rushed into the house. He could hear the rumble of voices in the kitchen. Jake's deep baritone and Dusty's with the slight twang from all his years of traveling…

He could hear Miller mumbling something and Little Jake's giggles and Taye's sweet voice…and something gripped his heart tightly, squeezing it so that he gasped for a moment at the intensity of the feeling. Longing? Yearning? Love…

No. He had no idea what love was…not when a mother could take off and leave her children after their father's death.

He had no idea if he was at all lovable himself. When his own mother hadn't loved him.

Sadie had. Sometimes too much when it came to her meddling. But he knew she only did that because she wanted what was best for them. The only problem was that what was best for him wasn't the best for Taye. *He* wasn't the best for her.

So instead of continuing down the hall to the kitchen, he stopped at the door to Sadie's suite. He would talk to her first. She had to have been aware of where Darlene was, and she probably even knew who those men were and if they were as related to him as they looked.

His knock at the door went unanswered. There wasn't even a yip out of Feisty like there usually was. Maybe they were out walking, but then the Chihuahua ran up and pawed at the door, whimpering to be let in.

So she thought someone was inside. Sadie?

He knocked again. "Grandma?"

There seemed to be some kind of answering whimper to Feisty's cries. Baker turned the handle and tried to push open the door, but something blocked it. He put his shoulder against it and shoved, and as he did, he peered through the crack and saw her lying on the floor.

"Grandma!" he exclaimed.

Feisty slipped inside, yapping and barking with concern for her human. Baker squeezed through the opening and dropped to his knees beside his grandmother.

She was breathing, but her breaths sounded labored and shallow. And her skin was so flushed, sweat rolling off her and matting her white hair around her face. He touched her wrist, where her pulse pounded wildly, and he counted the beats.

Over a hundred...

She was probably in A-fib. She needed oxygen and a defibrillator, but he didn't have the ambulance. He didn't even have his own truck with his first aid kit inside it.

He felt as helpless as he had the day of the crash. "Grandma," he said. "Hang in there. Come on..." He fumbled inside his pocket for his phone. He needed to get someone out here with a defibrillator because he had a feeling her heart was racing so much that it was only a matter of time before it stopped.

Instead of calling 9-1-1, he called the chief. "I found my grandma down at the ranch," he said. "I need a defibrillator out here ASAP. If you got anyone close..."

"I'll find someone, and I'll call 9-1-1 for you," the chief promised. "Help's on its way."

But would it arrive in time?

"DOGGY," LITTLE JAKE SAID, peering around the kitchen from where he sat on Taye's hip. One of his hands clutched her braid. "Doggy?"

Feisty had been here moments ago, but now she was barking down the hall. Anxiously barking… Taye thought she'd heard the door a short time ago. Had Ben and Emily come back inside? Or Katie and Caleb and Ian?

But they would have been in the kitchen by now.

And then she knew…

She should have checked on Sadie. She handed the toddler off to his bigger namesake and rushed down the hall. The door to Sadie's suite wasn't open all the way but enough that she could see through it, that she could see Baker leaning over his grandmother…doing chest compressions.

And Sadie… Who was always so strong, so larger than life…looked so pale and fragile and lifeless.

A scream burned at the back of Taye's throat, but she choked it down, knowing it wouldn't help. "What do you need?" she asked Baker.

He glanced up at her…and the look in his topaz eyes—the fear and the agony—reached inside her and clenched her heart. "I called for help. They promised they'd be here ASAP!"

But she could tell he was afraid it wouldn't be soon enough.

"I'm certified in CPR. I can help with chest compressions and mouth to mouth," she offered. She'd learned it when she'd worked at the diner, after one of the customers had had a heart attack. She squeezed through the door opening and dropped to her knees beside him. And as she did, she reached out and gripped his shoulder. She wished she could absorb his pain and fear, but it was too much. And she had so much of her own.

Sadie was the grandmother she'd never had, the mother she'd wished she had. Strong and fiercely loving…and so very wise.

They worked together to keep Sadie's heart beating, to keep breath in her lungs…and they were only vaguely aware that the others had gathered outside the door until someone said, "An ambulance is here!"

The paramedics were suddenly in the room, taking over the compressions, working a defibrillator, pushing Taye back—out of the way. Distancing her from Sadie and from Baker…until they were gone and she was left alone kneeling on the floor.

Limp from rotating breaths and chest compressions with Baker, she had to gather her strength before she could attempt to stand. Then they were there. Miller ran up to her, his gait only slightly uneven from his leg injury, and he grabbed her shoulders. "Miss Taye! They're taking Grandma away in an ambulance."

Ian rushed forward, too. During the time that she and Baker had been doing CPR, he and Caleb and Katie must have come into the house. "Miss Taye, will you take us to the hospital?"

Then Little Jake pushed past Katie and Juliet and Melanie and Dusty, who stood in the doorway. "Taye! Taye!" he said, his voice shaking while tears streamed down his face.

"I said they should stay here with Grandma Juliet," Dusty said, his voice gruff with emotion.

She could only imagine how upset he was and how badly he wanted to get to the hospital. So he probably wanted her to back him up on the boys staying at the ranch, maybe even hoped she'd help watch them. But they were scared. Their small bodies were shaking as badly as hers when she stood.

As if Katie sensed her hesitation, she said, "Emily is trying to get a hold of Beth Lancaster to ask—"

"We want to go, too!" Miller exclaimed. "We don't want to be left behind or lied to. We want to know the truth."

And instead of asking a question, Ian's head bobbed in agreement with his brother, and he added, "Even if it's bad."

Taye's chest expanded with a flood of love and respect for the bravery and strength of these young kids. Even Little Jake chimed in, "Gamma, Gamma, Gamma..."

He wanted to see her, wanted to make sure for himself that she was all right. Seeing Sadie lying on the floor like that, looking so lifeless, had scared Taye; she couldn't imagine how terrified the boys were, especially after having gone through this with their parents.

Even knowing that it probably wasn't her place, she said, "I'll bring them. We all need to be there."

Katie and Melanie looked doubtful as tears pooled in their eyes. "I don't think this is a good idea..." Katie began.

"We all need to stick together," Taye said, "that's what Sadie always says. We all need to stay together."

"At the ranch," Dusty clarified in a low

voice. "I don't know about taking them to the hospital."

"We took them all when Melanie went to the ER," Taye reminded everyone. But she understood why they were hesitating now. Melanie hadn't been in the danger that Sadie was now. While she'd been unconscious when they'd found her in the barn, she'd been breathing on her own; her heart had been fine. Sadie was not fine. And she might not make it…

"We want to go!" Miller vehemently insisted, and he clutched at Taye's hand, holding it tightly like he'd held Baker's that night they'd talked to Mrs. Lancaster. Anything to keep from drowning.

That was what Baker had called it. Taye wasn't so sure. They were a lot of people in this room that wanted to keep Miller afloat. She was the only one who was probably willing to let him struggle because it was what he wanted. "It's better for them to be there and know what's going on than left back here wondering and worrying and feeling helpless," she said. Then she drew in a deep breath and added an admission of her own. "I know what that feels like all too well from when I lost my mom."

Miller squeezed her hand and gave her a look of sympathy and gratitude that had her chest swelling again with love for this special kid.

While Katie, Melanie and Dusty stared at her as if shocked by what she'd shared, she unequivocally stated, "I'll bring them."

"Taye..." Katie murmured.

But Dusty, as if understanding that she somehow knew what was best for the boys, nodded. "Thank you, Taye," he said.

And she hoped that she wasn't making a terrible mistake.

LEM HAD MADE a terrible mistake. He'd known it the moment he'd started driving away from the ranch. But Sadie had been so insistent that he return to town to welcome his granddaughter home. Livvy had been so busy with med school and her residency that he hadn't seen her in years. Too many years...

He'd asked Sadie to come along with him, but she'd been exhausted after that family meeting. Too exhausted for him to have left her like he had. He should have stayed there, made sure she was really okay. But she wasn't and she wouldn't be until she knew what had happened to her son.

Until now…

Livvy laughed. "I'm thrilled for you, Grandpa, but I'm a little sad for myself that my eighty-year-old grandfather has a more active love life than I do."

"I really do like the food," Lem said. "I don't know about love…" But he had a feeling that he was falling. Maybe a part of him had always loved Sadie March…because she'd made him work harder, strive to be better than her since they were little kids. They weren't kids anymore, though.

And he had that uneasy feeling again, that sudden chill rushing over him that he shouldn't have left her. Then his cell phone vibrated inside his pocket. And he knew…

Even before he pulled it out and accepted Ben Haven's call, he knew… This was not going to be good news.

Something bad had happened.

"Lem," Ben said, his voice crackling out of the speaker. "We're on our way to the hospital, following Baker and Sadie in the ambulance. We can stop and pick you up on our way."

Because Ben was more than Lem's boss—he was one of Lem's closest friends—he knew how much Lem had come to care for

Sadie. "How is she?" he asked, fear gripping him so tightly he could barely breathe. "What happened?"

"I think it might have been a heart attack," Ben said, his voice cracking again but now with his own fear and pain. "Baker found her collapsed in her room. He and Taye did CPR until the ambulance got there."

"Don't stop for me, Ben. I can get myself..." But when he jumped up, he swayed a bit, overwhelmed with all the emotions racing over him.

"I'll drive you, Grandpa," Livvy offered. And into Lem's phone, she said, "We'll meet you at the hospital."

"I shouldn't have left her..." he muttered as foreboding closed around him, suffocating him. He wasn't having a heart attack, but he was afraid that his heart might break...if Sadie didn't survive. He wasn't sure that he would either.

CHAPTER SIXTEEN

BAKER COULDN'T KEEP doing this…riding in ambulances with members of his family. And he definitely couldn't lose another one. Especially not this one. The one who had always been there for him, who'd always loved him and had never let him down.

"Come on, Grandma," he said. "Come on, come around…"

He and Taye had kept up CPR until help had arrived, until the defibrillator had shocked Sadie's heart back into a normal rhythm. It was beating on its own now, at a normal pace. She was breathing on her own now, and getting extra oxygen through the tube in her nose, bringing her oxygen level back up. He hoped.

But how long had she been down?

Too long to come back to them?

She hadn't regained consciousness since he'd found her, not even since the defibrillator had brought her back. Had it taken too long for help to arrive? Just like it had for Dale?

He closed his eyes on that memory and the one of Dale's sons following him and Grandma and the paramedics out to the ambulance. Their small faces had been pinched with fear, tears streaming down their faces. They were so scared.

They couldn't lose anyone else.

He'd been smart this time. He hadn't made any promises he couldn't keep. He had just told them the truth. "Her heart is beating again, guys. We'll get her to the hospital and have the doctors check her out." Find out why she hadn't regained consciousness, not even yet.

They'd nodded grimly and then turned to run back into the house. And he knew to whom they were running, the same person to whom he wanted to run.

Taye.

She'd been at his side, working tirelessly next to him, with him, to save his grandmother. He hadn't been working alone like he had at the crash, and maybe for the first time since his mom had left him all those years ago, he hadn't felt alone.

Grandma had tried all those years to make

him feel like he hadn't been abandoned. That he was loved… Because she loved all her family fiercely. Maybe too fiercely.

Was that what had caused her heart attack? She'd been meddling so hard in all their lives, trying to make everyone happy again after their tragic loss, she hadn't been taking care of herself.

"Come on, Grandma," he said, speaking close to her ear. "You need to come back to us. You can't be done meddling yet. You have a lot more to do…and a lot to explain…" Because if anyone knew his mother had been staying at the Cassidy Ranch, Sadie Haven would have. There was very little his grandmother didn't know…like who those men were who looked so much like Jake and Ben.

"You're not getting off this easy," he said, and his pulse quickened when he noticed that her eyelids began to flutter a bit as if she was trying to lift them. "Come on, Grandma. You've always been there for me. You can't leave me now."

Not when he was reeling like he was from what he'd discovered at that ranch, from whom he'd discovered.

His mother.

And then she'd disappeared. Where had

she gone? To make sure the guys who'd left in the ambulance were all right? Were they all at the hospital in Willow Creek?

It was a small one. That was why Miller had had to be transferred to the hospital in Sheridan, which had the pediatric orthopedic surgeons on staff. But the guys from Cassidy Ranch had just had smoke inhalation and burns; they shouldn't have needed specialists.

Unless those burns were more severe than Baker had realized.

He was concerned about them, whoever they were, but his first priority was his grandmother right now. Her eyelids were no longer moving; she wasn't waking up. He needed her to regain consciousness, to make sure she hadn't suffered a stroke.

"Grandma, come on," he said. "You need to wake up. To let me know you're going to be okay…"

She had to be. He couldn't lose her. Not now.

Not ever.

"I'll be okay…" she murmured weakly.

His breath shuddered out in a sigh of relief. "Thank God."

"I'll be okay," she repeated, but her usually

strong voice was weak and raspy when she added, "if you do one thing for me."

"Anything, Grandma," he said. "What do you need? Water? Pain medication?"

She opened her eyes then and peered up into his face. "I need..." her voice trailed off weakly.

And he leaned closer. "What, Grandma? What do you need?"

"I need you..."

"Yes, what? What do you need me to do?" he asked anxiously, as he leaned even closer.

And finally she answered him, "I need you to marry Taye Cooper."

A laugh slipped out of him, releasing that pressure that had been on his chest since he'd found her lying on the floor. "Sheesh, Grandma, did you fake this whole thing?" he said, but he was just teasing. He knew all too well that she hadn't. "Just how far are you willing to go to manipulate people into doing what you want?"

She smiled, but it was weak, and then the smile slipped away and she admitted, "Sometimes too far."

"Is that what caused this?" he asked. "What happened?" If any of his brothers had upset her... "Did Dusty say something—"

She rolled her head back and forth on the gurney, shaking it. "No. But I overheard him talking about the fire at the Cassidy Ranch."

With his earlier suspicions confirmed, he said, "You knew my mother was there."

She gave a faint nod. "Yes, Dusty told me, when he came back to the ranch."

Anger and frustration momentarily gripped him, but he wasn't that surprised that his brother had known but hadn't said anything to him. This family kept too many secrets. "So you didn't know until recently?"

She nodded again before reaching out and clutching his forearm. "Is she all right?"

He shrugged. "I didn't talk to her. I just saw her…" And he felt that sucker punch of shock to his gut all over again. "She seemed fine. I was more concerned about the men."

She tensed. "What men?"

"You tell me," he said. "I thought I was looking at Jake and Ben for a minute. They look so much like us it's freaky." He shuddered a bit as he remembered how eerily similar they'd looked to his brothers.

Her eyes widened and she took a sharp-sounding breath. "They do? How many…?"

"Three of them," he replied. He checked her pulse rate, and his quickened because hers had. "But you need to wait to talk about this," he said. "You need to get checked out and treated."

"I need to know," she said. "I need to know... Are they hurt? Will they be okay?"

Baker's stomach tightened with dread. Grandma was a caring person, so even if they were strangers, she would have been concerned...but not this concerned.

"The firefighter wasn't hurt at all," he said. "But one of the other guys had his hands bandaged, and the third one was getting oxygen like the older guy..."

She sucked in another breath as her dark eyes widened. "Older guy? How old—what did he look like?"

"Like my dad if he would have lived..." But he remembered that funeral, remembered seeing his dad in the casket, and how devastating it had been that his father hadn't opened his eyes, that he hadn't looked at Baker the way he always had, with such love. "But even older...and the other guys were probably older than Jake."

She expelled a ragged breath and her body relaxed against the gurney. "He's alive..." Then she tightened her grasp on Baker's arm. "How badly was he hurt?"

He felt like he had with Miller during the aftermath of the crash. He wanted to calm her down, but unlike then, he really didn't know if he was lying or not this time. "I'm sure their injuries were minor, if anything. They might have already been released from the hospital by the time we get there."

When he glanced out the front window of the rig, he could see that they were pulling up to the hospital. Finally... Before the doors opened and she was whisked away to the ER, he had to know. "Who is he, Grandma?"

"My son."

"Son?" he echoed. Even though he'd noticed the resemblance, he was stunned. Shaken... "I thought my dad was an only child..."

She shook her head. "No. He was my second. I had an older son. Jessup..." Her voice cracked and trailed away on a sob as tears streamed from her eyes.

"Grandma," he managed, alarmed at her heartbreak. She was always so stoic, so strong.

The ambulance stopped, the doors opened and nurses and the paramedics with whom he'd ridden lifted Grandma out and rolled her through the open doors to the ER. He knew it was for the best. She needed to be treated. Maybe she would need a stent or a pacemaker...

She wasn't out of the woods yet.

And neither was he.

He felt lost, stunned...as he sat in the back of the rig and tried to absorb what she'd just revealed. Baker had a whole other branch of his family out there. An uncle and cousins and...

His mother. Why had she been with them and not him? Not his brothers? Why had she abandoned them?

That was how he felt now, all over again, sitting there alone. But he wasn't alone long before he heard the sound of running footsteps and he looked through the open doors to find Ian and Miller staring back at him. Ian scrambled up inside the rig and squeezed between the equipment to throw his skinny arms around Baker's neck, hugging him tightly.

Love flooded Baker's heart. It had only been a week since he'd seen them, but he'd missed them so much. So very much. But after that meeting with Mrs. Lancaster, he'd been so raw with emotion that he'd been worried they were, too. He wrapped his arms around Ian and held him closely.

Until Ian pulled back and asked, "Uncle Baker, where did Grandma go?"

"Yeah, where is she?" Miller asked, his body shaking, probably with fear. He hadn't jumped inside the rig. Maybe he hadn't wanted to get close to Baker. Or maybe he hadn't had the strength to get inside the truck, the strength to stand if Taye hadn't come up behind him, with Little Jake riding her hip. The seven-year-old leaned against her.

"What is it, Baker?" Taye asked. "What happened?"

"Did Grandma die?" Miller asked, his voice cracking with the tears that suddenly overflowed his hazel eyes.

Baker scooped up Ian, who had also begun to cry, and jumped down from the truck. He pulled Miller against him and assured him. "No, no, she's not dead. Her heart is beating strong and she was breathing well, and she regained consciousness. They just took her inside to treat her."

Miller pulled back and studied his face, as if trying to determine whether or not he was lying. And Baker felt that jab of guilt and regret that he had lied to his nephew once. "I'm telling you the truth," Baker assured him. "I will never lie to you again. I promise."

Miller studied him for another long moment before he nodded in acceptance. And the pressure in Baker's chest, the guilt he'd felt for that day, eased.

"She was doing really well when they wheeled her into the ER," he assured them all. So well that she'd been trying to get him to propose to Taye.

She studied him just as intensely as Miller had, her beautiful face taut with fear and exhaustion. He was exhausted, too, his legs a bit weak beneath his and Ian's weight. Performing CPR as long as they had was a lot of work. And when it was on someone you loved, it was unbearable. But doing it with her, having her help him, had made it bearable. She'd made him stronger.

Not strong enough to fight the feelings he was beginning to have for her, though...

The love.

As he acknowledged that emotion, he was so overwhelmed that he couldn't speak, could barely stand... He staggered back to sit on the back bumper of the rig.

"Uncle Baker!" Ian cried out in alarm.

Baker hadn't dropped him, but the kid

wriggled down from his arms and stared up at him. They all stared at him with concern.

"Are you okay?" Taye asked him.

He shook his head. He wasn't okay. Not now. He was falling in love.

That was something he'd vowed never to do for so many reasons. One of them was the woman he'd seen at the Cassidy Ranch. The woman who'd so easily abandoned him. He didn't just fear being abandoned again. He feared abandoning someone like she had, because she couldn't deal with the grief, the struggles.

Taye was right. He'd never really dealt with his. Not even that day with Mrs. Lancaster and the boys. All those years everyone had thought Dusty was the most like their mother, but it was really him.

He was the one who couldn't be trusted... to not run away when things got hard. And it seemed like lately, being a Haven was hard. Too hard...

HE WAS SCARING TAYE, and she'd already been terrified. Worse yet, he was also scaring the boys.

"Baker!" She stepped closer. "Are you all right?" The way he'd been staring at her had unnerved her. It was almost as if he was afraid of her. Or maybe he was just afraid. She could understand that; she was afraid for Sadie, too. But she'd believed him when he'd told the boys she had regained consciousness, that she was doing better.

"I'm fine," he finally replied. "Just tired."

"Unca Bake…" Little Jake babbled, and he reached out his hands toward his uncle.

A smile tugged at Baker's lips, and the fear dropped away for the moment. He stood up and reached for the toddler, hugging him close. And then he gruffly admitted, "I missed you guys."

"Why haven't you been back at the ranch?" Miller asked with his usual suspicion. "You weren't even at that family meeting this morning. And they would've let you go to it cuz you're old."

Baker's smile widened a bit.

"Were you fighting a fire?" Ian asked.

And Baker's smile slipped away. "Yes. I was."

"I thought I smelled smoke," Ian said.

Little Jake must have smelled it on Baker, too, because he reached for Taye again. She took him back into her arms. Then she glanced toward the open doors to the ER.

The rest of Baker's family had gone into the waiting room for news of Sadie's condition, but the boys had seen the ambulance and insisted on coming out here.

It was as if they'd known that Baker would still be inside. They were so drawn to him. Like they were to her.

And she wasn't sure how or when that had happened. She'd thought Emily was the kid whisperer or Old Man Lemmon.

She gasped as she thought of him. Had anyone told Lem? She had to find the rest of the Haven family almost as much as Baker needed to.

"Come on," she said. "Let's go inside…"

The boys listened to her first. Miller and Ian rushed through the open doors and into the hospital. Then as if he was one of the kids obeying her, Baker followed them inside the ER. They proceeded through it to the waiting room, where the other Havens, and thankfully Old Man Lemmon, had gathered. He looked as shaky as Baker seemed to be, but a young woman stood beside him, holding his arm with both of hers as if she was worried he might collapse.

Taye's own legs still weren't as steady as she would like. She slid an arm around Miller's shoulders—the boy continued to huddle close to her—holding him against her as much for her support as his.

She was also worried about Baker. He seemed so out of it, so in shock. But he visibly rallied himself as his family rushed up to him.

"How is she?" his oldest brother asked.

"Did she regain consciousness?" Dusty asked.

Baker nodded. "She came around," he said, "and the first thing she tried to do was…"

His family all stepped closer when he trailed off. "What?" Ben asked, his voice a little sharp with impatience.

Baker smiled faintly again before replying, "She tried to get me to propose to Taye."

Now Taye was the one in shock, so much so that she lost her breath for a moment at the thought of a real proposal from Baker Haven.

Everyone else laughed. Old Man Lemmon's was the heartiest; his deep belly laugh had the little boys turning quizzically toward him. Maybe they recognized that laugh as belonging to the town square Santa Claus they visited every year. At least it distracted them from what Baker had said, that his grandmother wanted him to propose to…*her*.

"Sounds like she's just fine, then," the old man said. "Just as sharp as she always is."

"Sharp or sneaky?" Ben asked with a chuckle of his own. He sounded relieved.

"Sneaky…" Baker repeated, and as he did, he turned away from his family as if he needed a moment to regroup. That must have been why he'd stayed out in the ambulance.

Was it just what had happened with Sadie that had him so upset? Or had he already been upset by what he'd seen at the Cassidy Ranch? She wanted to ask him, but before she could move closer to him, Emily approached her and held out her hands for Little Jake.

He ignored the teacher as he clung to Taye yet, one of his hands wrapped tightly around her braid. Miller and Ian ignored Emily, too, as they stared up at Taye.

"Are you going to marry Uncle Baker and become our aunt?" Ian asked. Apparently that Santa laugh hadn't distracted him long.

Miller's hazel eyes gleamed with hopefulness when he parroted his younger brother's question. "Are you?"

She forced herself to laugh. "No. He was just sharing Grandma Sadie's joke with everyone."

"She was joking?" Miller asked.

She better have been because Taye doubted there was any hope of Baker proposing to her for real. Not that she wanted him to.

"Yes," Emily said, coming to Taye's rescue. "And because she's well enough to joke, I'm sure she's going to be just fine. So you all don't need to worry."

"I'm not worried about Uncle Baker marrying Taye," Miller said, his forehead creasing with confusion. "I'd like her to be an aunt, too."

Every time Miller spoke or looked at her lately, it was as if he expanded her heart. He was such a sweetheart.

"Me, too," Ian said.

"Now you all sound like Grandma Sadie," Taye said. "But she was just kidding. And that's a good thing..." For so many reasons. Before they could keep pushing for that proposal, she handed Little Jake off to Emily. "We didn't have time to eat before we left the ranch. Why don't you go with Miss Emily to see what they have in the cafeteria."

"Are you hungry, Taye?" Emily asked.

Her stomach lurched at the thought of food. And she shook her head. "No, but they might be."

"We can see if they have cookies," Ian said.

And as if just realizing that his cousin wasn't there, he looked around the waiting room. "Where's Caleb?"

"He and Aunt Katie already headed to the cafeteria," Emily said. "He insisted on coming since his cousins were." She gave Taye a pointed look.

Apparently the teacher didn't approve of her bringing them. But they were handling the hospital well. Better than Baker was.

Ian took Emily's hand. "Let's go before Caleb eats all the cookies."

Miller hesitated a moment while he stared at Taye and then at Baker, as if he was worried about them. He really was the sweetest boy.

She smiled at him. "Go, you're probably hungry. I'll come get you when we know when Grandma can come home."

His eyes brightened. "She's coming home?"

Panic struck her that she might not. "We won't know for sure until her doctor comes out to talk to us. I'll let you know when he does."

He waited another long moment before nodding and heading off with Emily and his brothers. Baker hadn't joined his brothers yet. He stood off by himself, and they all eyed him warily as if uncertain how to approach him.

She wasn't uncertain. She walked over to where he stood near the Authorized Personnel Only door, as if he was about to step through it. As an EMT, he was authorized personnel. But he shouldn't have had to work on his own grandmother like he had.

"How are you *really* doing?" she asked him with concern.

He turned toward her, his topaz eyes glistening with tears, and admitted, "I'm drowning…"

She held out her hand toward him, offering it to him.

But he shook his head. "I don't want to pull you under with me."

It was too late, with the way he was looking at her like he'd looked at her by the ambulance, with such longing and… It was too late.

She was already drowning.

CHAPTER SEVENTEEN

BAKER COULD HAVE stared at Taye for hours, maybe forever…if his brothers hadn't interrupted them moments after she'd approached him in the waiting room.

"We need to talk to you," Jake said.

The sound of his older brother's voice, the solemnity of it, had Baker's stomach dropping. "Have you already talked to the doctor?" he asked anxiously. Had they been given bad news about Grandma?

Jake shook his head. "No. Nobody's talked to us since they brought her back."

"She hasn't been here long. They'll have to run some tests, maybe wait for a cardiologist to come in," Baker said. "It could be a while before we know for sure how she's doing…" He could admit that now that the kids were gone. He hadn't wanted to lie to them, but he hadn't wanted to scare them either.

He must have scared Ben, whose dark eyes widened with concern. "But you said she was pressuring you to propose. She had to be feeling better then…"

"Is it more serious than you would admit in front of the kids?" Dusty asked, and he cast a sideways glance at Taye.

Baker realized then that she was the reason the boys were here; she'd brought them. Maybe against the protests of his brothers. His respect for her increased. She *was* like Sadie, headstrong and fiercely protective. She'd done what she'd known was best for the boys. She hadn't wanted them worrying, like she'd worried so many years about her mom, and feeling as helpless as she'd felt then.

He shook his head, dismayed that his brother would think to exclude the kids again, to leave them guessing about what was going on with Sadie and imagining the worst, like he was now.

"No, I don't think it's more serious," Baker said. Finding her passed out and then having her heart stop had been serious enough. "She was weak, but she was lucid. Maybe a little too lucid…" He glanced at Taye.

His grandmother hadn't been wrong. He should propose to Taye Cooper, and he might have…if he knew he could give her the happily-ever-after she truly deserved. Even if he selfishly proposed, he doubted she would accept. She'd made it clear that she wasn't looking for anyone. They both had too much heartache in their pasts to really trust in happily-ever-after.

Then he remembered what else his grandmother had shared with him, whom she might have been looking for...

"Grandma told me something I didn't know," he said. "That I had no idea. I always thought Dad was an only child..."

"She told you about Uncle Jessup," Jake surmised.

Baker sucked in a breath, feeling suckerpunched again. Neither Ben nor Dusty looked surprised at the mention of this mysterious uncle. "You guys knew?" he asked, horrified. Once again he'd been left out of family business.

Just like his nephews...

"You would have known, too, if you'd shown up for the meeting I called this morning," Dusty said.

"That's when Jake and I found out," Ben said with a heavy sigh.

"And nobody thought to clue me in?" Baker asked. He stared at Dusty. When he'd said he couldn't make the meeting, his brother should have told him what it was about. *Whom* it was about.

"I tried to," Jake said. "But I wanted to do it in person. By the time I got to the firehouse, you were already gone on that call."

"To the Cassidy Ranch..." Dusty murmured. The color drained from his face. And Baker's gut twisted as he remembered. "Was anyone hurt?" Dusty asked.

Ben's throat moved as if he was struggling to swallow. Then, his voice sounding choked, he asked, "Did you see *her*?"

Baker glanced around for Taye, wishing now that he'd taken her hand. But his brothers had encircled him, and she'd slipped away. He needed her now because he felt like he was drowning again as he remembered recognizing his mother while she hadn't even noticed him. Maybe she'd forgotten all about him.

"Baker?" Dusty asked with concern. "Was she hurt? Did you see her?"

Before he could reply, the woman at the waiting room desk called out, "Family of Sadie Haven? You can see her now. The doctor is waiting in Sadie's room to speak to you all."

Her room? She was being admitted. He shouldn't have been surprised. He knew the heart attack had been serious, so serious that they might have lost her if he hadn't found her when he had.

Which was what the doctor confirmed when they all rushed off to the room number the attendant gave them. "From what the paramedics said, you're the only reason your grandmother is alive, Baker," Dr. Brower said. He knew him from the ER.

"Hasn't a cardiologist seen her?" Baker asked with concern. Why was the ER doctor doing the follow-up in her room?

"Not in person. He couldn't make it into the hospital. But he had me order tests and he read the results. He said her A-fib attack was so severe that her heart actually stopped beating. If you hadn't been there and performed CPR, she wouldn't have come back from that."

Sadie smiled up at Baker from the bed she lay in, which he and his brothers now surrounded. She reached out and grabbed his hand, squeezing it like Miller had that day they'd met with Mrs. Lancaster. Like he'd wanted to squeeze the hand Taye had offered him earlier.

Jake slapped his shoulder.

"Good work, baby brother," Ben said.

"I think she was, too," he said. "I didn't get a chance to talk to her. It was pretty chaotic with the fire and all." He hadn't even had a chance to process what he'd discovered at the Cassidy Ranch before coming home to find his grandmother collapsed. "I'll find out," he assured her. "As long as *you* rest…" He kept a steady gaze on her.

She nodded. "I feel better knowing that you saw him, that you saw *them*…that he's alive."

"Why wouldn't he have been?" Baker wondered. What had he missed in that family meeting?

"Lupus," she said. "He was diagnosed with lupus in his teens. The autoimmune disorder really affected his organs, weakening his kidneys and his heart…" Tears trickled out of her dark eyes and rolled down her face. "I was so scared that I was going to lose him… I was overbearing, overprotective."

"You? Grandma?" he teased.

But she didn't even manage a smile. "And I lost him anyway…when he ran away from me."

He squeezed her hand now. "But he's alive, and he apparently had some kids."

"Kids?" Jake asked. "What are you saying? We have cousins?"

"More like doppelgangers," Baker said. "At least for you and Ben. They're probably a little older than you both. The firefighter might have been younger."

"The firefighter?" Ben asked. "Guess it runs in the genes..."

But it didn't. Not anymore. At least not for Baker. He was done with treating family members. And now that he had so much more family. Before he could decide what he was going to do about his career, he had to find that family. Make sure they were okay after the fire. "I'll find them, Grandma," he assured her again.

She squeezed his hand. "Thank you."

He started to pull away, but she held tightly to him. She was definitely regaining her strength. "There's something else you can do for me," she said.

He tensed because he knew...

"Marry Taye Cooper," she persisted.

His brothers laughed. But he felt sick...with yearning. He wished he had more to offer Taye, but he couldn't give her the happy, uncomplicated life she deserved—not when his life just kept getting more and more complicated.

"Grandma, we're not really even dating,"

he admitted. "We just started acting like we were so you all would stop trying to push us together." He glanced from her to Ben, who'd orchestrated that firehouse visit.

Grandma snorted. "Neither you nor Taye are that good of actors," she said. "And Caleb told me you were kissing at the firehouse… when you didn't even know they were watching."

Heat climbed into his face as his family smiled at him, as if they all knew something he didn't know. But this wasn't like the big family secret. He was well aware of how he was beginning to feel about Taye Cooper. And apparently so was everyone else.

"You're definitely feeling like your old self," Ben said, and he leaned down to kiss Sadie's cheek.

She patted his face. "Speaking of old, where's that deputy mayor of yours? Anybody tell that old fool that I'm here?"

Ben smiled and nodded. "And he and his granddaughter are in the waiting room."

"Pretty girl that Livvy, and smart, too. You notice if any of your cousins were single?" she asked Baker.

Now he laughed. "Sheesh, Grandma, they

might not even know about you." Just like he and his brothers hadn't known about them.

Her shoulders slumped inside her hospital gown. "No, they probably don't."

"When you find them, you better not warn them," Ben advised him. "Or they won't want to meet us either."

Would they want to? Baker's mom had been living with them—that close to Ranch Haven—yet she hadn't even stopped by for a visit, to catch up with them. And even worse, she hadn't come to the funeral after Dusty had told her about Dale and Jenny.

He needed to find them all, but most of all, he needed answers from her. He needed to find out why she'd given up on her own family. On him...

Had his grief over his father been too much for her to handle even then, before he'd had so much more, so many other people to grieve? And if it was too much for his mom, he had no right to subject Taye to that, not after everything she'd been through with her own mother.

TAYE FELT ALONE when the Haven brothers left. Even though Lem and that young woman he'd introduced as his granddaughter, Olivia

Lemmon, were in the waiting room with her.
Or maybe it was just Baker leaving that made
her feel alone.

The hospital had checked Sadie into a
room. That meant that she wasn't well enough
to come back to the ranch yet. Would she be?
She was eighty. It might take her longer to recover from a heart attack or whatever she'd
had…if she recovered at all.

"Where is everyone?" Miller asked when
he limped into the waiting room just slightly
ahead of Ian and Caleb. Katie and Emily, with
Little Jake in her arms, followed closely behind them.

Melanie must have stayed back at the ranch
with her mother. Taye hoped she felt all right.
The last time they'd been here, the pregnant
woman had been the one who'd needed treatment. But she'd been able to come home.
Since Sadie had been checked into a room,
she was probably going to have to stay. How
would the boys handle that?

How would Taye? Every night, after Lem
left, Taye checked in on her in her suite, and
they always wound up talking about the boys
and the ranch and the family. But, despite
being included in all those meetings, Taye
wasn't really family. She hadn't been able to

go back with the brothers to see their grandmother.

"Where is everyone?" Miller asked again, anxiously.

She forced a smile for him. "Family was able to go back and see Grandma Sadie," she said.

"Family..." Miller murmured. "Are they having another *meeting*?"

She suspected that they were, and not just about Sadie's health but about what Baker had discovered at the Cassidy Ranch. His mother...

Poor Baker.

He must have been so shocked. And from what she'd overheard in the waiting room of their discussion before they'd been called back, his brothers hadn't been very sympathetic. He should have attended that family meeting, but she could understand why he'd hesitated, if he'd thought it was just another push to get him to meet with Mrs. Lancaster and the boys. He'd been so devastated after that first session.

And then he'd been the one to find Sadie... lying on the floor.

Her chest tightened with sympathy for him.

How much more emotional trauma could the man endure?

"Is this meeting about us?" Miller asked. "About Mrs. Lancaster?"

She shook her head. "I don't think so."

"What was this morning's meeting about?" Miller asked. "Is that why Grandma got sick?"

"I don't want to go to family meetings if they make you sick," Ian said. "You were at the meeting, Miss Taye. Are you sick?" And he rushed up to her, sliding his arm around her waist.

He was a bright kid, like his brother, so he'd probably noticed how shaky she'd been earlier after giving Sadie CPR. She wasn't going to lie to him or to Miller, whose body was tense as he waited for her answer, too. "I'm not sick, just tired," she told them.

"We can all head back to the ranch," a deep voice said as Jake joined them, sliding his arm around his red-haired bride. "They're keeping Sadie overnight, but she's going to be fine." He turned toward Lem, who'd rushed up to him and Ben and Dusty as they'd entered the waiting room. Baker wasn't with them. "She was asking about you, Lem, wondering if we'd told you she was here."

"She was asking for 'that old fool,'" Ben corrected his older brother.

And Lem laughed that deep belly laugh again. "She's feeling like her old self for sure, then."

Ben turned toward Lem's granddaughter. "You might want to make yourself scarce. I think she has plans for you, too."

"Plans for me?" the young woman nervously asked.

Lem patted her hand. "I'll explain later, honey. But now I'd like to go see Sadie, if that's all right…" He glanced at Ben.

"Of course it is," Ben assured him.

The older man hesitated for a moment.

"Go," his granddaughter urged him. "Go to Sadie."

Was Baker still with his grandmother? The boys peered around, too, as if looking for him. Had he left? Was it all too much for him just like Taye was worried that it was? And if it was too much, was there something Jake wasn't telling them? Was Sadie's condition more serious than he'd said?

The boys must have felt her tension because Miller and Ian were leaning against her now, each with an arm around her waist. Little Jake wriggled down from Emily's arms and started toward her. Until Baker walked into the room. Then Little Jake and his brothers ran toward him…like Taye wished she could.

"Unca Bake, Unca Bake!" Little Jake cried out, raising his arms.

Looking bemused, Baker picked up the toddler.

"Gamma, Gamma…" Little Jake repeated.

Tears stung Taye's eyes at how much the boys loved their great-grandmother, at how much she loved Sadie.

"Gamma is okay," Baker assured them. "In fact I'll sneak you up to visit her."

And now the tears threatened to fall, over how well Baker understood his nephews. He knew they would have to see her to believe that she was really okay, that she would come home…unlike their parents.

"Lem just went up," Jake said. "I don't think that's a good idea…"

"I should check with Mrs. Lancaster first," Emily added.

Baker shook his head. "No. I know what's best for them…" And as he said it, he looked stunned for a moment. As stunned as Taye was as she realized she'd fallen for Baker Haven. She hadn't wanted to fall for anyone.

Ever. Not after having a front-row seat to the aftermath of her mother's heartbreak.

And she knew that Baker would break her heart. He was going through too much right now, dealing with his guilt over Dale and Jenny and now with the realization that his mother had been this close to him…

He didn't have time for love. Time for her.

"Taye," he called out to her.

He and the boys stared at her, and she realized they must have been trying to get her attention. "Yes?"

"They want you to come with us to see Sadie."

They. Not him… He didn't want her. Not like she wanted him. But she had to push those feelings aside for now. Maybe forever. If she shared her feelings with Baker and he didn't return them, she would feel too awkward staying at the ranch, and she would have to quit her job and leave. But she hadn't fallen just for him; she'd fallen for all of them. While she would remain friends with Emily, Melanie and Katie, it wouldn't be the same as being at the ranch. With the boys…

She couldn't even contemplate not seeing them every day, not being with them. And now she knew what Baker had meant that

day when he'd warned her that it was too late.
He'd known then how much she loved his
nephews.

Like they were her own…like they were
her children.

CHAPTER EIGHTEEN

BAKER HAD SHOCKED himself with his declaration that he knew what was best for the boys. He'd shocked himself because he'd realized he was right. After weeks of doubting himself, of thinking that he was causing them more pain, he'd realized that he was the one who could ease their pain and their fears the most. Because he understood them best.

Taye understood them, too, after everything she'd gone through with her mom. He was pretty sure that she was the reason they were at the hospital—because she'd advocated for them. Baker was happy to do that now, even when the doctor protested that his nephews were too many visitors for Sadie.

Baker shook his head. "You don't know my grandma…"

"Let them in!" she bellowed from inside her room.

And Lem opened her door.

Miller and Ian rushed forward, with Caleb

following close behind. He must have come up with them, too. "Gamma, Gamma," Little Jake said as he wriggled down from Baker's arms and toddled into the room after his brothers and cousin.

Baker's brothers had come up behind him in the hall. Jake's big hand settled on his shoulder and squeezed. "You were right..." he murmured as he peered into the room.

Lem had lifted Little Jake into Sadie's bed while the other boys had gathered around her. She looked better, with color in her face, and her dark eyes shining with love. All the kids were smiling.

"You gotta take care of Feisty for me," she told Caleb, who solemnly nodded. "Make sure she doesn't take over my bed tonight. I'll be back in it tomorrow."

"She can sleep with me," Caleb offered.

"I sleep with you," Ian said.

"She can sleep with me," Miller offered. "I'll help take care of her, too, Grandma."

"Doggy," Little Jake said. "Doggy..." Did he want to sleep with Feisty, too?

"Baker," his grandmother called out, and he weaved his way around family members to approach her bed. "Are they here, at this hospital, too?"

He shook his head. He'd checked at the desk before rejoining his family in the waiting room. But he knew where they were. The ambulance had gone to the hospital on the other side of the Cassidy Ranch: Moss Valley. It was the opposite direction of Willow Creek.

"Maybe they're back at the ranch," Dusty said.

Baker didn't correct him. He didn't want his entire family rushing off to that other hospital, overwhelming the firefighter and his family after they'd just lost their home.

"Who are you talking about?" Miller asked.

"Nothing you need to worry about..." Dusty said.

And Miller glared at him. "That makes me worry more."

"Your grandma," Baker said. That was what Darlene was to them, though she'd never acted like it. She hadn't acted like a mother very long either.

Miller pointed at Sadie. "What about Grandma?"

"Not Grandma Sadie," Baker said. "Grandma Darlene. Your dad's mom. My mom."

Miller's brow creased with confusion. "I thought she was dead."

Baker shook his head. "I saw her…at that fire I was at today…and I saw some other guys that looked like us—"

"Baker!" Jake said, his voice sharp. "This is too much for them to understand. They don't need to deal with this, too, on top of—"

"No," Baker said, cutting off his older brother's protest. "No more leaving them out of family meetings. They're family. They've been through a lot—all of them." He swept his hand around at the little guys, including Caleb, who'd lost his dad a year ago. All that loss, all that pain, brought on a maturity far beyond their years. "They can understand this. Grandma Sadie had two sons," he explained. "My dad who died and another son…"

"Who ran away," Grandma finished for him when he trailed off because he hadn't wanted to bring up that pain for her again. "I didn't know where he was all these years. That's why I never talked about him."

"Now you know where he is?" Miller asked.

"He was at that ranch where the fire was," Baker said. "I'm not sure where he is now, but I'll find him and his sons." They could have been treated and released from that hospital in Moss Valley by now.

"We have more family?" Caleb asked, his blue eyes wide with awe. He loved being part of this family so much.

Baker hadn't always loved it. He'd felt lost, unseen, but maybe that had been his fault. Maybe he'd needed to stand up to his brothers sooner. "Yeah, buddy, we do."

"And you'll find them," Sadie said. It wasn't a question. She accepted that he would.

He wedged between his nephews and leaned over the bed to kiss her forehead. "Yes, I will."

"Can I go?" Miller asked.

"Me, too!" Ian said.

He smiled but shook his head. "You guys just promised to take care of Feisty tonight," he reminded them. "And it's getting late."

"We should get back to the ranch," Taye said. She'd agreed to come up to Sadie's room with him and the boys, but she'd held back.

Baker shook his head. Then he turned toward Jake and Katie. "Can you bring the boys back? I have something to ask Taye…"

"Are you going to propose like Aunt Emily did to Uncle Ben?" Caleb asked.

His breath left his lungs at the thought. And

he shook his head. "No… I want Miss Taye to go with me to look for my mom." He glanced at her, but her expression was unreadable.

"Okay," Ian said. Miller nodded, too, as if granting his permission for her to go with him.

What about hers?

Did she want to go?

Or was she worried that he was about to pull her under with him like he'd realized earlier? He knew that he shouldn't ask this of her, that he should bring one of his brothers instead. But she was the one he wanted. The one he needed. He worried that he might not have the nerve to confront his mother, to meet his uncle…

He needed Taye to do what she'd done with the boys. To push him to do the right thing no matter how hard it might be on him.

ALL TAYE HAD wanted was some distance from Baker, to process how she'd realized she felt about him. To figure out how to deal with those feelings… But then he'd been so sweet and honest with the boys, including them in that impromptu family meeting in Sadie's hospital room.

She knew how important that was to the

kids, because she'd been that kid who'd had no say in her own life, who'd been totally unaware of what was going on around her, with her parents, until her dad moved out and moved on and her mom had given up on living. For Taye, living with her dad and stepmother had been almost as bad because she'd been an outsider in what was supposed to be her home. In Sadie's hospital room with all that family, she'd felt like an outsider, too, until he'd included her. Until he'd asked her to go with him instead of his brothers.

She really should have refused and returned to the ranch. But instead she sat behind the wheel of her small SUV, and he sat just across the console from her, so close that his shoulder bumped against hers because his were so broad.

He was so big, his knees bumping up against the dash. The drive to Moss Valley was long and it was going to be uncomfortable for him in the close confines. Probably almost as physically uncomfortable for him as it was for her emotionally.

"You probably regret asking me to drive you now," she mumbled.

"Why?" he asked.

"Because Jake's and Dusty's and Ben's vehicles all have more room than mine," she pointed out.

"You fit all the boys in here," he said.

She smiled. "They're a lot smaller than you are."

"You're not," he said.

And she flinched as the remark reminded her of things her stepmother and sisters had said to her over the years. "Ouch."

"I didn't mean that as an insult," he said. "I meant that you don't have much more leg-room than I do. And your legs are probably as long as mine are…"

She glanced at him and noticed that he was staring at her legs, and even inside her jeans, her skin tingled. No. He hadn't been insulting her. She'd thought she'd stopped being sensitive about comments like that years ago. But because of how attractive she found Baker, she wanted him to find her attractive as well. Not that anything could ever come of that attraction.

"I put Little Jake's car seat behind the passenger seat, so you don't have as much room to push yours back as I do," she pointed out. "When I bought this, I figured I would be the only one riding in it." For at least as long as she had it. Maybe forever. She hadn't planned on having a family.

"Then Sadie convinced you to quit your job and move out to Ranch Haven," he said. "Why did you do that?"

She shrugged. "I knew Jenny and Dale and the boys from their visits to the diner. And when they died, I knew how hard it must have been on the boys. If there was anything I could do to help them, I wanted to…"

"You did. You have," he assured her. "Is that why you agreed to go with me to find my mom and my uncle and cousins? You want to help?"

"I do understand how you must feel," she said.

"But your mom died," he said. "Mine just ran away." He snorted derisively. "And she didn't even run that far…"

"My mom stayed in the same house, in her bed most of the time, but she was millions of miles away," Taye said. "Or maybe she was just stuck in the past, and she didn't want to move ahead, into the future. She didn't want to let go of that fairy-tale dream she'd had of happily-ever-after." That was how Baker reminded her of her mom. That he couldn't let the past go. She sighed and added, "She gave up long before she died."

"My mom did, too," he said. "She gave up all of us."

"She didn't have a choice with your dad," Taye pointed out. "He died, and maybe, like my mom, it was just more than she could handle."

He sucked in a breath as if she'd smacked him. "I always think about how hard it was on us, and how it was even harder when she left, too, but I never..."

"She lost her husband," Taye pointed out. "That's what made my mom give up, and he didn't even die." Maybe that would have been easier, though, because Michael Haven hadn't made the decision to leave; he hadn't found someone else.

"It doesn't matter how you lose someone," Baker intoned. "The loss still hurts..." Like when his mom had left.

That loss. That pain. Those were things Taye had vowed to never risk. To never fall for someone. But she found herself reaching across the console to cover his hand with hers. She'd offered it to him before, and he'd refused. This time he turned his over and entwined their fingers.

SADIE CLOSED HER eyes to rest for just a moment after everyone left her room. Her face was damp yet from the kisses that Little Jake had pressed against her cheek, acting like the doggy. Like Feisty. Tears stung her eyes over how he'd said over and over again, "Gamma, Gamma… Gamma…"

She loved those little guys so much. And she was so happy they were doing better. That was thanks to Baker. He was so fiercely protective of them. Such a good advocate for them.

Such a good guardian.

Baker had said she had other grandsons, duplicates of Ben and Jake. Did she have other great-grandchildren?

Jessup had kept himself and his kids from her all these years. When Baker found him, maybe he wouldn't want to see her. Maybe he hadn't forgiven her.

A sob slipped out of her throat and echoed in the silence of the room. Then a warm hand covered hers, squeezing it. And she opened her eyes to stare up into Lem Lemmon's slightly wrinkled face as he leaned over her bed. "Checking to see if I died?" she asked.

"Hoping you haven't," he said. "If you go before me…"

Her pulse quickened a little, and she held her breath, waiting for him to continue.

"…then I won't have any excuse to go out to the ranch to eat."

She laughed, like he'd probably meant her to, and the tears in her eyes dried up but for the one that had trickled down the cheek Little Jake had kissed so many times.

With his free hand, Lem reached out and brushed away the teardrop with the pad of his thumb. "Must've got something in your eye," he murmured, saving her pride for her.

The man knew her too well, maybe even better than her late husband had. How had Jake kept Jessup from her? How had he not told her that he'd been sending money to their runaway son?

Lem had been the one to tell her, and she'd been so angry that she'd taken it out on the messenger. She still regretted how she'd spoken to him that day, when he'd been nothing but a friend to her lately. Maybe more than a friend…

"What are you doing back here?" she asked. "I thought you were leaving with Livvy." He'd walked out with her family when they'd left, like he was leaving, too. But he hadn't said goodbye. She'd realized it then and had been hurting a bit. And it hadn't been just her pride.

She pressed her free hand over her heart.

And he tensed. "Are you all right? Should I get a nurse?"

She shook her head. "Calm down, old man, or you'll be having the next heart attack. I'm fine. I'm just worried."

"About Jessup and those grandkids you didn't know about?"

She nodded.

"I'm sure they're fine," he said.

"I wonder if I'll ever know..." she began.

"What do you mean? Baker will call and let you know the minute he finds them," he assured her.

She sighed. "I wonder if I'll ever get to meet them...to know them." She'd already lost so many years with them.

Lem leaned over the railing on her bed and brushed his lips across her forehead.

And she realized it wasn't just the years with her family that she'd lost. She'd wasted time with Lem, in a feud that had gone back to their school days so very long ago. She squeezed his hand. "What are you doing back here?" she asked again.

He shrugged. "Figured I better keep an eye

on you," he said. "The minute I leave you alone, you fall apart on me, woman."

She squeezed his hand harder, hard enough that he winced and chuckled. "I can still take you, Lem Lemmon," she warned him, reminding him of their schoolyard showdowns. She'd always been able to beat him and every other boy at arm wrestling.

"You already have me, Sadie March Haven," he informed her. "You've already taken me."

What was he saying? And why was she too scared to ask? He'd lost the love of his life, like she'd lost hers. Could they handle another loss like that? But he certainly didn't seem like he was ready to go anywhere. "So what are you going to do?" she asked. "Spend the night?"

He nodded. "Yup."

"Where?"

He pointed to a chair. "The nurse said that reclines. I usually spend most nights in my La-Z-Boy at home, so I'll be quite comfy there."

"But what will people say?" she asked. She didn't care about gossip. But as a politician, he probably did.

He chuckled. "If tongues get wagging,

Sadie, I guess I'll just have to make an honest woman of you…"

She wished she'd been honest with her family from the start. That she'd talked about Jessup to her grandsons, so that they wouldn't have been so shocked. Poor Baker. He must have been blindsided at the Cassidy Ranch. To see his mother…

And then those men…

"It's probably a little late for that, Lem," she said. And was it a little late for them?

They were eighty after all.

But, thanks to Baker, she wasn't dead. Not yet. And neither was Lem.

Baker. She smiled as she thought of him, of how he'd looked with his brother's kids, with Taye…like a family. Tears stung her eyes again, and she furiously blinked. "Must be a lot of dust in the air in here… I keep getting something in my eyes."

Lem smiled, leaned down and kissed her forehead again. "Close them, then. You should get some rest. It's been a long day."

Too long…

"I hope your snoring doesn't keep me awake," she grumbled faintly.

"You're going to have to get used to it,"

he replied softly, then released her hand and headed to that recliner.

She curled her fingers into her palm, surprised that they were tingling. Must have been the drugs they'd given her to regulate her heart. It didn't feel regulated, though.

It felt... Hopeful.

About Lem. And Baker and Taye and the little boys.

They weren't quite ready yet. She knew that. They both had their hang-ups because of their pasts, so they couldn't be pushed. They would have to come around to each other on their own. But they were getting there. Those circles they'd been making around each other were getting smaller and smaller so that they were getting closer and closer.

Baker had asked her to go with him. Of all the family he could have had accompany him, he'd picked her. No. Sadie had picked her a while ago for Baker, knowing that they would be good for each other.

That if anyone could heal Baker, it was Taye. And vice versa.

CHAPTER NINETEEN

THE HOSPITAL IN Moss Valley wasn't even as big as the small one in Willow Creek, so the lobby opened right onto the waiting room. When Baker and Taye walked into it, Baker heard her soft gasp of surprise. "Oh, my…"

He knew what had shocked her—that it was so eerily similar to the waiting room they'd just left. Not the decor but the people. All Havens. After talking to his grandmother, he knew it for a fact now. But he was struck again, like he'd been back at the Cassidy Ranch, at how much the men looked like his two oldest brothers. Tall and broad-shouldered with the same chiseled features and dark hair and eyes.

"It is like looking at Jake and Ben," Taye murmured. "But there are three of them…"

The other two men must have already been treated because they paced the waiting room. The one's hands were freshly bandaged and the other one had what appeared to be some minor burns on his forearms and hands, but he must have refused treatment.

The firefighter noticed Baker and separated from his brothers to walk over to him. "Is something else happening at the ranch?" he asked. "Did the fire spread anymore?"

"No, we didn't leave until all the hot spots were out," Baker assured him.

The guy tilted his head and glanced at Taye, and a crease formed between his dark eyebrows. "Then why…"

"I wanted to check on you all," Baker said, his gut churning with dread and indecision. Was this the right time? The right place? "How is your dad?"

The guy clenched his jaw so tightly that a muscle twitched in his cheek.

And Baker felt bad for prying. He thought about backing off, about leaving them alone, but before he could reconsider, his mother walked into the room. She must have been getting coffee from a vending machine in a back hall because she had a cup in each hand. When she saw him, she dropped those cups, splashing coffee all over the floor and her jeans.

"Darlene!" the bandaged man exclaimed. "Are you okay? Are you burned?"

She was trembling and staring at Baker.

"What's wrong?" the firefighter asked, glancing from one to the other.

"What's going on?" the third man asked, and as he approached, Baker noticed his holster and his badge. He was a sheriff's deputy. "Who are you?"

"Baker Haven," he replied. Then he pointed to his mother and added, "Darlene's youngest son."

"Darlene?" the lawman asked for verification.

And Baker, irritated and emboldened by her reaction, said, "I'm your cousin. Your father is…was…my dad's brother."

"Are you crazy?" the bandaged man asked. "What are you talking about? My dad doesn't have a brother. And Darlene is…was…my mother's friend."

"Baker Haven…" the firefighter said as if he recognized the name. Or maybe his story.

"What are you trying to pull?" the lawman asked, as he stepped closer to Baker as if he was going to cuff him.

And Taye stepped closer to him, too. "He's telling the truth," she said. "Ask her…"

Everyone turned back to Darlene, who just managed a weak nod.

"She might be hurt," Taye pointed out.

And Baker snapped into paramedic mode and crossed the room to her. The bandaged man was already there, trying to reach for her, but he flinched when he touched his hands against her shoulders.

Taye helped him steer his mother to a chair. Once she was sitting, Baker dropped to his knees in front of her and rolled up the damp legs of her jeans. The skin beneath was warm but not blistered or burning.

"I'm okay," she said, finally speaking, her voice just a faint rasp. Then she focused on Baker, and with her hands free now, she pressed her palms to his face and studied him. "It's really you…it's my baby…"

He sucked in a breath at the sharp jab to his heart. Then he jerked back, so that her hands fell away from his face, and he nearly fell to the floor from his crouch. "If that's how you really thought of me, how did you leave me?" he asked, his voice choked with the emotions overwhelming him. "How did you leave *us*?"

Tears streamed out of her hazel eyes, trailing over the faint lines in her face. "I—I can't do this right now…" she whispered.

Fury coursed through Baker with that helplessness Taye spoke of so often. As if she felt his emotions, she reached out and grasped his shoulder, squeezing it. But nothing could keep from him drowning right now—in his resentment. All these years he'd wondered how she was able to leave them when they'd already been suffering so much. And now that he'd found her, she still refused to answer him?

The other men moved closer, stepping between him and Darlene as if to protect her. "Now's not the time or the place to get into all of this," the firefighter said. "We're in a hospital waiting room, man."

"I was just in one, too," Baker informed them. "My grandmother..." Those emotions rushed up to choke him again, and he had to clear his throat. "*Our* grandmother had an attack. A-fib. Her heart stopped."

A cry slipped through Darlene's lips. "Not Sadie. Is she all right?"

Baker nodded. "She will be once she knows how her son is doing. That's why I came. She asked me to."

"He's being kept overnight for observation," Darlene said. "He had a heart transplant a few months ago, and they want to make sure his body can handle the smoke inhalation from the fire."

"Heart transplant," Baker echoed. From a few months ago…

Dale and Jenny had died a few months ago. His skin chilled before goose bumps lifted it. Could his brother's heart…

He couldn't let himself think it, couldn't think of Dale right now, or he would totally fall apart. Feeling like Midnight sometimes acted in that stall, wild enough to kick his way out, Baker jerked to his feet. He whirled and rushed out of the waiting room, through the automatic doors of the lobby and into the parking lot. Once outside, he gasped, drawing in gulps of night air…and he felt again like he was drowning…until Taye slid her arms around him, holding him close. She kept him afloat…or maybe she slipped under with him. He didn't know…and selfishly he didn't care.

He was just happy that he wasn't alone.

SHE HADN'T BEEN able to leave him alone. In the parking lot or even after their silent trip back to Ranch Haven. Knowing he wouldn't stay in the main house, she drove him to the foreman's cottage. And while he sat silently in the passenger's seat, she got out and, with her hand on his arm, helped him out and up the steps into the dark house.

He had to be in shock. Or maybe he was just so exhausted from the day that he could barely function. He'd been pulling double shifts for the past couple of weeks as well.

He wasn't taking care of himself…just like her mother hadn't. But unlike her mother, he was taking care of other people. He'd been fighting fires and rescuing people, like he'd rescued Sadie when she'd collapsed. If he hadn't found her when he had… She shuddered to think about losing such a wonderful, loving lady. But Sadie was going to be okay because of Baker.

Would he take any joy in that, any pride in knowing that he'd saved his grandmother? Or would he just wallow in the guilt of losing Dale and Jenny? And the pain of his mother's abandonment?

She shuddered again to think of how the woman had reacted to seeing him, to realizing he was her baby.

Darlene hadn't answered his question about why she'd left him and his brothers. And after his cousins had closed ranks to protect her, they'd had no choice but to leave. She hadn't wanted to drive him to the firehouse; he needed rest, not work.

Now she steered him through the door into

the bedroom. He collapsed onto the bed. And she knew he was exhausted. Physically and emotionally.

She closed the door and stepped out into the small living room. But when she started toward the door and where she'd parked her SUV outside it, she stopped at the couch. She couldn't leave him here alone.

Not like this…

He reminded her too much of her mother in those dark days when her mom hadn't been able to eat or talk or take care of herself at all. And Taye couldn't leave him alone and vulnerable like that.

She lay down on the couch. It was a little short, but it was soft. She bent her knees and curled up on her side, and she wished she was as exhausted as he was. While her body was weary, her mind kept whirling with all the events of the day.

Baker…

The boys…

Sadie…

Concern for them consumed her. Love for them.

She hadn't even realized how hard she'd fallen for the boys, how much they'd come to mean to her. And Sadie. Taye had started out just admiring her fierceness, her spirit, her loyalty, her strength. But then Sadie had become someone more than she wanted to emulate. She'd become someone she wanted in her life always.

And the boys… It was the same with them. She couldn't imagine leaving them, not being a daily part of their lives.

What about Baker…?

There was no room in her life, in her heart, for a man like him. One so tortured with guilt and regret. She couldn't go through what she had with her mother, watching someone she loved slip away to despair. Not again. She'd established a life she loved, had people in her life she loved, and she didn't want to lose that, to lose any of them. But somehow Baker, and his self-sacrifice and sweetness and care of his nephews, had snuck past her guard and into her heart. He'd made room for himself there.

Yet she just didn't see how it would work. And Baker wasn't interested in her as anything more than someone to keep him afloat as he dealt with all the trauma in his life. She was the one who'd fallen for him, not the other way around.

She emitted a soft sigh and gradually

drifted off to sleep…until a horrible sound jerked her awake. It was so primal, so tortured, that a cry of fear and sympathy slipped out of her lips as her skin chilled. Like that night she'd been walking near the barn, she thought it was an animal…until she realized it was coming from the bedroom where she'd left Baker.

She scrambled off the couch and rushed into the room. Uneasy, she flipped on the lights and found him sitting up in bed, staring straight ahead…but his eyes were unfocused. She knew he wasn't seeing her; he was seeing whatever he'd dreamed about, whatever had had him reacting with such distress.

"Baker!" she called his name, trying to bring him out of the nightmare.

But he didn't move, didn't react at all; he couldn't hear her. She drew closer to the bed and touched his shoulder, and he jerked as if she'd struck him.

"Baker," she said again, more softly.

He shook his head and expelled a long, ragged sigh before finally focusing on her. "What?" Then he glanced around as if he had no idea where he was or how he'd gotten there.

And maybe he didn't.

"Are you okay?" she asked.

He expelled another deep sigh. Then he drew in some steadying breaths before he nodded. "Yeah, yeah, I'm fine. I'm just..." He trailed off as he looked around again and then back at her. "What are you doing here?"

"I was worried about you," she said. "After you ran out of the waiting room, you were so out of it..."

He rubbed a hand over his face, as if trying to scrub away the tears he'd cried over his mother. Over all the revelations that had put him into the state of shock he'd been in. Was still in...apparently.

He closed his eyes, and she wondered for a moment if he was going to fall back to sleep. But when he opened them, tears glistened in them. "I'm sorry, Taye. I shouldn't have had you go with me..."

"Why did you?" she asked. He'd asked her why she'd agreed to come with him to Moss Valley, but she hadn't asked him why he'd wanted her to go. "Why me and not one of your brothers?"

He emitted a weary sigh. "Because you make me do the things I don't want to do."

She flinched. Was he still upset with her? "I'm sorry. I know you didn't want to talk with Mrs. Lancaster and the boys, but last night… I had no idea you didn't want to find your mother, your cousins, your uncle."

"I wanted to do it for Grandma," he said. "But I didn't really want to see the woman who took off after my dad died." His face flushed with anger. "I didn't want to see her with cousins I never knew about, with cousins she apparently helped raise…" He clenched his hands into fists. "…even though she didn't raise her own kids…"

"That's a lot of anger," she remarked. Maybe that was what had provoked the nightmare this time, not the guilt or grief he'd been feeling over Dale's and Jenny's deaths.

He nodded. "Yeah, I guess it is," he agreed. "It's better than that helpless feeling I had when my dad died and she left."

"I understand." All too well…

"I know you do," he said. "That's another reason I wanted you to go with me. But I'm sorry that I asked. I'm sorry that you had to be there to witness all that…" He gestured at himself, at his disheveled, sweat-damp hair. "All of this."

"What was the nightmare about?" she asked.

He shrugged. "I don't even know. I rarely remember them when I wake up."

"You need help for them," she said. "You can't go on like this…"

"I haven't had one in the week since the boys and I talked to Mrs. Lancaster," he said.

"So talk to her again," she urged him.

"What about you?" he asked.

She paused before nodding. "You can talk to me, too."

"I meant who do you talk to, Taye?" he asked.

She tensed. "Is this you deflecting again?" she asked. "Trying to change the subject off your problems."

He emitted a gruff chuckle. "Who's deflecting now I wonder…"

"You just woke up from a nightmare," she said. "You were nearly comatose after we left that hospital in Moss Valley. I had to get you out of the SUV and help you into the house." And she hadn't ever wanted to have to do that again, to watch someone give up right in front her. She was angry now that she'd put herself in this situation; that he'd put her in this situation. "You're the one with problems."

"Oh, I definitely have them," he heartily agreed. "And I was reeling ever since

I saw *her* at the ranch and *them* and then Grandma…" He shuddered.

And she felt a wave of guilt for not being more understanding. He'd had every reason to be in shock.

"I know," she said, and she bobbed her head in a quick nod. "And I understand—"

"I don't," he interrupted her. "I don't understand how a woman as warm and loving and nurturing as you are doesn't want more for herself."

She tensed again. "What are you talking about?"

"You," he said. "You need to be talking. I don't even think anyone else knows what you went through with your mom and stepmom and sisters…"

"Sadie does."

"Because you talked to her about it or because she figured it out as Sadie always does?" he asked skeptically. "Have you talked to Katie or Emily or Melanie?"

She felt that sting of guilt again over keeping secrets. She hadn't considered them secrets, though. She'd considered them a distraction. The boys were the focus for everyone; they had to be.

"They've all had a lot going on," she re-

minded him. "We all have." No one probably more than Baker. "And I don't like to
dwell in the past. I want to put it behind me
and not even think about it anymore, let alone
talk about it."

He smiled faintly. "Unlike me…who can't
seem to let it go." He released another sigh.
"I'm going to try." He straightened his shoulders. "No, I am going to *do* it. But what about
you…"

"What about me?" she asked. "I've put all
that behind me."

"Then why don't you want the fairy tale,
Taye?"

"Because that's all it is."

"So Katie and Jake aren't happy? Emily
and Ben aren't? Dusty and Melanie?"

She shook her head. "I didn't say that…"

"Then what's your hang-up? Why don't you
want what they have? Why do you want to
take care of other families but not your own?"

Her head snapped back like he'd slapped
her with the way he'd pointed out how she really wasn't one of them. She'd come to think
of the Havens—especially Miller, Ian and
Little Jake—as her own. Even Baker… But it
was clear that they would never get together.

She couldn't risk this kind of heartache. And her heart was aching, hurting…

"I don't want to wind up like my mother," she bit out. "Like you…"

"I know you don't want me," he assured her.

But that wasn't what she meant.

"But there are nice, uncomplicated guys out there who could make you happy," he said. "You deserve that, Taye."

"Katie's first husband was that kind of guy. Caleb's dad. And he died. Just like Dale and Jenny." There was no guarantee of happily-ever-after for anyone.

"And Katie survived and is in love again. And Dale and Jenny…" His voice cracked as he trailed off. "You want me to let go of the past. But you keep hanging on to it yourself." He surged up from the bed then and approached her.

And she stepped back, uncomfortable as she realized how alone they were out here. He wouldn't hurt her physically. But emotionally, he was already hurting her. He was already making her feel emotions she'd vowed she'd never risk feeling. Love…so much love that it scared her. She felt like screaming like he had from his nightmare. She wanted to run, but before she could even turn around, he touched her. Just his fingertips along her jaw.

He tipped her face up to his and stared deeply into her eyes. Then he brushed a soft kiss across her lips before he lifted his head and whispered, "You deserve so much more than you're letting yourself have. So much more."

CHAPTER TWENTY

SHE DESERVED SO much more than him. He'd
lied to her. Because Baker knew exactly what
his nightmare had been about.

Her.

Leaving.

Him and the ranch and the boys... Like
his mother had left him and his brothers all
those years ago.

In his dream the boys had been screaming
like they had in the aftermath of the crash,
in that upside-down SUV. And his scream
had echoed theirs. It burned yet in the back
of his throat even all these hours later, after
she'd left in the dark and driven up to the
main house. He breathed a little easier knowing that she was there for the boys. He had
to be, too. But he needed a little bit longer to
get his head together.

He'd given up on sleeping after she'd left,
and he stood now outside Midnight's stall.
The bronco's head extended over the door,

and Baker rubbed his hand along his neck. "Maybe you should put out a shingle offering counseling for a fee," Baker advised the horse. "It's easy to talk to you about my problems."

Taye was easy to talk to as well.

He'd told her the truth; he was going to get help in dealing with the past to make sure that he left it behind him. The crash. His deployments... Even his mother if that was where she was determined to stay: in the past. She obviously hadn't wanted a present or future with them.

He wanted a future with Taye, but he wasn't sure how much she could handle after growing up the way she had. Even after he got help, he might have nightmares from time to time.

Just as Midnight reared up and got restless from time to time. That restlessness was a part of the horse's nature. Like it was Baker's now. But he didn't want to run away from it or the ranch anymore.

Still, because of those nightmares, because of his past, he wasn't the man for Taye. She deserved a real prince, a guy who would treat her right and not complicate her life any more than it had been. But the thought of her leav-

ing him and the boys brought back that nightmare all over again.

As if Midnight felt the turmoil inside
Baker, he shifted restlessly in his stall, pawing the ground, rearing up…and that noise
escaped from him. That noise that Baker had
probably made that had had Taye rushing into
his room. He must have scared her.

"Stop spooking my horse," a deep voice
drawled as Dusty joined him at the stall.

Baker grinned. "I'm not the one riling him
up," he insisted. "We're friends now."

Dusty snorted. "What? You been bringing
him carrots, too?"

Baker chuckled. "No. He gets enough of
those from Caleb. I've just been boring him
with my problems."

Dusty reached out to rub Midnight's nose.
"Boring him or burdening him? Maybe that's
why he's rearing up."

"Maybe so," Baker admitted. "You still
going to take him away from all of this? You
still going to buy the Cassidy Ranch?"

Dusty nodded. "I wasn't buying it for the
house. I want the property and the barns."

"And that pretty mare." Baker had only
seen her for a moment in the shadows of the

barn, but her brown coat, stretched over lean muscles, had gleamed in the faint light.

"Yes," Dusty said.

Baker could see the operation that Dusty was going to have someday. "I understand why you want your own thing. Why you don't want to try to take Dale's place."

"Nobody can," Dusty said wistfully, and tears glistened in the hazel eyes that were so like Dale's, so like their mother's.

"You might want to explain that to Jake," Baker said.

"Nobody can take his place, but they can make their own," Dusty said. "Here on the ranch. With the boys. They can make their own place."

Baker released a ragged sigh. "I never thought I fit in here," he admitted, "with the rest of you. You all always knew what you wanted."

"You wanted to be a firefighter," Dusty said.

"I wanted anything that wasn't the ranch," Baker admitted.

"And now?" Dusty asked. "Now do you know what you want?"

He knew. But there wasn't much he could do about it. At least about Taye.

"Some answers," he said. "I found them last night." He shook his head. "But Mom wouldn't talk to me…" His chest ached as he remembered that encounter. "And I have a feeling our cousins didn't know any more about us than we knew about them."

Dusty nodded. "She called me… She wants to come over in a couple days and talk to us all."

"You think she'll show?" Baker asked doubtfully, refusing to get his hopes up like he used to when he was a little kid hoping she'd return for his birthday or Christmas.

Dusty's head bobbed in another nod. "Yeah, this time I think she will."

Unlike the funeral…

Unlike since he'd talked to her last…

Baker heard everything Dusty left unsaid. Like Baker had left so much unsaid with Taye last night. He hadn't thanked her for going with him. He hadn't thanked her for all she did for the boys, for his family…for helping him save Sadie.

He hadn't told her that he loved her.

He wasn't sure that he should. He was worried that if he did that, he'd spook her like Dusty had accused him of spooking Midnight. And she would run, just like his mother had all those years ago, leaving heartbroken little boys behind her.

He couldn't do that to her or to them. He couldn't cause them any more pain than they'd already suffered. He had to keep his feelings for her to himself.

TAYE HADN'T ATTEMPTED to go back to sleep after she returned to the main house. Instead she'd made some coffee and had probably had too many cups. Because she was so jittery, she jerked when she heard footsteps on the back stairwell and sloshed some of the hot brew over the rim. Sympathizing with Darlene Haven dropping those cups last night, she hissed at the pain and turned on the sink to run cold water over her fingers.

"Are you okay?" Emily asked with concern as she joined Taye at the counter.

She nodded and turned to look at the petite blonde woman. Emily's hair was tangled around her face, and she had dark circles beneath her eyes. "Are you?" Taye asked.

Emily nodded. "Just need coffee…"

"What happened?" Taye asked, alarm jabbing her. "Is Sadie all right?"

"Yes," Emily said. "Lem is going to drive her home later this morning from the hospital. She's fine. And the boys are finally asleep now."

"Finally?" Taye asked. "What happened?"

"You," Emily said.

Taye sucked in a breath. "What do you mean?"

"They wanted you," Emily said.

"Who?" Taye asked.

"All of them," Melanie murmured wearily as she descended the last few steps to join them in the kitchen. "I don't know when it happened, but you replaced all of us."

"Little Jake woke up with a nightmare and was inconsolable," Emily shared. "He wanted Taye or Unca Bake."

Tears stung Taye's eyes. "I'm sorry…" Her heart ached that she hadn't been there for him.

"Miller wound up taking him into bed with him and Feisty," Melanie shared.

"And then Ian and Caleb went into his room, too," Katie said as she joined them at the island. "They're all passed out on the floor in there now except for Feisty, who kept the bed to herself."

Taye reached for the coffeepot and mugs, and as she poured, she noticed her hands were shaking.

Katie put her hands over Taye's. "Are you okay? What's wrong?"

And the tears that had threatened her spilled over, running down her face. All three women surrounded her, wrapping her up in their arms as she wept.

She had never had support like this. When her mom had been sick, no one had helped her. With her stepmother and stepsisters, she'd had no allies—not even her dad. She wasn't used to this…to real family.

It didn't matter that they weren't related by blood or even by marriage. To her, they were Taye's family. So finally she opened up to them. She told them all about her childhood, about her past, and her fear of being like her mother, of not being strong enough to survive if she loved and lost.

"But Taye," Emily said. "You already did."

She blinked away the tears and asked, "What do you mean?" Did they know that she'd already fallen for Baker and that they had no future?

"Your mother," Emily said. "You lost your mom like I lost mine, and you survived without any support. I know what that's like. I know how much strength that takes."

"Sadie told me once that I'm stronger than

I think I am," Katie shared. "And she was right."

"You told me that," Melanie said.

"And I was right," Katie said with a smile.

Melanie smiled and nodded. "Yes, you were."

"And you, Taye," Emily said. "You're the strongest person I know."

She wished it was true, but she shook her head in denial. "Sadie Haven is. She's lost so much."

"And you're the most like Sadie," Emily said. "You're fiercely loving and loyal and nurturing and wise. Don't sell yourself short. Don't think you can't have it all."

The fairy tale…

Could she?

Was Baker right? Was that what she deserved? The only problem was, he didn't think she could have that with him. And she didn't want it with anyone else.

Two days had passed since Lem had driven her home from the hospital. Two days in which she was supposed to relax and recover…before Darlene visited. They'd warned her, like she needed a warning. Like Sadie March Haven was fragile.

Her heart had taken harder knocks than it had during whatever kind of attack she'd had. Not exactly a heart attack. A-fib, whatever that was. She didn't care. She would follow their instructions; it wasn't as if she had much choice.

They were all watching her like hawks, monitoring her medicine, her caffeine intake, her rest…like she could get any rest with them all hovering around her. Like she could rest before she saw Darlene.

Was she coming alone?

Dusty said she'd asked to visit on her own; she hadn't mentioned anyone else when she'd called him. Sadie could tell that none of Darlene's sons really expected her to show up. She remembered those early days when Darlene had called and promised she'd come back for the holidays or for their birthdays.

And she had never shown. So they'd told her—one by one—to stop contacting them. Poor Darlene… This was going to be even harder for her than them. Sadie understood that. They all had each other…and the women they loved.

They paced around the kitchen now. Restless. On edge. But Jake took comfort with Katie's hand in his. Ben with Emily anchored against his side. And Dusty, hovering around his pregnant wife.

Only Baker stood alone, near the glass doors to the patio, but he wasn't staring out of them. He was staring at the woman who stood behind the counter, fussing over platters of sandwiches and cookies that Juliet Shepard and Miller were helping her prepare.

Only Taye would turn this kind of tense, uncomfortable meeting into a party. She was such a special woman. And Baker obviously knew it.

Maybe he considered her too special. Maybe he didn't realize how special he was. He'd lobbied for the boys again, ensuring that the little ones were present. That no more family meetings were held without them.

But would this meeting even take place?

The doorbell rang, sending Feisty into a frenzy of yapping. Before Sadie could jump up from the table where she'd been sitting with the hearth at her back, Taye said, "I'll answer it."

And she disappeared down the hall only to return moments later, leading a smaller, sandy-haired woman. Darlene.

Despite nearly twenty years passing, she hadn't aged much. She was still as pretty as the young woman Michael had brought home to the ranch. Darlene had brought others along with her. She wasn't alone.

Three young men flanked her. With their dark hair and dark eyes, they all looked like Jake and Ben. Like their father...

He followed behind them. Jessup looked older than the teenaged boy who'd run away from her rules and restrictions. From her overbearing protectiveness...

Tears streamed down Sadie's face as she studied his. There were lines in it, so many more lines than she'd ever thought he would get. And the silver in his hair...

He was sixty years old. He'd lived.

A sob broke out of her throat. Lem, sitting next to her, squeezed her hand. But then Jessup was there, kneeling beside her, wrapping his arms around her. "Mom..." he murmured.

And she trembled at the word. Nobody had called her that since Michael had died.

"I'm so sorry," he said. "I'm so sorry..."

She leaned back and cupped his face in her hands, and like Little Jake had hers in the hospital, she pressed kisses against his cheek. "I thought you were dead," she admitted.

He released a ragged sigh. "I know. And there were many times I nearly was..." He

touched his chest. "That I would have been…
and I didn't want to put you through all that.
Not after you lost Michael and Dad… I didn't
want you to lose anyone else."

"But I did," she said. "I lost my grandson
and his sweet wife…"

Jessup's voice cracked when he said, "I
think I might have his heart." His hand was
still pressed against his chest, and Sadie covered it with hers.

"Dale would have liked that," she said even
as tears filled her eyes over the loss of her
grandson and Jenny.

A sob slipped out of Darlene then, and
her shoulders shook. While one of the men
wrapped his arm around her in support, Sadie
stood up and crossed over to her. And she
closed her arms around her, holding her close.
"Welcome home, honey…"

"How can you?" Darlene asked. "I thought
you hated me. That's why I left. I thought you
blamed me for Michael dying."

"Why?" Sadie asked. "That wasn't your
fault."

"But I was riding that tractor with him,"
Darlene said. "I distracted him, and he fell…
and…" Her voice cracked.

"That's why you left?" Sadie asked. "Because you thought we blamed you?"

Darlene nodded. "You most of all. I took your son away from you. And you'd already lost one."

"I could never hate you," Sadie said, and her heart broke to think of the guilt Darlene had been carrying around. "My son loved you so much, and no matter how short his life was, it was full of happiness—happiness that *you* brought him. No, Darlene, I could never hate you."

"That's why I went looking for Jessup," Darlene explained. "I wanted to give you back the son you lost. Michael told me about him, that Jessup was working as a rodeo bull fighter…"

Sadie sucked in a breath, then laughed. "Of course you were…" She'd wrapped him so tightly in bubble wrap that he would have sought out the most dangerous thing to do in retaliation.

"I was a fool," Jessup said. "I am so sorry for how I treated you, Mom. I had no idea how badly I had until I had kids of my own, though." His voice cracked with emotion, and he cleared his throat before continuing, "Before my oldest took off on me like I did on you."

She glanced at the three men who stood behind him and Darlene. "You have four sons?"

He nodded. "And here, let me introduce them…" He trailed off as his face flushed. "Uh, I changed my name after I ran away. I started calling myself JJ, and I took the last name Cassidy. It was my wife's. Colleen. She passed away from breast cancer probably around the same time Michael did."

He'd experienced so much loss, too, like she had. Sadie reached for his hand and grasped it in hers, holding it tightly. "I'm sorry, too," she said. "For so many things…"

"No," he said. "You have nothing to apologize for, Mom. All you've ever done is love us—all of us—so much that I know how much pain you were in over losing Michael and then Dad. And my health has been so touch-and-go over the years that I didn't want to reconnect with you only for you to watch me die."

"There are no guarantees in life," Sadie said. "But we can't stop living it because we're afraid…" And she looked beyond her son, then, to meet Baker's gaze and then Taye's.

Hopefully they would learn the lessons she had. That love was all that mattered. "And no amount of pain will ever take away from the love," she said. "Now introduce me to my grandsons."

CHAPTER TWENTY-ONE

BAKER STOOD YET near the patio doors, listening as his uncle introduced the firefighter, Colton Cassidy, and his twin, a cardiologist named Collin. The deputy, for the Moss Valley sheriff's department, had been named for Baker's dad. Michael March Cassidy, but he went by Marsh...something his older brother had called him when he was born. The oldest brother, the one who'd run away and had never returned, was Cash.

They were all older than Baker, like his brothers, and he felt a little lost in the shadows again like he had when he was growing up behind them. He also felt a little out of place...before he reminded himself that Ranch Haven was his place. And he was taking it.

"Jake," he said, drawing his older brother over toward him where he stood yet near the windows.

"Are you okay?" Jake asked.

"Yes, I am," he said. He was more okay than he'd been in a long time. Because Grandma was right, though it was doubtful that he would ever admit that to her. You couldn't stop living life because you were afraid. Had Taye heard that? "Are you okay?" he asked his oldest brother.

Jake released a ragged sigh. "I don't know. I'm reeling…"

Baker could relate; he'd felt that way yesterday. But he still advised Jake, "Don't. Don't do your Jake thing."

"My Jake thing?" his brother asked.

"Don't take on any more responsibility for anything," he said. "I want the job."

"What?"

"The foreman job," Baker reminded him. "It's mine."

Jake grinned and nodded. "Yeah, it is. I was just waiting for you to realize that."

"The boys are, too," Baker said.

And Jake's forehead creased with confusion. "What do you mean?"

"That day in the crash, Daddy told Uncle Baker to take care of us," Ian said.

Baker hadn't even noticed the five-year-old joining them, but he should have. Ian was pretty much his shadow whenever he was around. Miller was usually Taye's, but he approached them now, too, holding Little Jake's hand in his.

"What's going on?" Miller asked.

"We should discuss this, just adults," Jake said.

"No. This concerns them more than anyone else," Baker said, and he hoped they felt the way he did, that he'd finally come to accept. Everybody had been right that he was the only one who could reach them but not just in the therapy he planned to continue with them and on his own. They belonged together because they'd forged a bond that had brought them closer than he'd ever been with anyone else. He answered Miller, "I'm telling your uncle Jake that I want to be your primary guardian, that I want to take care of you and Ian and Little Jake."

Miller studied his face solemnly for a moment before he nodded. "That's okay with me as long as…"

Baker tensed. "What?"

"You marry Miss Taye," he finished, and he grinned.

"Sadie," Baker teased the seven-year-old. "You *really* are shrinking."

Miller's grin just widened. "You know you want to," he prodded Baker.

And he did. More than anything. But when he looked around the kitchen, the same heart of the home that she was, he didn't see her. She was gone. He needed to find her, to tell her what he'd done, what he wanted...

Her.

Before he could move, his mother was there, begging to be introduced to her grandsons. They accepted her readily before noticing that Caleb was eating all the cookies. Then they rushed off to the other side of the kitchen to get their share of the goodies Taye had made.

And Baker's heart filled with love for them.

"I'm sorry," Darlene said to him and to Jake, who stood stiffly in front of her. Ben and Dusty joined them. "I'm sorry I took off when you needed me most, when your father died."

"It was hard," Ben said, pulling no punches. "Losing you both like that."

"It was," Baker agreed. "But I understand. You felt guilty..." That same guilt had kept him from his nephews for too long. "You blamed yourself for something that wasn't your fault."

She shook her head, obviously unwilling to absolve herself of blame yet. She'd carried that a long time. "But it was my fault. I was with him."

A tractor accident. Baker could imagine what she'd seen, and how devastating that loss had been for her. He probably wasn't the only one who had nightmares.

"And I distracted him," she said.

"Mom, things just happen sometimes," he said. "Terrible things. We can't take responsibility for all of them. We need to focus on taking responsibility for the good things, too." Like the boys. He wanted responsibility for them. But they weren't all he wanted.

His mom's breath shuddered out in what sounded like relief. "I didn't think you would understand…"

"More than you know," he said. He hugged her, and as he did, his brothers slapped his back. They didn't say anything, though, as if they were too choked up. Tears trickled out of their eyes. When he released their mother, the others closed their arms around her, embracing her. Welcoming her home at last.

And Baker slipped away to find another woman he suspected was about to run.

SHE SHOULD RUN. She knew that. It was why Taye had fled the kitchen to hide in her room, to regroup and remind herself of what her friends had told her a couple of days ago.

She was stronger than she thought she was. As scary as falling in love was, it didn't have to end badly. It didn't have to end at all. She could have that happily-ever-after fairy-tale ending. If Baker loved her back.

She loved him so much, and her heart had hardly been able to handle all the emotion in the kitchen over the family reunion. She suspected Sadie's heart was stronger now than it had ever been. And Jessup had Dale's…

She remembered what Sadie had said in the kitchen during her reunion with her son. That no amount of pain could ever take away from the love. And that a person should not be too afraid to live.

Sadie had been speaking directly to her. And to Baker.

She still wanted them together. And Taye wanted that, too, so much that she didn't even mind the meddling. She wanted to live. She wanted Baker. So much…

Overwhelmed, she couldn't fight the tears anymore, and one slid down her cheek. Then a thumb was wiping it away as Baker cradled her face in his big hand. She hadn't even heard him open the door. She'd been sitting on her bed, struggling with her emotions, trying to find the strength to accept the challenge Sadie had not so subtly issued to her and Baker.

He knelt in front of her, staring up at her, and now she had no doubt. The love in his beautiful topaz eyes mirrored hers. So much love.

"What are you doing?" she asked. "You should be down there with all your family. With your mother."

He shook his head. "It's not all my family," he said. "Not without you, Taye."

She sniffled back her tears. "But you said you're not the guy for me," she reminded him.

"You deserve someone better," he said. "But you make *me* better—stronger and happier than I've ever been. And if you'll give me a chance, I'll try to make you stronger and happier than you've ever been."

"What about better?" she asked with a slight smile.

He shook his head. "You can't get any better than you already are…"

And she knew that with him, she was fully accepted exactly as she was. She wanted to make sure that he knew she accepted him the same way. "I don't care if you have nightmares, or if you take on more guilt and responsibility than you should. You are perfect to me just as you are, too, Baker Haven."

Tears shimmered in his eyes now. "You might change your mind about that…" he hedged. His face flushed. "I should have asked you before I did it…"

"Did what?" she asked.

"Told Jake that I want the boys, that I want to be their primary guardian."

"And just when I thought I couldn't love you more," she murmured, her heart swelling to hold it all, to hold all that he was.

"I love you, too," he said. "So very much…" And he leaned forward to brush a soft kiss across her lips.

Her breath caught, and she wanted to kiss him back. She wanted to kiss him forever. But she had to know; she had to ask, "What did the boys say about you being their primary guardian?"

"Ian thinks that's what his dad wanted," Baker said, "because after the crash, he heard Dale telling me to take care of them. I thought Dale just meant to focus on them, on their injuries and not his own…"

Because it had been too late to save him or Jenny. But maybe that wasn't what he meant. "Maybe Ian didn't misunderstand. Maybe his dad did want you to take care of them always," she suggested. "Maybe Dale did choose you."

"Of all my brothers?" he scoffed, shaking his head.

And she realized he had the same insecurities she had, that he'd never thought he was quite good enough just the way he was. That he'd lived in the shadows of his big brothers.

She nodded. "Jake cut himself off from everyone after breaking up with Katie in college, and he isolated himself, living out in the foreman cottage. Dusty was devoted to the rodeo and Ben to the town of Willow Creek. Dale had to know that you are the one who would give the boys the most of your time and attention. That you are the one the boys need."

"Just the boys?"

"I need you, too," she admitted.

"And I need you, Taye," he said.

"So are you proposing?"

He nodded.

"For real?"

"For a real relationship," he said. "For forever. Will you marry me, Taye Cooper?"

"Yes," she said. "I will marry you, and I will help you raise our boys."

"Our boys," he whispered, and then he kissed her...sweetly...with all the love in his heart.

"Did she say yes?" someone whispered.

Taye pulled back from her fiancé to stare over his shoulder at the other people who'd slipped into her room unnoticed. Miller. Ian and Little Jake. And, of course, Caleb, because he wouldn't have wanted to be left out.

The little blond-haired boy sighed. "They're kissing. Everybody's always kissing around here."

"You better warn your new Cassidy cousins," Baker said. "Better warn them what happens around Ranch Haven..."

"Kissing?" Caleb asked with another grimace.

"People fall in love," Baker said.

"With a little help from Sadie Haven," Taye crooned.

"We didn't need any help," Baker said. "All we needed was each other. And these guys." He wrapped his arms around his nephews, pulling them all in with her for a group hug.

And Taye had never felt so happy...just as he'd promised her. And she had no more fears or doubts. She knew that she'd found the guy for her. Not just one but four.

And that this happy ending was going to last forever.

* * * * *

Get 4 FREE REWARDS!

We'll send you 2 FREE Books plus 2 FREE Mystery Gifts.

FREE
Value Over
$20

Both the **Love Inspired®** and **Love Inspired® Suspense** series feature compelling novels filled with inspirational romance, faith, forgiveness and hope.

YES! Please send me 2 FREE novels from the Love Inspired or Love Inspired Suspense series and my 2 FREE gifts (gifts are worth about $10 retail). After receiving them, if I don't wish to receive any more books, I can return the shipping statement marked "cancel." If I don't cancel, I will receive 6 brand-new Love Inspired Larger-Print books or Love Inspired Suspense Larger-Print books every month and be billed just $6.49 each in the U.S. or $6.74 each in Canada. That is a savings of at least 16% off the cover price. It's quite a bargain! Shipping and handling is just 50¢ per book in the U.S. and $1.25 per book in Canada.* I understand that accepting the 2 free books and gifts places me under no obligation to buy anything. I can always return a shipment and cancel at any time by calling the number below. The free books and gifts are mine to keep no matter what I decide.

Choose one: ☐ **Love Inspired**
Larger-Print
(122/322 IDN GRHK)

☐ **Love Inspired Suspense**
Larger-Print
(107/307 IDN GRHK)

Name (please print)

Address   Apt. #

City   State/Province   Zip/Postal Code

Email: Please check this box ☐ if you would like to receive newsletters and promotional emails from Harlequin Enterprises ULC and its affiliates. You can unsubscribe anytime.

Mail to the **Harlequin Reader Service:**
IN U.S.A.: P.O. Box 1341, Buffalo, NY 14240-8531
IN CANADA: P.O. Box 603, Fort Erie, Ontario L2A 5X3

Want to try 2 free books from another series? Call 1-800-873-8635 or visit www.ReaderService.com.

*Terms and prices subject to change without notice. Prices do not include sales taxes, which will be charged (if applicable) based on your state or country of residence. Canadian residents will be charged applicable taxes. Offer not valid in Quebec. This offer is limited to one order per household. Books received may not be as shown. Not valid for current subscribers to the Love Inspired or Love Inspired Suspense series. All orders subject to approval. Credit or debit balances in a customer's account(s) may be offset by any other outstanding balance owed by or to the customer. Please allow 4 to 6 weeks for delivery. Offer available while quantities last.

Your Privacy—Your information is being collected by Harlequin Enterprises ULC, operating as Harlequin Reader Service. For a complete summary of the information we collect, how we use this information and to whom it is disclosed, please visit our privacy notice located at corporate.harlequin.com/privacy-notice. From time to time we may also exchange your personal information with reputable third parties. If you wish to opt out of this sharing of your personal information, please visit readerservice.com/consumerschoice or call 1-800-873-8635. **Notice to California Residents**—Under California law, you have specific rights to control and access your data. For more information on these rights and how to exercise them, visit corporate.harlequin.com/california-privacy.

LIRLIS22R3

HOMETOWN HEARTS ♥

YES! Please send me **The Hometown Hearts Collection** in Larger Print. This collection begins with 3 FREE books and 2 FREE gifts in the first shipment. Along with my 3 free books, I'll also get the next 4 books from the Hometown Hearts Collection, in LARGER PRINT, which I may either return and owe nothing, or keep for the low price of $4.99 U.S./ $5.89 CDN each plus $2.99 for shipping and handling per shipment*. If I decide to continue, about once a month for 8 months I will get 6 or 7 more books, but will only need to pay for 4. That means 2 or 3 books in every shipment will be FREE! If I decide to keep the entire collection, I'll have paid for only 32 books because 19 books are FREE! I understand that accepting the 3 free books and gifts places me under no obligation to buy anything. I can always return a shipment and cancel at any time. My free books and gifts are mine to keep no matter what I decide.

262 HCN 3432 462 HCN 3432

Name _____ (PLEASE PRINT)

Address _____ Apt. #

City _____ State/Prov. _____ Zip/Postal Code

Signature (if under 18, a parent or guardian must sign)

Mail to the **Reader Service:**
IN U.S.A.: P.O. Box 1867, Buffalo, NY. 14240-1867
IN CANADA: P.O. Box 609, Fort Erie, Ontario L2A 5X3

"I didn't even know they were sore at us!" a seaman
aboard the destroyer Monaghan said in awed tones, as the
Japanese bombs rained on Pearl Harbor. A B-17 pilot, com-
ing in from California, thought it was all a big celebration.
The battleship Nevada's band kept on playing THE STAR-
SPANGLED BANNER, while Japanese strafers sprayed her
decks with machine-gun fire. The ship's gambler on the
New Orleans canceled all debts and threw away his dice.
The war was on!

Here is the whole story of what really happened that day
at Pearl Harbor, the story that has baffled and fascinated
millions of Americans—Walter Lord's

Day of Infamy

"Historical milestone."

—Washington Post

"Unforgettable . . . Recommended."

—Library Journal

THE BANTAM WAR BOOK SERIES

This series of books is about a world on fire.

The carefully chosen volumes in the Bantam War Book Series cover the full dramatic sweep of World War II. Many are eyewitness accounts by the men who fought in a global conflict as the world's future hung in the balance. Fighter pilots, tank commanders and infantry captains, among many others, recount exploits of individual courage. They present vivid portraits of brave men, true stories of gallantry, moving sagas of survival and stark tragedies of untimely death.

In 1933 Nazi Germany marched to become an empire that was to last a thousand years. In only twelve years that empire was destroyed, and ever since, the country has been bisected by her conquerors. Italy relinquished her colonial lands, as did Japan. These were the losers. The winners also lost the empires they had so painfully seized over the centuries. And one, Russia, lost over twenty million dead.

Those wartime 1940s were a simple, even a hopeful time. Hats came in only two colors, white and black, and after an initial battering the Allied nations started on a long laborious march toward victory. It was a time when sane men believed the world would evolve into a decent place, but, as with all futures, there was no one then who could really forecast the world that we know now.

There are many ways to think about war. It has always been hard to understand the motivations and braveries of Axis soldiers fighting to enslave and dominate their neighbors. Yet it is impossible to know the hammer without the anvil, and to comprehend ourselves we must know the people we once fought against.

Through these books we can discover what it was like to take part in the war that was a final experience for nearly fifty million human beings. In so doing we may discover the strength to make a world as good as the one contained in those dreams and aspirations once believed by heroic men. We must understand our past as an honor to those dead who can no longer choose. They exchanged their lives in a hope for this future that we now inhabit. Though the fight took place many years ago, each of us remains as a living part of it.

DAY OF INFAMY
BY WALTER LORD

Illustrated with
Photographs and Maps

BANTAM BOOKS

NEW YORK • TORONTO • LONDON • SYDNEY • AUCKLAND

*This edition contains the complete text
of the original hardcover edition.*
NOT ONE WORD HAS BEEN OMITTED.

DAY OF INFAMY

*A Bantam Falcon Book / published by arrangement with
Holt, Rinehart & Winston, Inc.*

PRINTING HISTORY

*Henry Holt edition published March 1957
Three installments appeared in* LIFE *Magazine December 1956
Book-of-the-Month Club edition published March 1957
Bantam edition / January 1958
Bantam reissue / December 1991*

To Janet Cady

CONTENTS

Foreword

It happened on December 7, 1941.

One part of America learned while listening to the broadcast of the Dodger-Giant football game at the Polo Grounds in New York. Ward Cuff had just returned a Brooklyn kick-off to this 27-yard line when at 2:26 P.M. WOR interrupted with the first flash: the Japanese had attacked Pearl Harbor.

Another part of America learned half an hour later, while tuning in the New York Philharmonic concert at Carnegie Hall. Artur Rodzinski's musicians were just about to start Shostakovich's Symphony Number 1 when CBS repeated an earlier bulletin announcing the attack.

The concertgoers themselves learned still later when announcer Warren Sweeney told them at the end of the performance. Then he called for "The Star-Spangled Banner." The anthem had already been played at the start of the concert, but the audience had merely hummed along. Now they sang the words.

Others learned in other ways, but no matter how they learned, it was a day they would never forget. Nearly every American alive at the time can describe how he first heard the news. He marked the moment carefully, carving out a sort of mental souvenir, for instinctively he knew how much his life would be changed by what was happening in Hawaii.

This is the story of that day.

CHAPTER I

"Isn't That a Beautiful Sight?"

MONICA CONTER, a young Army nurse, and Second Lieutenant Barney Benning of the Coast Artillery strolled out of the Pearl Harbor Officers' Club, down the path near the ironwood trees, and stood by the club landing, watching the launches take men back to the warships riding at anchor.

They were engaged, and the setting was perfect. The workshops, the big hammerhead crane, all the paraphernalia of the Navy's great Hawaiian base were hidden by the night; the daytime clatter was gone; only the pretty things were left—the moonlight . . . the dance music that drifted from the club . . . the lights of the Pacific Fleet that shimmered across the harbor.

And there were more lights than ever before. For the first week end since July 4 all the battleships were in port at once. Normally they took turns—six might be out with Admiral Pye's battleship task force, or three would be off with Admiral Halsey's carrier task force. This was Pye's turn in, but Halsey was out on a special assignment that meant leaving his battleships behind. A secret "war warning" had been received from Washington—Japan was expected to hit "the Philippines, Thai, or Kra Peninsula or possibly Borneo"—and the carrier *Enterprise* was ferrying a squadron of Marine fighters to reinforce Wake Island. Battleships would slow the task force's speed from 30 to 17 knots. Yet they were too vulnerable to maneuver alone without carrier protection. The only other carrier, the *Lexington,* was off ferrying planes to Midway, so the battleships stayed at Pearl Harbor, where it was safe.

With the big ships in port, the officers' club seemed even gayer and more crowded than usual, as Monica Conter and Lieutenant Benning walked back and rejoined the group at the table. Somebody suggested calling Lieutenant Bill Silvester, a friend of them all who this particular evening was dining eight miles away in downtown Honolulu. Monica called him, playfully scolded him for deserting his buddies—the kind of call that has been placed thousands of times by young people late in the evening, and memorable this time only because it was the last night Bill Silvester would be alive.

Then back to the dance, which was really a conglomeration of Dutch treats and small private parties given by various officers for their friends: "Captain Montgomery E. Higgins and Mrs. Higgins entertained at the Pearl Harbor Officers' Club . . . Lieutenant Commander and Mrs. Harold Pullen gave a dinner at the Pearl Harbor Officers' Club . . ."—the Honolulu Sunday *Advertiser* rattled them off in its society column the following morning.

Gay but hardly giddy. The bar always closed at midnight. The band seemed in a bit of a rut—its favorite "Sweet Leilani" was now over four years old. The place itself was the standard blend of chrome, plywood, and synthetic leather, typical of all officers' clubs everywhere. But it was cheap—dinner for a dollar—and it was friendly. In the Navy everybody still seemed to know everybody else on December 6, 1941.

Twelve miles away, Brigadier General Durward S. Wilson, commanding the 24th Infantry Division, was enjoying the same kind of evening at the Schofield Barracks Officers' Club. Here, too, the weekly Saturday night dance seemed even gayer than usual—partly because many of the troops in the 24th and 25th Divisions had just come off a long, tough week in the field; partly because it was the night of Ann Etzler's Cabaret, a benefit show worked up annually by "one of the very talented young ladies on the post," as General Wilson gallantly puts it. The show featured amateur singing and dancing—a little corny perhaps, but it was all in the

name of charity and enjoyed the support of everybody
who counted, including Lieut. General Walter C. Short,
commanding general of the Hawaiian Department.

Actually, General Short was late. He had been trapped
by a phone call, just as he and his intelligence officer,
Lieutenant Colonel Kendall Fielder, were leaving for
the party from their quarters at Fort Shafter, the Army's
administrative headquarters just outside Honolulu. Lieutenant Colonel George Bicknell, Short's counterintel-
ligence officer, was on the wire. He asked them to wait;
he had something interesting to show them. The general
said all right, but hurry.

At 6:30 Bicknell puffed up. Then, while Mrs. Short
and Mrs. Fielder fretted and fumed in the car, the three
men sat down together on the commanding general's
lanai. Colonel Bicknell produced the transcript of a
phone conversation monitored the day before by the
local FBI. It was a call placed by someone on the Tokyo
newspaper *Yomiuri Shinbun* to Dr. Motokazu Mori, a
local Japanese dentist and husband of the paper's Honolulu correspondent.

Tokyo asked about conditions in general: about planes,
searchlights, the weather, the number of sailors around
. . . and about flowers. "Presently," offered Dr. Mori, "the
flowers in bloom are fewest out of the whole year. However, the hibiscus and the poinsettia are in bloom now."

The three officers hashed it over. Why would anyone
spend the cost of a transpacific phone call discussing
flowers? But if this was code, why talk in the clear about
things like planes and searchlights? And would a spy use
the telephone? On the other hand, what else could be
going on? Was there any connection with the cable recently received from Washington warning "hostile action
possible at any moment"?

Fifteen minutes . . . half an hour . . . nearly an hour
skipped by, and they couldn't make up their minds.
Finally General Short gently suggested that Colonel
Bicknell was "too intelligence-conscious"; in any case
they couldn't do anything about it tonight; they would
think it over some more and talk about it in the morning.

It was almost 7:30 when the general and Colonel Fielder rejoined their now-seething wives and drove the fifteen miles to Schofield. As they entered the dance floor, they scarcely noticed the big lava-rock columns banked with ferns for a gala evening—they were still brooding over the Mori call.

General Short had a couple of cocktails—he never drank after dinner—and worried his way through the next two hours. Perhaps it was the Mori call. Perhaps it was his troubles with training and equipment (there was never enough of anything). Perhaps it was his fear of sabotage. To General Short, Washington's warning had posed one overwhelming danger—an uprising by Hawaii's 157,905 civilians of Japanese blood, which would coincide with any Tokyo move in the Far East. He immediately alerted his command against sabotage; lined up all his planes neatly on the ramps, where they could be more easily guarded; and notified the War Department. Washington seemed satisfied, but the fear of a Japanese Fifth Column lingered—that was the way the Axis always struck.

By 9:30 he had had enough. The Shorts and the Fielders left the officers' club, started back to Shafter. As they rolled along the road that sloped down toward town again, Pearl Harbor spread out below them in the distance. The Pacific Fleet blazed with lights, and searchlight beams occasionally probed the sky. It was a moment for forgetting the cares of the day and enjoying the breathless night. "Isn't that a beautiful sight?" sighed General Short, adding thoughtfully, "and what a target they would make."

General Short's opposite number, Admiral Husband E. Kimmel, Commander in Chief of the Pacific Fleet—known as CINCPAC in the Navy's jargon of endless initials—had an even less eventful evening back in Honolulu. He was dining quietly at the Halekulani Hotel, a Waikiki landmark that maintained a precarious balance between charm and stuffiness. Several of the Navy's top brass lived there with their wives, and tonight Admiral and Mrs. Fairfax Leary were giving a small dinner, attended by the commander in chief. It was anything but a wild party—so slow, in fact, that at least two of the wives retreated to a bedroom upstairs for some refreshment with a little more authority.

But Admiral Kimmel was no party admiral anyhow. Hard, sharp, and utterly frank, he worked himself to the bone. When he relaxed, it was usually a brisk walk with a few brother officers, not cocktails and social banter. Proudly self-contained, he looked and acted uncomfortable in easygoing surroundings—he even disapproved of the Navy's new khakis as "lessening the dignity and military point of view of the wearer."

He was a difficult man to know, and his position made him more so. He had been jumped over 32 admirals to his present job. Relations were utterly correct, but inevitably there was a mild awkwardness—a lack of informal give-and-take—between himself and some of the men who had always been his seniors. Finally, there was his responsibility as CINCPAC—enough to kill the social inclinations in any man: refitting the fleet with the new weapons that were emerging, training the swarm of new recruits that were arriving, planning operations against Japan if hostilities should explode.

Admiral Kimmel had spent the early afternoon discussing the situation with his staff. The Japanese were now burning their codes . . . their fleet had changed call letters twice in a month . . . their carriers had disappeared. On the other hand, the Japanese would naturally take precautions at a time like this; and the lost carriers might not mean anything—Navy intelligence had already lost them 12 times the past six months. Whatever happened, it would be in southeast Asia—Washington, the official estimates, the local press, everybody said so. As for Hawaii, nobody gave it much thought. To free Kimmel's hands, defense of the base was left to the Army and to the Fourteenth Naval District, technically under Kimmel but run by Admiral Claude C. Bloch pretty much as his own show. Local defense seemed fairly academic anyhow. Only a week before, when Admiral Kimmel asked his operations officer, Captain Charles

McMorris, what the chances were of a surprise attack on Honolulu, the captain firmly replied, "None."

The staff meeting broke up about three o'clock. Admiral Kimmel retired to his quarters for the afternoon, went on to the Learys' party around 5:45. While they dined under the big hau tree on the Halekulani terrace, the admiral's driver waited in the car outside, slapping away at mosquitoes. At one point, Richard Kimball, the hotel manager, passed by and said he was sorry about the bugs. The driver replied he didn't mind the mosquitoes—it was the boredom that got him. If only the car had a radio. But it turned out he didn't need one tonight. The admiral left at 9:30, drove straight home, and was in bed by ten. It had been a long, tiring week, and tomorrow morning he had an early golf date with General Short.

Most of the officers stayed up later, but their evenings were hardly more spectacular. Rear Admiral Robert A. Theobald, commanding Destroyer Flotilla One, danced at the staid Pacific Club until midnight. Lieutenant Commander S. S. Isquith, engineering officer of the target ship *Utah*, played cards at the Hawaiian Bridge Center. Young Ensign Victor Delano—reared in the Navy and just out of Annapolis himself—spent a properly respectful evening at the home of Vice Admiral Walter Anderson, commander of Battleship Division Four.

The enlisted men were less circumscribed. Radioman Fred Glaeser from Pearl Harbor . . . Sergeant George Geiger from the Army's bomber base at Hickam Field . . . two thirds of Company M, 19th Infantry, from Schofield Barracks . . . thousands of others from posts scattered throughout the island of Oahu converged on Honolulu in a fleet of buses, jalopies, and ancient taxis.

Most were dropped at the YMCA, a convenient starting point. Then, after perhaps a quick one at the Black Cat Café across the street, they fanned out on the town. Some, like Chief M. G. Montessoro, patrolled the taverns of Waikiki Beach. Others watched "Tantalizing Tootsies," the variety show at the Princess. Most swarmed down Hotel Street—a hodgepodge of tattoo joints, shooting galleries, pinball machines, barber shops, massage parlors, photo booths, trinket counters—everything an enterprising citizenry could devise for a serviceman's leisure.

Juke boxes blared from Bill Leader's bar, the Two Jacks, the Mint, the New Emma Café. Thin shafts of light escaped around the drawn shades of hotels named Rex . . . Ritz . . . the Anchor. Occasional brawls erupted as the men overflowed the narrow sidewalks.

The Shore Patrol broke up a fight between two sailors from the cruiser *Honolulu;* caught a seaman from the *California* using somebody else's liberty card; arrested a man from the Kaneohe Naval Air Station for "malicious conversation." But the night was surprisingly calm—only five serious offenses as against 43 for the whole month so far.

The MPs had a quiet time too. They found perhaps 25 soldiers passed out—out of 42,952 in the islands—and these were sent to the Fort Shafter guardhouse to sober up. Otherwise, nothing special.

A surprisingly large number stuck to their ships, bases, and military posts. As the Army and Navy swelled with reservists, an ever-growing number of men seemed to prefer the simpler pleasures. At the Hickam post theater Private Ed Arison watched Clark Gable outwit oriental chicanery in *Honky Tonk.* In the big new barracks nearby, Staff Sergeant Charles W. Maybeck played Benny Goodmans and Bob Crosbys on his new phonograph. Up at Schofield, Private Aloysius Manuszewski had some beer at the PX, spent most of the evening writing home to Buffalo.

At Pearl Harbor, Boatswain's Mate Robert E. Jones joined the crowd at the Navy's new Bloch Recreation Center. It was a place designed to give the enlisted man every kind of relaxation the Navy felt proper—music, boxing, bowling, billiards, 3.2 beer. Tonight's attraction was "The Battle of Music," the finals of a contest to decide the best band in the fleet. As the men stamped and cheered, bands from the *Pennsylvania, Tennessee, Argonne,* and *Detroit* battled it out. The *Pennsylvania* band won; everybody sang "God Bless America"; and

the evening wound up with dancing. When the crowd
filed out at midnight, many still argued that the battleship *Arizona's* band—which had already been eliminated
—was really the best of all.

Slowly the men drifted back to their ships; the Hotel
Street bars closed down; the dances broke up—Honolulu's
strict blue laws took care of that. Here and there a few
couples lingered. Second Lieutenant Fred Gregg of
Schofield proposed to Evolin Dwyer and was accepted;
Ensign William Hasler of the *West Virginia* was not so
lucky, but he happily learned later that a woman can
change her mind. Lieutenant Benning drove Monica
Conter back to Hickam, where she was stationed. There
they laid plans for the following day—lunch, swimming,
a movie, some barbecued spareribs. Another engaged
couple, Ensign Everett Malcolm and Marian Shaffer,
drove to the Shaffer home high in the hills behind
Honolulu. He arranged to meet her for golf at one.

About 2:00 A.M. Ensign Malcolm started back for Pearl
Harbor but discovered he would never make the last
launch to his ship, the *Arizona.* So he headed instead for
the home of Captain D. C. Emerson. The old captain had
been senior dentist on the *Arizona,* and his congenial
bachelor establishment was a sort of shoreside bunkroom
for the ship's junior officers.

On arriving, Ensign Malcolm was quickly hailed in by
the captain, who sat on the floor with three other officers,
arguing about (of all things) Woodrow Wilson's Fourteen Points. Mildly bewildered, Malcolm joined in and
they were all still at it when the clock touched three.

Only the people who had to be up were now abroad.
Radioman Fred Glaeser couldn't find a bed at the Y,
resigned himself to a cramped night in his car. Lieutenant Kermit Tyler, a young pilot at Wheeler Field, was
up too—but he was already starting for work. He had
drawn the 4:00-8:00 A.M. shift in the Army's new inter-
ceptor center at Fort Shafter. Now as he rolled along
the road to town, he flicked on his car radio and listened
to KGMB playing Hawaiian records.

About 320 miles to the north, on the Japanese aircraft carrier *Akagi*, Commander Kanjiro Ono listened intently to the same program. He was a staff communications officer for Vice Admiral Chuichi Nagumo, commanding a huge Japanese task force of six carriers, two battleships, three cruisers, and nine destroyers that raced southward through the night. Admiral Nagumo was about to launch an all-out assault on the U. S. fleet at Pearl Harbor, and everything depended on surprise. He felt that if the Americans had even an inkling, the radio would somehow show it.

But there was nothing—nothing whatsoever, except the soft melodies of the islands. Admiral Nagumo settled back, relieved. There seemed a good chance that a great deal of hard work would not be wasted.

CHAPTER II

"A Dream Come True!"

TEN MONTHS HAD NOW PASSED since Admiral Isoroku Yamamoto, Commander of the Japanese Combined Fleet, remarked almost casually to Rear Admiral Takajiro Onishi, Chief of Staff of the Eleventh Air Fleet, "If we are to have war with America, we will have no hope of winning unless the U. S. fleet in Hawaiian waters can be destroyed."

Then he ordered Admiral Onishi to start studying the possibility of launching a surprise attack on Pearl Harbor. Onishi called in Commander Minoru Genda, a crack young airman, and ten days later Genda came up with his appraisal: risky but not impossible.

Yamamoto needed no further encouragement. A few trusted subordinates went quietly to work, and by May Rear Admiral Shigeru Fukudome of the Naval General Staff was able to toss a fat notebook at Rear Admiral Ryunosuke Kusaka.

"Go ahead, read it," invited Fukudome. Kusaka plunged into a mass of statistics on Pearl Harbor, but missed any operational plans. "That," said Fukudome, "is what I want you to do."

The job seemed overwhelming. The U. S. strength looked enormous. Hawaii was thousands of miles from Japan. There were airfields scattered all around Oahu—Hickam, Wheeler, Ewa, Kaneohe, probably others. Pearl Harbor itself was narrow and shallow, making it extremely difficult to get at the ships. On top of everything else, Vice Admiral Nagumo, commander of the First Air Fleet, and slated to lead any attack, was drag-

ging his feet. As his chief of staff, no wonder Kusaka
was discouraged.

"Don't keep saying, 'It's too much of a gamble,' just
because I happen to be fond of playing bridge and
shogi," Admiral Yamamoto cheerfully admonished. "Mr.
Kusaka, I am fully aware of your arguments. But Pearl
Harbor is my idea and I need your support." He added
that it would certainly help if Kusaka could win over
Admiral Nagumo.

Kusaka worked on, and somehow the project began to
make sense. Commander Genda did wonders with the
torpedo problem. All summer he experimented on the
Inland Sea, setting up short shallow torpedo runs. By
August he was trying out shallow-draft torpedoes at
Saeki. As for the short length of run—well, there was
Southeast Loch, a narrow arm of water that led like a
bowling alley straight to the battleship moorings in the
center of Pearl Harbor.

Everything was done in the darkest secrecy. One afternoon late in August, Lieutenant (j.g.) Toshio Hashimoto,
a young naval pilot, took some papers to his wing commander's office and found a group of high-ranking
officers poring over charts and maps of Pearl Harbor.
They were stamped *"Top Secret,"* and Lieutenant Hashimoto was appalled at his intrusion. Nobody rebuked him,
but he went away petrified by the mere knowledge of
such an enormous secret.

By the end of August, Admiral Yamamoto was ready to
unveil the scheme to a select few. Admiral Osami Nagano, Chief of the Naval General Staff, and 13 other key
officers were called to Tokyo and given the word. Then,
from September 2 to 13, they all tested the idea on the
game board at the Naval War College.

The attacking team "lost" two carriers; Admiral Nagano began complaining that December was too stormy;
Admiral Nagumo, commander of the all-important First
Air Fleet, still had cold feet. Other officers argued that
Japan could take southeast Asia without U. S. inter-
ference; that if America came in, the place to catch the
fleet was nearer Japanese waters.

But Yamamoto stuck to his guns—if war came, America was bound to be in it . . . her fleet was Japan's biggest obstacle . . . the best time to crush it was right away. By the time it recovered, Japan would have everything she needed and could sit back and hold out forever.

This logic won the day, and on September 13 the Naval Command issued the rough draft of a plan that combined Pearl Harbor, Malaya, the Philippines, and the Dutch East Indies in one huge assault.

Next, the training stage. One by one, men were tapped for the key jobs. Brilliant young Commander Mitsuo Fuchida was mildly surprised to be transferred suddenly to the carrier *Akagi*, having just left her the year before. He was far more amazed to be named commander of all air groups of the First Air Fleet. Commander Genda sidled up with the explanation: "Now don't be alarmed, Fuchida, but we want you to lead our air force in the event that we attack Pearl Harbor."

Lieutenant Yoshio Shiga and about a hundred other pilots got the word on October 5 from Admiral Yamamoto himself. He swore them to secrecy, told them the plan, urged them to their greatest effort.

The men practiced harder than ever—mostly the low, short torpedo runs that had to be mastered. The torpedoes themselves continued to misbehave in shallow water, diving to the bottom and sticking in the mud. Commander Fuchida wondered whether they would ever work. But Genda only grew more excited—once perfected, they would be the supreme weapon. And by early November he had succeeded. Simple wooden stabilizers were fitted on the fins, which would keep the torpedoes from hitting even the shallow 45-foot bottom of Pearl Harbor.

Meanwhile, other pilots practiced bombing techniques, for nobody except Genda was completely sold on torpedoes. Besides, the meticulous intelligence now pouring in from Consul General Nagao Kita in Honolulu showed that the battleships were often moored in pairs; torpedoes couldn't possibly reach the inboard ship. To penetrate tough armor-plated decks, ordnance men fitted fins on 15-inch and 16-inch armor-piercing shells. These converted missiles would go through anything.

While the pilots practiced and the inventors worked their miracles, Admiral Kusaka battled the red tape that snarls anybody's navy. Some time during October he flew to Tokyo to argue headquarters into giving him eight tankers for the task force that was now taking shape. It meant the difference between using four or six carriers, and at a time like this it seemed incredible that there should be any question about it. But headquarters hemmed and hawed, and it took several weeks to wangle the extra ships.

Thirty-three-year-old Suguru Suzuki, youngest lieutenant commander in the service, had a more stimulating job. Around the end of October he boarded the Japanese liner *Taiyo Maru* for an interesting journey to Honolulu. Instead of following her usual course, the ship sailed far to the north, crossed over between Midway and the Aleutians, and then cut south to Hawaii—exactly the course the task force planned to follow to avoid detection.

Lieutenant Commander Suzuki whiled away the trip taking reams of notes. He checked the winds, the atmospheric pressure, the roll of the vessel. Could a scouting seaplane be launched in these seas? It could. Would any special refueling problems arise? They would. He observed that during the entire voyage the *Taiyo Maru* didn't sight a single ship.

In Honolulu, Lieutenant Commander Suzuki spent a busy week. From occasional visitors to his ship he learned that the fleet wasn't now assembling at Lahaina Anchorage as it used to. He confirmed that the week end was a universally observed American institution. He picked up some choice titbits—structural data on the Hickam Field hangars, interesting aerial shots of Pearl Harbor taken October 21. These were made from a private plane that took up sight-seers at nearby John Rogers Airport. Anybody could do it.

Then back to Tokyo again, guardedly comparing notes with Lieutenant Commander Toshihide Maejima, who was also on board. Commander Maejima seems to have had much the same interests, but directed rather more toward submarines.

By now things were moving fast in Tokyo. November 3, Admiral Nagano's final blessing . . . November 5, Combined Fleet Top Secret Order Number 1, spelling out the plan . . . November 7, Admiral Nagumo officially named commander of the Pearl Harbor Striking Force. The same day Yamamoto tentatively set the date—December 8, or Sunday, December 7, Hawaii time. Good for a number of reasons: favorable moonlight . . . perfect coordination with the Malay strike . . . the best chance to catch the ships in port and the men off duty.

A few more people were let in on the secret. Admiral Kusaka confided in Commander Shin-Ichi Shimizu, a middle-aged supply officer. The problem: how to draw winter gear without attracting attention, when everybody else was getting ready for the tropics. Commander Shimizu's solution: requisition both summer and winter gear. He glibly told the startled depot that if war came, you never knew where you might go. Then he piled everything on the freighter *Hoko Maru* and chugged off to sea about November 15. Once out of sight, he swung north and made for Tankan Bay in the bleak, cold Kuriles—the secret rendezvous point for the Pearl Harbor Striking Force.

Admiral Nagumo himself was not far behind. His flagship, the carrier *Akagi*, left Saeki in the late evening of the 17th. His chief of staff, Admiral Kusaka, tingled with optimism. Only the day before, he had received a letter from his old housekeeper, telling of a pleasant dream— the Japanese submarine fleet had achieved a splendid surprise victory at Pearl Harbor. A strange dream for a housekeeper, but Admiral Kusaka thought it was a good omen.

On November 19 Lieutenant Commander Suzuki arrived back from his junket to Honolulu and took a fast launch to the battleship *Hiei*, anchored off Yokohama. Suzuki climbed aboard with his bulging brief case, and the *Hiei*, too, steamed off for Tankan.

One by one they slipped away. Always separately, never any apparent connection. Once out of sight, the sea simply swallowed them up. At the great Kure naval base a lively radio traffic crackled from the rest of the ships, designed to give the impression that the fleet was still at home. The regular carrier operators stayed behind to give these signals their usual "swing." (A wireless operator's touch is as distinctive as his handwriting.) The camouflage was so good it even fooled Admiral Kusaka, who bawled out his communications man for breaking radio silence, only to find the "message" was a fake concocted back home.

One by one they glided into Tankan Bay—the lumbering carriers *Akagi* and *Kaga;* the huge new flattop *Zuikaku;* the light carriers *Hiryu* and *Soryu;* the old battleships *Hiei* and *Kirishima;* the crack new cruisers *Tone* and *Chikuma;* nine destroyers led the light cruiser *Abukuma;* three screening submarines; the eight tankers finally wangled from headquarters. Last to arrive in the twilight of November 21 was the great carrier *Shokaku,* which had put on such an effective masquerade of turbine trouble that she was almost late.

Now they were all there—32 ships incongruously packed in a desolate harbor. Snow crowned the mountains that ringed the cold, gray bay. Three lonely radio masts stood against the sky. Three small fishermen's huts and one bare concrete pier were the only other traces of civilization. Even so, Nagumo took no chances—no shore leaves, no rubbish overboard. When Seaman Shigeki Yokota got the *Kaga's* garbage detail, he had to burn it right beside the pier.

Commander Shimizu and the other supply ship skippers gradually transferred food, clothes, and thousands of drums of fuel oil to the task force. Five-gallon tins of oil were crammed into every empty space. When all was loaded, Shimizu told his crew to stay put until December 10: "Go fishing. Do anything you want, but you can't leave the area." Then he transferred to the *Akagi*—he couldn't resist going along for the ride.

Admiral Nagumo held a last conference on the *Akagi*

on the night of the 23rd. Lieutenant Commander Suzuki
told about his interesting trip to Honolulu. Commander
Fuchida, who would lead the air strike, scribbled away
at his notes. The meeting ended with a toast of *sake* and
three *banzais* for the emperor.

On the 25th Yamamoto ordered the fleet to get going
the following day, and inevitably Admiral Nagumo spent
a restless last night. At 2:00 A.M. he finally called in
Lieutenant Commander Suzuki, apologized for waking
him, and said he just had to check one point again:
"You're absolutely certain about not spotting the U. S.
Pacific Fleet in Lahaina?"

"Yes, Admiral."

"Nor is there any possibility that it might assemble at
Lahaina?"

Suzuki reassured him and went back to bed, deeply
moved by the sight of the old admiral, all alone with his
worries, pacing away the night in his kimono.

At dawn Suzuki left the *Akagi* and stood on the shore
waving good-by as the anchor chains rattled upward and
the ships got under way. On the bridge of the *Akagi*
Admiral Kusaka tugged at his coat collar to escape the
bitter wind that swept the cheerless morning.

An unexpected hitch arose when a piece of cable
snarled in the *Akagi's* propeller, but a diver got it free
in half an hour, and by 8:00 A.M. the whole task force
was clear of the harbor. As the *Akagi* glided by, a patrol
boat's blinkers flashed through the gloom, "Good luck
on your mission."

Commander Gishiro Miura, the *Akagi's* navigation
officer, certainly needed it. He had no easy job in
weather like this—pounding seas, steady gales, the thick-
est kind of fog. Miura was famous throughout the fleet
for his sloppy, easy-going amiability; but it was all gone
now. He stood stern and tense on the bridge. He wore a
pair of shoes instead of his usual carpet slippers.

Most of the time the ships managed to keep in formation: the carriers in two parallel columns of three . . .
the eight tankers trailing behind . . . the battleships and
cruisers guarding the flanks . . . the destroyers screening

the whole force . . . the subs scouting far ahead. But at
night the tankers, not used to this sort of work, would
stray far and wide. Every morning the destroyers herded
them back to the fleet.

The second day out, Admiral Nagumo and Kusaka
clung to the plunging bridge of the *Akagi*, trying as
usual to round up the tankers. Suddenly Nagumo blurted,
"Mr. Chief of Staff, what do you think? I feel that I've
undertaken a heavy responsibility. If I had only been
more firm and refused. Now we've left home waters and
I'm beginning to wonder if the operation will work."

Admiral Kusaka came up with the right answer: "Sir,
there's no need to worry. We'll make out all right."

Nagumo smiled. "I envy you, Mr. Kusaka. You're such
an optimist."

Admiral Nagumo must have felt even more discouraged when they first tried refueling on the 28th. This
turned out to be dangerous, back-breaking work. As the
ships bucked and plunged, the big hoses running from
the tankers would snap loose and whiplash across the
deck. Several crewmen were swept overboard, but
nothing could be done about it.

By the 30th they were getting better at refueling, but
now they had another problem. As the weather grew
worse, oil drums stored on the deck of the light carrier
Hiryu spilled, turning her into a skating rink. Commander Takahisa Amagai, the flight deck officer, wrapped
straw rope around his boots to keep from falling, but
barked his shins anyhow.

On they plowed, through nerve-wracked days and
sleepless nights. Admiral Kusaka cat-napped in a canvas
chair on the *Akagi's* bridge. Her chief engineer, Commander Yoshibumi Tanbo, did the same far below. He
and his 350 men rarely left the engine room, lived in a
life of oil and sweat beside their beloved machines. Mess
attendants carried down all their meals—usually rice balls
with pickled plums and radishes, wrapped in bamboo
bark.

Everyone grew more and more restless. From the
bridge of the *Akagi* Admiral Kusaka watched the pilots

endlessly check their planes, warm up the engines, run through daily calisthenics. On the *Shokaku*, Commander Hoichiro Tsukamoto never knew that time could pass so slowly—his mind was always wandering to his watch or clock. Captain Tadataka Endo, the ship's doctor, whiled away the hours playing *shogi* and *go*. On the *Hiryu*, everyone speculated about the gauze mask that Group Leader Lieutenant Haita Matsumura wore over his mouth. He mumbled something about the unhealthy climate, and they marked him off as a hopeless hypochondriac.

But they speculated most of all on where they were going. Fighter pilot Yoshio Shiga on the *Kaga* was sure it would be in the north—all the planes had been changed to winter oil. Lieutenant (j.g.) Sukao Ebina, the *Shokaku's* junior medical officer, guessed Dutch Harbor. Commander Tanbo down in the *Akagi's* engine room enjoyed a special advantage: he knew how far she could go on the fuel she carried. It all added up to the Philippines.

Hardly anybody yet knew the truth. Last-ditch negotiations were being conducted by Japanese envoys in Washington, trying to win for Japan a free hand in Asia. If these talks unexpectedly succeeded, orders would be sent to Nagumo to turn around and come home. And if this were done, the world must never know what almost happened. So at this point Nagumo couldn't risk telling anybody.

But it was far more likely that the attack would come off; so the main job was to keep the fleet from being discovered. No waste could be thrown overboard—it might leave a tell-tale track. The ships used the highest grade fuel to keep smoke at a minimum. The empty oil drums were carefully stowed away. Complete blackout and strict radio silence. On the *Hiei*, Commander Kazuyoshi Kochi, chief communications officer for the whole task force, disconnected an essential part of his transmitter, put it in a wooden box, and used it as a pillow whenever he managed to get in some sleep.

They had several bad scares. Once Tokyo radioed that

an unknown submarine had been detected. The fleet hastily changed course, only to discover that it was all a mistake. Another night Admiral Kusaka suddenly spotted a light in the sky, thought it might be an unknown aircraft. It turned out to be a spark from the *Kaga's* funnel. She got a stiff warning to be more careful.

One morning the report spread that a Soviet ship was cruising nearby, en route from San Francisco to Russia. Every ship went on alert, but nothing came of it. Nor was there any way of checking such reports—Nagumo would not allow any planes in the air for fear of disclosing the fleet's presence.

Arguments rambled over what to do if they were spotted by a neutral ship. At least one member of Nagumo's staff cheerfully advised, "Sink it and forget it."

On December 2 this sort of bull session ended abruptly. The day before, the imperial council had decided on war, and now Admiral Yamamoto radioed the task force: "Climb Mount Niitaka." It was code for "Proceed with the attack."

Another message later that day confirmed the date: "X-Day will be 8 December"—which was, of course, Sunday, December 7, in Hawaii.

At last the men were mustered and told. On the *Kaga*, Seaman Shigeki Yokota, a 23-year-old farm boy, was frightened but philosophical. Down in the heat and noise of the *Akagi's* engine room Commander Tanbo's men drank a quiet toast of *sake* . . . somehow no one felt like more than one cup. But most of the crew howled *banzais* and shared Seaman Iki Kuramoti's ecstasy: "An air attack on Hawaii! A dream come true!"

Next morning everyone seemed to take a new lease on life. The pilots were briefed on their specific assignments —the Army airfields at Hickam and Wheeler . . . Schofield Barracks . . . the naval air stations at Kaneohe and Ford Island . . . the Marine base at Ewa . . . the U. S. fleet. On the *Akagi*, Admiral Kusaka produced a beautiful plaster-of-Paris relief map of Pearl Harbor. Previously, he had kept it under lock and key in his stateroom, accessible only to a few top officers; now he had it in-

stalled on the hangar deck, where everybody could use
it. On the *Kaga* the pilots played identification games.
An air officer would hide silhouettes of the American
ships behind his back. Then he would flash them one at
a time for the fliers to name. Lieutenant Yoshio Shiga
just never could get the *Utah*.

The fliers were now pampered by everybody—daily
baths, special rations of fresh milk and eggs. Despite all
the Shinto cult could do, these were promptly converted
into American milkshakes.

On the flagship, Admiral Nagumo worried more than
ever about being discovered. He was indeed in a ticklish
spot. If sighted by the enemy at any time before December 6, he was to turn around and go home. If sighted
on the 6th, he was to use his own judgment. Only on
the 7th was he committed, no matter what happened.

In the radio room of the *Hiei*, Commander Kochi
listened intently to detect any sign that the Americans
were onto the game. The intercepts were very reassuring.

Soon a flow of messages began to arrive from home,
so important that Kochi let his staff do the monitoring,
and devoted his own attention entirely to Tokyo. Yamamoto was relaying the latest Honolulu intelligence on the
U. S. fleet. On December 3 he radioed:

"November 28—0800 (Local Time) Pearl Harbor:
2 Battleships (*Oklahoma, Nevada*); 1 Aircraft carrier
(*Enterprise*); 2 Class-A Cruisers; 12 Destroyers Depart. 5 Battleships; 3 Class-A Cruisers; 3 Class-B
Cruisers; 12 Destroyers; 1 Seaplane Carrier Enter . . ."

The following day Nagumo refueled and crossed the
international date line. This made no difference to the
Japanese, who always kept their watches on Tokyo time,
but to an American it explains why it is December 3
again.

By evening the fleet was 900 miles north of Midway
. . . 1300 miles northwest of Oahu. Admiral Nagumo
began veering southeast. On the *Hiei*, Commander Kochi

caught another useful message relayed by Tokyo from Honolulu:

"November 29 P.M. (Local Time) Vessels Anchored in Pearl Harbor: A-Zone (Between Navy Arsenal and Ford Island) KT (NW dock Navy Arsenal) Battleships, *Pennsylvania, Arizona;* FV (Mooring buoy) Battleships, *California, Tennessee, Maryland, West Virginia.* KS (Navy Arsenal Repair Dock) Class-A Cruiser *Portland . . ."*

More refueling on the 4th, and another morsel from Honolulu: "Unable to ascertain whether air alert has been issued. There are no indications of sea alert . . ."

On the 5th, part of the fleet refueled most of the day and night. Admiral Kusaka then ordered three of the tankers to withdraw and wait for him to return. It was one of those sentimental moments the Japanese love so well, and the crew kept waving their caps as the tankers slowly disappeared. Down below Commander Shimizu— the supply officer who was just along for the ride—wistfully listened to a Japanese program, Mrs. Hanako Muraoka's "Children's Hours." It was now so faint that he finally gave up and twirled the dial until he caught some American music. It came in bright and lively.

At dawn on the 6th Kusaka refueled the rest of the task force, then once again the ships that had been refueled the day before. His idea was to have the tanks as full as possible for the day of the attack. By late morning the job was done, and the five remaining tankers also withdrew. More fond farewells.

Meanwhile Yamamoto had radioed a final, stirring call to arms: "The moment has arrived. The rise or fall of our empire is at stake . . ."

Everyone who could be spared assembled on deck, and on each ship the message was read to all hands. Speeches followed, and cheers split the air. Then up the *Akagi's* mast ran the same "Z" flag flown by Admiral Heihachiro Togo at his great victory over the Russians in 1905. Down in the *Akagi's* engine room Chief Engineer Tanbo

couldn't see it happen, but as he listened over the voice
tube, his heart pounded and tears came to his eyes. He
still regards it as his most dramatic single moment during
the entire war.

It was hardly the moment for an earache. But as Group
Leader Lieutenant Rokuro Kijuchi resumed briefing a
group of pilots on the flight deck of the *Hiryu*, he felt a
throbbing pain. He went to the ship's doctor and got the
bad news—he couldn't go; he had mastoids.

The fleet was now some 640 miles due north of Oahu.
With the slow tankers gone, it could make its final thrust
southward. Shortly before noon Admiral Kusaka turned
his ships and gave the order: "Twenty-four knots, full
speed ahead!"

By 3:00 P.M. they had closed the gap to 500 miles. And
in the radio room of the *Hiei*, Commander Kochi had a
new message from Honolulu: as of 6:00 P.M., December
5, Pearl Harbor contained "8 battleships; 3 Class-B
Cruisers; 16 Destroyers. Entering Harbor, 4 Class-B
Cruisers (*Honolulu* Type); 5 Destroyers."

At 4:55 P.M. the submarine *I-72*, already on the scene,
sent some up-to-the-minute information: "American fleet
is not in Lahaina waters."

So they were either still at Pearl or had just left for
sea. Nagumo's staff hashed it over. Lieutenant Commander Ono, the admiral's intelligence officer, pointed
out that five of the battleships had been in port eight
days; he was afraid they would be gone now. But Chief
of Staff Kusaka, who was a bug on statistics, didn't think
they would leave on a week end.

Commander Genda, the enterprising torpedo specialist,
bemoaned the absence of carriers, but Ono comforted
him that a couple of them might return at the last
minute. Genda cheered up: "If that happened, I don't
care if all eight battleships are away."

Late that evening another reassuring message from
Honolulu: "No barrage balloons sighted. Battleships are
without crinolines. No indications of an air or sea alert
wired to nearby islands ..."

The deceptive measures obviously were working. And

Tokyo must have felt quite self-satisfied, for everything possible had been done. The authorities had even brought busloads of sailors from the Yokosuka Naval Barracks and paraded them conspicuously all over town on sight-seeing tours.

At 1:20 A.M. a last message was relayed by Tokyo from Honolulu:

> "December 6 (Local Time) Vessels moored in Harbor: 9 Battleships; 3 Class-B Cruisers; 3 Seaplane Tenders; 17 Destroyers. Entering Harbor are 4 Class-B Cruisers; 3 Destroyers. All Aircraft Carriers and Heavy Cruisers have departed Harbor . . . No indication of any changes in U. S. Fleet or anything else unusual."

More regrets that the carriers were gone. Some even wondered whether the raid should be called off. But Admiral Nagumo felt there was no turning back now. Eight battleships were bound to be in port, and it was time to stop worrying "about carriers that are not there."

A last restless night of peace settled over the darkened ships as they pounded on toward Oahu, now less than 400 miles away. On the *Kaga,* Fighter Pilot Shiga took a tub bath, prepared a complete new change in clothing before retiring. Pilot Ippei Goto, who had just been promoted, laid out his new ensign's uniform for the first time. On the *Hiryu,* Bomber Pilot Hashimoto put his things in order and tried to get some sleep. But he kept tossing in his bunk. Finally he got up, went to the ship's doctor, and talked him out of some sleeping pills.

They must have worked, for when Commander Amagai, the *Hiryu's* flight deck officer, dropped by a little later to see how his boys were getting on, they were all sound asleep.

He then went up to the hangar deck and carefully checked the wireless in each plane. To make doubly sure that nobody accidentally touched a set and gave away the show, he slipped small pieces of paper between each transmitter key and its point of contact.

On the *Akagi*, Lieutenant Commander Ono hunched over his radio and continued his all-night vigil, monitoring the Honolulu radio stations. Two . . . 2:30 . . . 3:00 A.M. passed; still there was just KGMB playing Hawaiian songs.

Some 360 miles to the south, Lieutenant Commander Mochitsura Hashimoto, special torpedo officer of the Japanese submarine *I-24*, sat listening to the same radio program. The *I-24* was one of 28 large cruising subs that had been stationed off Oahu. They were to catch any U. S. warships lucky enough to escape to sea.

Also listening to the program in the *I-24* was Ensign Kazuo Sakamaki, who had just turned 23 the day they left Japan. Sakamaki lived dreams of naval glory, but so far he was just a passenger. He was skipper of a two-man midget sub, which the *I-24* carried papoose-style on her afterdeck.

There were five of these midgets altogether, each carried by a mother sub. The plan was to launch them shortly before the air attack. With luck they might sneak inside the harbor and bag a ship or two themselves.

The whole idea had an implausible touch that didn't appeal to the superpractical Admiral Yamamoto. But it also had that touch of military suicide dear to the Japanese heart, and finally Commander Naoji Iwasa persuaded the high command to incorporate the midgets —by now called the "Special Naval Attack Unit"—into the over-all plan. Then, since Iwasa had thought it up, he was put in charge.

At first Yamamoto set an important condition—the midgets couldn't enter Pearl Harbor itself . . . they might give away the show before it began. But Commander Iwasa insisted that they could sneak in undetected, and finally Yamamoto relented on this point too.

Commander Iwasa quickly whipped his project into shape. Five long-range cruising subs were stripped of their aircraft and catapults and fitted instead with the new secret midgets. Four big clamps and one auxiliary clamp held them in place. Each of the midgets was about 45 feet long, carried two torpedoes, ran on storage batteries, and required a two-man crew.

The crews—hand-picked and trained for more than a year—gathered in the Naval Command's private room at Kure Naval Base on the morning of November 16. There they learned that the great day was at hand, that they would sail on the 18th for Hawaii.

The following night Ensign Sakamaki took a last stroll through Kure with his classmate and fellow skipper, Ensign Akira Hirowo. At a novelty shop they each bought a small bottle of perfume. In the best tradition of the old Japanese warriors, they planned to put it on before going to battle. Then they could die gloriously—as Sakamaki explained, "like cherry blossoms falling to the ground."

Next morning they were off. Straight across the Pacific they sailed, cruising about 20 miles apart. Usually they ran submerged by day, on the surface at night. During these evening runs Sakamaki and his crewman, Seaman Kyoji Inagaki, would climb all over the midget, making sure that everything was all right. In his enthusiasm, Sakamaki was twice washed overboard. Fortunately he had remembered to tie himself to the big sub with a rope; so each time he was hauled in, dripping but full of pep, ready to go back to work.

On December 6 they sighted Oahu. After nightfall they surfaced and eased closer to shore. Finally they lay to in the moonlight, about ten miles off Pearl Harbor. From the conning tower Commander Hashimoto studied with interest the red and green lights off the port ... the glow of Honolulu itself ... the illuminated twin towers of the Royal Hawaiian Hotel ... and all the way to his right the Elks Club that glittered and twinkled at the foot of Diamond Head.

So at last they were there. Sakamaki and Inagaki ran through the million details that needed last minute checking. Suddenly they discovered the gyrocompass wasn't working. This was important—without it they

couldn't navigate under water. Sakamaki corralled the
I-24's gyrocompass man, ordered Inagaki to help him
on the repair job, and went below for a last nap.

About 12:30 A.M. he left his bunk and wandered up
to the conning tower for a little fresh air. Oahu was
darker now and seemed wrapped in haze. The stars
were out, and the moon beat on a choppy, restless sea.

He went below and checked on the gyrocompass.
Inagaki and the specialist were getting nowhere. Sakamaki's heart sank and he wondered whether this was
just bad luck or if he had somehow failed. In any case,
he was determined to go on.

He packed his personal belongings and wrote a farewell note to his family. In it he thoughtfully included
a lock of hair and one of his fingernail parings. He
cleaned up and changed to his midget submarine uniform—a leather jacket and *fundoshi*, which was a sort of
Japanese G-string. He sprinkled himself with the perfume he bought at Kure and put on a white *hashamaki*,
the Japanese warrior's traditional headband. Then he
made the rounds of the sub, embracing the crew. By
now it was well after 3:30 A.M., the time the midgets
were meant to start for Pearl Harbor.

CHAPTER III

"Gate Open—White Lights"

AT 3:42 A.M. the small mine sweeper *Condor* was plying her trade just outside Pearl Harbor, when watch officer Ensign R. C. McCloy suddenly sighted a strange white wave to port. It was less than 100 yards away, gradually converging on the *Condor* and moving toward the harbor entrance. He pointed it out to Quartermaster B. C. Uttrick, and they took turns looking at it with McCloy's binoculars. They decided it was the periscope of a submerged submarine, trailing a wake as it moved through the water.

Soon it was only 50 yards away—about 1000 yards from the entrance buoys. Then it apparently saw the *Condor*, for it quickly veered off in the opposite direction. At 3:58 the *Condor's* signal light blinked the news to the destroyer *Ward*, on patrol duty nearby: "Sighted submerged submarine on westerly course, speed nine knots."

The message came to Lieutenant (j.g.) Oscar Goepner, a young reserve officer from Northwestern University, who had just taken over the watch. He had been on the *Ward* doing this sort of inshore patrol work for more than a year, but tonight was the first time anything like this had ever happened. He woke up the skipper, Lieutenant William W. Outerbridge.

For Outerbridge it was more than his first sub alert —it was his first night on his first patrol on his first command. Until now his naval career had been very uneventful, considering a rather colorful background. He had been born in Hong Kong—the son of a British merchant captain and an Ohio girl. After his father's

death, the widow moved back home, and Outerbridge
entered Annapolis, Class of 1927. He managed to scrape
through, and spent the next 14 years inching up from
one stripe to two—it was always a slow climb in the
prewar Navy.

Until a few days before, he had been executive officer
on the destroyer *Cummings,* where all the officers were
Academy men except one reservist. Now he was the
only Academy man on a ship full of reservists. He recalled how sorry he had felt for the *Cummings'* lonely
reserve officer. Now the tables were turned—Goepner
still recalls how sorry everybody on the *Ward* felt for
Outerbridge, alone among the heathens.

On reading the *Condor's* message, Outerbridge sounded
general quarters, and the men tumbled to their battle
stations. For the next half-hour the *Ward* prowled about
—her lookouts and sonar men straining for any sign of
the sub. No luck. At 4:43 A.M. the crew were released,
and most of them went back to bed. The regular watch
continued to search the night.

Four minutes later the gate in the antitorpedo net
across the harbor entrance began to swing open. This
always took eight to ten minutes; and it wasn't until
4:58 A.M. that a crewman noted in the gate vessel log,
"Gate open—white lights."

At 5:08 the mine sweeper *Crossbill,* which had been
working with the *Condor,* passed in. Normally the gate
would now be closed again—this was always supposed
to be done at night—but the *Condor* was due in so soon,
it just didn't seem worth the trouble.

By 5:32 the *Condor* was safely in, but still the gate
stayed open. The tug *Keosanqua* was due to pass out
around 6:15 A.M. Once more it didn't seem worth the
trouble to close the gate, only to open it again in a little
while.

As the *Condor* closed up shop, the *Ward* radioed for
a few final words of advice that might help her carry
on the search: "What was the approximate distance
and course of the sub you sighted?"

"The course was about what we were steering at the time, 020 magnetic, and about 1000 yards from the entrance."

This was far to the east of the area first indicated, and Outerbridge felt he must have been looking in the wrong place. Actually, the *Condor* was talking about two different things. Her first message gave the sub's course when last seen; this new message gave it when first seen. She never explained that in between times the sub had completely changed course.

So the *Ward* moved east, combing an area where the sub could never be. And as she scurried about, she remembered at 5:34 to acknowledge the *Condor's* help: "Thank you for your information . . . We will continue search."

The radio station at nearby Bishops Point listened in on this exchange, but didn't report it to anybody—after all, a ship-to-ship conversation between the *Ward* and the *Condor* was none of their business. The *Ward* didn't report anything either—after all, the *Condor* didn't, and she was the one who said she saw something. She must have decided it wasn't a sub after all.

In any event, it wasn't the sub piloted by Ensign Kazuo Sakamaki. He wasn't even ready to leave until 5:30, a good two hours behind schedule. Meanwhile there had been more futile last-minute efforts to fix the broken gyroscope. Then another round of ceremonial good-bys.

When the *I-24's* skipper, Lieutenant Commander Hiroshi Hanabusa, asked if the broken gyrocompass had altered his plans, Sakamaki proudly replied, "Captain, I am going ahead." And then, carried away by it all, they both shouted, "On to Pearl Harbor!"

Dawn was just breaking when Sakamaki and Inagaki left the bridge of the *I-24* and scrambled aft along the catwalk to their midget. Each man held a bottle of wine and some lunch in his left hand, and shook a few more hands with his right. As Sakamaki's friend, Ensign

Hirowo observed when climbing into his midget on the *I-20,* "We must look like high school boys happily going on a picnic."

Sakamaki was far beyond such mundane thoughts. He and Inagaki said nothing as they climbed up the side of the small sub, squirmed through the hatch in the conning tower, and slammed it shut behind them.

The *I-24* slowly submerged, and the crew took their stations to release the four big clamps that held the midget. Quietly they waited for the signal.

Sakamaki and Inagaki were waiting too. Their electric motor was now purring, and they could feel the mother sub picking up speed to give them a better start.

Suddenly there was the terrific bang of the releasing gear, and they were off on their own. Immediately everything went wrong. Instead of thrusting ahead on an even keel, the midget tilted down, nearly standing on end. Sakamaki switched off the engines and began trying to correct the boat's trim.

CHAPTER IV

"You'd Be Surprised What Goes on Around Here"

LIEUTENANT HARAUO TAKEDA, 30-year-old flight officer on the cruiser *Tone*, was a disappointed, worried man as the Japanese striking force hurtled southward, now less than 250 miles from Oahu.

He was disappointed because last-minute orders kept him from piloting the *Tone's* seaplane, which was to take off at 5:30 A.M., joining the *Chikuma's* plane in a final reconnaissance of the U. S. fleet. And he was worried because—as the man in charge of launching these planes—he feared that they would somehow collide while taking off. True, the two ships were some eight miles apart, but it was still pitch black. Besides, when the stakes are so high, a man almost looks for things to worry about.

Nothing went wrong. The planes shot safely from their catapults and winged off into the dark—two small harbingers of the great armada that would follow. Admiral Nagumo planned to hit Pearl Harbor with 353 planes in two mighty waves. The first was to go at 6:00 A.M.—40 torpedo planes . . . 51 dive bombers . . . 49 horizontal bombers . . . 43 fighters to provide cover. The second at 7:15 A.M.—80 dive bombers . . . 54 high-level bombers . . . 36 more fighters. This would still leave 39 planes to guard the task force in case the Americans struck back.

By now the men on the carriers were making their final preparations. The deck crews—up an hour before the pilots—checked the planes in their hangars, then brought them up to the flight decks. Motors sputtered and roared as the mechanics tuned up the engines. On the *Hiryu*, Commander Amagai carefully removed the pieces of paper he had slipped into each plane's wireless transmitter to keep it from being set off by accident.

Down below, the pilots were pulling on their clean underwear and freshly pressed uniforms. Several wore the traditional *hashamaki* headbands. Little groups gathered around the portable Shinto shrines that were standard equipment on every Japanese warship. There they drank jiggers of *sake* and prayed for their success.

Assembling for breakfast, they found a special treat. Instead of the usual salted pike-mackerel and rice mixed with barley, today they ate *sekihan*. This Japanese dish of rice boiled with tiny red beans was reserved for only the most ceremonial occasions. Next, they picked up some simple rations for the trip—a sort of box lunch that included the usual rice balls and pickled plums, emergency rations of chocolate, hardtack, and special pills to keep them alert.

Now to the flight operations rooms for final briefing. On the *Akagi* Commander Mitsuo Fuchida, leader of the attacking planes, sought out Admiral Nagumo: "I am ready for the mission."

"I have every confidence in you," the admiral answered, grasping Fuchida's hand.

On every carrier the scene was the same: the dimly lit briefing room; the pilots crowding in and spilling out into the corridor; the blackboard revised to show ship positions at Pearl Harbor as of 10:30 A.M., December 6. Time for one last look at the enemy line-up; one last run-down on the charts and maps. Then the latest data on wind direction and velocity, some up-to-the-minute calculations on distance and flying time to Hawaii and back. Next a stern edict: no one except Commander Fuchida was to touch his radio until the attack began. Finally, brief pep talks by the flight officers, the skippers, and, on the *Akagi*, by Admiral Nagumo himself.

A bright dawn swept the sky as the men emerged, some wearing small briefing boards slung around their necks. One by one they climbed to the cockpits, waving good-by—27-year-old Ippei Goto of the *Kaga*, in his brand-new ensign's uniform . . . quiet Fusata Iida of the *Soryu*, who was so crazy about baseball . . . artistic Mimori Suzuki of the *Akagi*, whose Caucasian looks invited rough teasing about his "mixed blood." When it was Lieutenant Haita Matsumura's turn, he suddenly whipped off the gauze mask which had marked him as such a hypochondriac. All along, he had been secretly growing a beautiful mustache.

Commander Fuchida headed for the flight leader's plane, designated by a red and yellow stripe around the tail. As he swung aboard, the crew chief handed him a special *hashamaki* headband: "This is a present from the maintenance crews. May I ask that you take it along to Pearl Harbor?"

In the *Agaki's* engine room, Commander Tanbo got permission and rushed topside for the great moment—the only time he left his post during the entire voyage. Along the flight decks the men gathered, shouting good luck and waving good-by. Lieutenant Ebina, the *Shokaku's* junior surgeon, trembled with excitement as he watched the motors race faster and the blue exhaust smoke pour out.

All eyes turned to the *Akagi*, which would give the signal. She flew a set of flags at half-mast, which meant to get ready. When they were hoisted to the top and swiftly lowered, the planes would go.

Slowly the six carriers swung into the wind. It was from the east, and perfect for take-off. But the southern seas were running high, and the carriers dipped 15 degrees, sending high waves crashing against the bow. Too rough for really safe launching, Admiral Kusaka thought, but there was no other choice now. The Pearl Harbor Striking Force was poised 230 miles north and slightly east of Oahu. The time was 6:00 A.M.

Up fluttered the signal flags, then down again. One by one the fighters roared down the flight decks, drowning the cheers and yells that erupted everywhere. Commander Hoichiro Tsukamoto forgot his worries as navigation officer of the *Shokaku*, decided this was the greatest moment of his life. The ship's doctors, Captain

Endo and Lieutenant Ebina, abandoned their professional dignity and wildly waved the fliers on. Engineer Tanbo shouted like a schoolboy, then rushed back to the *Akagi's* engine room to tell everybody else.

Now the torpedo planes and dive bombers thundered off, while the fighters circled above, giving protection. Plane after plane rose, flashing in the early-morning sun that peeked over the horizon. Soon all 183 were in the air, circling and wheeling into formation. Seaman Iki Kuramoti watched, on the verge of tears. Quietly he put his hands together and prayed.

For Admiral Kusaka it had been a terrible strain, getting the planes off in these high seas. Now they were on their way, and the sudden relief was simply too much. He trembled like a leaf—just couldn't control himself. And he was embarrassed, too, because he prided himself on his grasp of Buddhism, *bushido*, and *kendo* (a form of Japanese fencing)—all of which were meant to fortify a man against exactly this sort of thing. Finally he sat on the deck—or he thinks possibly in a chair— and meditated Buddha-fashion. Slowly he pulled himself together again as the planes winged off to the south.

At the main target of this onslaught, the only sign of life was a middle-aged housewife driving her husband to work. Mrs. William Blackmore headed through the main Pearl Harbor gate . . . past the Marine sentry, who checked her windshield sticker . . . and headed down to the harbor craft pier. Mr. Blackmore—16 years in the Navy and presently chief engineer of the tug *Keosanqua*—was to get under way at 6:00 A.M. to meet the supply ship *Antares* and take over a steel barge she was towing up from Palmyra.

As Mrs. Blackmore dropped her husband, the first gray light of morning gave the rows of silent warships an eerie, ghostly look. "This," she observed, "is the quietest place I've ever seen."

"You'd be surprised what goes on around here," Blackmore replied cheerfully, and he jumped aboard the tug for another day's work.

The *Keosanqua* moved down the harbor, through the long narrow entrance channel, and past the open torpedo net, which was kept open still longer for whenever the tug should return. It was now 6:30 A.M. and the *Antares* was already in sight, towing the barge about a hundred yards behind her. The *Ward* hovered about a mile away, and a Navy PBY circled above, apparently looking at something.

Seaman H. E. Raenbig, the *Ward's* helmsman, was looking at something too. As the *Antares* came up from the southwest and crossed the *Ward's* bow to port, he suddenly noticed a curious black object that seemed to be fastened to the towline between the *Antares* and her barge. They were about a mile away, and so he asked Quartermaster H. F. Gearin to use his glasses for a closer look.

Gearin immediately saw that the black object was not hanging on the hawser but was merely in line with it. Actually, the object was in the water on the far side of the *Antares*. He showed it to Lieutenant Goepner, who said it looked like a buoy to him, but to keep an eye on it.

Gearin did, and about a minute later said he thought it was a small conning tower. It seemed to be converging on the *Antares'* course, as though planning to fall in behind the barge. At this point the Navy patrol bomber began circling overhead. Goepner needed no further convincing.

"Captain, come on the bridge!" he shouted. Outerbridge jumped from his cot in the chartroom, pulled on a Japanese kimono, and joined the others. He took one look and sounded general quarters. It was just 6:40 A.M.

Seaman Sidney Noble stumbled out of his bunk in the forecastle for the second time in three hours—so sleepy he could barely wipe the sand from his eyes. He pulled on dungarees, shoes but no socks, and a blue shirt, which he didn't bother to button. Then he joined the other men racing up the ladder to their battle stations.

Gunner's Mate Louis Gerner stayed below long enough to slam and dog the hatch leading to the anchor engine room, then dashed after the rest. As he ran aft toward his station in the after well deck, Outerbridge leaned over the bridge railing and frantically waved him away from Number 1 gun, which was now swinging out, trained on the conning tower ahead.

Along the afterdeck Ensign D. B. Haynie ran past Number 2, 3, and 4 guns, shouting to the men to break out the ammunition. He might have spared himself the trouble at Number 3. Seaman Ambrose Domagall, the first loader, had been on duty as bridge messenger. As soon as general quarters sounded, he went directly to the gun, yanked open the ready rack, and was waiting with a three-inch shell in his arms when the rest of the crew rushed up.

Outerbridge had signaled "All engines ahead full," and the old *Ward* was now surging forward—bounding from five to ten to 25 knots in five minutes.

"Come left," he called to Helmsman Raenbig, and the 1918 hull wheezed with the strain as she heeled hard to port. Outerbridge headed her straight for the gap between the barge and the conning tower, now some 400 yards off the *Ward's* starboard bow.

At this point the *Antares* caught on—her blinker flashed the news that she thought she was being followed. Up above, the PBY dropped two smoke pots to mark the sub's position.

To Ensign William Tanner, pilot of the PBY, this was simply the act of a good Samaritan. He had been on the regular morning patrol when he first spotted the submarine. It was well out of the designated area for friendly subs. His immediate reaction—"My God, a sub in distress!"

Then he saw the *Ward* steaming in that direction. Quickly he swooped down and dropped his two smoke bombs. They would help the *Ward* come to the rescue. From his position this was the best he could do for the sub.

The *Ward* didn't need any markers—the submarine

was just to starboard, pointing straight at the ship. It was running awash, with the conning tower about two feet out of water. In the choppy sea the men caught brief glimpses of a small cigar-shaped hull. They were utterly fascinated. Chief Commissary Steward H. A. Minter noticed that it was painted a dingy green. Quartermaster Gearin saw a layer of small barnacles . . . Helmsman Raenbig noticed moss on the conning tower . . . most of the men thought it looked rather rusty. Everyone agreed there were no markings on the squat, oval conning tower.

Curiously enough, the sub didn't seem to see the *Ward* at all. It just kept moving ahead, trailing the *Antares* at about eight or nine knots.

"Commence firing," Outerbridge ordered. They were now only 100 yards away and Boatswain's Mate A. Art, captain of Number 1 gun, knew they were much too close to use his sights. So he aimed the gun like a squirrel rifle and let her go. It was exactly 6:45 A.M. when this first shot whistled over the conning tower and plunged into the sea beyond.

They were better squirrel hunters at Number 3 gun on the galley house roof. Gun Captain Russell Knapp gave his order to fire about 30 seconds later, with the target less than 50 yards away. The shell hit the base of the conning tower, just where it touched the water. The sub staggered but came on.

Now it was right alongside, sucked almost against the ship. For an instant it seemed to hang there—long enough to give Gunner's Mate Louis Gerner an indelible picture of the glass in its stubby periscope—and then it was behind them, writhing and spinning in the *Ward's* wake.

Four quick whistle blasts told Chief Torpedoman W. C. Maskzawilz to release his depth charges. One . . . two . . . three . . . four rolled off the stern. Huge geysers erupted and the sub was instantly swallowed in a mountain of foam. Maskzawilz, who set the pistols at 100 feet, noted with satisfaction that the sub "seemed to wade right into the first one."

Up in the PBY Ensign Tanner was doing some soul-searching. Helping the sub might be the decent thing to do, but his orders were very strict—"Depth bomb and sink any submarines found in the defensive sea area without authority." Now he looked down, the *Ward* was doing just that. A pang of hesitation, and Tanner made another run. This time he dropped some depth bombs of his own.

All these fireworks were watched with mild interest by the men on the tug *Keosanqua*. She loafed about two miles away, just off the harbor mouth, still waiting to pick up the *Antares'* barge. Like everybody else on board, Engineer Blackmore thought it was merely some early-morning practice.

On the *Ward,* Lieutenant Goepner had a far more harrowing thought. He had the awful feeling that it might be an American sub. Of course, it shouldn't have been there and, of course, it didn't look like anything he had ever seen before; but could there have been a mistake?

In the PBY, Ensign Tanner had the same feeling. He and his copilot, Ensign Clark Greevey, assured each other that orders were orders. But if Tanner's judgment was wrong, a lot of good that would do. He could see the court-martial now. And he could see himself labeled for the rest of his life as the man who sank the American sub. In a wave of youthful self-pity he began picturing himself trying to get any job anywhere. As the plane resumed its patrol, he grimly reported the sinking to the Kaneohe Naval Air Station and settled back to await the inevitable end of his career.

Only Outerbridge seemed absolutely confident. In fact, he decided that the report radioed at 6:51 A.M. wasn't strong enough. It ran: "Depth-bombed sub operating in defensive sea area." This might imply just a periscope sighting or a sonar contact. Throughout the years there had been too many spars and whales bombed for headquarters to get overly excited about a message like that. But the *Ward* had seen the sub itself, and that was the all-important point to put over. It was the one hope of stirring up some action, instead of the standard "verify and repeat."

So Outerbridge quickly drafted another message. At 6:53 he again radioed the Fourteenth Naval District Headquarters. This time the report ran: "Attacked, fired on, depth-bombed, and sunk, submarine operating in defensive sea area." He felt that "fired on" was the key phrase. Now they would know he used his guns. Now they would know that he at least saw something.

Even Outerbridge didn't go all the way. He might have reported this extraordinary encounter in the clear instead of in code, and thus saved a few minutes. He might have used his blinker to signal the harbor control tower. He might have sent the more jolting message that was drafted but ended up crumpled in his file—it began with the words: "Sighted conning tower of strange sub, fired two rounds at point-blank range . . ." But at least he did something. At least he was willing, when other men were hypnotized by peace, to announce that he had blasted the daylights out of someone.

Whoever it was, it wasn't Ensign Sakamaki. At 6:30 he and Inagaki were still trying to correct their boat's trim. It was no easy job. Only one man at a time could wriggle on his stomach along the cramped tunnel that led fore and aft from the control room. They took turns slithering back and forth . . . shifting lead ballast, twisting the dials that released the air and filled the tanks with water. It took an hour to get the sub back on an even keel.

At last they started off again and even found time for a spot of lunch. They sat facing each other in the tiny control room, munching rice balls and exchanging cups of grape wine. As they finished, they grasped each other's hands and again pledged success.

Ten minutes later Sakamaki, peeking through the periscope, was appalled to see that they were approximately 90 degrees off course. With the gyrocompass out of order, he was depending on an auxiliary compass, which he thought would at least show the right directions. Apparently it was out of order too.

He tried to reset his course with his periscope, but it wasn't much help. Blindly the sub moved this way and that, always seeming to end up in the wrong direction. His hands grew wet with sweat. It was now about 7:00 A.M., and Ensign Kazuo Sakamaki was still a long way from the mouth of Pearl Harbor.

CHAPTER V

"Well, Don't Worry About It"

IT WAS AN UNEVENTFUL MORNING at the Army's Opana radar station near Kahuku Point on the northern tip of Oahu. Normally Privates Joseph Lockard and George Elliott made 25 plane contacts during the regular 4:00 to 7:00 A.M. watch, but this Sunday there was hardly anything.

The Opana station was one of five mobile units set up at strategic points around the perimeter of Oahu. They were all linked to an information center at Fort Shafter, which kept track of the plots picked up by the stations. The system could pick up any plane within 150 miles—when it worked. But it had just started operating around Thanksgiving and was still full of bugs. Lockard, Elliott, and the others spent most of their time training and making repairs.

At first they practiced from 7:00 A.M. to 4:00 P.M. But after Washington's warning of November 27, they went on duty every morning from four to seven—General Short felt these were the critical hours. Then they trained until 11:00 and knocked off for the day. On Sundays they worked only the four-to-seven shift. To the men this was simply a change in hours, not a change in routine or approach.

It was all very casual at Opana. This was the most remote of the five stations, and the six men who ran it were left pretty much to themselves. They had a small camp at Kawaiola, nine miles down the coast, and commuted to work by pickup truck. They were meant to work in three-man shifts, but this Sunday they decided that a two-man shift would do. Lockard served as

operator, Elliott as both plotter and motorman. The
regular motorman stayed in the sack.

They went on duty at noon December 6. They had
the double job of guarding the set with a .45 pistol
and seven rounds of ammunition, and running it during
the four-to-seven watch the following morning. That
night they set the alarm for 3:45 A.M., tuned in the
set on schedule at 4:00, and spent the next three hours
waiting for something to happen. There was a flicker
or so around 6:45—apparently a couple of planes were
coming in from the northeast about 130 miles away—
but nothing more than that. They weren't surprised
when the Shafter Information Center phoned at 6:54
and told them they could start closing up.

At the information center, Lieutenant Kermit Tyler,
the only officer on duty, was having an equally quiet
time. Usually the place was quite busy as the five stations phoned in their contacts and the spotters moved
little arrows around the big wooden plotting table. It
was all make-believe, for the other services hadn't yet
assigned liaison officers to help screen out friendly
planes, but still it made for lively practice. The control
officer would plan the interception of the "enemy." His
assistant, the pursuit officer, would relay his orders to
mythical squadrons of Army fighters. Sometimes they
even practiced with real planes.

But this Sunday there was little action. Few contacts;
nobody to evaluate the planes that were spotted; no
control officer to direct any interception. Except for the
enlisted men at the plotting table, only the pursuit officer, Lieutenant Tyler, was on hand. But with nobody
to give him orders and no planes to relay orders to, he
had nothing to do. Nor did he really know what he
was meant to do—he had only drawn this duty once
before.

Actually, he was there purely for training. Major Kenneth Bergquist—in charge of the radar network—wanted
the young pilots to learn as much about the systems
as possible, so they could use it more effectively in interception work. Since the center had to operate from

four to seven anyhow, this was a good chance to brush up. Today was Tyler's turn, and it was enough if he kept his eyes peeled.

For the first two hours nothing happened. Around 6:10 one of the stations finally phoned in a contact, and the spotters began shoving their arrows around the board. At 6:45 some plots began to show up 130 miles north of Oahu—not much, but enough to make Lieutenant Tyler wander over and see how the clerk would mark them on the daily record. They showed up as little hen scratches pointing toward Oahu. Then suddenly it was 7:00 A.M., and everyone went off to breakfast.

Tyler was left alone in the room. For one of those reasons known only to the Army, his orders ran from 4:00 to 8:00—an hour beyond everybody else's. He settled back alone—no one to obey . . . no one to command . . . and now no one even to talk to.

The 7:00 A.M. closing time made little difference to Privates Lockard and Elliott at Opana. They were at the mercy of the breakfast truck. It usually came about seven, but a man couldn't set his watch by it. With this in mind, they decided to keep the set running until the truck came. Elliott wanted to practice operating the set. After two weeks in the outfit, he could do the plotting pretty well, but still was no operator. Lockard was willing to teach him.

At 7:02 Elliott sat down and began fiddling with the controls. Lockard leaned over his shoulder and started explaining the various echoes or blips. Suddenly a blip flashed on the screen far bigger than anything Lockard had ever seen before. It was almost as big as the main pulse the unit always sent out. So big he thought the set was broken . . . that somehow the main pulse and mileage scale had gotten out of kilter. It was a pinball machine gone haywire.

He shoved Elliott aside and took over the controls himself. Quickly he saw there was nothing wrong with the set—it was just a huge flight of planes. By now Elliott was at the plotting table, and in a few seconds they nailed down the position: 137 miles to the north, three degrees east.

At 7:06 Elliott tried the headphones that connected directly with one of the spotters in the information center. The line was dead. Then he tried the regular Army circuit. After the clicks and hums and wheezes that are the overture to any phone call in Hawaii, he finally got through to the information center switchboard operator, Private Joseph McDonald. McDonald worked in a small cubicle just outside the plotting room and remained on duty even though the center was now closed.

Breathlessly Elliott broke the news: "There's a large number of planes coming in from the north, three degrees east."

McDonald thought there was nobody left at the information center, so he wrote down the message and turned around to time it by the big clock on the plotting room wall. Through the open door he suddenly noticed Lieutenant Tyler, sitting alone at the plotting table—there was someone in the building after all.

McDonald took the message to the lieutenant. Helpfully he explained that it was the first time he had ever received anything like this—"Do you think we ought to do something about it?" He suggested they call the plotters back from breakfast. They didn't get too much practice, and this certainly seemed "an awful big flight."

Tyler was unimpressed. McDonald returned to the switchboard and called back Opana. This time he got Lockard, who was excited too. The blips looked bigger than ever; the distance was shrinking fast—7:08 A.M., 113 miles . . . 7:15 A.M., 92 miles. At least 50 planes must be soaring toward Oahu at almost 180 mph.

"Hey, Mac!" he protested when McDonald told him the lieutenant said everything was all right. Then Lockard asked to speak directly to Tyler, explaining he had never seen so many planes, so many flashes, on his screen.

McDonald traipsed back to Tyler: "Sir, I would appreciate it very much if you would answer the phone."

Tyler took over, listened patiently, and thought a minute. He remembered the carriers were out—these might be Navy planes. He recalled hearing the radio on his way to work; remembered that it stayed on all night whenever B-17s came in from the coast—these might be Flying Fortresses. In either case, the planes were friendly. Cutting short any further discussion, he told Lockard, "Well, don't worry about it."

Lockard was now in no mood to keep on; he thought they might as well shut down the set. But Elliott wanted to practice some more, so they followed the flight on in—7:25 A.M., 62 miles . . . 7:30 A.M., 47 miles . . . 7:39 A.M., 22 miles. At this point they lost it in the "dead zone" caused by the hills around them.

Conveniently, the pickup truck arrived just then to take them back to Kawaiola for breakfast. They slammed shut the doors of the mobile unit, turned the lock, hopped in the truck, and bounced off down the road at 7:45.

At the Shafter Information Center Private McDonald was still uneasy. He asked Lieutenant Tyler what he really thought of the blips, and was glad to hear the lieutenant say, "It's nothing." Shortly after 7:30 another operator took over the switchboard, and as McDonald left the building he suddenly stuck the original Opana message in his pocket. He had never done anything like this before, but he wanted to show it to the fellows.

Alone again in the plotting room, Lieutenant Tyler settled back to wait out the last dragging minutes of his own tour of duty. He had no qualms about the Opana message, and although he didn't know it, on one count at least he was absolutely right—the all-night radio did mean some B-17s were coming in from the mainland. At this very moment 12 of the big bombers were approaching from the northeast.

But the planes that showed upon the Opana screen were a little less to the east, far more numerous, and at this moment infinitely closer.

Commander Mitsuo Fuchida knew they must be nearly there—they had been in the air now almost an hour and a half. But a carpet of thick white clouds stretched endlessly below, and he couldn't even see the ocean to check the wind drift. He flicked on the radio direction finder and picked up an early-morning program from Honolulu. By twisting his antenna he got a good bearing on the station and discovered he was five degrees off course. He made the correction, and the other planes followed suit.

They were all around him. Behind were the other 48 horizontal bombers. To the left and slightly above were Lieutenant Commander Kakwichi Takahashi's 51 dive bombers. To the right and a little below were Lieutenant Commander Shigeharu Murata's 40 torpedo planes. Far above, Lieutenant Commander Shigeru Itaya's 43 fighters provided cover. The bombers flew at 9000 feet, the fighters as high as 15,000. All of them basked in the bright morning sun that now blazed off to the left.

But below, the clouds were still everywhere. Fuchida began to worry—would it be as bad over Pearl Harbor? If so, what would that do to the bombing? He wished the reconnaissance planes would report—they should be there by now. And then through the radio music he suddenly heard a weather broadcast. He tuned closer and caught it clearly: ". . . partly cloudy . . . mostly over the mountains . . . ceiling 3500 feet . . . visibility good."

Now he knew he could count on the clouds to break once he reached Oahu. Also that it would be better to come in from the west and southwest—those clouds over the mountains made an eastern approach too dangerous. Then, as if to cap this run of good luck, the clouds below him parted, and almost directly ahead he saw a white line of surf breaking against a rugged green shore. It was Kahuku Point, Oahu.

Lieutenant Toshio Hashimoto, piloting one of Fuchida's bombers, was simply charmed. The lush green island, the clear blue water, the colored roofs of the little houses seemed in another world. It was the kind of scene one likes to preserve. He pulled out his camera and snapped some pictures.

For fighter pilot Yoshio Shiga, this warm, sunlit land had a deeper meaning. Back in 1934 he had been to Honolulu on a naval training cruise . . . a visit full of good times and pleasant memories. To see Oahu again, still so green and lovely, gave him a strange, nostalgic feeling. He thought about it for a moment, then turned to the business at hand.

The time had come to deploy for the attack, and Commander Fuchida had a difficult decision to make. The plan provided for either "Surprise" or "Surprise Lost" conditions. If "Surprise," the torpedo planes were to go in first, then the horizontal bombers, finally the dive bombers, while the fighters remained above for protection. (The idea was to drop as many torpedoes as possible before the smoke from the dive bombing ruined the targets.) On the other hand, if the raiders had been detected and it was "Surprise Lost," the dive bombers and fighters would hit the airfields and anti-aircraft defenses first; then the torpedo planes would come in when resistance was crushed. To tell the planes which deployment to take, Commander Fuchida was to fire his signal gun once for "Surprise," twice for "Surprise Lost."

Trouble was, Commander Fuchida didn't know whether the Americans had caught on or not. The reconnaissance planes were meant to tell him, but they hadn't reported yet. It was now 7:40 A.M., and he couldn't wait any longer. They were already well down the west coast and about opposite Haleiwa. Playing a hunch, he decided he could carry off the surprise.

He held out his signal pistol and fired one "black dragon." The dive bombers began circling upward to 12,000 feet; the horizontal bombers spiraled down to 3500; the torpedo planes dropped until they barely skimmed the sea, ready for the honor of leading the assault.

As the planes orbited into position, Fuchida noticed

that the fighters weren't responding at all. He decided that they must have missed his signal, so he reached out and fired another "black dragon." The fighters saw it this time, but so did the dive bombers. They decided it was the second "black dragon" of the "Surprise Lost" signal. Hence, they would be the ones to go in first. In a welter of confusion, the High Command's plan for carefully integrated phases vanished; dive bombers and torpedo planes eagerly prepared to slam into Pearl Harbor at the same time.

They could already see it on their left. Lieutenant Shiga was attracted by the unusual color gray of the warships. Commander Itaya was struck by the way the battleships were "strung out and anchored two ships side by side in an orderly manner." Commander Fuchida was more interested in counting them—two, four, eight. No doubt about it, they were all there.

CHAPTER VI

"Joe, This Is One for the Tourist!"

Thirteen-year-old James B. Mann, Jr., stood with his father, squinting at the planes that circled high above their beach house at Haleiwa on the northwest coast of Oahu. The Manns liked to come to Haleiwa for a restful week end, but this morning there was no rest at all. First the planes set off their two pug dogs; then the barking woke the family up. Mrs. Mann thought it might be that Lieutenant Underwood from Wheeler Field—he was always buzzing the beach—but Mr. Mann and Junior quickly discovered that it was a much bigger show.

More than 100 planes were orbiting about, gradually breaking up into smaller groups of three, five, and seven. Soon, several fighters dropped down low enough for Junior to observe, "They've changed the color of our planes." Then the fighters sped off to the east, down the road toward Schofield and Wheeler Field. Now the other groups were flying away too, and by 7:45 A.M. they had all disappeared.

Twelve miles further south, another 13-year-old, Tommy Young, was surf-casting with his father off Maile Beach. Suddenly Tommy's attention was attracted by the drone of airplane motors. Looking up, he saw a big formation of silvery planes flying southeast. His father counted 72 of them.

Fourteen miles to the southeast, two other young fishermen were trying their luck in Pearl Harbor. Thirteen-year-old Jerry Morton and his kid brother Don, 11, sat on the enlisted men's landing at Pearl City, a peninsula that juts southward into the middle of the anchorage. Like most service children, Jerry and Don regarded Pearl Harbor not as a naval base but as a huge, fascinating play pool. Almost every morning when they weren't at school, they ran down to the landing— only 200 yards from the house—and let out a ball of string. Occasionally a gullible perch took a chance; rarely anything worthy of the dinner table. But there were always the ships, the planes, the sailors—a wonderful kaleidoscope that never grew dull.

This morning they set out as usual—barefoot, khaki pants rolled up, T-shirts stuffed in their pockets as soon as their mother wasn't looking. Little gusts of wind stirred the harbor waters, but the sun poked through the clouds often enough to make the day hot and lazy. It was a typical Sunday morning, except for one thing: incredibly, the fish were biting. By 7:45 the boys had used up all their bait, and Don was dispatched to the house for more. Jerry, the senior partner, lolled in the morning sun.

Around him, the ships of the Pacific Fleet lay in every direction. To the north and east, little nests of destroyers clustered about their tenders at anchor. To the southeast, most of the cruisers pointed into the Navy Yard piers. Still further to the south, the cruiser *Helena* lay at 1010 dock . . . then the battleship *Pennsylvania*, sharing Drydock No. 1 with two destroyers. To their west was another destroyer, high in the floating drydock . . . and finally, completing the circle, more destroyers, the repair ship *Medusa*, and the aircraft tender *Curtiss* lay moored offshore.

Dominating the whole scene—and squarely in the middle of the harbor—was Ford Island, where Don and Jerry's stepfather, Aviation Ordnanceman Thomas Croft, had duty this Sunday at the seaplane hangars. The Navy PBY patrol planes were based here; also the carrier planes when they were in port. The carriers themselves moored along the northwest side of the island, while the battleships used the southeast side.

This Sunday, of course, the carriers were all at sea, and the moorings opposite Pearl City offered little in the way of excitement—only the old cruisers *Detroit* and *Raleigh* . . . the ex-battleship *Utah,* now demoted to target ship . . . the seaplane tender *Tangier.* But on the far side of the island a thrilling line of masts and funnels sprouted from "Battleship Row"—*Nevada, Arizona, Tennessee, West Virginia, Maryland, Oklahoma,* and *California* were all there.

Other less glamorous craft elbowed their way into the picture. The "honey barge" *YG-17* crawled from ship to ship, collecting garbage. The tanker *Neosho* squatted toward the southern end of Battleship Row. The cruiser *Baltimore*—a veteran of Teddy Roosevelt's Great White Fleet—lingered in rusty retirement, anchored among the sleek destroyers in East Loch. The poky little seaplane tender *Swan* perched on a marine railway near the cruisers (Radio Operator Charles Michaels estimates she could do 12.6 knots with a clean bottom and all laundry aloft). The old gunboat *Sacramento* hovered nearby—her tall, thin smokestack looked like something designed by Robert Fulton. The ancient mine layer *Oglala* lay next to the cruiser *Helena* at 1010 dock. She had the romantic past of a Fall River liner, but it was all over now. These days she was almost always tied up; once so long that a family of birds built a nest in her funnel.

The large and the small, the mighty and the meek, they all added up to 96 warships in Pearl Harbor this Sunday morning.

Assembled together, the U. S. Pacific Fleet was a big family—yet it was a small family too. Most of the men knew everybody else in their line of work, regardless of ship. Walter Simmons, who served a long hitch as mess attendant on the *Curtiss,* recalls that it was almost impossible for him to board any other ship in the fleet without meeting someone he knew.

In these prewar days everybody stayed put. Chief Boatswain's Mate Joseph Nickson had been on the *San Francisco* nine years; Chief Jack Haley on the *Nevada* 12 years. Ensign Joseph Taussig, brand-new to the ship, thought that several of the chief petty officers on the

Nevada had been there before he was born. These old chiefs played an important part in keeping the family spirit. They were almost like fathers to the young ensigns—taught them beer baseball in the long, dull hours when nothing was happening; called them "Sonny" when no one else was listening. But they were also the first to accept an officer's authority, and believed implicitly in the Navy chain of command.

For the officers it was a small world too. Year after year they had come from the same school, taken the same courses, followed the same careers, step by step. They too knew one another's service records and "signal numbers" by heart. They all shared the same hard work, wardroom Cokes, starched white uniforms, Annapolis traditions. Like all true professionals, they were a proud, sensitive, tightly knit group.

But signs were beginning to appear that this small, little world might be in for a change. Reservists were now pouring in from the various training programs. They were enthusiastic enough, but they lacked the background of Navy tradition. Where they were involved, sometimes the old way of doing things just wouldn't work.

Doris Miller, a huge mess attendant on the *West Virginia*, was one of the regulars faced with this problem of reconciling the old with the new. Every morning he had the colossal job of waking up Ensign Edmond Jacoby, a young reservist from the University of Wichita. At first Miller used to yank at Jacoby, much like a Pullman porter arousing a passenger. This was fine with Jacoby, but an Annapolis man reminded Miller that an enlisted man must never touch an officer. Faced with the problem of upholding an ensign's dignity and still getting Jacoby up, Miller appeared the following morning with a brilliant solution. Standing three inches from Jacoby's ear, he yelled, "Hey, Jake!" and fled the room.

This Sunday morning Doris Miller had no problems. Ensign Jacoby was off duty and free to sleep. Miller was working as mess attendant in the junior officers' wardroom, but there were only two officers on hand and there wasn't much to do.

It was just about as easy for the other men on duty. At 1010 dock Coxswain Ralph Haines was touching up the bright work on Admiral William Calhoun's gig. The admiral, who gloried in the title "COMTRAINRON 8" (Commander Training Squadron Eight), ran a group of supply ships. He had been scheduled to arrive this morning on the *Antares,* but for some reason was late.

On the *Nevada,* Ensign Taussig was officer of the deck. He whiled away the time trying to think of something useful to do. It occurred to him that one boiler had been carrying the burden all four days the ship had been in port. He ordered another lit off.

On the *Arizona,* Coxswain James Forbis had a working party on the fantail, rigging the ship for church services. The awning flapped and snapped in the breeze, and standing on the shore waiting to go out, Fleet Chaplain William A. Maguire made a mental note to have an extra windbreak rigged to keep his altar things in place. But the sun was warm, the clouds were high, and all things considered, the day was perfect. Turning to his assistant, Seaman Joseph Workman, Maguire burst out, "Joe, this is one for the tourist!"

The men off duty seemed to agree. On ship after ship they were getting ready to go ashore. Some, like Seaman Donald Marman of the cruiser *Honolulu,* were preparing for Catholic mass at the base arena. Others, like Signalman John Blanken on the *San Francisco,* were headed for swimming at Waikiki. Ensign Thomas Taylor on the *Nevada* hoped to get in some tennis. The *Helena* marine detachment was warming up for softball. Ensign William Brown had a very special project in mind as he stood on the deck of his PT boat, which was loaded on the tanker *Ramapo* for shipment to the Philippines. His wife was coming over in two weeks, and he had just rented a little house in town. This would be the perfect day to fix the place up.

The less ambitious loafed about the decks. On the

St. Louis, Seaman Robert McMurray watched his mates playing checkers. Pharmacist's Mate William Lynch on the *California* remembered this was his sister's birthday, and began planning a letter to her. Machinist's Mate R. L. Hooton sat on a bucket in front of his locker on the *West Virginia,* enjoying some snapshots just received from his wife. They were of his eight-month-old son whom he had never seen.

Storekeeper Felder Crawford sat on his desk in the *Maryland's* supply room, absorbed in that great American institution, the Sunday comics: Dagwood was having his usual troubles with Mr. Dithers . . . Daddy Warbucks' private plane made a forced landing, leading the Asp to observe, "I have never trusted the air" . . . Navy Bob Steele successfully deflected a surprise air attack on his destroyer by an unidentified navy.

A number of the men turned their thoughts to Christmas—there were only 15 more shopping days left. Yeoman Durrell Conner sat in the flag communications office of the *California* wrapping presents. Seaman Leslie Short climbed up to one of the *Maryland's* machine-gun stations, where he wasn't likely to be disturbed, and addressed his Christmas cards.

On every ship there were men still at breakfast. Captain Bentham Simons of the *Raleigh* lounged in a pair of blue pajamas, sipping coffee in his cabin. On the *Oklahoma,* Ensign Bill Ingram, son of Navy's great football coach, ordered poached eggs. Quartermaster Jim Varner took a large bunch of grapes from the serving line on the repair ship *Rigel,* then retired below to enjoy them properly. He hung them from the springs of an empty upper bunk and climbed into the lower, lay there happily plucking the grapes and wondering what to do the rest of the day.

The shoreside breakfasts offered more variety, fewer restrictions. At the target repair base, Seaman Marlin Ayotte's meal showed real faith in his cooking—four eggs, bacon, two bowls of cereal, fruit, toast, three cups of coffee. At the civilian workers' cantonment—affectionately known to the residents as "Boystown"—Ben Rottach entertained a couple of friends from the *Raleigh* at a breakfast of ham and eggs with whisky chasers.

In the repair shops and at Drydock No. 1, a few luckless souls had duty. Civilian yard worker Harry Danner struggled to align the boring bars on the *Pennsylvania's* starboard propeller shafts. But there was a Sunday spirit even about the men at work. At the main Pearl Harbor gate, for instance, the Marine guard was getting ready to have its picture taken by Tai Sing Loe, who seemed to be the whole Navy's unofficial photographer. He was a wonderfully colorful Chinese, who stalked his prey wearing a huge elephant hunter's hat.

Just down the road from the Pearl Harbor gate—a few hundred yards closer to Honolulu—lay the main entrance to Hickam Field, where the Army bombers were based. Normally there was a good deal of practice flying here, including some friendly buzzing of the Navy next door. The carrier planes, in turn, would occasionally stage mock raids on Hickam. But this morning all was quiet. The carriers were at sea, and the bombers were lined up in neat rows beside the main concrete runway.

General Short's sabotage alert was in full force, and obviously the best way to guard the planes was to group them together, out in the open. So there they all were— or at least all that mattered, for only six of the B-17s could fly . . . only six of the 12 A-20s . . . and only 17 of the 33 outmoded B-18s.

Their hangars stood silent and empty along the Pearl Harbor side of the field (there were only boondocks on the Honolulu side); but the control tower, near the left end of the hangar line, hummed with excitement. Captain Gordon Blake, the tall, young base operations officer, had been in his office since seven. Next, his friend, Major Roger Ramey, arrived. Then Colonel Cheney Bertholf, adjutant general of the Hawaiian Air Force. Finally, even the base commandant, Colonel William Farthing, steamed up. Everybody who was in the know wanted to see the B-17s arrive from the mainland. They were new, fabulous planes; to have 12 of them come at once was a big event indeed. Down on the field, Captain

Andre d'Alfonso, medical officer of the day, prepared his
own special welcome. As soon as they arrived, his job
was to spray them with Flit guns.

Elsewhere hardly anything was going on. Sergeant
Robert Hey began dressing for a rifle match with Captain J. W. Chappelman. Captain Levi Erdmann mulled
over the base tennis tournament. Nurse Monica Conter—
in between dates with Lieutenant Benning—took pulses
and temperatures at the new base hospital. Private Mark
Layton squeezed under the 7:45 breakfast deadline, but
most of the men didn't even try. At the big new consolidated barracks, Staff Sergeant Charles Judd lay in
bed, reading an article debunking Japanese air power in
the September issue of *Aviation* magazine.

It was the same story at Wheeler Field—the Army
fighter base in the center of the island. Here, too, the
planes were lined up in neat rows—62 of the Army's
brand-new P-40s. Here, too, most people were still in
bed. Two exceptions—Lieutenants George Welch and
Ken Taylor, a couple of pilots stationed at the small
Haleiwa air strip on the west coast of the island. Welch
and Taylor had come over for the weekly Saturday
dance. Then they got involved in an all-night poker
game. Now Welch was arguing that they should forget
all about bed and drive back to Haleiwa for an early-
morning swim. This debate was perhaps the liveliest
thing happening at Wheeler.

Just to the north, the five big quadrangles of Schofield
Barracks were equally quiet. Many of the men in the 24th
and 25th Divisions were on week-end pass to Honolulu;
others had straggled home in the early hours and were
dead to the world. A few, like Sergeant Valentine Lemanski, were in the washroom fumbling with toothpaste,
towels, and shaving kits. There never seemed enough
space on the washbowl shelves. But in the nearby officers'
housing area, Colonel Virgil Miller's little girl Julia was
up, fed, and dressed in her Sunday best. Now she was
about to enter the family car on her way to church with
her mother and brother.

It was also time for church at Fort Shafter, the Army's

administrative center near Honolulu. Pfc. William Mc-
Carthy joined a group approaching the Catholic chapel.
But many of the men stayed in bed or lolled in the
morning sunshine. Colonel Fielder, feeling fresh and
rested after his early evening with General Short, had
pulled on blue slacks and a blue sport shirt. He was
about to drive over to the windward side of the island
for a picnic at Bellows Field.

Bellows was a small Army fighter base near the eastern
end of Oahu. It had only two small squadrons, and only
12 of the planes were modern P-40s, but all of them were
lined up just as neatly as the planes at Hickam and
Wheeler. The men were all taking it easy or planning
the usual Sunday projects.

Five miles farther up the coast lay the Kaneohe Naval
Air Station, the only other post on the windward side of
Oahu. Thirty-three of the Navy's new PBYs operated out
of here. This morning three of them were out on patrol.
The others were in the hangars or riding at anchor in
the choppy blue water of Kaneohe Bay.

At 7:45 this lazy Sunday morning Kaneohe looked as
serene as any of the Army airfields. Mess Attendant
Walter Simmons was setting the table in the officers'
wardroom, but nobody had turned up to eat. Lieutenant
Commander H. P. McCrimmon, the post medical officer,
was sitting in his office with his feet on his desk, wondering why the Sunday paper was late.

That was what the people in Honolulu were wondering, too. Normally they counted on the *Advertiser* as an
indispensable part of Sunday breakfast, but this morning
the presses had broken down after running off only 2000
copies. The papers already printed had gone to Pearl
Harbor for distribution among the ships. Everyone else
was simply out of luck. Getting something repaired on
Sunday in Honolulu was a tall order, although Editor
Ray Coll worked hard at the problem.

Across town, Editor Riley Allen of the *Star-Bulletin*
had no press troubles and his afternoon paper didn't
come out on Sunday, but he was miles behind on his
correspondence. This morning he hoped to catch up, and

now sat in his office dictating to his secretary, Winifred
McCombs. It was her first day on the job, and at 7:45
A.M. she perhaps wondered whether she had been wise
in leaving her last position.

Most of the people in Honolulu were enjoying more
civilized hours, many of them sleeping off the island's
big football week end. Saturday afternoon the University
of Hawaii beat Willamette 20-6 in the annual Shrine
game, and the victory had been celebrated in standard
mainland fashion. Now the fans bravely faced the morning after. Webley Edwards, manager of radio station
KGMB and a popular broadcaster himself, tackled a
grape and soda. It looked like a constructive way to start
the new day.

In sharp contrast to Oahu's Sunday morning torpor,
the destroyer *Ward* scurried about off the entrance to
Pearl Harbor. A lot had happened since she polished off
the midget sub. At 6:48 A.M. she sighted a white sampan
well inside the restricted area. She scooted over to investigate, and the sampan took off. Quickly overhauled,
the sampan's skipper, a Japanese, shut off his engines and
waved a white flag. This struck Outerbridge as rather
odd—these sampans often sneaked into the restricted
area for better fishing, but when caught the surrender
was rarely so formal. On the other hand, the skipper had
already heard plenty of firing and might be just em-
phasizing his own peaceful inclinations. In any case, the
Ward started escorting the offender toward Honolulu to
turn him over to the Coast Guard.

At 7:03 A.M. the *Ward* picked up another sub on her
sound apparatus. Outerbridge raced over to the spot indicated, unloaded five depth charges, and watched a
huge black oil bubble erupt 300 yards astern. Then back
to the sampan. Everyone remained at general quarters,
and Outerbidge alerted Fourteenth Naval District Headquarters to stand by for further messages.

At headquarters, all of this fell into the lap of Lieutenant Commander Harold Kaminsky, an old reservist
who had been in the Navy off and on ever since he was

an enlisted man in World War I. Regularly in charge of net and boom defenses, he took his Sunday turn as duty officer like everyone else. This morning he held down the fort with the aid of one enlisted man, a Hawaiian who understood little English and nothing about the teletype.

Due to various delays in decoding, paraphrasing, and typing, it was 7:12 by the time Commander Kaminsky received the *Ward's* 6:53 message about sinking the submarine. First he tried to phone Admiral Bloch's aide but couldn't reach him. Then he put in a call to the admiral's chief of staff, Captain John B. Earle. The phone woke up Mrs. Earle, and she immediately put her husband on the wire. To Kaminsky, the captain sounded astonished and incredulous. Captain Earle later recalled that he first felt it was just one more of the sub "sightings" that had been turning up in recent months. On the other hand, this did seem too serious to be brushed off—it was the first time he heard of a Navy ship firing depth charges or anything else at one of these contacts. So he told Kaminsky to get the dispatch verified, also to notify the CINCPAC duty officer and Commander Charles Momsen, the Fourteenth Naval District operations officer. Earle said he would take care of telling Admiral Bloch.

The admiral was on the phone by 7:15. Captain Earle relayed the news, and the two men spent the next five or ten minutes trying to decide whether it was reliable or not. In the course of passing from mouth to mouth, the message had lost the point Outerbridge tried to make by saying he "fired on" the sub, hence must have seen it. Now neither Bloch nor Earle could tell whether this was just a sound contact or whether the *Ward* had actually seen something. Finally they made up their minds. Since they had asked the *Ward* to verify, since Commander Momsen was investigating, and since they had referred the matter to CINCPAC, they decided (using Captain Earle's phrase) "to await further developments."

Meanwhile Kaminsky had notified CINCPAC Headquarters over at the sub base. The assistant duty officer, Lieutenant Commander Francis Black, estimated that he

got the call around 7:20. He relayed the report to the
duty officer, Commander Vincent Murphy, who was
dressing in his quarters on the spot. Murphy asked,
"Did he say what he was doing about it? Did he say
whether Admiral Bloch knew about it or not?"

Nothing had been said on these points, so Murphy told
Black to call back and find out. He dialed and dialed,
but the line was always busy. By now Murphy was
dressed and told Black, "All right, you go to the office
and start breaking out the charts and positions of the
various ships. I'll dial one more time, and then I'll be
over."

The line was still busy, so Murphy told the operator to
break in and have Kaminsky call the CINCPAC office.
Then he ran on down to get there in time for the call.

Small wonder Kaminsky's line was busy. After talking
to Black, he had to phone Commander Momsen, the district operations officer. Then Momsen said to call Ensign
Joseph Logan. Then a call to the Coast Guard about that
sampan the *Ward* caught. Then Momsen on the line
again at 7:25—have the ready-duty destroyer *Monaghan*
contact the *Ward*. Then a call to Lieutenant Ottley to
get the Honolulu harbor gate closed. Phone call by
phone call, the minutes slipped away.

Commander Murphy dashed into his office a little
after 7:30 to find the phone ringing. But it wasn't the
call that he expected from Kaminsky; it was a call from
Commander Logan Ramsey, the operations officer at
Patrol Wing (Patwing) 2, the Ford Island headquarters
for all Navy patrol plane work. Ramsey was bursting
with news—a PBY reported it had just sunk a sub about
a mile off the Pearl Harbor entrance. Murphy told him
he already had a similar report, and for the next minute
or so the two men compared notes.

The PBY message had been sent by Ensign Tanner.
It was logged in at seven o'clock, but there had been
the usual delays in decoding, then the usual incredulity.
Commander Knefler McGinnis, who was Tanner's commanding officer and in charge of Patwing 1 at Kaneohe,
felt it must be a case of mistaken identity. He checked

to make sure that all information on U. S. subs was in the hands of the patrol planes. Ramsey himself received the message around 7:30 from the Patwing 2 duty officer, and his first reaction was that some kind of drill message must have gotten out by mistake. He ordered the duty officer to request "authentication" of the message immediately. But to be on the safe side he decided to draw up a search plan and notify CINCPAC—that was what he was doing now.

As Murphy hung up, the phone began ringing again. This time it was Kaminsky, finally on the wire. He assured Murphy that Bloch had been told . . . that the ready-duty destroyer was on its way to help . . . that the stand-by destroyer had been ordered to get up steam. Murphy asked, "Have you any previous details or any more details about this attack?"

"The message came out of a clear sky," Kaminsky replied.

Murphy decided he'd better call Admiral Kimmel, and by 7:40 CINCPAC himself was on the telephone. The admiral, who had left Mrs. Kimmel on the mainland as a defensive measure against any diverting influences, lived alone in a bare new house at Makalapa, about five minutes' drive away. As soon as he heard the news, he told Murphy, "I'll be right down."

Next, Ramsey phoned again, asking if there was anything new. Murphy said there wasn't, but warned him to keep search planes available, in case the admiral wanted them.

Now Kaminsky was back on the wire, reporting the *Ward's* run-in with the sampan. He had already told Earle, and the captain regarded it as evidence that nothing was really the matter—if there was a submarine around, what was the *Ward* doing escorting a mere sampan to Honolulu? He apparently didn't realize that the submarine incident was at 6:45, and the *Ward* had considered it definitely sunk.

Commander Murphy thought the sampan report was sufficiently interesting to relay to Admiral Kimmel, and he put in another call about 7:50.

Out in the harbor, Lieutenant Commander Bill Burford made the best of things as skipper of the ready-duty destroyer *Monaghan*. She was due to be relieved at eight o'clock, and Burford had planned to go ashore. In fact, the gig was already alongside. Then at 7:51 a message suddenly came in from Fourteenth Naval District Headquarters to "get under way immediately and contact *Ward* in defensive sea area." The message didn't even say what he should prepare for, but obviously it might be a couple of hours before he would be free again to go ashore.

Whatever was in store for the *Monaghan*, the other ships in Pearl Harbor had only morning colors to worry about. This ceremony was always the same. At 7:55 the signal tower on top of the Navy Yard water tank hoisted the blue "prep" flag, and every ship in the harbor followed suit. On each ship a man took his place at the bow with the "jack," another at the stern with the American flag. Then, promptly at 8:00, the prep flag came down, and the other two went up. On the smaller ships a boatswain piped his whistle; on the larger a bugler sounded colors; on the largest a band might even play the National Anthem.

As the clock ticked toward 7:55, all over the harbor men went to their stations. On the bridge of the old repair ship *Vestal*, Signalman Adolph Zlabis got ready to hoist the prep flag. On the fantail of the sleek cruiser *Helena* at 1010 dock, Ensign W. W. Jones marched to the flagstaff with a four-man Marine honor guard. On the big battleship *Nevada*, the ship's band assembled for a ceremony that would have all the trimmings. The only trouble was, the officer of the deck, Ensign Taussig had never stood watch for morning colors before and didn't know what size American flag to fly. He quietly sent an enlisted man forward to ask the *Arizona* people what they were going to do. While everybody waited around, some of the bandsmen noticed specks in the sky far to the southwest.

Planes were approaching, and from more than one direction. Ensign Donald L. Korn, officer of the deck on the *Raleigh*, noticed a thin line winging in from the northwest. Seaman "Red" Pressler of the *Arizona* saw a string approaching from the mountains to the east. On the destroyer *Helm*, Quartermaster Frank Handler noticed another group coming in low from the south. The *Helm*—the only ship under way in all of Pearl Harbor—was in the main channel, about to turn up West Loch. The planes passed only 100 yards away, flying directly up the channel from the harbor entrance. One of the pilots gave a casual wave, and Quartermaster Handler cheerfully waved back. He noticed that, unlike most American planes, these had fixed landing gear.

As the planes roared nearer, Pharmacist's Mate William Lynch heard a *California* shipmate call out, "The Russians must have a carrier visiting us. Here come some planes with the red ball showing clearly."

Signalman Charles Flood on the *Helena* picked up a pair of binoculars and gave the planes a hard look. They were approaching in a highly unusual manner, but all the same there was something familiar about them. Then he recalled the time he was in Shanghai in 1932, when the Japanese Army and Navy invaded the city. He remembered their bombing technique—a form of glide bombing. The planes over Ford Island were diving in the same way.

In they hurtled—Lieutenant Commander Takahashi's 27 dive bombers plunging toward Ford Island and Hickam . . . Lieutenant Commander Murata's 40 torpedo planes swinging into position for their run at the big ships. Commander Fuchida marked time off Barbers Point with the horizontal bombers, watching his men go in. They were all attacking together instead of in stages as originally planned, but it would apparently make no difference—the ships were sitting ducks.

A few minutes earlier, at 7:49 A.M., Fuchida had radioed the signal to attack: "To . . . to . . . to . . . to . . ." Now he was so sure of victory that at 7:53—even before the first bomb fell—he signaled the carriers that the surprise attack was successful: "Tora . . . tora . . . tora . . ."

Back on the *Akagi*, Admiral Kusaka turned to Admiral Nagumo. Not a word passed between them. Just a long, firm handshake.

CHAPTER VII

"I Didn't Even Know They Were Sore at Us"

COMMANDER LOGAN RAMSEY jumped from his desk at the Patwing 2 Command Center on Ford Island. He had been working out a search plan for the sub reported by the PBY when a single dive bomber screamed down on the seaplane ramp at the southern tip of the island. It looked like a young aviator "flathatting," and both he and the duty officer tried to get the offender's number. But they were too late, and Ramsey remarked that it was going to be hard to find out who it was. Then a blast . . . a column of dirt and smoke erupted from the foot of the ramp.

"Never mind," said Ramsey, "it's a Jap."

The plane pulled out of its dive and veered up the channel between Ford Island and 1010 dock. It passed less than 600 feet from Rear Admiral William Furlong as he paced the deck of his flagship, the antique mine layer *Oglala*. The admiral took one glance at the flaming orange-red circle on the fuselage and understood too. He shouted for general quarters, and as SOPA (Senior Officer Present Afloat), he hoisted the signal, "All ships in harbor sortie." The time was 7:55 A.M.

Now two more planes screeched down. This time the aim was perfect. Parts of the big PBY hangar at the head of the ramp flew in all directions. Radioman Harry Mead, member of a utility plane squadron based on the island, couldn't understand why American planes were bombing the place. Seaman Robert Oborne of the same outfit had a plausible explanation: it was an Army snafu. "Boy," he thought, "is somebody going to catch it for putting live bombs on those planes."

All this passed unnoticed by Ensign Donald Korn of the cruiser *Raleigh,* moored on the northwest side of Ford Island at one of the berths normally used by the carriers. He was turning over his deck watch to Ensign William Game and couldn't see much of anything happening down by the seaplane ramp. But he did have a fine view of the valley leading up the center of Oahu. At 7:56 he noticed some planes flying in low from that direction.

Now they were gliding past the algarroba trees at Pearl City. Splitting up, two headed for the *Utah* just astern, one for the *Detroit* just ahead, and one for the *Raleigh* herself. Ensign Korn, thinking the planes were Marines on maneuvers, called out his antiaircraft crews to practice with them. The men were just taking their stations when the torpedo struck home about opposite the second funnel. A shattering roar, a sickening lurch. Through a blinding mixture of smoke and dirt and muddy water, men caught a brief glimpse of the *Raleigh's* splintered church launch; it had been easing alongside where the torpedo hit. The *Detroit* got off scot-free, but the *Utah* shuddered under two solid blows. Watching from the destroyer *Monaghan* several hundred yards to the north, Boatswain's Mate Thomas Donahue thought that this time the U.S. Army really had a hole in its head.

A fifth plane in this group saved its torpedo, skimmed across Ford Island, and let fly at the *Oglala* and *Helena,* moored side by side at 1010 dock—the berth normally used by the battleship *Pennsylvania,* flagship of the whole Pacific Fleet. The torpedo passed completely under the *Oglala,* moored outboard, and barreled into the *Helena* midships—her engine-room clock stopped at 7:57. The concussion burst the seams of the old *Oglala* alongside, hurling Musician Don Rodenberger from his upper bunk. He could only think that the ancient boilers had finally exploded.

Ensign Roman Leo Brooks, officer of the deck on the *West Virginia* across the channel, was thinking along these same lines. He, too, was in no position to see the plane diving on the seaplane hangars or on the ships moored across Ford Island. All he saw was the sudden eruption of flames and smoke at 1010 dock. He lost no time—in seconds the ship's bugler and PA system were blaring, "Away the fire and rescue party!"

Even the men who saw the planes couldn't understand. One of them was Fireman Frank Stock of the repair ship *Vestal,* moored beside the *Arizona* along Battleship Row. Stock and six of his mates had taken the church launch for services ashore. They moved across the channel and into Southeast Loch, that long, narrow strip of water pointing directly at the battleships. On their right they passed the cruisers, nosed into the Navy Yard piers; on the left some subs tucked into their berths. As they reached the Merry's Point landing at the end of the loch, six or eight torpedo planes flew in low from the east, about 50 feet above the water and heading down the loch toward the battleships.

The men were mildly surprised—they had never seen U. S. planes come in from that direction. They were even more surprised when the rear-seat gunners sprayed them with machine-gun bullets. Then Stock recalled the stories he had read about "battle-condition" maneuvers in the Southern states. This must be the same idea—for extra realism they had even painted red circles on the planes. The truth finally dawned when one of his friends caught a slug in the stomach from the fifth plane that passed.

On the *Nevada* at the northern end of Battleship Row, Leader Oden McMillan waited with his band to play morning colors at eight o'clock. His 23 men had been in position since 7:55, when the blue prep signal went up. As they moved into formation, some of the musicians noticed planes diving at the other end of Ford Island. McMillan saw a lot of dirt and sand go up, but thought it was another drill. Now it was 7:58—two minutes to go—and planes started coming in low from Southeast Loch. Heavy, muffled explosions began booming down the line . . . enough to worry anyone. And then it was eight o'clock.

The band crashed into "The Star-Spangled Banner."
A Japanese plane skimmed across the harbor . . . dropped
a torpedo at the *Arizona* . . . and peeled off right over
the *Nevada's* fantail. The rear gunner sprayed the men
standing at attention, but he must have been a poor shot.
He missed the entire band and Marine guard, lined up
in two neat rows. He did succeed in shredding the flag,
which was just being raised.

McMillan knew now but kept on conducting. The
years of training had taken over—it never occurred to
him that once he had begun playing the National
Anthem, he could possibly stop. Another strafer flashed
by. This time McMillan unconsciously paused as the
deck splintered around him, but he quickly picked up
the beat again. The entire band stopped and started
again with him, as though they had rehearsed it for
weeks. Not a man broke formation until the final note
died. Then everyone ran wildly for cover.

Ensign Joe Taussig, officer of the deck, pulled the
alarm bell. The ship's bugler got ready to blow general
quarters, but Taussig took the bugle and tossed it overboard. Somehow it seemed too much like make-believe
at a time like this. Instead he shouted over the PA system
again and again, "All hands, general quarters. Air raid!
This is no drill!"

Ship after ship began to catch on. The executive officer
of the supply ship *Castor* shouted, "The Japs are bombing us! The Japs are bombing us!" For an instant Seaman Bill Deas drew a blank and wondered whether the
man was speaking to him. On the submarine *Tautog*,
the topside anchor watch shouted down the forward
torpedo hatch, "The war is on, no fooling!"

Everybody was racing for the alarm signals now. On
the little gunboat *Sacramento* in the Navy Yard, Seaman
Charles Bohnstadt dashed over to pull the switch, lost
the race to a mess attendant. On the cruiser *Phoenix*, out
where the destroyers were moored, the loud-speaker had
just announced, "Lay up to the quarter deck the Catholic
church party"— then the general alarm bell drowned out
anything else. On Battleship Row the *Maryland's* bugler

blew general quarters over the PA system, while the ship's klaxon lent added authority.

The *Oklahoma's* call to arms needed no extra punch. First came an air raid alert; then general quarters a minute later. This time the voice on the PA system added a few well-chosen words, which one crew member recalls as follows: "Real planes, real bombs; this is no drill!" Other witnesses have a less delicate version of the last part. The language alone, they say, convinced them that this was it.

But on most ships the men down below still needed convincing. Even as the torpedo hit, Fireman Joseph Messier of the *Helena* was sure the alarm bell was just another of the executive officer's bright ideas to get the crew to go to church.

"This is a hell of a time to hold general drills," echoed through the firemen's quarters of the *California*, the signalmen's compartment on the *San Francisco*, the after "head" on the *Nevada*. On the destroyer *Phelps* Machinist's Mate William Taylor engaged in a sort of one-man slowdown. He deliberately took plenty of time getting dressed. Then he ambled topside, yawned, and strolled toward the stern to get a drink of water before going below to his station in the boiler room. As he started down the after gangway, a chief gunner's mate came charging down behind him, shouting, "Get to hell out of the way—don't you know we're at war?" Taylor thought to himself, "You mumbling jackass, isn't this drill enough without added harassment from you?"

Commander Herald Stout, skipper of the destroyer-mine-craft *Breese*, was even more annoyed. He had left standing orders never to test general quarters before eight on Sunday. When the alarm sounded, he left his breakfast to chew out the watch.

Captain Harold C. Train, Admiral Pye's chief of staff on the *California*, was sure the alarm had been set off by mistake. And on the destroyer *Henley* it really was a mistake. Her crew was normally mustered on Sundays at 7:55 by sounding the gas-attack alarm; this morning someone pressed the wrong button—general quarters.

Chaplain Howell Forgy of the cruiser *New Orleans* also thought someone had blundered. He drifted to his station in sick bay completely unconcerned. A moment later the ship's doctor arrived and hesitantly remarked, "Padre, there's planes out there and they look like Japs."

The word spread faster. A boatswain dashed into the CPO wardroom on the *Maryland*, sat down white as a sheet: "The Japs are here . . ." As Ensign Charles Merdinger of the *Nevada* pulled on his clothes, someone outside his stateroom yelled, "It's the real thing; it's the Japs!" With that, Merdinger stepped completely through his sock. Watertender Samuel Cucuk looked into the "head" on the destroyer tender *Dobbin*, called to Fireman Charles Leahey, "You better cut that short, Charlie, the Japs are here."

A few skeptics still held out. In the *Honolulu's* hoist room Private Roy Henry bet another Marine a dollar that it was the Army, pulling a surprise on the Navy with dummy torpedoes. The men in the repair ship *Rigel's* pipe and copper shop remained unperturbed when a seaman wearing only underwear burst in with the news—they figured the fellow was pretending he was crazy so he could get back to the Coast. When a sailor on the *Pennsylvania* said the Japs were attacking, Machinist's Mate William Felsing had a snappy comeback: "So are the Germans."

The last doubts vanished in an avalanche of shattering evidence. Pharmacist's Mate William Lynch took a skeptical metalsmith to his porthole on the *California*, pointed to the chaos erupting outside. The man sagged away, sighing, "Jesus Christ . . . Jesus Christ." On the *West Virginia* a sailor spattered with fuel oil ran by Ensign Maurice Featherman shouting, "Look what the bastards did to me!"

One and all, they accepted it now—some with a worldly grasp of affairs, some with almost ingenuous innocence. Captain Mervyn Bennion, skipper of the *West Virginia*, calmly remarked to his Marine orderly, "This is certainly in keeping with their history of surprise attacks." A seaman on the destroyer *Monaghan* told Boatswain's Mate Thomas Donahue, "Hell, I didn't even know they were sore at us."

Down the corridors . . . up the ladders . . . through the hatches the men ran, climbed, milled, and shoved toward their battle stations. And it was high time. The alarm was no sooner given when the *Oklahoma* took the first of five torpedoes . . . the *West Virginia* the first of six. These were the golden targets—directly across from Southeast Loch. Next the *Arizona* took two, even though a little to the north and partly blocked by the *Vestal.* Then the *California* got two, even though far to the south and a relatively poor target. Only the inboard battleships seemed safe—*Maryland* alongside *Oklahoma* and *Tennessee* beside *West Virginia.*

As the torpedoes whacked home, the men struggled to keep going, sometimes fell in jumbled heaps. On the *West Virginia* Ensign Ed Jacoby went out like a light when one of the first explosions toppled a steel locker over his head. Seaman James Jensen kept his feet through the first two blasts, but the next two hurled him into another compartment, and a fifth knocked him out. Quartermaster Ed Vecera, trying to get from the quarterdeck aft to his post on the bridge, ran a regular obstacle course: torpedoes . . . Japanese strafing . . . watertight doors slammed in his face . . . a tide of men who always seemed headed the other way. Finally he fell in behind Captain Bennion, and for a while everything opened up to let the skipper pass. But soon they were separated, and Vecera was shunted off in another direction. Somehow he got to the main deck and was stopped again. He never made it to the bridge.

On the *Helena,* the mess hall crashed around Machinist's Mate Paul Weisenberger, as he struggled toward his post in the forward engine room. A table, unhooked from the overhead, bounced off his shoulder. By the time he picked himself up, the next door forward was dogged shut. He had to settle for the after engine room instead.

The mess hall on the *Oglala*—racked up by the same torpedo—was a shambles too. Broken glass and china

littered the deck, as Musician Frank Forgione dashed
through barefoot on his way to his station in the sick
bay. He cut his feet terribly—never even noticed it until
hours later.

Worst of all was the *Oklahoma*. The second torpedo
put out her lights; the next three ripped open what was
left of her port side. The sea swirled in, driving Seaman
George Murphy from his post in the print shop on third
deck as soon as he got there. His group retreated midships, slamming a watertight door behind them. The list
grew steeper, and within seconds the water was squirting
around the seams, filling that compartment too. As the
ship heeled further, Chief Yeoman George Smith shifted
over to a starboard ladder to reach his battle station.
Everybody else had the same idea. In the flicker of a
few emergency lamps men pushed and shoved, trying
to climb over and around each other on the few usable
ladders. It was a dark, sweat-smeared nightmare.

No matter how bad things were, men remembered to
take care of absurd details. Radioman Robert Gamble
of the *Tennessee* ignored the old shoes beside his bunk,
went to his locker, and carefully put on a brand-new pair
to start the war right. The *Nevada* musicians put their
instruments away before going to their stations. (Exception—one man took along his cornet and excitedly
threw it into a shell hoist along with some shells for the
antiaircraft guns above.)

On the other hand, there was always the danger of
forgetting something important. As Radioman James
Lagerman raced for his battle station in the Ford Island
Administration Building, he kept saying again and again
to himself, "Just gotta try to remember this date . . ."

In the confusion many of the ships—unlike the *Nevada*
—never carried out morning colors. Others did, but in
somewhat unorthodox fashion. On the sub alongside the
oil barge *YO-44*, a young sailor popped out of the conning tower and ran to the flagstaff at the stern. Just then
a torpedo plane roared by, the rear-seat man swiveling
his guns. The sailor scurried back to the conning tower,
hugging the flag. Next try, he clipped it on; then another

plane sent him diving back to shelter. Third time he got it up—just before another plane sent him ducking for cover again. The men on *YO-44* laughed and clapped and cheered.

But at the sub base headquarters a few yards away, Chief Torpedoman's Mate Pete Chang, in charge of the Navy's Submarine Torpedo School, could only watch with sickened admiration as the Japanese planes grooved one strike after another down the narrow alley of Southeast Loch. It was a real demonstration for the reluctant students who had to watch it, and Chang didn't hesitate to draw on it for material to be used in future lectures.

At CINCPAC Headquarters in the sub base administration building, Commander Vincent Murphy was still phoning Admiral Kimmel about the *Ward's* sampan report when a yeoman burst into the room: "There's a message from the signal tower saying the Japanese are attacking Pearl Harbor, and this is no drill." Murphy relayed the message to his boss, then told the communications officer to radio the Chief of Naval Operations, the C-in-C Atlantic Fleet, the C-in-C Asiatic Fleet, and all forces at sea: AIR RAID ON PEARL HARBOR. THIS IS NO DRILL. The message went out at 8:00 A.M., but Admiral Bellinger had radioed a similar message to all ships in the harbor at 7:58; so Washington already knew.

Murphy now phoned Commander Ramsey over at Patwing 2 and optimistically asked how many planes were available. The commander showed a keen grasp of the situation: "I don't think I have any, but I'm scraping together what I can for search."

In the Navy housing areas around Pearl Harbor, people couldn't imagine what was wrecking Sunday morning. Captain Reynolds Hayden, enjoying breakfast at his home on Hospital Point, thought it was construction blasting—then his young son Billy rushed in shouting, "They're Jap planes!" Lieutenant C. E. Boudreau, drying down after a shower, thought an oil tank had blown up near his quarters behind Bloch Arena until a Japanese plane almost grazed the bathroom window. Chief Petty Officer Albert Molter, puttering around his Ford Island flat, thought a drill was going on until his wife Esther called, "Al, there's a battleship tipping over."

As 11-year-old Don Morton scuffed back to his house in Pearl City for more fishing bait, an explosion almost pitched him on his face. Then another, and still another. He scrambled home and asked his mother what was happening. She just told him to go fetch his brother Jerry. He ran out to find several planes now gliding by at house-top level. One was strafing the dirt road, kicking up little puffs of dust. Don was scared to go any further. As he ran back to the house, he saw his next-door neighbor, a Navy lieutenant, standing in his pajamas on the grass, crying like a child.

Up on the hill at Makalapa, where the senior officers lived, Admiral Kimmel ran out to his yard right after Commander Murphy reported the attack. He stood there for a minute or two, watching the planes make their first torpedo runs. Near him stood Mrs. John Earle, wife of Admiral Bloch's chief of staff. At one point she remarked quietly, "Looks like they've got the *Oklahoma*."

"Yes, I can see they have," the admiral answered

In a house directly across the street—and just a little down the hill—Mrs. Hall Mayfield, wife of Admiral Bloch's intelligence officer, buried her head in the pillow and tried to forget the noise. Makalapa was just being developed, and since it was on the side of an old volcano, they had to do a lot of dynamiting through the lava. It occurred to Mrs. Mayfield that they must now be blasting the hole for her mailbox post.

But the pillow was useless. Mrs. Mayfield surrendered and opened her eyes. Her Japanese maid Fumiyo was standing in the doorway . . . each hand clutching the frame, the long sleeves of her kimono making her look curiously like a butterfly. Fumiyo was trying to say something, but the noise drowned it out. Mrs. Mayfield jumped out of bed and went to her. "Oh, Mrs. Mayfield," Fumiyo was saying, "Pearl Harbor is on fire!"

Glancing through a window, she saw her husband in pajamas, standing on the back lawn. He was leveling binoculars on the harbor, which lay below the house.

Seconds later the two women joined him. Mrs. Mayfield's first words were a bit of wifely advice: "Hall, go right back inside and put in your teeth."

The captain's dentures were quickly forgotten as she watched the smoke billow up in the harbor. His wistful suggestion that it might be a drill failed to convince her. When two planes flashed by with the rising-sun insignia, all three of them turned and dashed back to the house.

Captain Mayfield was now pawing about his closet, hurling clothes and hangers in every direction. Mrs. Mayfield chose this moment to make a fatal mistake. "Why," she asked, "don't the Navy planes do something?"

The captain's glare showed that her question was treason. "Why," he yelled back, "doesn't the *Army* do something?"

In the control tower of Hickam Field just east of Pearl Harbor, Colonel William Farthing was still waiting for the B-17s from the mainland when he saw a long, thin line of aircraft approaching from the northwest. They looked like Marine planes from Ewa Field. As they began diving, Farthing remarked to Colonel Bertholf, "Very realistic maneuvers. I wonder what the Marines are doing to the Navy so early Sunday."

Watching the same show from the parade ground nearby, Sergeant Robert Halliday saw a big splash go up near Ford Island; he decided the Navy was practicing with water bombs. Then one of the bombs hit an oil tank, which exploded in a cloud of smoke and flames. A man said some poor Navy pilot would get into trouble for that. At this point a plane suddenly swooped down on Hickam—a rising sun gleamed on its fuselage. Somebody remarked, "Look, there goes one of the red team."

Next instant, the group was scattering for cover. The plane dropped a bomb and followed it into the huge maintenance hangar of the Hawaiian Air Depot. It was the first in a long line of bombers diving on Hickam from the south. No one is completely sure whether these planes, or those pulling out of their dives on Ford Island, reached Hickam first. Within seconds, both groups were everywhere at once—strafing the men and the neat rows of planes . . . dive-bombing the hangars and buildings.

In the mess hall at the center of Hickam's big, new consolidated barracks, Pfc. Frank Rom yelled a frantic warning to the early risers eating breakfast. It was too late. Trays, dishes, food splattered in all directions as a bomb crashed through the roof. Thirty-five men were wiped out instantly; the injured crawled to safety through the rubble—including one man wounded by a gallon jar of mayonnaise.

In the barracks, where most of the men were still asleep, the first explosions at Pearl Harbor woke up Corporal John Sherwood. Cursing the Navy, he got up and looked for something to read. As he padded about, he glanced out the window just in time to see the Hawaiian Air Depot get pasted. He took off in his shorts for a safer place, shouting, "Air raid! It's the real thing!"

Someone dashing through the barracks woke up Sergeant H. E. Swinney. Only then did he notice the bomb bursts and low-flying aircraft. Even so, he was more curious than alarmed. But he half sensed something was wrong—the barracks were never that empty on Sunday. He got up and slipped downstairs to investigate. In the hallway a group of men were chattering in excited whispers. He could get nothing out of them and looked around for a better clue. Near a doorway he saw a man with a Springfield rifle; then another man came in with blood running down his face. Swinney peeked out just in time to see a Zero fighter streak by Hangar 7. At last he caught on—he recalls it was almost the way an idea used to come to a comic-strip character, complete with light bulb above the head.

The men were desperately trying to get to their stations now. Some never made it—Private Mark Creighton, pinned down by strafers, dived into a latrine and hugged a toilet bowl for shelter. Others got there too late— Pfc. Emmett Pethoud found that the plane he had to guard was already blown to bits. More bombs were coming, so he ducked under a table—but not before he carefully replaced a phone receiver that had fallen off its hook.

A few were able to carry out their duties. Pfc. Joseph Nelles, the Catholic chaplain's assistant, was returning from early-morning mass when the planes struck. His first thoughts were to safeguard the Blessed Sacrament in the chapel. He ran back and must have just reached the altar when the chapel took a direct hit and vanished in the blast.

While Pearl and Hickam rocked with explosions, all was still quiet at Wheeler Field, the Army's fighter base in the center of the island. Staff Sergeant Francis Clossen, changing his clothes for a date at Waikiki, glanced out his third-floor window in the main barracks, saw a line of six to ten planes come through Kole Kole Pass to the west. They banked left and disappeared, blending into the background of the Waianae Mountains.

They circled back, joined others coming in from the northwest, and charged down on the field. At 8:02 A.M., Pfc. Arthur Fusco, guarding some P-40s with his rifle, froze in his tracks as the first dive bomber peeled off. He recognized those red balls and rushed into the hangar for a machine gun. He couldn't break the lock of the armament shack, but by now it made no difference.

Pfc. Carroll Andrews flattened against his barracks wall as bullets tore through the men's lockers, shattered and splintered the windows around him. Somebody yanked Pfc. Leonard Egan from his cot in one of the tents along the hangar line, and for a moment he stood dazed and naked watching the dive bombers and strafers at work. Then he grabbed his shoes and a pair of coveralls and started running.

In the housing areas families poured into their back yards in pajamas and bathrobes. A man wrapped in a bath towel raced up the post's main street. In the officers' club, Lieutenant Welch and Taylor stopped debating whether to go swimming. Welch grabbed the phone and called Haleiwa, where their P-40s were kept. Yes, the planes were all right . . . yes, they would be gassed up and loaded right away. Welch slammed down the receiver, hopped into Taylor's car, and the two careened off to Haleiwa, prodded along by a strafing Zero.

Just north of Wheeler, Major General Maxwell Murray, commanding the 25th Division, heard a plane diving over his quarters in the General's Loop at Schofield Barracks. He rushed to the window determined to report the pilot. The plane zoomed by only 75 yards away, but the general couldn't catch the number. So he ran to the front door, glancing at his watch—he would at least get the landing time. To his surprise the plane dropped a bomb.

Private Lester Buckley was unloading manure nearby at the Schofield compost heap. He took one look at flames billowing up from Wheeler, jumped in his wagon, and raced back to the barracks so fast that the pitchforks rattled out.

In the barracks, Pfc. Raymond Senecal, jolted from his sleep, thought the engineers were blasting. He got out of bed and found the air full of strange-looking airplanes with fixed landing gear. Soon they were diving on the big Schofield quadrangles, where most of the men ate and slept. Senecal saw the bright red circles clearly, but still he couldn't quite believe it. Turning to his sergeant, he offered the advice of a true citizen-soldier: "Get someone on the telephone . . ."

Corporal Maurice Herman ran out on his barracks porch and started cranking away at the air raid siren. Down below, the Sunday morning chow lines wound through the quadrangle. It was an incongruous picture— heads raised to view the planes . . . excited discussions . . . questions being yelled to Herman on the porch . . . and every man reluctant to give up his place in the chow line. Then a plane swept by, raking the lines of men. Wild confusion, as the men scattered for their guns and stations.

Bugles began sounding. Corporal Harry Foss thought the old call to arms did more than anything else to pull the men together in the 65th Combat Engineers. Private Frank Gobeo of the 98th Coast Artillery didn't know how to blow call to arms, but he made a brilliant substitution that brought the men swarming from the barracks—he blew pay call.

Supply Sergeant Valentine Lemanski of 27th Infantry rocketed down the stairs of Quadrangle D, found the men in his company had already smashed open the supply room doors. A young private in the 19th Infantry seized a Browning Automatic Rifle (known as a BAR in the Army) and shot off a clip while still in the building. Some men in the 27th Infantry couldn't get guns at all—their sergeant refused to issue the ammunition because a sign said it couldn't be released without orders from the adjutant.

In the radar information center at Fort Shafter, Lieutenant Tyler had heard the first explosions just before his watch ended at eight. He strolled outside and for a moment or so watched what appeared to be "Navy practice at Pearl." Then he heard a few bursts of antiaircraft fire, somewhat closer. He hung around even though his watch was now over, and a few minutes after eight got a call from Sergeant Storry up at the base: "There's an air attack at Wheeler Field." Tyler knew just what to do: he instantly recalled the headset operators.

General Short listened with interest to the bedlam in his quarters nearby. He decided that the Navy must be having some kind of battle practice. The explosions increased, and he wandered out on his *lanai* for a look. There was a lot of smoke to the west, but he couldn't make much out of it. Then Colonel Philips, his chief of staff, burst in at 8:03 with the news—Hickam and Wheeler had just phoned that this was "the real thing."

Pfc. William McCarthy felt the Catholic chapel at Shafter shake and tremble with every explosion. The windows rattled all through mass and the sermon. Right after the sermon a GI ran up to the priest and told him what was happening. Quickly the padre turned to the congregation: "God bless you all, the Japanese are attacking Pearl Harbor. Return to your units at once."

Twelve miles away—across the Koolau Mountains and on the windward side of Oahu—Lieutenant Commander H. P. McCrimmon heard some low-flying planes roar past the dispensary at the Kaneohe Naval Air Station.

Someone in the room mentioned Army maneuvers, and McCrimmon got up to get a better look. Three planes were flying in close formation at about treetop height, shooting tracer bullets. They made three separate passes at the hangars two blocks away, always firing their guns as they approached. Soon black smoke began pouring from one of the buildings. McCrimmon immediately sent an ambulance to the fire in accordance with base regulations.

Another plane flew by, flashing those telltale red circles. This time McCrimmon told his yeoman to "call up Pearl Harbor and ask for some help." The call went through, but Pearl said this was one day they couldn't lend a hand. McCrimmon next called his wife and told her not to pick him up when his duty ended—the place was under attack. Her cheerful reply: "Oh, come on home; all is forgiven."

In the officers' mess a little farther away from the hangars, Attendant Walter Simmons had just finished setting up the tables when the firing began. He had a few minutes to kill and went out to watch the show. After he saw the burning hangar, he darted back in, collared an officer who had just appeared for breakfast, and the pair of them rushed off to the pilots' sleeping quarters— a two-man task force faced with the formidable job of waking up several hundred aviators Sunday morning.

Ensign George Shute burst into Ensign Hubert Reese's room, shouting, "Some damn Army pilot has gone buster —he's diving on BOQ and shooting!" He held out a warm bullet as evidence.

Reese looked out the window, saw the red circles, and joined the little group spreading the alarm. He woke up Ensign Bellinger, who reacted promptly: "Are you guys drunk? Get out and leave me alone!" Now it was Bellinger's turn to look. Then he too was running up and down the halls, banging on doors, spreading the word.

"They is attacking! They is attacking!" shouted a cook, who had joined the group, as he crashed into Ensign Charles Willis' room beating a cake pan with a spoon.

Five pilots crowded into Willis' car and started off for the hangars. Bullets ripped through the roof, the men piled out, then back in again when Willis found that the car still worked. They reached the hangar this time, but just barely. As they got out, another strafer hit the car and this time the gasoline tank went up. It was nothing compared to the blaze they found around them: 33 planes—everything at Kaneohe except the three PBYs on patrol—were burning.

The story was much the same at Ewa Field, the Marine base west of Pearl Harbor. Captain Leonard Ashwell, officer of the day, first sensed something was wrong when he saw two lines of torpedo bombers cruising eastward along the coast toward the Navy base. Unlike almost everybody else in Hawaii, he instantly recognized them. As he ran to sound the alarm, 21 Zeroes barreled in over the Waianae Mountains and began shooting up the base.

Some headed for the planes parked in neat rows; others for the hangars and roadways. One strafer caught Lieutenant Colonel Claude Larkin, base commander, just coming to work in his 1930 Plymouth jalopy. Larkin didn't even turn off the motor—he catapulted out of the car and into a roadside ditch as the plane swept past. Then he scrambled back in and raced for the base about a mile away. He arrived by 8:05, but 33 of his 49 planes were blazing wrecks.

At Waikiki Mrs. Larkin had already put in a big day. She and the colonel had finally found an apartment, and this morning she was moving everything over from the Halekulani Hotel, where they had set up temporary quarters. Other Halekulani guests were enjoying a typical, quiet Sunday morning. Captain J. W. Bunkley of the *California* slipped into his swimming trunks for a prebreakfast dip. Correspondent Joseph Harsch of *The Christian Science Monitor* awoke hearing sounds of explosions in the distance. They immediately reminded him of the air raids they used to have when he was in Berlin the winter before. He woke his wife and told her, "Dar-

ling, you often have asked me what an air raid sounds
like. Listen to this—it's a good imitation."

"Oh, so that's what it sounds like," she replied. Then
they both dozed off to sleep again.

Most of Honolulu was equally uninterested. Author
Blake Clark heard the noise at his home on Punahou
Street, wrote it off as artillery practice. When he came
down to breakfast, he was disturbed only because the
Sunday *Advertiser* hadn't come. He walked down to
Blackshear's drugstore, picked up an early edition, and
came back to enjoy it. When the Japanese cook began
talking about planes outside, he strolled onto the *lanai*
with Mr. and Mrs. Frear, who shared the house. There
were plenty of planes, all right, and Mr. Frear observed
that it was just as well in times like these.

Some civilians couldn't help learning. Jim Duncan,
foreman for a private contractor at Pearl, was taking
flying lessons from Tommy Tommerlin, an inter-island
pilot who gave instruction on the side. This was the day
for Duncan's cross-country check flight, and now they
were cruising leisurely around the island in the Hui Lele
Flying Club's yellow Aeronca.

They had just passed the Mormon Temple near
Kahuku Point when they heard machine-gun fire and
the plane gave a heavy lurch. Then it happened again.
At first Duncan thought some playful Army pilot was
trying to scare him, but he changed his mind as he saw
the red tracers pouring toward him and heard the bullets
chopping into his fuselage. Two planes had come up
from below, firing and passing so close that they tossed
him about in their backwash. Now they turned and were
charging back down on him. As they swerved by, he
saw for the first time the orange-red circles on the wings.
Nothing ever looked bigger.

Duncan dived for the shoreline, hoping to find cover
by hugging the steep hills that came almost down to the
sea. It was a good decision—the Japanese planes circled
once or twice, then flew off to rejoin the armada heading for Pearl. The crippled Aeronca limped down the

coast, over the *pali*, and back to the John Rogers Airport, the civilian field just east of Hickam and Pearl Harbor.

Another amateur pilot, lawyer Roy Vitousek, had almost as much trouble right over John Rogers. He, too, had gone up in an Aeronca for an early-morning spin, taking along his son Martin. They were just getting ready to land again when they saw the first explosion on Ford Island. Some planes were circling nearby, but Vitousek didn't link them to the blast. Now more explosions ripped the harbor . . . then the hangars at Hickam . . . and if he still had any doubt, he knew for certain when he saw some planes flying below him and caught a glimpse of the rising sun.

Two of the planes came after Vitousek, and he gunned the Aeronca out to sea, hoping nobody would go to very much trouble just to get him. He was right—the two Japanese gave him a perfunctory burst and turned to John Rogers instead. At the first break Vitousek himself went into Rogers, landed, and found the place seething with indignation: "Did you see those fools? They must be drunk, practicing with live ammunition!"

For a long time the field tried its best to conduct normal business. When the dispatcher announced the 8:00 A.M. inter-island flight to Maui, the passengers filed through the gate as usual. Among them went Dr. Homer Izumi, a physician from the Kula Sanitarium on Maui, who had been in Honolulu on business. His hosts, Dr. and Mrs. Harold Johnson, saw him off as he boarded the plane, gingerly carrying a box of his favorite cookies. Waving good-by through the cabin window, he noticed somebody running across the field from the Andrew Flying Service hangar. The plane door opened and everyone was ordered out.

Dr. Izumi climbed down and went back to the Johnsons. There had been more strafing—civilian pilot Bob Tyce had been killed—and the Johnsons urged Dr. Izumi to drive home with them. But he guessed it was nothing . . . the plane was sure to leave soon.

Dr. Izumi guessed wrong. The place was soon in chaos—smoke, shrapnel, strafers everywhere. When a big plane droned toward him from the sea, he dived for a palm tree in the middle of the parking circle. His first thought—protect the cookies; his second—if only he had kissed his son Allen good-by the day he left Maui.

CHAPTER VIII

"I Can't Keep Throwing Things at Them"

UP IN THE *Maryland's* FORETOP, Seaman Leslie Vernon
Short had abandoned his hopes of a quiet morning addressing Christmas cards. After a quick double-take on
the planes diving at Ford Island, he loaded the ready
machine gun and hammered away at the first torpedo
planes gliding in from Southeast Loch.

In the destroyer anchorage to the north, Gunner's
Mate Walter Bowe grabbed a .50-caliber machine gun
on the afterdeck of the *Tucker* and fired back too. So
did Seaman Frank Johnson, who was sweeping near
the bridge of the destroyer *Bagley* in the Navy Yard.
Seaman George Sallet watched the slugs from Johnson's
gun tear into a torpedo plane passing alongside, saw
the rear gunner slump in the cockpit, and thought it
was just like in the movies.

Others were firing too—the *Helena* at 1010 dock . . .
the *Tautog* at the sub base . . . the *Raleigh* on the
northwest side of Ford Island. Up in the *Nevada's* "bird
bath," a seaman generally regarded as one of the less
useful members of the crew seized a .30-caliber machine
gun and winged a torpedo plane headed directly for
the ship. It was to be an important reprieve.

Here and there other guns joined in, but at first they
were pitifully few. A "Number 3 condition of readiness"
was in effect—that meant one antiaircraft battery in each
sector—and orders had been given to man additional
guns on the battleships. But whatever the official direc-
tives, the men actually on the ships recall no difference
from any other peacetime Sunday.

On some ships key men were still ashore—five of the battleship captains . . . 50 per cent of the destroyer officers. On others, men were pinned down by strafing, blocked by watertight doors, dazed by the suddenness of it all. Seaman Robert Benton, a sight-setter of a five-inch gun on the *West Virginia*, stood helplessly at his post—the rest of the gun crew never did appear. Yeoman Alfred Horne waited alone so long on the signal bridge of the sub tender *Pelias* that he finally gave up. He started back down the ladder, almost into the arms of the skipper, who thundered, "Where the hell do you think you're going?"

There were more delays once the men reached their stations. First, the canvas awnings that stretched over the decks and guns. On the *Sacramento* Watertender Gilbert Hawkins found himself carefully untying each knot—he just couldn't shake off the peacetime way of doing things. Finally a cook ran up and slashed the lines with a butcher's knife.

Other men struggled to get guns and ammunition. At Ford Island a supply officer took a firm stand: no .30-caliber machine guns without a BuSandA 307 Stub Requisition. On the *Helm* a gunner's mate asked Commander Carroll's permission to get the keys to open the magazine locks. The skipper said, "Damn the keys—cut the locks!"

On the *New Orleans* they used fire axes to smash open the ammunition ready boxes. The *Pennsylvania* locks were knocked off by a gunner's mate who walked around swinging a big hammer—he had been bombed by the Japanese on the gunboat *Panay* in 1937 and announced he wasn't going to be caught again. On the *Monaghan* Boatswain's Mate Thomas Donahue—relieved of all duties to return to the mainland—ran back to his old job as captain of No. 4 gun. While the ammunition locks were being sawed off, Donahue whiled away the time slinging wrenches at low-flying planes. Then somebody called up from the magazine and asked what he needed. "Powder," he called back, "I can't keep throwing things at them."

They took him literally and sent up powder without shells. Nothing daunted, he used a drill shell for his first shot at the enemy—at least it was better than a wrench.

On the afterdeck of the *Detroit*, men banged their three-inch shells against the gun shields to get the protector caps off the fuses, and Aviation Metalsmith George Dorfmeister wondered why the whole ship didn't go up in smoke. On the *Bagley*, a five-inch gun crew trained on a low-flying strafer . . . Seaman George Sallet squeezed the trigger . . . and nothing happened. Somebody on the *Honolulu* just astern yelled and pointed to the barrel—nobody had taken out the tampion, a decorative brass plug that seals the barrel when not in use. Whereupon, the crew on one of the *Honolulu's* after guns forgot their own tampion—but here it didn't seem to matter: the first shot blew it out, and on they fought.

More and more guns were firing now, but ten priceless minutes had passed. At a time like this, they made a life-and-death difference on Battleship Row.

Another plane glided toward the *Nevada*. Again the machine guns in her foretop blazed away. Again the plane wobbled and never pulled out of its turn. The men were wild with excitement as it plowed into the water alongside the dredge pipe just astern. The pilot frantically struggled clear and floated face up past the ship. But this time they got him too late. Marine Private Payton McDaniel watched the torpedo's silver streak as it headed for the port bow. He remembered pictures of torpedoed ships and half expected the *Nevada* to break in two and sink enveloped in flames. It didn't happen that way at all. Just a slight shudder, a brief list to port.

Then she caught a bomb by the starboard antiaircraft director. Ensign Joe Taussig was at his station there, standing in the doorway, when it hit. Suddenly he found his left leg tucked under his arm. Almost absently he said to himself, "That's a hell of a place for a foot to be," and was amazed to hear Boatswain's Mate Allen

Owens, standing beside him, say exactly the same words aloud.

In the plotting room five decks below, Ensign Charles Merdinger at first felt that it was all like the drills he had been through dozens of times. But it began to seem different when he learned through the phone circuit that his roommate Joe Taussig had been hit.

The men on the *Arizona*, forward of the *Nevada*, hardly had time to think. She was inboard of the *Vestal*, but the little repair ship didn't offer much protection—a torpedo struck home almost right away—and nothing could stop the steel that rained down from Fuchida's horizontal bombers now overhead. A big one shattered the boat deck between No. 4 and 6 guns—it came in like a fly ball, and Seaman Russell Lott, standing in the antiaircraft director, had the feeling he could reach out and catch it. Another hit No. 4 turret, scorched and hurled Coxswain James Forbis off a ladder two decks below.

The PA system barked, "Fire on the quarter-deck," and then went off the air for good. Radioman Glenn Lane and three of his shipmates rigged a hose and tried to fight the fire. No water pressure. They rigged phones and tried to call for water. No power. All the time explosions somewhere forward were throwing them off their feet.

Alongside, the *Vestal* seemed to be catching everything that missed the *Arizona*. One bomb went through an open hatch, tore right through the ship, exploding as it passed out the bottom. It flooded the No. 3 hold, and the ship began settling at the stern. A prisoner in the brig howled to be let out, and finally someone shot off the lock with a .45.

Forward of the *Arizona* and *Vestal*, the *Tennessee* so far was holding her own; but the *West Virginia* on the outside was taking a terrible beating. A Japanese torpedo plane headed straight for the casemate where Seaman Robert Benton waited for the rest of his gun crew. He stood there transfixed—wanted to move but couldn't. The torpedo hit directly underneath and sent

Benton and his headphones flying in opposite directions. He got up . . . ran across the deck . . . slipped down the starboard side of the ship to the armor shelf, a ledge formed by the ship's 15-inch steel plates. As he walked aft along the ledge, he glanced up, saw the bombers this time. Caught in the bright morning sun, the falling bombs looked for a fleeting second like snowflakes.

The men below were spared such sights, but the compensation was questionable. Storekeeper Donald Brown tried to get the phones working in the ammunition supply room, third deck forward. The lines were dead. More torpedoes—sickening fumes—steeper list—no lights. Men began screaming in the dark. Someone shouted, "Abandon ship!" and the crowd stampeded to the compartment ladder. Brown figured he would have no chance in this clawing mob, felt his way to the next compartment forward, and found another ladder with no one near it at all. Now he was on the second deck, but not allowed any higher. Nothing left to do, no place else to go—he and a friend brushed a bunch of dirty breakfast dishes off a mess table and sat down to wait the end.

Down in the plotting room—the gunnery nerve center and well below the water line—conditions looked just as hopeless. Torpedoes were slamming into the ship somewhere above. Through an overhead hatch Ensign Victor Delano could see that the third deck was starting to flood. Heavy yellowish smoke began pouring down through the opening. The list grew steeper; tracking board, plotting board, tables, chairs, cots, everything slid across the room and jumbled against the port bulkhead. In the internal communications room next door, circuit breakers were sparking and electrical units ran wild. The men were pale but calm.

Soon oily water began pouring through the exhaust trunks of the ventilation system. Then more yellow smoke. Nothing further could be done, so Delano led his men forward to central station, the ship's damage control center. Before closing the watertight door behind him, he called back to make sure no one was left. From

nowhere six oil-drenched electrician's mates showed up
—they had somehow been hurled through the hatch
from the deck above. Then Warrant Electrician Charles
T. Duvall called to please wait for him. He sounded
in trouble and Delano stepped back into the plotting
room to lend a hand. But he slipped on some oil and
slid across the linoleum floor, bowling over Duvall in
the process. The two men ended in a tangled heap
among the tables and chairs now packed against the
"down" side of the room.

They couldn't get back on their feet; the oil was
everywhere. Even crawling didn't work—they still got
no traction. Finally they grabbed a row of knobs on
the main battery switchboard, which ran all the way
across the room. Painfully they pulled themselves uphill,
hand over hand along the switchboard. By now it was
almost like scaling a cliff.

In central station at last, they found conditions almost as bad. The lights dimmed, went out, came on
again for a while as some auxiliary circuit took hold.
Outside the watertight door on the lower side, the water
began to rise . . . spouting through the cracks around
the edges and shooting like a hose through an air-test
opening. Delano could hear the pleas and cries of the
men trapped on the other side, and he thought with
awe of the decision Lieutenant Commander J. S. Harper,
the damage control officer, had to make: let the men
drown, or open the door and risk the ship as well as
the people now in central station. The door stayed
closed.

Delano suggested to Harper that he and his men
might be more useful topside. For the moment Harper
didn't even have time to answer. He was desperately
trying to keep in touch with the rest of the ship and
direct the counterflooding that might save it, but all
the circuits were dead.

The counterflooding was done anyhow. Lieutenant
Claude V. Ricketts had once been damage control officer
and liked to discuss with other young officers what
should be done in just this kind of situation. More or

less as skull practice, they had worked out a plan among themselves. Now Ricketts began counterflooding on his own hook, helped along by Boatswain's Mate Billingsley, who knew how to work the knobs and valves. The *West Virginia* slowly swung back to starboard and settled into the harbor mud on an even keel.

There was no time for counterflooding on the *Oklahoma*, lying ahead of the *West Virginia* and outboard of the *Maryland*. Lying directly across from Southeast Loch, she got three torpedoes right away, then another two as she heeled to port.

Curiously, many of the men weren't even aware of the torpedoes. Seaman George Murphy only heard the loud-speaker say something about "air attack" and assumed the explosions were bombs. Along with hundreds of other men who had no air defense stations, he now trooped down to the third deck, where he would be protected by the armor plate that covered the deck above. Seaman Stephen Young never thought of torpedoes either, and he was even relieved when the water surged into the port side of No. 4 turret powder handling room. He assumed that someone was finally counterflooding on that side to offset bomb damage to starboard.

The water rose . . . the emergency lights went out . . . the list increased. Now everything was breaking loose. Big 1000-pound shells rumbled across the handling rooms, sweeping men before them. Eight-foot reels of steel towing cable rolled across the second deck, blocking the ladders topside. The door of the drug room swung open, and Seaman Murphy watched hundreds of bottles cascade over a couple of seamen hurrying down a passageway. The boys slipped and rolled through the broken glass, jumped up, and ran on.

On the few remaining ladders, men battled grimly to get to the main deck. It was a regular log jam on the ladder to S Division compartment, just a few steps from open air. Every time something exploded outside, men would surge down the ladder, meeting head-on another crowd that surged up. Soon it was impossible to move in either direction. Seaman Murphy gave up even trying. He stood off to the side—one foot on deck, the other on the corridor wall, the only way he could now keep his footing.

Yeoman L. L. Curry had a better way out. He and some mates were still in the machine shop on third deck amidships when the list reached 60 degrees. Someone spied an exhaust ventilator leading all the way to the deck, and one by one the men crawled up. As they reached fresh air, an officer ran over and tried to shoo them back inside, where they would be safe from bomb splinters. That was the big danger, he explained: a battleship couldn't turn over.

Several hundred yards ahead of the *Oklahoma*—and moored alone at the southern end of Battleship Row —the *California* caught her first torpedo at 8:05. Yeoman Durrell Conner watched it come from his station in the flag communications office. He slammed the port-hole shut as it struck the ship directly beneath him.

Another crashed home farther aft. There might as well have been more—the *California* was wide open. She was due for inspection Monday, and the covers had been taken off six of the manholes leading to her double bottom. A dozen more of these covers had been loosened. The water poured in and surged freely through the ship.

It swept into the ruptured fuel tanks, contaminating the oil, knocking out the power plant right away. It swirled into the forward air compressor station, where Machinist's Mate Robert Scott was trying to feed air to the five-inch guns. The other men cleared out, calling Scott to come with them. He yelled back, "This is my station—I'll stay here and give them air as long as the guns are going." They closed the watertight door and let him have his way.

With the power gone, men desperately tried to do by hand the tasks that were meant for machines. Yeoman Conner joined a long chain of men passing powder and shells up from an ammunition room far below. Stifling fumes from the ruptured fuel tanks made their work harder, and word spread that the ship was under gas attack. At the wounded collecting station in the crew's reception room Pharmacist's Mate William Lynch smashed open lockers in a vain search for morphine. Near the communications office a man knelt in prayer under a ladder. Numb to the chaos around him, another absently sat at a desk typing, "Now is the time for all good men . . ."

Around the harbor nobody noticed the *California's* troubles—all eyes were glued on the *Oklahoma*. From his bungalow on Ford Island, Chief Albert Molter watched her gradually roll over on her side, "slowly and stately . . . as if she were tired and wanted to rest." She kept rolling until her mast and superstructure jammed in the mud, leaving her bottom-up—a huge dead whale lying in the water. Only eight minutes had passed since the first torpedo hit.

On the *Maryland* Electrician's Mate Harold North recalled how everyone had cursed on Friday when the *Oklahoma* tied up alongside, shutting off what air there was at night.

Inside the *Oklahoma* men were giving it one more try. Storekeeper Terry Armstrong found himself alone in a small compartment on the second deck. As it slowly filled with water, he dived down, groped for the porthole, squirmed through to safety. Seaman Malcolm McCleary escaped through a washroom porthole the same way. Nearby, Lieutenant (j.g.) Aloysius Schmitt, the Catholic chaplain, started out too. But a breviary in his hip pocket caught on the coaming. As he backed into the compartment again to take it out, several men started forward. Chaplain Schmitt had no more time to spend on himself. He pushed three, possibly four, of the others through before the water closed over the compartment.

Some men weren't even close to life as they knew it, but were still alive nevertheless. They found themselves gasping, swimming, trying to orient themselves to an upside-down world in the air pockets that formed as the ship rolled over. Seventeen-year-old Seaman Willard Beal fought back the water that poured into the steering engine room. Seaman George Murphy splashed about the operating room of the ship's dispensary . . .

wondering what part of the ship had a tile ceiling . . . never dreaming he was looking up at the floor.

Topside, the men had it easier. As the ship slowly turned turtle, most of the men simply climbed over the starboard side and walked with the roll, finally ending up on the bottom. When and how they got off was pretty much a matter of personal choice. Some started swinging hand over hand along the lines that tied the ship to the *Maryland,* but as she rolled, these snapped, and the men were pitched into the water between the two ships. Seaman Tom Armstrong dived off on this side—his watch stopped at 8:10. Tom's brother Pat jumped off from the outboard side. Their third brother Terry was already in the water after squeezing through the porthole on the second deck. Marine Gunnery Sergeant Leo Wears slid down a line and almost drowned when someone used him as a stepladder to climb into a launch. His friend Sergeant Norman Currier coolly walked along the side of the ship to the bow, hailed a passing boat, and stepped into it without getting a foot wet. Ensign Bill Ingram climbed onto the high side just as the yardarm touched the water. He stripped to his shorts and slid down the bottom of the ship.

As Ingram hit the water, the *Arizona* blew up. Afterward men said a bomb went right down her stack, but later examination showed even the wire screen across the funnel top still intact. It seems more likely the bomb landed alongside the second turret, crashed through the forecastle, and set off the forward magazines.

In any case, a huge ball of fire and smoke mushroomed 500 feet into the air. There wasn't so much noise—most of the men say it was more a "whoom" than a "bang"—but the concussion was terrific. It stalled the motor of Aviation Ordanceman Harand Quisdorf's pickup truck as he drove along Ford Island. It hurled Chief Albert Molter against the pipe banister of his basement stairs. It knocked everyone flat on Fireman Stanley H. Rabe's water barge. It blew Gunner Carey Garnett and dozens of other men off the *Nevada* . . . Commander Cassin Young off the *Vestal* . . . Ensign Vance Fowler

off the *West Virginia*. Far above, Commander Fuchida's
bomber trembled like a leaf. On the fleet landing at
Merry's Point a Navy captain wrung his hands and
sobbed that it just couldn't be true.

On the *Arizona*, hundreds of men were cut down in
a single, searing flash. Inside the port antiaircraft director, one fire control man simply vanished—the only place
he could have gone was through the narrow range-finder
slot. On the bridge Rear Admiral Isaac C. Kidd and
Captain Franklin Van Valkenburgh were instantly killed.
On the second deck the entire ship's band was wiped
out.

Over 1000 men were gone.

Incredibly, some still lived. Major Allen Shapley of
the Marine detachment was blown out of the foremast
and well clear of the ship. Though partly paralyzed,
he swam to Ford Island, detouring to help two shipmates along the way. Radioman Glenn Lane was blown
off the quarter-deck and found himself swimming in
water thick with oil. He looked back at the *Arizona*
and couldn't see a sign of life.

But men were there. On the third deck aft Coxswain
James Forbis felt skinned alive, and the No. 4 turret
handling room was filling with thick smoke. He and his
mates finally moved over to No. 3 turret, where conditions were a little better, but soon smoke began coming
in around the guns there too. The men stripped to their
skivvie drawers and crammed their clothes around the
guns to keep the smoke out. When somebody finally
ordered them out, Forbis took off his newly shined shoes
and carefully carried them in his hands as he left the
turret. The deck was blazing hot and covered with oil.
But there was a dry spot farther aft near No. 4 turret,
and before rejoining the fight, Forbis carefully placed
his shoes there. He lined them neatly with the heels
against the turret—just as though he planned to wear
them up Hotel Street again that night.

In the portside antiaircraft director, Russell Lott
wrapped himself in a blanket and stumbled out the
twisted door. The blanket kept him from getting

scorched, but the deck was so hot he had to keep hopping from one foot to the other. Five shipmates staggered up through the smoke, so he stretched the blanket as a sort of shield for them all. Then he saw the *Vestal* still alongside. The explosion had left her decks a shambles, but he found someone who tossed over a line, and, one by one, all six men inched over to the little repair ship.

At that particular moment they were lucky to find anyone on the *Vestal*. The blast had blown some of the crew overboard, including skipper Cassin Young, and the executive officer told the rest to abandon ship. Seaman Thomas Garzione climbed down a line over the forecastle, came to the end of it, and found himself standing on the anchor. He just froze there—he was a nonswimmer and too scared to jump the rest of the way. Finally he worked up enough nerve, made the sign of the cross, and plunged down holding his nose. For a nonswimmer, he made remarkable time to a whale boat drifting in the debris.

Signalman Adolph Zlabis dived off the bridge and reached a launch hovering nearby. He and a few others yelled encouragement to a young sailor who had climbed out on the *Vestal's* boat boom and now dangled from a rope ladder five feet above the water. Finally the man let go, landed flat in the water with a resounding whack. The men in the launch couldn't help laughing.

Still on board the *Vestal*, Radioman John Murphy watched a long line of men pass his radio room, on their way to abandon ship. One of the other radiomen saw his brother go by. He cried, "I'm going with him," and ran out the door. For no particular reason Murphy decided to stay, but he began feeling that he would like to get back home just once more before he passed on.

At this point Commander Young climbed back on the *Vestal* from his swim in the harbor. He was by no means ready to call it a day. He stood sopping wet at the top of the gangway, shouting down to the swimmers and the men in the boats, "Come back! We're not giving up this ship yet!"

Most of the crew returned and Young gave orders to cast off. Men hacked at the hawsers tying the *Vestal* to the blazing *Arizona*. Inevitably, there was confusion. One officer on the *Arizona's* quarter-deck yelled, "Don't cut those lines." Others on the battleship pitched in and helped. Aviation Mechanic "Turkey" Graham slashed the last line with an ax, shouting, "Get away from here while you can!"

Other help came from an unexpected source. A Navy tug happened by, whose skipper and chief engineer had both put in many years on the *Vestal*. They loyally eased alongside, took a line from the bow, and towed their old ship off toward Aiea landing, where she could safely sit out the rest of the attack.

When the *Arizona* blew up, Chief Electrician's Mate Harold North on the *Maryland* thought the end of the world had come. Actually he was lucky. Moored inboard of the *Oklahoma*, the *Maryland* was safe from torpedoes and caught only two bombs. One was a 15-inch armor-piercing shell fitted with fins—it slanted down just off the port bow, smashing into her hull 17 feet below the water line. The other hit the forecastle, setting the awnings on fire. When a strafer swept by, Chief George Haitle watched the firefighters scoot for shelter. One man threw his extinguisher down a hatch, where it exploded at the feet of an old petty officer, who grabbed for a mask, shouting, "Gas!"

The *Tennessee*, the other inboard battleship, had more trouble. Seaman J. P. Burkholder looked out a porthole on the bridge just as one of the converted 16-inch shells crashed down on No. 2 turret a few feet forward. The porthole cover tore loose, clobbered him on the head, and sent him scurrying through the door. Outside he helped a wounded ensign, but couldn't help one of his closest friends, who was so far gone he only wanted Burkholder to shoot him.

Another armor-piercing bomb burst through No. 3 turret farther aft. Seaman S. F. Bowen, stationed there as a powder carman, was just dogging the hatch when the bomb hit. It wasn't a shattering crash at all. Just a ball of fire, about the size of a basketball, appeared overhead and seemed to melt down on everyone. It seemed to run down on his skin and there was no way to stop it. As he crawled down to the deck below, he noticed that his shoe strings were still on fire.

Splinters flew in all directions from the bombs that hit the *Tennessee*. One hunk ripped the bridge of the *West Virginia* alongside, cut down Captain Mervyn Bennion as he tried to direct his ship's defense. He slumped across the sill of the signal bridge door on the starboard side of the machine-gun platform. Soon after he fell, Ensign Delano arrived on the bridge, having finally been sent up from central station. As Delano stepped out onto the platform, Lieutenant (j.g.) F. H. White rushed by, told him about the captain, and asked him to do what he could.

Delano saw right away it was hopeless. Captain Bennion had been hit in the stomach, and it took no medical training to know the wound was fatal. Yet he was perfectly conscious, and at least he might be made more comfortable. Delano opened a first-aid kit and looked for some morphine. No luck. Then he found a can of ether and tried to make the captain pass out. He sat down beside the dying man, holding his head in one hand and the ether in the other. It made the captain drowsy but never unconscious. Occasionally Delano moved the captain's legs to more comfortable positions, but there was so little he could do.

As they sat there together, Captain Bennion prodded him with questions. He asked how the battle was going, what the *West Virginia* was doing, whether the ship and the men were badly hit. Delano did his best to answer, resorting every now and then to a gentle white lie. Yes, he assured the captain, the ship's guns were still firing.

Lieutenant Ricketts now turned up and proved a pillar of strength. Other men arrived too—Chief Pharmacist's Mate Leak . . . Ensign Jacoby from the flag radio room . . . Lieutenant Commander Doir Johnson from the forecastle. On his way up, Johnson ran across big Doris

Miller, thought the powerful mess steward might come in handy, brought him along to the bridge. Together they tenderly lifted Captain Bennion and carried him to a sheltered spot behind the conning tower. He was still quite conscious and well aware of the flames creeping closer. He kept telling the men to leave him and save themselves.

In her house at Makalapa, Mrs. Mayfield still couldn't grasp what had happened. She walked numbly to a window and looked at Admiral Kimmel's house across the street. The Venetian blinds were closed, and there was no sign of activity. Somehow this was reassuring . . . surely there would be some sign of life if it was really true. It didn't occur to her that this might be one morning when the admiral had no time for Venetian blinds.

By now Captain Mayfield was in his uniform. He took a few swallows of coffee, slopping most of it in the saucer, and dashed for the carport. He roared off as the CINCPAC official car screeched up to the admiral's house across the street. Admiral Kimmel ran down the steps and jumped in, knotting his tie on the way. Captain Freeland Daubin, commanding a squadron of submarines, leaped on the running board as the car moved off, and Captain Earle's station wagon shot down the hill after them.

In five minutes Admiral Kimmel was at CINCPAC Headquarters in the sub base. The admiral thought he was there by 8:05; Commander Murphy thought it was more like 8:10. In either case, within a very few minutes of his arrival, the backbone of his fleet was gone or immobile—*Arizona*, *Oklahoma*, and *West Virginia* sunk . . . *California* sinking . . . *Maryland* and *Tennessee* bottled up by the wrecked battleships alongside . . . *Pennsylvania* squatting in drydock. Only the *Nevada* was left, and she seemed a forlorn hope with one torpedo and two bombs already in her.

Nor was the picture much brighter elsewhere. On the other side of Ford Island the target ship *Utah* took a heavy list to port as her engineering officer, Lieutenant

Commander S. S. Isquith, pulled his khakis over his pajamas. The alarm bell clanged a few strokes and stopped; the men trooped below to take shelter from bombing. Isquith sensed the ship couldn't last, and he had the officer of the deck order all hands topside instead.

The men were amazingly cool—perhaps because they were used to being "bombed" by the Army and Navy every day. When Machinist's Mate David Gilmartin reached the main deck, he found the port rail already under water. Twice he crawled up toward the starboard side and slid back. As he did it a third time, he slid by another seaman who suggested he throw away the cigarettes. To Gilmartin's amazement he had been trying to climb up the slanting deck while holding a carton of cigarettes in one hand. Relieved of his handicap, he made the starboard rail easily.

As the list increased, the big six-by-twelve-inch timbers that covered the *Utah's* decks began breaking loose. These timbers were used to cushion the decks against practice bombing and undoubtedly helped fool the Japanese into thinking the ship was a carrier unexpectedly in port. Now they played another lethal role, sliding down on the men trying to climb up.

As she rolled still further, Commander Isquith made a last check below to find anyone who might still be trapped—and almost got trapped himself. He managed to reach the captain's cabin where a door led to the forecastle deck. The timbers had jammed the door; so he stumbled into the captain's bedroom where he knew there was a porthole. It was now almost directly overhead, but he managed to reach it by climbing on the captain's bed. As he popped his head through the porthole, the bed broke loose and slid out from under him. He fell back, but the radio officer, Lieutenant Commander L. Winser, grabbed his hand just in time and pulled him through. As Isquith got to his feet, he slipped and bumped down the side of the ship into the water. Half dead with exhaustion, harassed by strafers, he was helped by his crew to Ford Island.

Others never left the ship—Fireman John Vaessen in the dynamo room, who kept the power up to the end; Chief Watertender Peter Tomich in the boiler room, who stayed behind to make sure his men got out; Lieutenant (j.g.) John Black, the assistant engineer, who jammed his foot in his cabin door; Mess Attendant Smith, who was always so afraid of the water.

Of the other ships on this side of Ford Island, the *Tangier* and *Detroit* were still untouched, but the *Raleigh* sagged heavily to port. Water swirled into No. 1 and 2 firerooms, flooded the forward engine room, contaminated the fuel oil, knocked out her power. In the struggle to keep her afloat, no one even had time to dress. As though they went around that way every day, Captain Simons sported his blue pajamas . . . Ensign John Beardall worked the port antiaircraft guns in red pajamas . . . others toiled in a weird assortment of skivvies, *aloha* shirts, and bathing trunks. Somehow they didn't seem even odd: as Signalman Jack Foeppel watched Captain Simons in the admiral's wing on the bridge, he only marveled that any man could be so calm.

Ford Island, where all these ships were moored, was itself in chaos. Japanese strafers were now working the place over, and most of the men were trying to make themselves as small as possible. Storekeeper Jack Rogovsky crouched under a mess hall table nibbling raisins. The men in the air photo laboratory dived under the steel developing tables. Some of the flight crews plunged into an eight-foot ditch that was being dug for gas lines along the edge of the runway. This is where Ordnanceman Quisdorf's unit was hiding when he and another airman arrived in the squadron truck. But they didn't know that—they thought they had been left behind in a general retreat. They decided their only hope was to find a pair of rifles, swim the north channel, and hole up in the hills until liberation.

Nor was there much room for optimism in the Navy Yard. On the ships at the finger piers, the stern gunners had a perfect shot at the torpedo planes gliding down

Southeast Loch, but most of them had little to shoot with. The *San Francisco* was being overhauled; all her guns were in the shops; most of her large ammunition was on shore. The repair ship *Rigel* was in the same fix. The *St. Louis* was on "limited availability" while radar was being installed; her topside was littered with scaffolding and cable reels; three of her four five-inch antiaircraft guns were dismantled.

The little *Sacramento* had just come out of drydock, and in line with drydock regulations most of her ammunition lockers had been emptied. The *Swan* plugged away with her two three-inch guns, but a new gun earmarked for her top deck was still missing. A pharmacist's mate stood on the empty emplacement, cursing helplessly. The other ships were having less trouble, although there was little power on the *New Orleans*, and to Seaman L. A. Morley on the *Honolulu* just about everything seemed "secured for the week end."

On all these ships the men had more time for reflection than their mates along Battleship Row. On the *New Orleans* the ship's gambler and "big operator" sat at his station, reading the New Testament. (Later he canceled his debts and loans; threw away his dice.) A young engineer on the *San Francisco*—with nothing to do because her boilers were dismantled—appeared topside, wistfully told Ensign John E. Parrott, "Thought I'd come up and die with you." Machinist's Mate Henry Johnson on the *Rigel* remarked that now he knew how a rabbit felt and he'd never hunt one again. A few minutes later he lay mortally wounded on the deck.

Their very helplessness turned many of the men from fear to fury. Commander Duncan Curry, strictly an old Navy type, stood on the bridge of the *Ramapo* firing a .45 pistol as the tears streamed down his face. On the *New Orleans* a veteran master at arms fired away with another .45, daring them to come back and fight. A man stood near the sub base, banging away with a double-barreled shotgun.

A young Marine on 1010 dock used his rifle on the planes, while a Japanese-American boy about seven years old lit a cigarette for him. The butt of his cigarette was burning his lips, but he never even noticed it. As he fired away, he remarked aloud, "If my mother could see me now."

Ten-ten dock itself was a mess, littered with debris from the *Helena* and *Oglala* alongside. In the after engine room of the torpedoed *Helena*, Chief Machinist's Mate Paul Weisenberger fought to check the water that poured aft through the ship's drain system. The hit had also set off the ship's gas alarm; its steady blast added to the uproar. Marine Second Lieutenant Bernard Kelly struggled to get ammunition to the guns. In keeping a steady supply flowing, it was a tossup whether he had more trouble with the damage or with conscientious damage control men, who kept shutting the doors.

Topside was a shambles. The *Helena's* forecastle, which had been rigged for church, looked as if a cyclone had passed. The *Oglala*, to starboard, listed heavily; her signal flags drooped over the *Helena's* bridge. Across the channel, Battleship Row was a mass of flames and smoke. Above the whole scene, a beautiful rainbow arched over Ford Island.

Just below 1010 dock, the *Pennsylvania* and destroyers *Cassin* and *Downes* sat ominously unmolested in Drydock No. 1. Likewise the destroyer *Shaw* in the floating drydock, which was a few hundred yards to the west. Aboard the *Pennsylvania* the men waited tensely. Lieutenant Commander James Craig, the ship's first lieutenant, checked here and there, making sure they would be ready when the blow came—or at least ready as a ship out of water could be. He told Boatswain's Mate Robert Jones and his damage control party to lie face down on the deck. He warned them that their work was cut out, and to be prepared for the worst.

On deck, the gunners were getting in a few licks in advance. For Gunner's Mate Alvin Gerth, captain of one antiaircraft gun crew, it was already hard, dangerous work. The electrical system had gone haywire, and he could fire by percussion only. On top of that, the ammunition was so old, he had a lot of misfires. Normally he could throw them over the side, but the ship was in drydock, so that was out of the question, He piled them on deck behind the mount, gradually transferring the area into a little arsenal wide open to the sky. Not very safe to do, but he figured his time was up anyhow.

It was much the same on the ships anchored in the harbor. Radioman Leonard Stagich sat by his set on the destroyer *Montgomery* writing prayers on a little pad. In the transmitter room of the aircraft tender *Curtiss*, Radioman James Raines sat with three other men listening to the steady booming outside. No orders, so they just waited. With the doors and portholes dogged down and the ventilators off, it grew hotter and hotter. They removed their shirts and took turns wearing the heavy headphones. Still no orders. They kept moving about the room, squatting in different places, always wondering what was going on outside. From time to time the PA system squawked meaningless commands to others on the ship, which only made them wonder more. Still no orders.

But the most exasperating thing to those at anchor was just sitting there. It took time to build up enough steam to move—an hour for a destroyer, two hours for a larger ship. Meanwhile, they could only fire their guns manually, dodge the strafers, and watch (to use their favorite phrase) "all hell break loose."

The destroyer *Monaghan* had a slight edge on the others. As the ready-duty destroyer, her fires were already lit; and then of course she had been getting up steam since 7:50 to go out and contact the *Ward*. Commander Bill Burford would be able to take her out in a few minutes now, but at a time like this, that seemed forever.

At the moment the destroyer *Helm* was still the only ship under way. Twenty minutes had passed since Quartermaster Frank Handler genially waved at that aviator flying low up the channel. After the first explosion Commander Carroll quickly sounded general quarters . . . swung her around from West Loch . . . caught Admiral Furlong's sortie signal . . . and was now ready to get up and go. Turning to Handler, he said, "Take her out. I'll direct the battery."

Handler had never taken the ship out alone. The channel was tricky—speed limit 14 knots—and the job was always left to the most experienced hands. He took the wheel and rang the engine room to step her up to 400 rpm. The engine room queried the order and he repeated it. The ship leaped forward and raced down the channel at 27 knots. To complicate matters, there wasn't a single compass on board; everything had to be done by seaman eye. But Handler had one break in his favor—the torpedo net was still wide open. So the *Helm* rushed on, proudly guided by a novice without a compass breaking every speed law in the book.

By this time Handler was game for anything; so he took it in his stride when at 8:17 he came face to face with a Japanese midget sub. He saw it as the *Helm* burst out of the harbor entrance—first the periscope, then the conning tower. It lay about 1000 yards off the starboard bow, bouncing up and down on the coral near the buoys. The *Helm's* guns roared, but somehow they never could hit the sub. Finally it slid off the coral and disappeared. The *Helm* flashed the news to headquarters: "Small Jap sub trying to penetrate channel."

Signal flags fluttered up all over Pearl Harbor, telling the ships of the fleet. From the bridge of the burning *West Virginia*, Ensign Delano read the warning and sighed to himself, "Oh, my God—that too!"

As the *Helm* began patrolling off the harbor entrance, Quartermaster Handler noticed several big Army bombers circling Hickam Field, trying to land. Japanese planes nipped at them from all sides—Handler could see the bullets ripping off big chunks of metal—but the pilots went about their business as though it happened every day.

The B-17s were coming in from the mainland—12 planes in the 38th and 88th Reconnaissance Squadrons under Major Truman Landon. It was a long flight for those days—14 hours' flying time. To save gas, the planes were flying separately instead of in formation. They also were stripped down—no armor or ammunition, their guns in cosmoline.

Even so, some of the B-17s barely made Oahu. On Lieutenant Karl Barthelmes' plane one of the crew accidentally flicked a switch, which threw the plane north of its course, and by the time they figured out why, the gas needle wobbled at zero. Barthelmes turned hard south, and as he approached Oahu around 8:00 A.M., he was suddenly overtaken by 12 to 15 light planes marked with large red circles. They flew above, under, and alongside the B-17, apparently escorting the big plane in. The bomber's crew sighed with relief, removed the lifebelts they had put on while the plane was off course. They waved their thanks, but the pilots of the other planes were apparently too preoccupied to respond.

About the same time Major Landon was also flying in from the north. He had let one of his crew practice navigation most of the way, and they were heading west 150 miles north of Oahu when Landon finally took over. As he turned southward and approached the island, a flight of nine planes came straight at him, flying north. For an instant he too thought it was a reception committee. Then a burst of gun-fire, a quick glimpse of the red circles told him the truth. He pulled up into the clouds and shook off any pursuit.

Most of the B-17s had no advance notice, Major Richard Carmichael flew in over Diamond Head, pointing out the sights to his West Point classmate Colonel Twaddell, the weather officer. As they passed along Waikiki Beach, they could see the smoke over Pearl, but assumed the Navy was practicing. Other pilots saw the smoke too—Lieutenant Bruce Allen thought there was an unusual amount of cane burning . . . Lieutenant Robert Ramsey thought it was some sort of big celebration.

They drew closer, and the devastation spread below them. Sergeant Albert Brawley gazed at the blazing rows of planes at Hickam and wondered whether some hot fighter pilot had crashed, setting them all on fire. Lieutenant Charles Bergdoll still thought it was a drill, complete with smoke pots and mock bombing, until he saw the remains of a smashed B-24 burning beside the runway. He knew the Army would never wreck anything so expensive.

Now the planes were asking for landing instructions from the tower. A calm, flat voice gave wind direction, velocity, the runway on which to land, as though it were any other day. Occasionally the voice observed without emotion that the field was under attack by "unidentified planes."

Lieutenant Allen was the first to land. Then came Captain Raymond Swenson's plane. As it circled in, a Japanese bullet exploded some magnesium flares in the radio compartment, which set the whole plane on fire. It bounced down heavily . . . the blazing tail section broke off . . . and the forward half skidded to a stop. Lieutenant Ernest Reid, the copilot, reacted to habit and set the parking brakes as usual. The crew all reached shelter except Flight Surgeon William Schick. A Zero riddled him as he ran down the runway.

Now it was Major Landon's turn to come in. The same nasal voice in the tower told him to "land from west to east." and added laconically that there were three Japanese planes on his tail. With this encouraging news he came on in, landing safely at 8:20.

As the planes rolled to a stop, the men jumped out and raced for the boondocks on the Honolulu side of the field. Sergeant Brawley lay in the keawa bushes, listening uneasily as the bullets thudded around him. Lieutenant George Newton picked a swamp, Lieutenant Ramsey a drainage ditch. Lieutenant Allen tried to disappear into grass three inches high. Lieutenant Homer Taylor ran the opposite way, winding up in some officer's house under a couple of overturned sofas. The officer's wife and children huddled there too, and every time a Japanese plane roared by, a small boy tried to get out from under the sofa and look outside. He would nearly get to the end of the sofa, then Taylor would grab an ankle and drag him back just in time. This duel continued until the end of the raid.

Taylor had the right idea—nothing was immune. Even the Snake Ranch, the new beer garden for enlisted men, exploded in a shower of glass and lumber. The only thing saved was a recording of "San Antonio Rose"— when the place was later rebuilt, it was the only record the old-timers allowed.

The base fire department was now in action, but no firemen ever operated under greater handicaps. Bombs blasted the water mains, then the fire house itself. As Hoseman Howard King manned one of the engines, his crew chief, Joe Clagnon, suddenly yelled to look out. Before King could move, there was a blinding flash and something that felt like a ton of bricks. Lying in the smoke, he saw dimly the twisted engine, Clagnon dying, his own leg shattered. He begged a passing GI to put a tourniquet around his leg; the man said dazedly that he was sorry but he didn't have a handkerchief.

Through it all Fire Chief William Benedict calmly directed his men, munching an apple. Soon he was hit but the wound was minor. Then he was hit worse, but he got up again and continued supervising the work. The third time he stayed down, but as they carried him away badly injured, he was still munching the apple.

Some of the casualties were needless. One first sergeant, in a well-meaning attempt to organize his unit, lined them up on the edge of the parade rounds just outside the big barracks. The target was too inviting to miss—a couple of Zeroes peeled off and strafed the men.

Perhaps it didn't make much difference—the strafers seemed just as interested in individuals. One Zero caught a lineman up a telegraph pole. He yanked out his spurs and slid down the pole, as the wood splintered around him. Another strafer stitched up Hangar Avenue, sawed right through the cab of a swerving truck. Searching out targets, the planes swooped unbelievably low. Completely absorbed in his work, one pilot forgot about flying. As he skimmed along the parking ramp, his propeller tips flecked the asphalt . . . his belly tank scraped off and went scooting down the ramp. He finally pulled up—hitting the hills beyond the field, according to one man . . . crashing into the sea, according to another . . . getting away with it completely, according to a third.

It's a wonder anybody noticed. The dive bombers were concentrating on the hangars, and most men were trying to get out of the area. A pack of men headed across the ball field for the post school building. A strafer caught up with them as they crossed the diamond—Private J. H. Thompson got two bullet holes in his canteen, one of his buddies in the bill of his cap, and others got off far worse. Corporal John Sherwood joined 200 others in a wild dash from the big barracks, which were perilously close to the hangars. They headed across the parade grounds for the post exchange, encouraged along by the inevitable Zero. Sherwood, a compact little man, was clad only in undershorts and must have been a spectacular figure. His sergeant, Wilbur Hunt, still recalls how he paused in his work and wondered how anybody that short could run that fast. Today Sherwood denies he ran, but says he passed at least a hundred who did.

From the shelter of the PX, Corporal Sherwood watched a master sergeant pedal furiously by on a bicycle. Head down, feet pumping hard, all the time shooting a .45 pistol in the air, he seemed curiously like a cowboy in a Wild West movie. Perhaps there was something of that spirit in the air, for out in the open near the married men's quarters a group of small children were leaping up and down shrieking, "Here come the Indians!"

Gradually, fear and panic gave way to anger. A wounded man outside Hangar 15 kept shaking his fist at the sky in helpless rage. Sergeant George Geiger was bitterly mad, searched for a gun—any gun. He found one in the barracks supply room, but there was no ammunition. Then he heard there was a supply of arms at the main gate. When he got there, everything was gone excet a .45 pistol holster. He took it, later gave it to a man who had a pistol but no holster.

Guns began to appear. Sergeant Stanley McLeod stood on the parade ground, hammering away with a Thompson submachine gun . . . Staff Sergeant Doyle

King fired another from under a panel truck . . . Technical Sergeant Wilbur Hunt set up 12 .50-caliber machine guns in fresh bomb craters near the barracks. His gunners turned up from an unexpected source. A bomb had blown off a corner of the guardhouse, releasing everybody. The prisoners dashed over to Hunt and said they were ready to go to work. It was just as he thought —the ones who are always in trouble are the ones you want with you when the going gets tough. He put them on the guns right away.

Wheeler had its guardhouse heroes too. All the prisoners were turned loose, and two of them helped man a machine gun on the roof. At the main barracks men broke down the supply room doors, and three guns were firing from the narrow back porch. Somebody had set up another out in the open, toward the main road. Pfc. Arthur Fusco helped set one up in front of a hangar, but by now all the smoke made it useless. At one point he took cover in the hangar office, and was surprised to hear the phone ringing. He automatically picked up the receiver. A post wife was on the other end, asking what all the noise was about.

Most of the men had no idea what to do or where to go. Staff Sergeant Francis Clossen, like the men at Hickam, was at least sure the hangar line was a poor choice. He ran toward the road, fell down, limped on. Then a solicitous chaplain stopped him, thinking he was wounded. That out of the way, he climbed a fence . . . lost his shoes . . . and lunged into some keawa bushes. At least a dozen others had reached the patch before him.

Pfc. Carroll Andrews was one man with a definite objective. A sergeant told him to hit for Schofield. He and a buddy started off through the noncom housing area, running in short spurts between the strafing. Once they ducked into the kitchen of an empty house. Bullets ripped the stove, and they marveled at the splintered porcelain—it was the first time they realized how the stuff could shatter.

On they ran, and then another interruption. This time

it was a soldier who had seen Andrews playing the organ for Catholic services. He asked Andrews to help him say the Catholic's Act of Contrition. He explained he hadn't been to mass or confession for years and needed to make an emergency peace. Andrews stopped and repeated the words with him.

They dashed on. Soon a Filipino woman ran up with a tiny baby. She too had seen Andrews in Church, wanted him to baptize the baby. By now mildly exasperated, Andrews asked her why she didn't do it herself. She said she wasn't sure how. So he went in another empty house, tried the kitchen faucets (they didn't run), found a bottle of cold water, and baptized the baby. The mother burst into tears and ran off.

They finally reached Schofield about 8:30. At this point it was an odd place to go for protection. The planes were gone now—they were finished with this whole area by 8:17—but the post was in enormous confusion. The various antiaircraft units were trying to get going to their assigned positions, but there were often difficulties. The men in Battery B, 98th Coast Artillery, couldn't get trucks to tow their guns to Wheeler Field until the raid was all over. When they were issued machine-gun ammunition, they found it was 1918 stuff— so old the belts came to pieces in the loading machine. With the Japanese likely to return any minute, Private Lester Buckley—back safely from his compost heap— opened the gates of the corral, so that at least his mules would have a chance.

At Wahiawa, a small town next to Wheeler and Schofield, Mr. and Mrs. Paul Young listened to the explosions nearby. The Youngs were Koreans and ran a small laundry in a shed attached to their house. They had just put in a big night at mah-jongg, and Mr. Young was all for staying in bed. But Mrs. Young was curious and finally walked down to the Wheeler gate to find out what was going on. The sentry had a quick answer: "Get back home. Don't you know there's a war on?"

Mrs. Young ran back, calling out the news. Mr. Young and his brother, Sung do Kim, then got up and

came down to watch the show. Suddenly they saw a
plane flying up the road from Pearl Harbor, looking
for something to strafe. Mrs. Young sensed trouble,
and they all took cover, except for their old Chinese
hired man. He stayed outside, nonchalantly rolling some
Bull Durham. The plane got him before he could finish
making the cigarette.

They ran out and dragged the old man in. Mrs. Young
scolded him like a naughty child, asked him why he
didn't come inside with them. He replied he couldn't
talk because it hurt so much.

Now a dogfight began. Stray bullets whined about the
house—one smashed a window; another nicked the wash-
ing machine; another bored a hole through the door
where Mrs. Young was peeking out. The family,
crouched under the ironing table, caught occasional
glimpses of the planes through the skylight. Suddenly
there was an ear-splitting roar. A Japanese plane sheared
off the top of the eucalyptus tree in their yard, crashed
in a pineapple field just beyond. The American fighter
that shot it down disappeared off toward the mountains.
Mrs. Young, of course, couldn't know it, but Lieutenants
Welch and Taylor had reached Haleiwa, taken off in
their P-40s, and were now in business.

At Haleiwa, eight miles away, there was now plenty
of other action. Two B-17s had lumbered up from the
south and were circling above. Captain Chaffin and
Major Carmichael had given up trying to land in the
shambles at Hickam. After rejecting Wheeler and Ewa
for the same reasons, they finally decided on Haleiwa,
which the Japanese apparently didn't know about. The
little strip was only 1200 feet long—certainly not inviting—but they were almost out of gas and there was no
other choice. Down they came, somewhat surprisingly,
to perfect landings.

They taxied as close as they could to a clump of trees,
but they were already too late. A Zero had seen them
land and came over to investigate. Somebody yelled a
warning, and Major Carmichael and his classmate,
Colonel Twaddell, dived under a big rock on the beach.

A
Portfolio
OF
Maps
AND
Photographs

MAPS:

> *Pearl Harbor with the locations of the U.S. warships bombed by the Japanese on December 7, 1941. Route of Japanese attack force.*

PHOTOGRAPHS:

> *Navy and Army photographs taken in action, as well as some revealing pictures captured from the Japanese. This portfolio recounts, briefly and pictorially, the attack on Pearl Harbor from start to finish.*

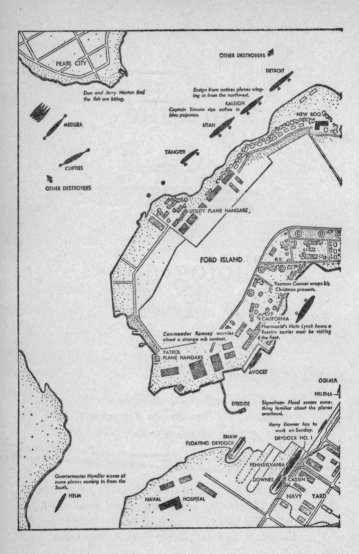

PEARL CITY

Don and Jerry Morton find the fish are biting.

OTHER DESTROYERS

DETROIT

Ensign Korn notices planes winging in from the northwest.

RALEIGH

Captain Simons sips coffee in blue pajamas.

UTAH

NEW ORL

MEDUSA

TANGIER

CURTISS

OTHER DESTROYERS

UTILITY PLANE HANGARS

FORD ISLAND

Yeoman Conner wraps his Christmas presents.

CALIFORNIA

Pharmacist's Mate Lynch hears a Russian carrier must be visiting the fleet.

Commander Ramsey worries about a strange sub contact.

PATROL PLANE HANGARS

AVOCET

OGLALA

HELENA

DREDGE

Signalman Flood senses something familiar about the planes overhead.

Harry Danner has to work on Sunday.

SHAW

FLOATING DRYDOCK

DRYDOCK NO. 1

PENNSYLVANIA

DOWNES   CASSIN

Quartermaster Handler waves at some planes coming in from the South.

HELM

NAVAL   HOSPITAL

NAVY YARD

114

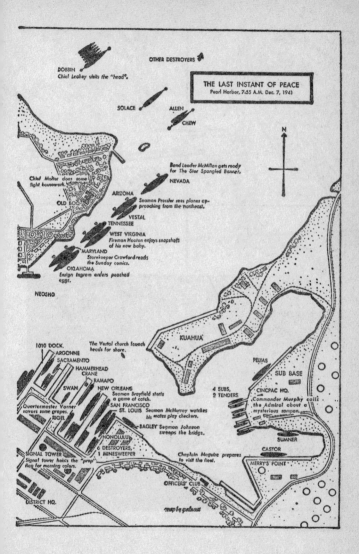

THE LAST INSTANT OF PEACE
Pearl Harbor, 7:55 A.M. Dec. 7, 1941

OTHER DESTROYERS

DOBBIN
Chief Leahy visits the "head".

SOLACE
ALLEN
CHEW

N

Band Leader McMillan gets ready
for The Star Spangled Banner.

Chief Molter does some
light housework.

NEVADA

ARIZONA
Seaman Prosser sees planes approaching from the northeast.

OLD BOO
VESTAL
TENNESSEE
WEST VIRGINIA
Fireman Hooton enjoys snapshots
of his new baby.

MARYLAND
Storekeeper Crawford reads
the Sunday comics.
OKLAHOMA
Ensign Ingram orders poached
eggs.

NEOSHO

KUAHUA

1010 DOCK.
ARGONNE
SACRAMENTO
HAMMERHEAD
CRANE
RAMAPO
SWAN
NEW ORLEANS
Seaman Brayfield starts
a game of catch.
SAN FRANCISCO
ST. LOUIS Seaman McMurray watches
his mates play checkers.
BAGLEY Seaman Johnson
sweeps the bridge.
HONOLULU
6 DESTROYERS,
1 MINESWEEPER

The Vestal church launch
heads for shore.

Quartermaster Varner
savors some grapes.
RIGEL

SIGNAL TOWER
Signal tower hoists the "prep"
flag for morning colors.

DISTRICT HQ.

PELIAS
SUB BASE

4 SUBS,
2 TENDERS
CINCPAC HQ.
Commander Murphy calls
the Admiral about a
mysterious sampan.

SUMNER
CASTOR

Chaplain Maguire prepares
to visit the fleet.

MERRY'S POINT

OFFICERS' CLUB

map by galand

115

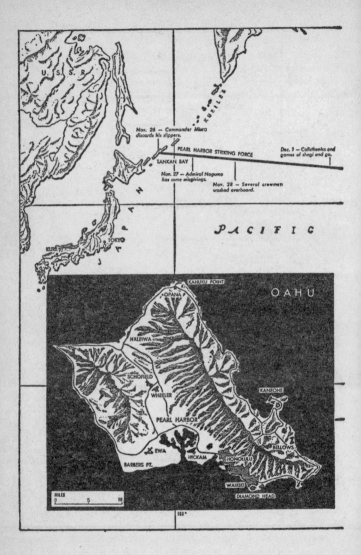

Nov. 26 — Commander Miura
discards his slippers.

TANKAN BAY

PEARL HARBOR STRIKING FORCE

Dec. 1 — Calisthenics and
games of shogi and go.

Nov. 27 — Admiral Nagumo
has some misgivings.

Nov. 28 — Several crewmen
washed overboard.

U. S. S. R

KURILES

PACIFIC

KURE

TOKYO

JAPAN

OAHU

KAHUKU POINT

OPANA

HALEIWA

SCHOFIELD

WHEELER

KANEOHE

PEARL HARBOR

EWA

HICKAM

BELLOWS

BARBERS PT.

HONOLULU

WAIKIKI

DIAMOND HEAD

MILES
0   5   10

158°

116

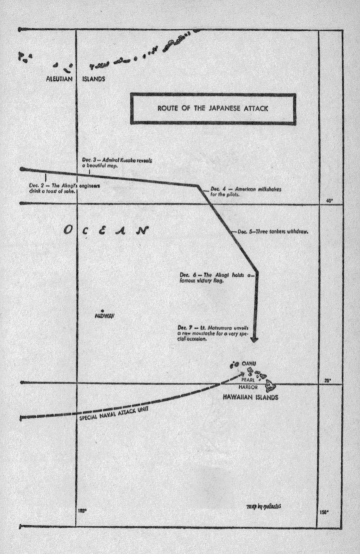

ROUTE OF THE JAPANESE ATTACK

ALEUTIAN ISLANDS

Dec. 3 — Admiral Kuaoka reveals a beautiful map.

Dec. 2 — The Akagi's engineers drink a toast of sake.

Dec. 4 — American milkshakes for the pilots.

O C E A N

Dec. 5 — Three tankers withdraw.

Dec. 6 — The Akagi hoists a famous victory flag.

MIDWAY

Dec. 7 — Lt. Matsumura unveils a new moustache for a very special occasion.

OAHU

PEARL HARBOR

HAWAIIAN ISLANDS

SPECIAL NAVAL ATTACK UNIT

map by pelacioi

40°

20°

180°

150°

117

The Zero was probably low in ammunition—he gave Haleiwa a perfunctory burst and flew off. But a Pacific comber took care of Carmichael and his friend. It rolled in, completely drenching them. It even ruined Carmichael's watch.

At Kaneohe on the windward side, a strafing Japanese plane cost Ordnanceman Homer Bisbee his watch too, but much more indirectly. As he dived for cover off the seaplane ramp, he noticed he was swimming with his good watch on. At first he held his arm up out of the water; next, he put the watch in his white cap and laid it on the ramp. When he came out from under a few minutes later, the cap was still there, but the watch was missing.

Almost anything could have happened to it—the ramp was an inferno. Again and again the dive bombers strafed the 26 PBYs lined up in neat rows, the four others moored in the bay. Several small boats servicing the planes at anchor were riddled too, and one man had to swim all the way across Kaneohe Bay to reach safety. Only one gun was firing back—Chief Aviation Ordnanceman John Finn had mounted a machine gun on an instruction stand far out on the ramp. He hammered away at the strafers in a shower of blazing gasoline from the planes parked around him. A bullet clipped him in the heel, but he kept on firing.

The pilots and flight crews struggled to salvage what was left. Ensign C. S. Malwein got a tractor, and with two other men struggled to save a plane that wasn't burning yet. A Japanese fighter swooped down to stop them, and the wing fabric was soon a mass of flames.

Another Zero cut down Aviation Machinist's Mate Robert Ballou as he ran out on the ramp with a rifle. Two of his buddies put him on a cot and set off for a truck being used as an ambulance. They were spotted right away. Flat on his back, Ballou watched the tracer bullets smoke by; he found it especially disconcerting when he realized the men had set the cot down and were running for cover. He jumped up and outran them both.

About 8:15 A.M. the planes flew off to the north. The

quiet was anything but restful. So far there had been no
bombing, and everyone sensed that this was what would
happen next. Sure enough, around 8:30—Ensign Reese
remembered glancing at his watch—nine horizontal
bombers appeared, flying in close formation. Dirt, metal,
cement, glass flew in all directions as they dropped their
load. Then another formation appeared but saved their
bombs perhaps for a better target—Kaneohe's two new
hangars were wrecked by now.

All was still serene at Bellows Field, the Army's fighter
base only six miles down the coast. Captain John P.
Joyce, the officer of the day, was shaving in the officers'
club just before 8:30, when a single plane buzzed the
field once, firing about 50 rounds. A private of the medical detachment was hit in bed in the tent area. A messenger drove off to tell Major L. D. Waddington, the
base commander, who lived about a mile away, but
even this rather startling event didn't seem to stir much
excitement. Certainly not enough to keep Private Raymond McBriarty from going to church as usual at 8:30.
Like everybody else, he hadn't paid much attention to
the strafing plane. But then as he sat in the pew with
more time to meditate, he began to think how strange it
was.

Outside, a big B-17 was coming in downwind on the
short 2600-foot strip. Lieutenant Robert Richards was
another of the bomber pilots who wanted no part of
Hickam—three of his crew had been wounded already.
So on the tower's advice, he was now trying Bellows.
With a damaged plane almost out of gas, he decided to
get down as quickly as possible, and got away with a
downwind landing.

At this point Hickam finally notified Bellows about
the attack. Major Waddington hurried on over to get the
defense organized, and about the same time nine Japanese planes—apparently attracted by Richards' B-17—
dropped by and shot up the field.

Other enemy planes kept on top of Ewa, the Marine
air base west of Pearl. There were no antiaircraft guns,
no planes that could fly, no chance to do anything. Lieu-

tenant Colonel Larkin, the base commander, watched from under a truck, and most of his men were pinned down just as effectively.

Up above, Lieutenant Yoshio Shiga raked Ewa with his Zero fighter. He noticed a Marine standing beside a disabled plane and charged down, all guns blazing. The man refused to budge . . . kept firing with a pistol. Shiga still considers him the bravest American he ever met.

Lieutenant Shiga was also impressed by the B-17. He watched one of the big bombers shake off a swarm of Zeroes and lumber on safely to Hickam. He made a mental note that in the days ahead the Flying Fortress was going to be a hard plane to knock out.

Perhaps the visitors' biggest surprise was the antiaircraft fire, which was now coming to life. As Commander Fuchida's 50 horizontal bombers approached Battleship Row in a long, single line from the south, he felt they looked entirely too much like ducks in a shooting gallery. If he were doing it again, they would come in some other way.

As they neared the target, Fuchida traded positions with the lead bomber in his squadron. This plane had a specially trained bombardier, and when he released his bombs the other planes would follow suit. All the squadrons operated the same way.

Everything depended on perfect timing. When Fuchida saw the third plane in his group get out of line and prematurely drop its bomb, he was thoroughly annoyed. The man had a reputation for carelessness anyhow. Fuchida scribbled, "What happened?" on a small blackboard and waved it at the culprit. The pilot indicated that he had been hit, that the bomb lines had been shot away, and Fuchida was filled with remorse.

The squadron flew on. The *Nevada* was its particular target, and everybody waited for the lead plane to release. It never did. They ran into clouds at the crucial moment and had to try again. Next time around there was too much smoke over the *Nevada*, so Fuchida picked the *Maryland* instead. This time there was no trouble.

The lead plane released and the others followed suit. Fuchida peeked down and felt sure he had two hits.

Lieutenant Toshio Hashimoto, leading one of the rear squadrons, had an even more difficult time. The backwash of the planes in front kept throwing his group off. Then the lead plane miscalculated its range and signaled the others to hold everything. As they circled for another run, the expert bombardier Sergeant Umezawa bowed his apologies.

There were other errors over which the planes had no control. Their map of the area was made in 1933, and the efforts to up-date it hadn't been too successful. The new Navy tank farm was noted, but a 1936 artist's conception of Hickam had been accepted as gospel, so that the map showed eight pairs of hangars instead of the five actually built. The map also put the underground gasoline system where the baseball field was—at one time it had indeed been planned for there. Also, the administration building—a vital center—was labeled the officers' club and hence not touched. This mistake arose because dances were held there while the permanent club was being built. Whatever the other successes of Japanese agents, apparently they weren't invited to dances at Hickam.

But all in all, Fuchida had good reason to be satisfied. As the first attack wave wound up its work around 8:30, he could weigh what had been done to the fleet and the airfields against his own losses: five torpedo planes . . . one dive bomber . . . three fighters.

Admiral Nagumo was also taking stock of the striking force, now hovering about 200 miles north of Oahu. Brief radio flashes from the planes gave a pretty good picture: 8:05 A.M., torpedoes successfully dropped . . . 8:10 A.M., 30 planes hit, 23 on fire . . . 8:16 A.M., large cruiser hit . . . 8:22 A.M., battleship hit . . .

Once again everyone went into ecstasy. In the *Akagi's* engine room Commander Tanbo's firemen hugged each other with joy as the news filtered down. Up on deck, Seaman Iki Kuramoti shouted in glee. But tough Commander Hoichiro Tsukamoto, navigation officer of the

Shokaku, lived in fear of being caught by American planes. He knew the carriers were easy targets; he didn't know how little was left to hit them.

Admiral Yamamoto was also serious as he waited for results in the operations room of his flagship *Nagato* back at Kure. The minutes ticked away on the large nautical clock that hung on the wall. Yamamoto had almost finished his second cigarette when the first word came in. As the results piled up, the rest of the room buzzed with excitement, but Yamamoto rarely changed expression. One intercepted U. S. message spoke of ships operating around the harbor. "Good!" exclaimed Rear Admiral Matome Ugaki, "that means our midget subs are getting through!" Yamamoto merely nodded. Actually he still felt the midget submarines were a mistake, that it was a waste of manpower to sacrifice men at the outset of war.

He may have been right—certainly Ensign Sakamaki was getting nowhere. Coming in for another try at the harbor entrance, he got close enough to a patrolling destroyer to see the white uniforms of the crew. It apparently picked him up too, for several depth bombs thoroughly shook up the sub. One of them stunned Sakamaki and filled the sub with fumes and a thin white smoke. When he came to, he withdrew to check his damage. Nothing seriously wrong, so he tried again. According to Sakamaki, he made three separate attempts to get by charging, depth-bombing American destroyers before ending up briefly on the coral reef just outside the harbor entrance.

American memories and records suggest no such spirited engagement. Between the *Ward's* contact at 6:45 and the time the *Helm* saw the midget on the coral at 8:17, there was only one sub report—the sound contact made by the *Ward* at 7:03.

If Sakamaki was confused or mistaken, it's quite understandable. The air in the sub was vile, the batteries were leaking, the smoke getting worse. And there is certainly no question about one thing he recalls seeing. Once, as he twisted his periscope toward Pearl Harbor, he saw columns of black smoke towering toward the sky. "Look! Look!" he cried.

Seaman Inagaki was completely overjoyed: "Just look at that smoke!"

They clasped each other's shoulders and solemnly pledged, "We'll do the same!"

CHAPTER IX

"You Don't Wear a Tie to War"

THE *Breese* SAW IT FIRST. From her anchorage off Pearl City, the old destroyer-minecraft sighted a conning tower turning up the west side of Ford Island just after 8:30. The *Medusa* and *Curtiss* saw it a few minutes later, and signal flags fluttered from all three yardarms.

The *Monaghan* caught the warning right away. The ready-duty destroyer had now cleared her nest and was heading down the west channel, the first ship to get going. A signalman turned to Commander Bill Burford: "Captain, the *Curtiss* is flying a signal that means, 'Submarine sighted to starboard.'"

Burford explained it was probably a mistake . . . such a thing could easily happen in all the confusion of gunfire and burning ships.

"Okay, Captain—then what is that thing dead ahead of us that looks like an over-and-under shotgun?"

The skipper squinted through the smoke and was amazed to see a small submarine moving toward them on the surface several hundred yards ahead. In its bow were two torpedo tubes, not side by side as usual, but one directly above the other. They seemed to be pointed directly at the *Monaghan*.

By now everybody was firing. The *Curtiss* pumped a shell right through the conning tower at 8:40—decapitating the pilot, according to her gunners; clipping off his coat button, according to *Monaghan* men. The *Medusa* was firing too, but at the crucial moment the powder hoist broke on the gun that had the best shot. The *Monaghan's* own guns were blazing as she rushed at the sub, but the shot missed and hit a derrick along the shore.

The midget missed too. It failed to get the *Curtiss* with one torpedo; the other whisked by the charging *Monaghan* and exploded on the Ford Island shore. The *Monaghan* rushed on, and everybody else held their fire as Burford tried to ram. He grazed the conning tower, not really a square blow, but hard enough to spin the sub against the *Monaghan's* side as she surged by. Chief Torpedoman's Mate G. S. Hardon set his depth charges for 30 feet and let them go. They went off with a terrific blast, utterly destroying the sub and knocking down nearly everybody on deck. Fireman Ed Creighton thought the ship had at least blown up its own fantail.

But she hadn't. Instead, the *Monaghan* rocketed on, now too late to make her turn into the main channel leading to sea. She drove ashore at Beckoning Point, piling into the derrick already set on fire by her guns. Fireman Creighton ran to the bow and manned a hose; others wrestled the anchor free. Burford backed off, turned, and steamed out to sea while the nearby ships rang with cheers.

The whole harbor was on the upsurge. A trace of jauntiness—even cockiness—began to appear. Three men in a 50-foot launch hawked .30 and .50-caliber ammunition off the foot of Ford Island as if they were selling vegetables. A bomb hit a mobile "gedunk" wagon on 1010 dock, and men from the *Helena* dashed ashore to gather up the free pies, ice cream, and candy bars. A number of seamen sneaked away from their regular stations on the *Whitney* to take a turn at the machine guns —like patrons of a shooting gallery. When a gun crew on the *Blue* winged a plane, everyone stopped work, danced about shaking hands with one another.

A strange exhilaration seized the men at the guns. Not knowing of war, they compared it to football. Marine Gunner Payton McDaniel on the *Nevada* sensed the tingle of going onto the field at game time. Ensign Martin Burns on the *Phoenix* felt the excitement of the scrimmage. When the *Honolulu* and *St. Louis* winged a plane, Machinist's Mate Robert White could only com-

Japanese crewmen cheer attacking planes as they take off
from carriers.

Raid begins. Japanese torpedo plane climbs after direct hit on *Oklahoma*.

Battleship Row as the Japanese pilots saw it. A captured
photograph.

(Top) Oil gushes from the *Oklahoma, West Virginia, Arizona* after direct hits.

(Bottom) Three days later—*Oklahoma* turned turtle, *West Virginia* awash, *Arizona* blown apart.

Height of attack. *West Virginia* sunk, *Tennessee* damaged.

Rescue of swimmers from *West Virginia*.

Torpedoed *Utah* rolls over in her berth

Arizona burning after direct bomb hit.

Arizona, fires out, sunk with 1102 men.

Pearl Harbor alert, a wall of antiaircraft fire meets second Japanese attack wave.

The *Nevada* beached on Waipio Point.

Destroyer *Shaw* exploding in dry dock.

Japanese midget sub beached off Bellows Field.

Japanese fighters seen from unarmed B-17 arriving from California.

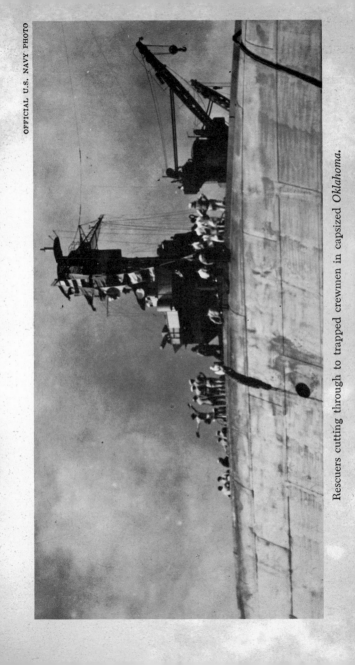

Rescuers cutting through to trapped crewmen in capsized *Oklahoma*.

Burning barracks in background, the bullet-torn American flag still flies over Hickam Field.

pare the cheers to Navy scoring against Army. And in fact, when the Marine gunners on the *Helena* knocked down a plane, Captain Bob English shouted from the bridge, "The Marine team scored a touchdown!"

In their excitement men performed astonishing feats. Woodrow Bailey, a sailor on the *Tennessee,* chopped a a ten-inch hawser in half with one stroke. Gun Captain Alvin Gerth and two other men did the job of 15 men at one of the *Pennsylvania's* five-inch guns. Kenneth Carlson ran up vertical ladders on the *Selfridge* with a bandoleer of .50-caliber machine-gun shells slung over each shoulder—normally he could handle just one of the 75-pound belts. A man on the *Phelps* adjusted a blue-hot 1.1 gun barrel by twisting it with his hands—didn't even notice the heat.

There were fiascoes too. When an old chief on the *St. Louis* cleared some Navy Yard rigging from the ship's foremast, other crew members paused to watch with delight a Mack Sennett classic—he was chopping away the scaffold he stood on. The *Argonne* gunners shot down their own antenna, then almost got the Fourteenth Naval District signal tower. Next a hole appeared in the powerhouse smokestack. Seaman Don Marman says the *Helena* fired the shot; Marine Gunner McDaniel of the *Nevada* also claims the honor. Other shells—with the fuses defective or not set at all—whistled off toward downtown Honolulu.

Little matter. At the moment all anybody cared about was keeping the guns. going. The *Tennessee's* five-inch guns fired so fast that paint hung from the overheated barrels in foot-long strips. On the *Pennsylvania* Gunner's Mate Millard Rucoi was busy ramming shells when a man at the next five-inch gun began waving his arms, as though describing a shapely woman. Rucoi was too busy for frivolity and there was too much noise for conversation, so he just shook his fist and went on ramming. Finally the man came over and shouted to come and look at his gun barrel—it was so hot it was wavy. He asked Rucoi whether he should keep shooting. The answer was easy: "Hell, yes, keep her going."

Nothing was allowed to interfere. At 1010 dock, tugs towed the sinking *Oglala* clear of the *Helena* to a new berth farther astern. As the lines between the two ships were cast off, Admiral Furlong appeared on the *Oglala's* bridge and wandered into the line of fire of a *Helena* five-incher. A very young boatswain's mate stuck his head out of the gunport: "Pardon me, Admiral, sir! Would you mind moving from the wing of the bridge so we can shoot through there?"

Lieutenant Commander Shigekazu Shimazaki got a real reception when he arrived with the second attack wave at 8:40. There were no torpedo planes this time—just 54 high-level bombers, 80 dive bombers, and 36 fighters. The level bombers would concentrate on Hickam and Kaneohe, but the dive bombers screamed down on Pearl, searching for targets that hadn't been plastered.

The *Maryland* and *Helena's* newly installed 1.1 guns now swung into action and bagged three planes right away. On the *Castor*, Quartermaster William Miller listened with clinical interest to the new weapon. It wasn't a bark like the three-inch guns, or an ear-blasting crack like the five-inchers—just a muffled, persistent pom-pom that was somehow very reassuring. On the *West Virginia*, Ensign Ed Jacoby was more surprised than reassured; these guns had been a constant headache in practice—they were always breaking down—but this morning they worked like a charm.

A dive bomber crashed near Ford Island, just off the dock normally used by the *Tangier* . . . another into the main channel near the *Nevada* . . . another off Pearl City, not far from the destroyer-minecraft *Montgomery*. Chief Machinist's Mate Harry Haws sent Seaman D. F. Calkins in the destroyer's whaleboat to investigate. The pilot was sitting on the wing, but refused to be rescued. As the gig drew alongside, he pulled a pistol. He had no chance to use it—Calkins shot first.

In their anger and excitement the men shot at anything that flew. This had already been learned by the B-17s coming into Hickam. Now it was discovered by 18 planes flying into Ford Island on a routine scouting mission from the carrier *Enterprise*.

The big ship had been due back at 7:30 A.M. from her trip to Wake, but heavy seas held up the refueling of her destroyers, and at 6:15 she was still some 200 miles west of Oahu. So the early-morning scouting flight took off as usual—13 planes from Scouting Squadron 6; four from Bombing Squadron 6; one additional reconnaissance plane. They were to sweep the 180-degree sector ahead of the ship, then land at Ford Island. Ensign Cleo Dobson and the other married pilots were delighted—they couldn't go ashore until the *Enterprise* docked, but they could at least call their wives.

The planes droned off. It must have been about 8:00 A.M. when they all heard Ensign Manuel Gonzales yell over the radio, "Don't shoot! I'm a friendly plane!" No one ever saw him again.

Lieutenant (j.g.) F. A. Patriarca's patrol took him north to Kaui, and as he swung back toward Oahu shortly after eight, he noticed planes orbiting northward in the distance. It looked like the Army on maneuvers. When he reached Oahu, he learned the truth and gunned his plane out to sea, calling again and again over the radio: "White 16—Pearl Harbor under attack. Do not acknowledge." He headed back for the *Enterprise*, but the carrier—now under radio silence—had changed course and disappeared. Running out of gas, Patriarca finally crash-landed in a pasture at Kaui.

The warning was too late for some of the pilots. Japanese fighters racked up Ensigns Bud McCarthy, John Vogt, and Walter Willis; only McCarthy escaped alive. Navy antiaircraft fire took care of Ensign Edward Deacon; he crashed into the sea, but both he and his rear-seat man were saved. Then a Zero caught Lieutenant (j.g.) Clarence Dickinson's plane. The rear-seat man was shot, but Dickinson bailed out. Landing in a dirt bank just west of Ewa Field, he stumbled to the main road. He hoped at least to catch a ride to Pearl.

The rest of the pilots somehow squeaked into Ewa or Ford Island. Lieutenant Earl Gallaher arrived over

Pearl about 8:35, decided it was hopeless and made for Ewa instead. Ensign Dobson happened along and decided that was a good idea too. They touched down, and a Marine ran up shouting, "For God's sake, get into the air or they'll strafe you too!" Taking off again, they circled about for a few minutes, finally headed into Ford Island when it looked like a lull.

As Dobson dropped his wheels to land, every gun in the Navy seemed to open up on him. Tracers flew by. A pom-pom shell burst under his right wing, throwing the plane on its side. He dropped his seat down . . . hid behind the engine . . . and dived for the runway. At 50 knots extra speed, he shuddered to think that his tires might be shot. But he made it all right, scooted the whole length of the runway, ground-looped to a stop just short of a ditch.

There was nothing dazed or stunned about Ford Island now. Some of the men were dragging damaged planes clear of the burning hangars. Others were salvaging the guns and setting up pillboxes. One ordnance-man had to improvise his mount out of some sewer pipe. There still weren't enough guns to go around, and Chief Storekeeper Bonett—a quiet, unassuming man who was supposed to know nothing about weapons—was busy assembling .30-caliber machine guns in the paint storage building.

Others rallied around the oil-soaked men who struggled ashore from Battleship Row. Many of them headed for a spot near the gas dock, where the beach shelved off gradually. Chief Albert Molter dragged in a tall ensign, still wearing binoculars, who had passed out just short of the beach. As he tugged away, he saw another man swimming in, using only one arm. Molter thought he must be using a cross-chest carry on someone else, and helpfully called out that the water was shallow. The man murmured his thanks and stumbled to his feet —he was carrying a large canned ham.

The wounded were quickly taken in tow—some to the tennis courts, which had been turned into a receiving station; others to the mess hall, where they lay on tables yet to be cleared of breakfast. Seaman Thomas Malmin, who drove the bus that ran around the island, took the worst hit to the dispensary. Once he picked up an ensign—no apparent wounds but in a state of complete shock. He couldn't speak, couldn't hear, fought desperately to stay in the bus when it reached the building. Another time he gave four colored men a lift. They were all badly hurt but wouldn't let anybody touch them or aid them in any way. They kept together in the bus and helped each other out at the end—still going it alone.

The dispensary was quickly swamped, and the men piled up in the patio—sprawling, sopping bundles that looked completely out of place on the bright, clean tiles. A young girl, perhaps 14, went around trying to get their names, but she just couldn't bear to look.

The service families opened their larders and wardrobes for the men who weren't wounded. An officer walked about in seaman's jumpers; a sailor with him wore a T-shirt, swallow-tailed coat, and full-dress "fore and aft" admiral's hat. Like the other good Samaritans, Mrs. Pat Bellinger had raided her husband's trunk.

Off Ford Island, a weird flotilla dodged Japanese strafers, darted in and out of the burning oil, picking up the men still swimming. Boatswain's Mate A. M. Gustchen maneuvered Admiral Leary's barge with all the professional polish an admiral's coxswain should have. Musician Walter Frazee, who had never steered a boat before, handled a launch from the *Argonne*. Chief Jansen brought his honey barge in close, fighting fires on the *West Virginia*. A water barge turned up to redeem a mildly tarnished past. For some time it had been the crew's custom to give any ship more than its quota of fresh water—if the ship made it worthwhile. A suggested rate of exchange was 10,000 gallons for a big dressed turkey, sixty dozen eggs, with a few extra items to sweeten the deal. Just the day before, such a transaction was worked out with the *Curtiss;* in fact, the turkey was in the oven at the very moment the Japanese struck. Now, all thoughts of a Sunday feast were forgotten, as the barge rushed to help the swimmers.

They were all types. When Seaman Albert Jones idled his motor for a second to spread sand for better footage, a sailor in the water screamed hysterically—he was sure he would be forgotten. Another man swam over and did his best to help. It wasn't easy, for he had just lost his own arm.

Ensign Maurice Featherman of the *West Virginia* lay exhausted on the deck of a harbor tug and didn't care whether he lived or died. His shipmate, Ensign John Armstrong, appeared from nowhere in starched whites —looking as if he had just stepped out of the Harvard Club. Kneeling at Featherman's side, he set about injecting his friend with the will to live: "Mo, history is being made now, and you and I are in the middle of it, and our actions might affect the outcome."

Few men thought in such terms, but more and more acted as if they did. Chief Radioman Thomas Reeves hung on alone in a burning passageway of the *California*, trying to pass ammunition by hand, until he fell unconscious and died. The ship had taken a bad hit around 8:25, and flames raged along the second deck. As Ensign Herbert Jones lay wounded in their path, he calmly explained to two friends that he was done for anyhow and they must leave him.

On the bridge of the tanker *Neosho*—lying between the *California* and the rest of Battleship Row—Commander John Phillips prepared to move his ship from the area. As her engineers lit off the boilers and the blowers cut in, Aviation Machinist William Powers jumped with fright—that rising whine sounded just like bombs in the movies. By 8:35, some of the *Neosho's* crew had joined air station personnel in the job of chopping the lines. Slowly she cleared the dock and backed up Battleship Row to the fuel depot on the other side of the channel.

Actually the Japanese weren't interested in the *Neosho*. When one strafer flew down Battleship Row, he even held fire while passing the tanker—just a waste of good bullets. He might have cared more had he known she was still half loaded with high-octane aviation gas.

Next up the line, the *Oklahoma* lay bottom-up, but her men were by no means out of the fight. Marine Sergeant Thomas Hailey reached Ford Island, volunteered for a mission in a small unarmed plane. They gave him a rifle and sent him up. The mission: locate the Japanese fleet. The plane had no luck and returned five hours later. For Hailey it was an especially uncomfortable trip because he still had on only the oil-soaked underwear he wore from the *Oklahoma*.

Most of her survivors settled for the *Maryland*. A seaman covered with oil tagged after Chief Gunner's Mate McCaine, calling, "What can we do, Chief?" Marine Sergeant Leo Wears found a shorthanded gun on the main deck, appointed himself a member of its crew. Ensign Bill Ingram took over another gun that seemed to need help. As he worked away, someone on the bridge hollered down, telling him that on the *Maryland* an officer was expected to wear his cap when he fought. There were plenty of them lying around, so Ingram put one on, paused long enough to wave cheerfully in the general direction of the bridge.

The *Maryland's* own crew were just as busy. Mess Attendant Arvelton Baines, who had been in the brig for fighting with civilians, worked to get ammunition topside until he passed out from exhaustion. A hulking Marine sergeant—nicknamed "Tiny," as usual—rammed a five-inch antiaircraft gun with his hand when the hydraulic hammer got stuck. The men sweated away, oblivious of the flames blown toward them, above them, in fact all around them from the burning *West Virginia* and *Arizona*. Under the circumstances, Chief George Haitle was mildly astonished when an officer drew a gun and threatened to shoot the first man caught lighting a cigarette.

Men on the *West Virginia* were even more surprised when they too were chewed out for smoking. The ship was now a sea of flames—ammunition exploding everywhere, bullets and shells flying all over the place. Everything aft of the foremast was lost in choking smoke. Abandon ship had been ordered, and her port bow was level with the water, when Ensign Thomas A. Lombardi arrived from shore leave around 8:50. He stepped aboard and stood rooted in his tracks—could this litter of clothing, bedding, bodies, and debris be the same neat deck he had left the night before?

It was no weirder a picture than the one he made himself. As he pitched in to help the wounded, he was still wearing his white dinner jacket, black tie, and tuxedo pants. They didn't matter, but he needed something far more effective than the black evening pumps he still wore. Then a miracle—he stumbled over a pair of rubber boots lying on deck. And an even greater miracle (for Lombardi was an old Syracuse football player with frame and feet to match)—they were size 13, a perfect fit.

On the signal bridge, Ensign Delano also had an unexpected windfall in the way of apparel—he picked up the only helmet he ever found that fitted. He clapped it on and checked two idle machine guns mounted forward of the conning tower. They seemed in good shape, so he recruited a young officer, a seaman, and Mess Attendant Doris Miller to get them going. The first two would do the firing; Miller would pass the ammunition. Next time Delano looked, Miller had taken over one of the guns and was happily blazing away. The big steward had no training whatsoever in machine guns, and at least one witness felt he was a bigger menace than the Japanese. But there was nothing wrong with his heart, and it was the only time Delano had ever seen him smile, except the day he won that big fight as the *West Virginia's* heavyweight boxer.

As fast as men could be spared, Delano packed them off to help the *Tennessee* alongside. Others thought of it themselves and crawled across on the ten-inch hawsers. When a *Tennessee* gun captain asked one *West Virginia* ensign what fuse setting to use, he got an impatient reply: "To hell with fuse settings—shoot!" More shells sailed off for downtown Honolulu.

Everyone at least agreed there was no time for technicalities. Captain Charles E. Reordan fought the *Tennes-*

see in his Panama hat. Crew members gladly recruited Private Harry Polto, a soldier who happened to be visiting aboard, and assigned him to a five-inch gun. Men tossed scores of empty shell cases overboard with carefree abandon, forgetting completely the swimmers struggling alongside. But through all the scorn for details, the seaman's prerogative to gripe was carefully preserved. Few seemed to mind Yeoman Duncan grumbling that his new whites had been ruined by a broken steam pipe.

Even the twisted, burning *Arizona* still showed signs of fight. Boatswain's Mate Barthis and most of those still living stood on the fantail, dropping life rafts to the men in the water. Coxswain Forbis gave a hand until Barthis said nothing more could be done. Then he dived in—his watch stopped at 8:50. Radioman Glenn Lane was already in the water, had been swimming ever since the big explosion blew him overboard. He could have reached the shore easily but wanted some more interesting way to stay in the fight.

Suddenly he saw it right before his eyes. The *Nevada* was swinging out . . . getting under way . . . moving down the harbor. He paddled over to meet her. Someone tossed him a line, yanked him aboard. Two other *Arizona* seamen were hauled up the same way, and all three were assigned to a five-inch gun on the starboard side. The *Nevada* steamed on down the channel, gliding past the burning wrecks, proudly heading for the sea.

It seemed utterly incredible. A battleship needed two and a half hours to light up her boilers, four tugs to turn and pull her into the stream, a captain to handle the whole intricate business. Everybody knew that. Yet here was the *Nevada*—steam up in 45 minutes, pulling away without tugs, and no skipper at all. How could she do it?

She had certain advantages. It might normally take two and a half hours to get up steam, but two of her boilers were already hot. One was the boiler that normally provides power for a ship at her mooring. Ensign Taussig had lit the second during that last peacetime

watch, planning to switch the steam load later. Now
his efficiency paid off. Both boilers had plenty of steam
—giving the *Nevada* some 90 minutes' jump in getting
away. Hard work in the fire room made up the difference.

And four tugs might normally be needed to ease the
ship out, but in a pinch their role could be filled by a
good quartermaster. The *Nevada* had a superb one—
Chief Quartermaster Robert Sedberry.

It was the same with leadership. Captain Scanland and
his executive officer might be ashore, but the spark was
supplied by Lieutenant Commander Francis Thomas,
the middle-aged reservist who was senior officer present.
As damage control officer, Thomas was down in central
station when he heard that the engine room was ready.
He put a yeoman in charge of central station, vaulted
up the tube to the conning tower, and took over as
commanding officer.

Chief Boatswain Edwin Joseph Hill climbed down to
the mooring quay, cut loose an ammunition lighter
alongside, and cast off. The *Nevada* began drifting
away with the tide, and Hill had to swim to get back
on board. But after 29 years in the Navy, he wasn't
going to miss this trip.

In the wheelhouse Sedberry backed her until she
nudged a dredging pipeline strung out from Ford Island.
Then ahead on the starboard engines, astern on the
port, until the bow swung clear of the burning *Arizona*.
Now ahead on both engines, with just enough right
rudder to swing the stern clear too. She passed so close,
Commander Thomas felt he could almost light a cigarette from the blazing wreck.

So she was on her way—and the effect was electric.
Photographer J. W. Burton watched from the Ford
Island shore . . . Lieutenant Commander Henry Wray
from 1010 dock . . . Quartermaster William Miller from
the *Castor* in the sub base—but wherever men stood,
their hearts beat faster. To most she was the finest thing
they saw that day. Against the backdrop of thick black
smoke, Seaman Thomas Malmin caught a glimpse of

the flag on her fantail. It was for only a few seconds, but long enough to give him an old-fashioned thrill. He recalled that "The Star-Spangled Banner" was written under similar conditions, and he felt the glow of living the same experience. He understood better the words of Francis Scott Key.

It was less of a pageant close up. All kinds of men compose even a great ship's crew, and they were all there on the *Nevada*. As the Japanese planes converged on the moving ship, Seaman K. V. Hendon spied a pot of fresh coffee near the after battle dressing station; he paused and had a cup. A young seaman stood by one of the five-inch casemate guns, holding a bag of powder close to his chest—he explained that if he went, it was going to be a complete job. One officer beat on the conning tower bulkhead, pleading, "Make them go away!" Ensign Taussig, his left leg hopelessly shattered, lay in a stretcher near the starboard antiaircraft director. Turning to Boatswain's Mate Allen Owens, he remarked, "Isn't this a hell of a thing—the man in charge lying flat on his back while everyone else is doing something."

As the *Nevada* steamed on, all the Japanese planes at Pearl Harbor seemed to dive on her. At 1010 dock, Ensign David King watched one flight of dive bombers head for the *Helena*, then swerve in mid-attack to hit the battleship instead. Another group shifted over from Drydock No. 1. Soon she was wreathed in smoke from her own guns . . . from bomb hits . . . from the fires that raged amidships and forward. Sometimes she disappeared from view, when near-misses threw huge columns of water high in the air. As Ensign Delano watched from the bridge of the *West Virginia*, a tremendous explosion erupted somewhere within her, blowing flames and debris far above the masts. The whole ship seemed to rise up and shake violently in the water.

Another hit on the starboard side slaughtered the crew of one gun, mowed down most of the next group forward. The survivors doubled up as best they could— three men doing the work of seven. It was all the more difficult because Chief Gunner's Mate Robert E. Lin-nartz—now acting as sight-setter, pointer, and rammer-man—had himself been wounded.

In the plotting room far below, Ensign Merdinger got a call to send up some men to fill in for the killed and wounded. Many of the men obviously wanted to go—it looked like a safer bet than suffocating in the plotting room. Others wanted to stay—they preferred to keep a few decks between themselves and the bombs. Merdinger picked them at random, and he could see in some faces an almost pleading look to be included in the other group, whichever it happened to be. But no one murmured a word, and his orders were instantly obeyed. Now he understood more clearly the reasons for the system of discipline, the drills, the little rituals, the exacting course at Annapolis, the gold braid—all the things that made the Navy essentially autocratic but at the same time made it work.

The *Nevada* was well beyond Battleship Row and pretty far down 1010 dock when she encountered still another obstacle. Half the channel was blocked by a long pipeline that ran out from Ford Island to the dredge *Turbine*, lying squarely in midstream. Somehow Quartermaster Sedberry snaked between the dredge and the shore. It was a fine piece of navigation and a wonderful arguing point for Captain August Persson of the dredge. The Navy had always made him unhook the pipeline every time the battleships came in or out, claiming there wasn't enough room to pass. Captain Persson had always claimed they could do it if they wanted. Now he had his proof.

The Japanese obviously hoped to sink the *Nevada* in the entrance channel and bottle up the whole fleet. By the time she was opposite the floating drydock, it began to look as though they might succeed. More signal flags fluttered on top the Naval District water tower—stay clear of the channel. Still lying in his stretcher near the starboard director, Ensign Taussig was indignant. He was sure they could get to sea. In fact, he felt the ship was all right—she looked in bad shape only because someone down below was counterflooding her starboard bow instead of stern. Sitting by his five-inch casemate gun, Marine Sergeant Inks had different ideas. He had been in the Corps forever and knew trouble when he saw it. He was gloomily muttering that the ship would never get out.

In any case, orders were orders. Thomas cut his engines and nosed her into Hospital Point on the south shore. The wind and current caught her stern and swung her completely around. Chief Boatswain Hill, who had cast off a long 30 minutes before, now went forward to drop anchor. Then another wave of planes dived on the *Nevada* in one final, all-out fling. Three bombs landed near the bow. Hill vanished in the blast—the last time Thomas saw him, he was still working on the anchor gear.

It was now nine o'clock, and the hour had come for the ships in drydock—the flagship *Pennsylvania* in Drydock No. 1, with the destroyers *Cassin* and *Downes* lying side by side just ahead of her; the destroyer *Shaw* in the new floating drydock a few hundred yards to the west.

The three ships at the main drydock fought under a special handicap. The water had been pumped out, dropping their decks to a point where the high sides of the drydock blocked most of the view. This was noticed right away by George Walters, a civilian yard worker operating a traveling crane that ran on rails along the side of the dock. From his perch 50 feet up, Walters saw the first planes dive on Ford Island. Like everybody else he thought it was a drill and caught on only when he saw the PBYs crumble.

He looked down and realized that the men lolling in the sun on the *Pennsylvania, Cassin,* and *Downes* were aware of none of this. He yelled but nobody paid attention. He threw a wrench, but that only made them angry. As the attack spread all over the harbor, they finally understood.

When the Japanese turned their attention to the *Pennsylvania,* Walters decided to capitalize on the ship's predicament. He devised a unique defense. He ran his crane back and forth along the ship, hoping to protect it and ward off low-flying planes. A forlorn hope perhaps, but after all this was a crane taking on an air force.

At first, Walters' contribution infuriated the *Pennsylvania* gunners, who felt he was only spoiling their aim. Gradually they learned to use him. They discovered that, sitting in their trough, they couldn't see the planes soon enough anyhow. The crane's movements at least gave them a lead on where a plane might next appear. Then they could set their guns and be ready when it came. Walters was just completing his transition from goat to hero when a Japanese bomb blasted the dock, putting him out of business.

It, of course, made no real difference: planes were swarming on the drydock from every direction. On the *Pennsylvania*, Gun Captain Alvin Gerth pumped out shells directly over the heads of the next gun crew forward. He had adjusted the gun to shoot a little below the safety cutout, and every time he fired, the blast would knock down the other gun captain. He in turn would jump up, run back, and kick Gerth in the seat of his pants. This went on and on.

On the *Pennsylvania*, too, there was a new jauntiness in the air. Electrician's Mate James Power took time out for a quick glance at his home-town paper, the Odessa, Texas, *Times*. He just had to know the score of the big Thanksgiving game between Odessa High and Midland. When he saw that Odessa had won for the first time in ten years, he jumped and hollered with joy.

More bombs rained down, and Captain Charles Cooke of the *Pennsylvania* began to worry about the drydock gate. He realized that a direct hit would let in a rush of water, pushing his ship into the destroyers lying ahead. To guard against this, he ordered the drydock partially flooded and sent Lieutenant Commander James Craig to tighten up the mooring line. Craig carried out the job in nimble, skillful fashion . . . paying no attention to the bullets that whipped the ground around him. He seemed to live a charmed life. At 9:06 he stepped back on board, just in time to be killed by a 500-pound bomb that shattered the starboard casemate he was passing through.

Boatswain's Mate Robert Jones rushed up to help the men hit by the blast. He gently pulled a blanket over one seaman who was obviously dead. The man thrashed out with both hands, yanked the blanket from his face: "I've got to breathe, ain't I?"

The dock was flooding fast when yard worker Harry Danner suddenly realized he had left his lunch tin down in the pit. He started back but was too late. It was sailing away into the *Cassin* and *Downes*, carried along by the inrush of water, just the way Captain Cooke figured a loosely moored battleship might do. When Danner finally reached the top of the dock, the *Pennsylvania* was still smoking from her bomb hit. He decided she could use some help and rushed up the gangplank. After a brief encounter with the duty officer, who couldn't grasp the idea of a civilian manning a gun, he got on board and joined one of the five-inch antiaircraft crews.

As the *Pennsylvania* fought on, a record player could be heard in one of the ship's repair shops. It had apparently been on when the attack started, and no one bothered to turn it off. Now, in the midst of this early-morning nightmare, it repeated over and over again the pleasant strains of Glenn Miller's "Sunrise Serenade."

Up ahead the *Cassin* and *Downes* seemed to catch everything that missed the *Pennsylvania*—a bad hit at 9:06 . . . another at 9:15. By the time the drydock was flooded, both destroyers were heavily on fire. Explosions racked their decks, and a big blast ripped the *Cassin* at 9:37. She sagged heavily to starboard and rolled slowly over onto the *Downes*. Seaman Eugene McClarty got out from under just in time, and as he streaked onto the drydock, another bomb crashed behind him, shaking the gangway loose. It fell into the drydock as McClarty pulled one sailor to his feet; but two other shipmates were too late, and plunged on down into the blazing caldron.

On the quarter-deck of the *Downes* a single sailor hung on, manning a .50-caliber machine gun. Watching from the *Pennsylvania*, Gunner's Mate Millard Rucoi wondered how long any man could stand that kind of heat. He soon had his answer. As the flames swept closer, the sailor seemed to have a harder and harder time keeping his head up. Finally he dropped to his knees, head down, but with one hand still hanging on the trigger of the gun. That's the way Rucoi last saw him when the flames and smoke closed off the view.

The *Shaw* was having just as much trouble in the floating drydock to the west. A bad hit around 9:12 . . . fire spreading toward her forward magazine . . . a fantastic explosion about 9:30. It was the Fourth of July kind—a huge ball of fire ballooned into the air; bits of flaming material arched and snaked across the sky, trailing white streamers of smoke behind. Once again the whole harbor paused to take in the scene. Seaman Ed Waszkiewicz watched from the Ford Island seaplane ramp, nearly half a mile across the bay. At this distance he knew he was at least safe—until he looked up at the sky. One of the *Shaw's* five-inch shells was tumbling end over end, arching directly at him. He dived behind a fire truck as the shell hit the concrete ramp several feet away. It didn't explode, merely bounced a hundred yards along the ramp and clanged into one of the hangars.

Ensign David King also took in the show from his station on the *Helena*. The gun mounts, mattresses, and bodies flying through the air reminded him strangely of the dummies and clowns fired from a gun in a circus. Only this time, he mused, no one would land in a net.

By now many of the planes were shifting over to the seaplane tender *Curtiss*, lying off Pearl City on the other side of Ford Island. A little earlier the *Curtiss* had clipped a bomber, which crashed into her starboard seaplane crane—perhaps the war's first kamikazi. In any case, it started bad fires, and these may have attracted the pilots hungry for a new kill.

Sealed in the transmitter room, the *Curtiss'* four radiomen couldn't see any of this, but they could hear the bombs coming closer and they could feel the ship shudder from near-misses. Radioman R. E. Jones was on the battle phones and couldn't move, but the other three could. and did. James Raines squatted between the transmitters; on his left crouched Dean B. Orwick; right in front of him, Benny Schlect—three men packed together in a space 30 inches wide.

Raines never really noticed any noise—the incredible thing was the hole that suddenly appeared in the deck right in front of him and no hole above. How could a bomb do this without coming through the overhead?

Then he noticed his left shoe was missing . . . then that Schlect was dead and Orwick hurt. The room filled with smoke as Jones ran over to help. Together they got Orwick to the door, undogged it, and laid him outside. Jones went back to try to move Schlect, and Raines stayed with Orwick. There was little he could do—a shot of morphine . . . a tourniquet . . . a few comforting words. Orwick asked quietly, "My foot's gone, isn't it?" Raines said yes it was, but everything would be all right. Corpsmen were there now, and they carried Orwick away. To his deep sorrow, Raines later learned that Orwick didn't pull through. Also, he was quite surprised to hear that he had broken his own back.

On the beleaguered *Raleigh*, Captain Simons watched the bomber crash into the *Curtiss* around 9:10, saw another plane in the same formation let go two bombs at his own ship. The first missed; the second was a perfect strike. It landed aft between a couple of gun crews . . . grazed an ammunition ready box . . . passed through the carpenter shop . . . through a bunk on the deck below . . . through an oil tank . . . through the bottom of the ship . . . and exploded in the harbor mud.

The *Raleigh* took a bad list to port, and from then on the battle was to keep from capsizing. The first step was to get rid of all topside weight. The planes went off on a scouting trip; everything else went over the side— catapults, torpedo tubes, torpedoes, booms, ladders, boat skids, chests, stanchions, anchors, chains, rafts, boats, everything. All the time Captain Simons kept a yeoman busy with pencil and paper, carefully plotting where everything fell, so it could be recovered later. Then he got some pumps from the Navy Yard, another from the *Medusa* . . . stuffed life belts into the holes . . . borrowed four pontoons . . . warped a lighter alongside. He also found time to send Carpenter R. C. Tellin with an acetylene torch to help Commander Isquith investigate some mysterious tappings coming from inside the hull of the overturned *Utah*.

While this work was getting under way, the *Raleigh* never stopped firing. Captain Simons thought his 1.1 guns had a lot to do with the plane that struck the *Curtiss* . . . another that crashed north of Ford Island . . . two more that fell near Pearl City . . . and a fifth that blew to bits in mid-air.

But there always seemed to be more—Simons watched another plane bomb the *Dobbin*, moored with her destroyers off the northern end of Ford Island. The bomb just missed the big tender, exploding off her starboard side. But a near-miss could do a lot of damage. Shrapnel slashed across her afterdecks, gouging the mainmast and smokestack . . . ripping a whaleboat to splinters . . . wrecking a refreshment stand . . . cutting down the crew at No. 4 gun.

Twenty-two-year-old Fireman Charles Leahey watched the blood trickle around the corner of the gun mount, and he thought about the Navy planes that drowned out the sound track every night there was a movie: "They always come around when we're having a show; where in the hell are they now?"

Just east of the *Dobbin*, the hospital ship *Solace* was getting ready for a busy day. In the main operating room, Corpsman T. A. Sawyer was breaking out drapes, getting the sterilizers started. Near him a nurse stood by, occasionally peeking through an uncovered porthole at the battle raging outside. Heavily influenced by the movie comedian Hugh Herbert, she would exclaim, "Woo-woo, there goes another one!" when a Japanese plane was hit. Another nurse was tearing long strips of adhesive for holding dressings in place after surgery; a near-miss rocked the ship, hopelessly entangling her in the tape. Out on the promenade deck a chief petty officer, clearly all thumbs, was hard at work rolling bandages.

A steady stream of launches began unloading the injured, sometimes escorted by shipmates and friends. Seaman Howard Adams of the *Arizona* helped carry a buddy to the operating room. He took one look, turned to the rail, and was sick. But he came back, asking if he could help. It was a big decision, for that day he chose his career—medical work.

A few hundred yards north of the *Solace*, the destroyer *Blue* cast off and moved slowly down the east channel toward the harbor entrance. As she passed Battleship Row, Machinist's Mate Charles Etter helped toss lines to the men still swimming in the water. Some were hauled aboard, but others couldn't hang on and fell back into the thick oil that spread over the channel. There was no time to stop for a second try.

The men on the blazing wrecks cheered the *Blue*, and the other destroyers, too, as one by one they glided by. As fast as they built up enough steam to move, they got under way—no waiting for skippers who still were on shore. The *Blue* sailed under Ensign Nathan Asher—his complement of officers was three other ensigns. *Aylwin* was handled by Ensign Stanley Caplan, a 26-year-old University of Michigan chemistry graduate in civilian life.

Outside the harbor, Quartermaster Frank Handler watched and waited on the bridge of the *Helm*. For 40 long minutes she and the *Ward* had been out there alone. For all anyone knew, the whole Japanese Navy might be just over the horizon. When would help come?

The first destroyer burst out of the channel just about nine o'clock. It was the *Monaghan*, fresh from her brush with the midget. Then the *Dale* . . . the *Blue* . . . the *Henley* . . . the *Phelps* . . . men soon lost track. Perhaps not much to start a war on, but there would be more to follow.

With a splintering crash Admiral Leary's special mahogany gangway sailed over the side of the cruiser *Honolulu* and broke in half on the dock. It was the first thing 30 men headed for, when word was passed to strip the ship of unnecessary equipment and prepare to sortie.

The *Honolulu* was warped alongside the *St. Louis* in one of the Navy Yard's finger piers, and as the men cast off the lines between the two ships, a dive bomber charged down on them. Seaman Don Marman ducked under the narrow space between the Number 1 turret overhang and the deck—there was about a two-foot clearance. He never knew so many men could get in so small a spot at one time. The bomb plunged through the concrete pier on the port side and exploded next to the ship. It holed her oil tanks, pushed in the armor plating, and made any sortie impossible. Perhaps she couldn't have gone anyhow, for in the excitement of casting off, one man chopped away the power line to the dock. Since the *Honolulu* didn't have enough steam yet to supply her own power, this knocked out her lights and all the electrical gear for operating the guns.

The same thing happened on the *New Orleans* at the next pier. Hot cables danced on the decks, the lights went out, the ammunition hoists ground to a halt. So the men formed human chains to pass the shells and powder from the magazines to the guns. As they sweated away in the dark, Chaplain Howell Forgy did his best to encourage them. He passed out apples and oranges . . . stopped and chatted with the gun crews . . . patted Seaman Sam Brayfield on the back . . . told him and the others that they couldn't have church this morning, but "praise the Lord and pass the ammunition."

Nobody chopped the cables that gave the *St. Louis* power, but nothing else was spared. A shopfitter dropped down over the starboard side and burned off the gangway with an acetylene torch. Somebody else chopped loose the water hose, leaving a 12-inch hole in the side of the ship; Shopfitter Bullock welded a plate over it in ten minutes. Up on the bridge, Captain George Rood signaled the engine room, and the *St. Louis* began backing out at 9:31 A.M.—the first cruiser under way.

As she pulled out, Captain Rood called down to the wardroom and requested some water. The strafing was especially heavy, but Pharmacist's Mate Howard Myers took pitcher and glass up the exposed ladder and served it properly. For the men on the *St. Louis,* nothing was too good for Captain Rood.

As the ships began pulling out, the men caught on shore raced to get back in time. Admiral Anderson tore through red lights in his official car. Admirals Pye and Leary got a lift from Richard Kimball, manager of the Halekulani. When Admiral Pye noticed one of the B-17s circling above, Kimball recalls him exploding: "Why they've even painted 'U. S. Army' on their planes!"

Ensign Malcolm of the *Arizona* drove his overnight host, Captain D. C. Emerson, and as the car hit 80, the old captain tapped Malcolm on the shoulder: "Slow down, kid; let's wait'll we get to Pearl to be killed."

Commander A. M. Townsend of the *St. Louis* chugged along as best he could in a '29 jalopy. Entering the main gate, he gradually overhauled a man running toward the fleet landing. It was a friend he hadn't seen for ten years.

Yeoman Charles Knapp of the *Raleigh* and eight other sailors piled into a taxi at the YMCA. Hundreds of others caught in town did the same. Manuel Medeiros' Pearl Harbor Drivers' Association kept at least 25 cabs shuttling back and forth—Driver Tony Andrade alone took six loads.

There were no taxis on the dusty country road where Lieutenant (j.g.) Clarence Dickinson stood after parachuting from his burning plane. He resorted to an old American expedient—hitchhiking. After a while a pleasant middle-aged couple drove up in a blue sedan. Mr. and Mrs. Otto F. Heine were on their way to breakfast with friends at Ewa, completely unaware of any battle. It took a few minutes to grasp that this hitchhiker was different —that he had just been shot down from the sky. At first

Mrs. Heine said politely that there really wasn't time to help him, that their friends were already waiting. But when the facts sank in, she bubbled with solicitude. Mr. Heine drove on toward Pearl without saying much. As they rounded the closed end of the harbor, strafers raked the car in front of them. He took one hand from the wheel and gently pushed Mrs. Heine's head under the dashboard.

The strafing planes were doing their best to paralyze the traffic now converging on Pearl Harbor. Radioman Frederick Glaeser wasn't convinced it was a real attack until a dive bomber gave his car a burst about three miles from the main gate. Jack Lower, a civilian electrician, was a little closer when the planes got interested in him. He was with a group of other workers, riding in the back of an open truck. Every time a plane approached, the men would hammer on the cab roof, the truck would stop, and everybody would scatter—behind palm trees, in the bushes, under the truck, anywhere. When the plane was gone, they would jump back in and start off again. It took 20 minutes to go two miles.

Even more snarls resulted from the average American's knack of creating his own traffic jams. A vegetable truck stalled and tied everybody up for a while. Word spread that a Fifth Columnist did it, but more likely some frightened farmer was trying to get to safety. About a mile from the gate everyone was held up by cross-traffic slanting off to Pearl City and Ewa. Two columns of cars sat bumper to bumper. In one line Commander Jerry Wiltse, skipper of the *Detroit*, waited in his station wagon. The car opposite him in the other line contained an old chief and his wife. When Wiltse's line began to move, it was too much for the chief. He jumped out and got in the commander's car, as his abandoned wife screamed, "But you know I don't know how to drive!"

Near the gate Commander Wiltse stopped again, this time picked up an aviator running alongside the road. It was Lieutenant Dickinson, who had left the Heines' sedan at the Hickam turn-off rather than involve them in the Pearl Harbor jam. When Wiltse reached the officers' club landing, Dickinson hopped out and eventually found still another ride to the landing opposite Ford Island.

Out on the main road, more jams developed. Finally Captain A. R. Early, commanding Destroyer Squadron One, jumped from his car and told a traffic cop to throw all cars without Pearl Harbor tags into the cane fields. To his surprise, the officer did it. There had been a feud between the Navy and the local police for years, and ordering that cop around was the only pleasure Captain Early got from the day.

When he finally reached the Navy Yard, Captain Early methodically put his car in its assigned parking space, carefully locked it, and then went on to the officers' landing. It was full of men trying to get rides to their ships . . . trying to find where their ships were . . . and, in some cases, trying to grasp the fact that their ships were gone forever. Commander Louis Puckett, supply officer of the *Arizona*, sat in the grass near the landing with four or five other officers from the ship. They just didn't know what to do.

A steady stream of launches ferried the men out to the ships and Ford Island. Commander McIsaac, skipper of the *McDonough*, gave Admiral Anderson a lift to the *Maryland* in his launch. The admiral marveled at the fearless, debonair spirit of the men in the launch; Commander McIsaac was pretty impressed by the admiral's own poise—he even had the little bag he liked to carry ashore.

It wasn't always possible to show such poise. A dive bomber screeched down on Seaman P. E. Bos' launch, and it was a tossup whether to dive overboard or stay in and take a chance. Bos was one of the ones who stayed—the machine gun missed them by inches. Shrapnel holed the crash boat taking Seaman Joseph Smith to the *Dale*, and the men abandoned it by the old coal docks. They all switched to another boat and chased the *Dale* out to sea. They never caught up with her. Nor did Lieutenant Commander R. H. Rogers, skipper of the *Aylwin*, who pursued Ensign Caplan in a motor launch.

It was all right with Captain Early, the squadron commander. He only wanted to get his destroyers out, and he was quite satisfied as he stood on the shore at 9:30 and saw that he now had on his hands more unemployed skippers than ships.

Pearl Harbor had no monopoly on hectic efforts to get back to duty. The men who pulled on their clothes, gulped coffee, kissed their wives, and dashed off to Hickam were just as frantic. Master Sergeant Arthur Fahrner couldn't find any collar insignia, and Mrs. Fahrner didn't help—she was forever handing him a tie.

"We're at war," he kept telling her; "you don't wear a tie to war."

First Lieutenant Warren Wilkinson meticulously pinned on all his insignia but started his car too abruptly. His chin banged against the horn button and it stuck. For a few seconds he drove on toward his squadron hangar, then couldn't stand it any longer. In the midst of the bombing and strafing he got out, raised the hood, and disconnected the horn.

By the time Wilkinson reached the hangar area, the dive bombing had tapered off and the field seemed strangely quiet. Sergeant H. E. Swinney wandered out from Hangar 11 and joined a group of men looking at a big bomb crater nearby. Sidewalk superintendents appeared everywhere, inspecting the damage, taking uneasy sidelong glances at the bodies that sprawled on the grass.

Near the barracks across the street, Sergeant Robert Hey put down his Tommy gun for a breather; then about nine o'clock he got word that the high-level bombers were coming. At first he couldn't see them at all. Then he saw antiaircraft bursts to the south above Fort Kamehameha. Soon he could make out the planes themselves—tiny specks far above the puffs of smoke. They were flying in a perfect V, never had to break formation. As he watched the planes pass over, he heard a faint rustling sound which kept getting louder. He yelled a warning, dived across the sidewalk into the dirt next to the barracks. Two of the bombs hit less than 50 feet away, and the fragments whizzed by, just over his head.

There was no warning in Hangar 15. Sergeant Swinney had returned from his inspection tour and was checking a damaged B-18. Under the plane some men were changing a bullet-riddled tire. Nearby the crew chief was explaining how the wheel was assembled to some mechanic who had chosen this particular moment to learn his trade a little better.

The bomb plunged through the roof with a deafening roar. The hangar went totally dark, and Swinney thought to himself that this was the end. Then the smoke and dust cleared, and an encouraging shaft of sunlight streamed through the hole. So he was alive after all— but he now had the terrifying feeling that everyone else had completely disintegrated. It was an illusion, however, for after he had groped his way out—alive and unhurt—he saw several dead lying where he had stood.

Corporal John Sherwood was working outside Hangar 15 when the high-level attack began. For some reason he headed for Hangar 13—a poor choice, since it had not yet been damaged. But he found a good corner in the engineering office, lay down, and waited. For the first time that morning he even had a chance to pray. As the bombs thundered closer, two young lieutenants—both crying like children—ran in and tried to dislodge him. Sherwood told them to go find their own corner. The hangar took several hits, and Sherwood realized he was in the wrong place after all. He ran out, leaving the lieutenants free to take any corner they liked.

At the base hospital Nurse Monica Conter also had to fight for her cover. Lying on the floor with other nurses, doctors, and patients, she had seized the galvanized lid of a brand-new garbage can and was holding it over herself. Someone kept tugging, trying to get it, but she managed to hang on.

Once again, good shelter was at a premium. Private Bert Shipley joined four men in a manhole who were firing at the planes with rifles. They knew they wouldn't hit anything, but it made them feel better. Some cooks in the bombed-out mess hall holed up in the freezer. More bombs hit the building, and they were all killed

by concussion. Private John Wilson dived under the edge
of a one-story frame building. He was glad to find the
shelter, but it was even better to be there with his buddy
Stan Koenig. He kept thinking if he was going to be
killed, he wanted some friend to know about it.

Hickam couldn't do much about the high-level attack,
but when the dive bombers returned around 9:15, the
men fought bitterly with what was left. One airman
manned a .30-caliber machine gun in the nose of a
damaged B-18 and kept firing until the plane burned
out from under him.

As fast as men fell at the machine guns on the open
parade ground, others rushed out to take their place,
and then they too would fall. Old-timers, like Sergeant
Stanley McLeod . . . young recruits, like Corporal Billy
Anderson of Virginia, lay there side by side. A few men
somehow survived. Staff Sergeant Chuck Middaugh, a
burly 235-pound roughneck always in trouble, grabbed
a .30-caliber machine gun in his hands and fired away
until he got a plane.

On the ball diamond two men set up a machine gun
on a tripod between home plate and some trees along
the edge of the field. It looked like a pretty safe spot
with a good field of fire. Suddenly a wave of planes
roared out of the sky, saturating the field with bombs
. . . scoring a direct hit on the gun . . . killing both men
instantly. They had no way of knowing that the Japanese
were sure the ball diamond was clever camouflage for
Hickam's underground gasoline system.

Other bombs did put the system briefly out of action.
They hit a water main near its real location, and since it
worked by water, it could no longer operate. The damage
was serious, but Staff Sergeant Guido Mambretti, the
Petroleum Section's maintenance man, bet Major Rob-
bins a bottle of cognac he could get the thing working
again. He did too, but he still hasn't collected.

While Mambretti toiled away, volunteers rushed up
and moved several loaded tank trucks out of the storage
area. Other volunteers turned up who had no connection
at all with Hickam. Major Henry Sachs, an ordnance

specialist passing through on his way to the Middle East, dashed to the Hickam cargo pier and took on the job of unloading the SS *Haleakala,* a munitions ship full of dynamite and hand grenades. A Hawaiian motorcycle club appeared, on the hunch they might be useful. One of the members, a huge, fat native, attached himself to Captain Gordon Blake, who was trying to disperse the B-17s. They made quite a pair bouncing along the runway—the Hawaiian resplendent in *aloha* shirt and rhinestone-studded cyclist belt; Blake seated behind, hanging on for dear life.

In between motorcycle trips, Blake tried to guide the B-17s still in the air to some place where they could land. One put down on Kahuku Golf Course; another suddenly turned up at Wheeler. As the pilot climbed out, Colonel William Flood, Wheeler base commander, told him dead-pan to get back up and find the Japanese fleet. The pilot looked depressed: "You know, Colonel, we just came over from California."

"I know, but, son, there's a war on."

"Okay," the pilot sighed, "if I can just get a cup of coffee, we're off."

Flood couldn't bear to keep the joke going any longer, told the pilot to get some sleep and he'd use him tomorrow.

It's hard to say how many planes really did get up from Wheeler. General Howard Davidson, commanding all the fighters, thought about 14. Air Force records indicate no P-40s and only a handful of worthless P-36s. Perhaps the general was counting in Welch and Taylor, who landed three different times for ammunition and then took off again.

These two were having a busy morning. After reaching Haleiwa, they had rushed straight for their planes. No briefing or checking out—Major Austin, the squadron commander, was off deer hunting, and they didn't bother with Lieutenant Rogers, the acting CO. They just took off.

First they flew down to Barbers Point, where the Japanese were said to be rendezvousing. Nobody there.

Just as well—there hadn't been time to belt up enough ammunition. So they dropped by Wheeler to get some more. By nine o'clock they were almost ready to take off again when seven Japanese planes swept in from Hickam for one last strafing run. Welch and Taylor gunned their P-40s and flew straight at them. Both men were up and away before the Japanese could give chase. Instead, the P-40s managed to get into the Japanese flight pattern and shot two down—one was the plane that grazed the eucalyptus tree behind Mr. Young's laundry.

Then Welch and Taylor headed for Ewa, where they had seen some dive bombers at work. It was a picnic. Between them, they got four more before Taylor had to land with a wounded arm. Welch stayed on and picked off another.

They had plenty of cooperation from the ground. Ewa, like the other airfields, was bounding back. Sergeant Emil Peters and Private William Turner manned a machine gun in one of the disabled planes; Sergeant William Turrage manned another; Sergeant Carlo Micheletto was firing too, until a low-flying strafer cut him down.

A piece of shrapnel nicked Lieutenant Colonel Larkin, the base commander, and Captain Leonard Ashwell became another casualty when he sped off on a bicycle to check some sentries. He forgot about a barbed-wire fence, careened into it, and arose somewhat the worse for wear. As Pharmacist's Mate Orin Smith treated the wounded, he himself was hit in the leg. He patched it up and rejoined his ambulance, which eventually accumulated 52 bullet holes.

On the windward side of the island, Bellows tried to fight back too, but a group of Japanese fighters gave the men little chance. Lieutenant George Whitman took up the first P-40 about nine o'clock, and six Zeroes got him right away. Next they pounced on Lieutenant Hans Christianson before he could even get off the ground. Then they caught Lieutenant Sam Bishop just after he took off. He managed to crash-land into the ocean and swim to safety. The attack was over before anybody else tried his luck.

None of the planes could even fly at nearby Kaneohe. The horizontal bombers took care of everything the strafers missed. Then there was a lull, and the bull horn bellowed for all hands to fight the hangar fires. Aviation Ordnanceman Henry Popko joined a wave of men who surged forward to answer the call. Halfway there, the strafers met them, and the men had to scatter. Seaman "Squash" Marshall raced for cover with the bullets snapping at his heels. It was another of those classic dashes that seemed to catch everyone's fancy. He actually outran a Zero for 100 yards, according to one man, then zagged to one side as the bullets plowed straight on. The men who watched set up a huge cheer—just as if someone had hit a home run at a ball game.

By 9:30 the dive bombers were back, but now everybody seemed to have some kind of gun. Ensign Hubert Reese and his friend Joe Hill sat in their clump of weeds, popping away with rifles. Others had mounted machine guns on water pipes, on tail-wheel assemblies, on anything. Big, friendly Aviation Machinist's Mate Ralph Watson cradled a .30-caliber weapon in his arms, kept it going long after he was hit.

Suddenly all guns began to concentrate on one fighter. Everyone had the same idea at once—it seemed like telepathy. Smoke began pouring from the plane. It kept on diving, motor wide open. Ensign Reese wondered if the pilot was crazy—it was hard to believe they were actually shooting one down. But it was true. The pilot never pulled up. As he hit the hillside, there was a cloud of dirt, a burst of fire in the air, and the plane completely disintegrated.

It wasn't the gunfire or bombing; it was the door that swung to and fro from the concussion that bothered Lieutenant Commander McCrimmon as he operated on his third patient at the Kaneohe dispensary. The man had a bad stomach wound, and Commander McCrimmon just couldn't concentrate. Finally he had a sailor hold the door steady so he could finish the operation.

He was scrubbing up for the next patient, when he suddenly realized what he had done. The door had distracted him so much he had sewed the wrong parts of the stomach together. Before the man came out of ether, McCrimmon had him back on the table, reopened the wound, corrected the error, and sewed him back up.

Three miles away, Mrs. McCrimmon stood in the yard beside the house, watching the planes dive on Kaneohe. The McCrimmons lived on the beach, and pretty soon 27 Japanese planes came flying down the coast, so low overhead she could see the white scarves worn by some of the pilots. Her two little boys waved and waved, but none of the pilots took any notice.

The Navy families on Ford Island had no time to watch and wave. The war surged all around them. Some huddled in the strong, concrete Bachelor Officers' Quarters. Others brought Cokes and cigarettes for the men swimming ashore. Chief Albert Molter turned his home into a first-aid station. He had about 40 there— all soaking wet, all covered with oil, most suffering from shock, some burned very badly. He borrowed a first-aid kit from the big crate the Boy Scouts used as a clubhouse. He broke open the canned fruit and juice he was keeping in case of emergency. He raided the linen closet for sheets, towels, blankets. He gave away all his civilian clothes—he didn't expect to wear them soon again anyhow.

At the senior officers' housing quarters on Makalapa, Mrs. Mayfield and her maid Fumiyo went next door, to sit out the raid with Mrs. Earle. They were soon joined by Mrs. Daubin, the only other wife on the hill. In the Earles' living room the women built a makeshift shelter by turning over two big bamboo sofas and piling all the cushions on top. In the course of this construction work Fumiyo whispered: "Mrs. Mayfield, is it—is it the *Japanese* who are attacking us?"

Mrs. Mayfield told her yes, as kindly as she could.

The shelters and defensive measures varied from house to house. Mrs. Mary Buethe, a young Navy wife, grabbed her children and hid in a clothes closet every time she heard a plane. At the Hickam NCO quarters, Mrs. Walter Blakey preferred her bathtub. Mrs. A. M. Townsend filled her tub with water and some pails with sand at her house in the "Punchbowl" section of town. Mrs. Claire Fonderhide, whose husband was at sea in a submarine, sat with a .45 automatic and waited. Mrs. Joseph Cote's little boy Richard used his gun too—he filled a water pistol with green paint and fired it all over the place.

Mrs. Carl Eifler, wife of an infantry captain, couldn't find her little boy. He had completely disappeared, the way little boys will. She busied herself, packing a suitcase, filling jugs with water, emptying the medicine cabinet, all the time wondering where her child could be. He finally sauntered home, but things looked so black by now, her thoughts were following a new channel: "Do I allow myself and my boy to be taken or do I use this pistol?" While she tried to make up her mind, she washed the bathroom woodwork.

Mechanically, other wives also went about their daily chores. Mrs. William Campbell, whose husband was in the Navy, carefully washed his whites and was hanging them on the line when an amazed Marine sentry saw her and chased her to cover.

Mrs. Melbourne West, married to an Army captain, did her ironing. She had this incessant feeling that her husband would need a lot of clean shirts if there was going to be a war.

As the service families numbly adjusted to war, much of Honolulu carried on as usual. The people in close touch with the Army and Navy knew all too well by now; but for the thousands with little contact—or perhaps out of touch for the week end—the world was still at peace.

Mrs. Garnett King called her local garage: could they wash the family car? They said they were pretty busy right now, but could take it in the afternoon. While explosions boomed in the distance, civilian Arthur Land helped transfer 20 gallons of salad from a caterer's truck to his own car—this was the day of the Odd Fellows Picnic. As the noise gradually subsided later in the morning, Mr. Hubert Coryell remarked to another civilian friend, "Well, that was quite a show." Then he went off to archery practice.

People somehow ignored the most blatant hints. Second Lieutenant Earl Patton, off duty for the day, was out with friends in a chartered fishing boat when a plane plunged into the sea nearby. Assuming it was an accident, they headed for the spot to help the pilot. Then another plane swooped by, strafing them with machine guns. One of the party was even nicked, but Patton charitably assumed the second plane was just attracting their attention to the first.

Walking home from church, Mrs. Patrick Gillis saw the side of a house blown in . . . figured someone's hot-water heater had exploded. Mrs. Cecilia Bradley, a Hawaiian housewife, was in the yard feeding her chickens when she was wounded by a piece of flying shrapnel. She thought it was somebody deer hunting in the hill behind her house. Mrs. Barry Fox, living on Kaneohe Bay, awoke to the sound of explosions, looked out, and saw strange-looking planes circling the base, flames boiling up, a wall of smoke. She decided it was a smoke-screen test. She didn't become really alarmed until she turned on the radio at 9:30 and didn't hear the news. That was the time she always listened to the latest bulletins, and this morning there was only music.

One by one they gradually learned. Stephen Moon, a Chinese 12-year-old, was at early mass on Alewa Heights—he planned to go on to the school club picnic at Kailua. Near the end of the service his mind began to wander, and his eyes strayed out the window. Right above Alewa Heights two planes were in a dogfight. But that was common, and he thought nothing of it. He glanced a little to the left and saw black puffs of smoke in the sky. That was strange—he knew the practice ammunition always left white smoke. As his attention drifted back to church, he became aware of a completely changed atmosphere. Right in the middle of the service, parents were slipping in and hurriedly taking their children out. He knew there was something wrong now, for the grownups were whispering and acting very mysteriously. The mass ended, and instead of the regular hymn, everyone stood and sang "The Star-Spangled Banner."

But it was all too deep for Stephen. Still thinking about the picnic, he strolled off toward a friend's house. Then a plane roared down from the sky and shot at a car driving toward Pearl. He spun around and ran home as hard as he could. His mother was glad to see him too; she had been looking for him everywhere.

Captain Walter Bahr, one of Honolulu's crack harbor pilots, also noticed the black puffs of smoke as he went out to meet the Dutch liner *Jagersfontein,* inbound from the West Coast. The pier watchman explained it was probably the Navy practicing. But he had a curious sense of urgency when he boarded the ship at 9.00 A.M. No one told him anything, but he sensed danger in all that noise and smoke. He brought her in fast. They were about at the harbor entrance when bombs began to fall, and columns of water shot up around them. Since Holland was already at war, the *Jagersfontein* was armed and the Dutch crew knew exactly what to do. They peeled the canvas covers from the guns and began firing back—the first Allies to join the fight.

A scrappy young flyweight boxer named Toy Tamanaha listened to the gunfire as he walked down Fort Street to the Pacific Café for breakfast around 9:30. He didn't think much of it—there was always shooting going on. Somebody in the café said it was war, but Toy remained unconvinced. Then somebody said all carpenters had been called to their jobs. Toy's close friend Johnny Kawakami was a carpenter, so Toy advised him to get going, and sauntered off himself to the Cherry Blossom Sweet Shop on Kukui Street for a popsicle. He was just inside when it happened—a blinding blast hurled him right out into the street. Vaguely he heard yells of help. He noticed his left leg was missing. He thought, "Maybe I only lost one leg." He was wrong—the other was gone too—but just before he blacked out, it was nice to hear someone come up and say, "Toy, you'll be all right."

There were explosions all over Honolulu—the Lewers and Cooke Building in the heart of town . . . the Schu-

man Carriage Company on Beretania Street . . . Kuhio
Avenue near Waikiki Beach . . . a Japanese community
out McCully Street. Four Navy Yard workers were
blown to pieces in their green '37 Packard at the corner
of Judd and Iholena. The same blast killed a 13-year-old
Samoan girl sitting on her front porch watching the gunfire.

Many of the people in Honolulu later believed the explosions were bombs. (Some of them still do: in the
words of one witness, "As the years pass, the bombs keep
dropping closer.") But careful investigation by ordnance
experts revealed that antiaircraft shells caused every one
of the 40 explosions in Honolulu, except for one blast
near the Hawaiian Electrical Company's powerhouse.

In their excitement, gunners on the *Tennessee, Far-
ragut,* and probably other ships forgot to crank in fuses.
Other ships like the *Phoenix* had trouble with bad fuses.
Others like the *Nevada* fired some shells that exploded
only on contact. As one *Nevada* gunner explained, if the
shell missed, it still had to come down somewhere.

But even the shells didn't do a complete job of waking
up Honolulu. At Police Headquarters, Sergeant Jimmy
Wong's blotter reflected a good deal of consternation
about the explosions—the first was a complaint phoned
in at 8:05 by Thomas Fujimoto, 610 E Road, Damon
Tract, that a bomb had interrupted his breakfast. But
there were also more familiar entries, indicating nor-
malcy far into the morning: "10:50 A.M. A man reported
to be drunk and raising trouble at Beretania and Alapai."

As the uproar increased, Editor Riley Allen of the *Star-
Bulletin* gallantly struggled to get out an extra. He was a
fast, if unorthodox, typist. This morning he was at his
best—one hand punching madly, the other rooting out
the keys that piled up in a hopeless snarl. The papers
were on the street by nine-thirty; the headline: WAR!
OAHU BOMBED BY JAPANESE PLANES.

At her home on Alewa Drive, Mrs. Paul Spangler heard
the newsboys shouting "Extra!" She had no ready change
and debated whether to raid the money she set aside for
church collection. She finally did.

Back at the *Star-Bulletin* office, Editor Allen got a call from an exasperated policeman. Would he recall his newsboys—they might get hurt. They had gone to Pearl Harbor to sell their papers.

Anyone still in doubt learned by radio. At 8:04 KGMB had interrupted a music program with the first word—a call ordering all Army, Navy, and Marine personnel to report to duty. The call went out again at 8:15 and 8:30. By then KGU was on the air too, calling doctors, nurses, defense workers to report for emergency duty. The first explanation came at 8:40—"A sporadic air attack had been made on Oahu . . . enemy airplanes have been shot down . . . the rising sun has been sighted on the wingtips." This only confused many listeners, who thought "sporadic" meant "simulated."

It took time to sink in, even if a person understood "sporadic." Some people tuned in between bulletins, heard only a gospel service or the incidental music that was used to fill in. Reassured, they turned off their sets again. Others harked back to Orsen Welles' broadcast of the Martian invasion . . . they weren't going to bite on this one.

Webley Edwards was at KGMB by now and did his best to gear the station to the crisis. But it was hard to drop some peacetime practices that were done almost by instinct. The records played between the bulletins sometimes seemed hideously incongruous. Once the song was "Three Little Fishes," a popular melody of the time that began:

"Down in the meadow in the iddy biddy poo
Thwam thwee little fishies and a mamma fishie too."

As people continued to phone, continued to ask questions, continued to be doubtful, Edwards grew more and more exasperated. Finally a call came from Allan Davis, a prominent businessman and member of the station's Board of Directors. When he too asked if it wasn't really a maneuver, Edwards burst out, "Hell, no, this is the real McCoy!"

Davis sounded really shocked . . . mumbled "Oh, oh," and hung up.

The effect was so impressive that Edwards decided to use the same words on the air. That might be the way to get people to really believe the news. Starting about 9:00 A.M., he repeated again and again that the attack was the "real McCoy"—so often that most people who listened to the Honolulu radio that day remember little else.

As they sat by their sets, many of the listeners found themselves paying special attention to the tone in Edwards' voice. They seemed to be searching for some extra clue that would tell them how serious the situation was. Mrs. Mayfield thought he sounded hoarse with suppressed excitement. Joan Stidham thought he was tense.

Edwards had at least one very disappointed listener. Sitting in the wardroom of the Japanese carrier *Akagi*, Commander Shin-Ichi Shimizu tuned in the radio to see how the Americans would react to the attack. Soon the announcer began breaking in with orders for different units to report to duty, but his voice was calm, and in between times the station continued to play music. It was a big anticlimax. The announcer wasn't nearly as excited as Shimizu.

CHAPTER X

"I Want Three Volunteers: You, You, and You"

HIGH ABOVE PEARL HARBOR, the last raiders wheeled off to the west, vanishing as mysteriously as they had appeared. On the *Nevada,* Commander Thomas moved off the mud of Hospital Point, and with the aid of tugs backed across the channel to the hard, sandy bottom of Waipio Penninsula. Word was passed releasing the men from battle stations, and Musician C. S. Griffin began groping his way up from the third deck forward. When he finally stepped into the bright morning sun, he glanced at his watch—it said 10.00 A.M.

For the first time men realized what a strain it had been. Boatswain's Mate K. V. Hendon ran into one of his best friends, who had been working a five-inch gun all morning. The man was so dazed he couldn't recognize anybody—all he could still see were planes. The men in the antiaircraft gun shack passed cigarettes around, omitting as usual the cleancut member of the team, who, as far as they knew, didn't smoke or drink or even take coffee. Shakily he said, "I think I'll have one of those."

Ensign John Landreth emerged from the port antiaircraft director, felt a curious numbness. Training and discipline had seen him through, but in the back of his mind the question kept revolving, "What is this really? A dream, perhaps, or is it really me shooting at other men and they shooting at me? What is this really?"

Perhaps indeed it was a dream, thought Pfc. John Fisher, a young MP at Fort Shafter. And when no one was looking, he even pinched himself, hoping he would wake up and find everything was all right. As Staff Ser-

163

geant Frank Allo surveyed Hickam's smoldering wreckage, he felt like a small boy looking at his dog lying in
the road after it had been hit by a car: it was simply
unbelievable that such a thing could have happened.

But there was little time for reflection. A man had to
think fast just to stay alive on the burning, sinking ships.
When the *Oglala* finally rolled over on her port side at
ten o'clock Admiral Furlong slid down toward the low
side of her deck. He showed the timing of a trapeze
artist, hopping nimbly ashore as the side of the deck
rolled flush with the edge of 1010 dock. Officially, it was
said the *Oglala's* seams had been sprung by the torpedo
that holed the *Helena;* but there are men who still claim
the old Fall River boat really "sank from fright."

Across the channel, it was time to abandon the *West
Virginia* too. Fires raged out of control around the conning tower and foremast, igniting the paint work, trapping Lieutenant Ricketts and the others still on the
bridge. Ensign Lombardi got a hose going, and a seaman
played it on the little group. Then Ensign Hank Graham
tossed up a line, and the men came down hand over hand
to the desk. Ensign Delano was cut off from the rest; he
finally crawled forward on the searchlight platform and
used the turrets as a giant stepladder to reach the deck.
He jumped overboard and swam for Ford Island, trying
to keep ahead of the oil burning on the water.

"Help! Help! I can't swim any farther," called a
familiar voice somewhere behind. It was an old chief
petty officer, known to be a poor swimmer. Delano was
now too weak to do any towing, but at least he could
encourage the man. As he turned his head, the old chief
thrashed by, arms and legs flying through the water, still
yelling that he couldn't swim any longer. He reached
shore five minutes before Delano.

Ensign Jacoby plunged off the *West Virginia's* forecastle, still wearing shoes, uniform, and even cap. He
swam under the burning oil, emerged beyond it, and
headed for a launch from the *Solace.* But his waterlogged
clothes dragged him down, and the burning oil crept

after him faster than he could swim. A sailor in the launch dived in to help—apparently forgetting that he couldn't swim at all. They were rapidly drowning each other when someone else in the launch knotted some sheets together, tossed out the improvised line, and dragged them both in. It was close—as they were hauled aboard, the bow of the launch was already starting to burn.

Ensign Vance Fowler, the *West Virginia's* disbursing officer, abandoned ship far more stylishly. He pushed off in a raft and moved swiftly to shore, using his cash ledger as a paddle.

Seaman George Murphy had no use for a paddle, trapped in the dispensary of the overturned *Oklahoma.* He and some 30 others were in a triangular-shaped air space with about a three-foot ceiling. Carpenter John A. Austin had a flashlight, and they played it around, trying to figure out where they were. None of them yet understood that the ship had turned over . . . that the tile overhead was really the deck.

For over an hour they didn't even try to get out. They could cling to a coaming around the tile without constant swimming, and it seemed best just to wait. They all assumed help was on the way—never dreaming they were far below the surface of Pearl Harbor.

Time went on, and they began to wonder. Eventually someone kicked a porthole under the water, and the men took turns ducking down and investigating it. They were still reluctant to dive through, because many of the ship's portholes led only to void space, and nobody wanted to get trapped that way.

Finally there was no choice. The air grew foul, and it was clear they couldn't live in the compartment. One by one they began squeezing through. It was a slow process. The porthole hung the wrong way (that's how they learned the ship was upside down), and every time anybody tried it, one man had to go under water and hold it open for the other to escape.

Nothing could help the man who first found the porthole. He was simply too big for the 14-inch opening. He bobbed back up, completely broken. Several others began shouting and calling out prayers.

Seaman Murphy barely made it. He had to try three times before he finally squeezed through and kicked out from the ship. He popped to the surface and was picked up by a launch from the *Dobbin* shortly after ten o'clock. The thing that really amazed him was not his escape but the scene in the harbor. The men in the compartment had all assumed that the *Oklahoma* was the only ship damaged.

There was no problem abandoning the *California*. As the burning oil drifted down the harbor, engulfing her stern, Captain Bunkley gave the order at 10:02 A.M., and the men swarmed ashore. But the wind blew the burning oil clear, and by 10:15 Captain Bunkley was trying to get everybody on board again to fight the fires. Yeoman Durrell Conner abandoned his efforts to evacuate some files, and watched an officer appeal to the men on shore. He gave quite a pep talk, saying that the *California* was a good ship, and if they would all come back and fight the fire, he thought they could save her.

The men seemed a little slow, and Conner had an inspiration. Noting the flag had not been raised, he grabbed a seaman and together they hoisted the colors on the fantail. A big cheer went up, and men began streaming back.

The upturned *Utah* was of course beyond hope, but the banging within her hull told Commander Isquith that he might at least save someone trapped inside. So he worked away with Machinist Szymanski, who knew all about welding . . . Watertender H. G. Nugent, who knew the structure of the ship's hull . . . and Chief Motor Machinist Terrance MacSelwiney, who wanted so much to help. Strafers bothered them at first, but then the raid died down, and cutting outfits arrived from the *Raleigh* and *Tangier*. They traced the noise to the dynamo room and went to work. After an hour they had an 18-inch hole and yelled to whoever was inside to stand clear so they could pound the plating in. When they finished, out popped Fireman John Vaessen, who had kept the lights going until it was too late to get out.

Unlike the men in the *Oklahoma* dispensary, Vaessen knew right away that the ship was upside down. He set out for the bottom with a flashlight and an open-end wrench for tapping signals. When he reached the double bottom, he had to undo 20 bolts to get through to the outer skin of the ship. Here he enjoyed a stroke of the incredible luck that sometimes helps a brave man in danger. His wrench just happened to fit the bolts.

Down in the plotting room of the *Nevada*, Ensign Merdinger wasn't yet trapped, but his agile mind began thinking along those lines. The room was five decks down. The regular lights were out, and the emergency system cast a weird green glow. The ventilation was gone, and to save their breath, the men lay down, phones strapped to their heads. Some were stripped to the waist; others still wore their shirts. Merdinger noted the beads of sweat glistening in the pale green light and thought what a dramatic movie it would make of men trapped in a submarine.

His thoughts passed through various phases, taking the form of silent prayers. At first he hoped he wouldn't be wounded. As things grew worse, he hoped that, if wounded, he at least wouldn't be permanently crippled. Finally, he reached the point where he was completely prepared to give his life. He prayed only that he might die—and he knew he was guilty of a cliché—like an officer and a gentleman, an inspiration to his men.

Certainly there was nothing to encourage him in the reports drifting down from above. The plotting room was a sort of clearinghouse for information, and all the news seemed bad. He heard about the *Oklahoma*—and the *Nevada* started to list. The *Arizona* blew up—and fire spread close to the *Nevada's* magazines. Every disaster on the other ships seemed to stalk his own. And now, to top it off, the bridge was calling for anyone who could speak Japanese. That suggested even more unpleasant possibilities.

Topside, Ensign John Landreth heard the radio say

the Japanese were landing on Diamond Head. Radioman
Peter La Fata of the *Swan* picked up even worse news:
they had taken Waikiki.

The danger lay not to the east but to the west, according to rumors heard by the *Arizona* survivors at the
Navy receiving station—in fact, 40 Japanese transports
were off Barbers Point. It was worse than that; they were
already landing men at Waianae Beach, someone told
Gunner's Mate Ralph Carl on the *Tennessee*.

Others claimed the Japanese were really landing to
the north. At the Navy Yard, civilian worker James
Spagnola heard that the entire north shore was lost. At
Schofield, Lieutenant Roy Foster got word that a major
assault would be launched on Schofield and Wheeler
within 30 minutes to an hour. Marine Sergeant Burdette
Odekirk heard that Schofield had fallen.

As if seaborne invasion wasn't enough, other reports
spread that Japanese paratroopers were raining down
from the skies—at Nanakuli Beach to the northwest . . .
in the sugar-cane fields southwest of Ford Island . . . in
the Manoa Valley, northwest of Honolulu. A man could
spot them by the rising sun sewed on their backs . . .
or by the red patch on the left breast pocket . . . or by
the rising sun shoulder patch. In any case, they were
wearing blue coveralls.

At Kaneohe, Mess Attendant Walter Simmons lost
no time taking off his own blue dungarees. Orders were
to change to khakis, but Simmons and most of the others
had none. So they boiled vats of strong coffee, dipped in
their whites, made khakis that way. Next report—the
Imperial Marines landing on the west shore were in
khaki. All hands change to whites. Later, the force
landing to the east was in white. Back to blues.

These were not men who had lost their heads—they
were acting on the best information available. An official Army circuit monitored at Kaneohe reported sampans landing troops at the Navy Ammunition Depot . . .
transports to the north . . . eight enemy battleships
70 miles away The Navy's harbor circuit was just as

active. On the *Vestal* Radioman John Murphy logged in messages that Japanese troops were landing on Barbers Point . . . paratroopers dropping in Nuuanu Valley . . . Honolulu's water supply had been poisoned.

Later, some radiomen felt the Japanese must have used Army and Navy frequencies, filling the air with false reports. But the outgoing logs of the various official message centers show that most, if not all, of the traffic was authentic:

1146. From Patwing. Enemy troops landing on north shore. Blue coveralls, red emblems.

1150 COM14 to CINCPAC. Parachutists landing at Barbers Point.

In the present frame of mind, small incidents were easily misinterpreted and then exaggerated. The *Helm* firing at the midget quickly became a Japanese task force bombarding the shore. When Fort Kamehameha, under the same illusion, began firing at the *Helm*, that just proved it.

It was the same with the paratroopers. Lieutenant Dickinson and Ensign McCarthy bailing out of their flaming planes were quickly spotted as two . . . 20 . . . 200 enemy soldiers. And once the idea was planted, the power of suggestion did the rest. Honolulu Police Headquarters got a frantic call that parachutists were landing on St. Louis Heights. Sergeant Jimmy Wong called for a National Guard Company and sent up Patrolman Albert Won. The Guard never arrived, but Won got there, armed with a .38. Luckily, all he found was a kite dangling from a tree.

Even more frightening reports were now pouring in. The local Japanese were rising, it was said, and Fifth Columnists were on the loose. Sergeant Wong got a call at 10:08 A.M. that two Japanese with a camera were on Wilhelmina Rise. He sent a squad car, found only a couple out walking. McKinley High School reported

saboteurs—two pedestrians happened to be passing the
ROTC building. But the stories spread faster than they
could possibly be disproved or checked.

On the seaplane tender *Swan*, Radioman Peter La
Fata heard that Japanese drivers were making milk de-
liveries with radio transmitters concealed in the cans to
beam in the raiding planes. Mrs. McCrimmon heard that
it happened at Kaneohe. Private Sydney Davis heard that
it was Hickam where the milk trucks went, and they
drove up and down the hangar line knocking the tails off
planes. Lieutenant George Newton also heard it was
Hickam, and that a warrant officer shot the milkman
when he boasted, "Well, I guess we Japanese showed
you." Radioman Douglas Eakar heard that the sides of
the truck dropped down and Japanese machine-gunners
sprayed the field.

Other rumors described how the local Japanese had
ringed Oahu with white sampans—presumably to show
the pilots that they had the right island. Additional
reports told of arrows cut in the cane fields, helpfully
pointing out the last 20 miles to Pearl Harbor. Under
the circumstances, Corporal Maurice Herman wasn't
surprised when all communications failed at his infantry
outfit's command post. Along with everybody else, he
supposed Japanese saboteurs had cut the wires. A careful
check uncovered the break right next to the command
post itself. A soldier pitching a pup tent had needed a
piece of line and cut it out of the unit's radio coil.

Worst of all was the report that Fifth Columnists
were poisoning the water. At Ewa the post dentist
spread a canvas cover over the base water tower, hoping
to frustrate the saboteurs. Others heard that it was too
late for preventive measures—the water was already
contaminated. Mrs. Arthur Gardiner, a Navy wife, tried
in vain to find a way of explaining the development to
her thirsty two-year-old. Fifteen-year-old Jackie Bennett
ordinarily didn't drink much water—now she was never
thirstier. Storekeeper H. W. Smith heard the rumor
after he had already quenched his thirst. He became
violently ill and thought what an inglorious way to die

for his country. They were quite clinical at the Hickam dispensary. Lieutenant Colonel Frank Lane had Saliva, the hospital's mascot dog, nailed up in a crate, then gave him a pan of water to see what would happen. The experiment failed when Saliva wouldn't drink. As the day wore on, people grew too thirsty to care . . . drank the water anyhow and, of course, with no aftereffects.

In all the excitement over spies and Fifth Columnists, almost everybody forgot about Japanese Consul General Kita. Soon after the attack started, Reporter Lawrence Nakatsuka of the *Star-Bulletin* went up to the consulate to get Mr. Kita's comments, but had little luck. The consul simply said he didn't believe there was an attack. Nakatsuka returned to the office, and as soon as the *Star-Bulletin's* extra was run off, he went back to the consulate with a copy. If it wasn't adequate evidence, it might at least be a conversation piece.

Meanwhile AP Correspondent Eugene Burns tipped off the police that the consulate might be worth checking. Robert Shivers, the local FBI man, was urging the same thing, having failed to interest the Army or Navy in the matter. It was around eleven o'clock by the time Lieutenant Yoshio Hasegawa—the ranking officer of Japanese ancestry—got under way. He arrived with two carloads of men, to find Consul General Kita lounging around the back yard in slacks, with Reporter Nakatsuka still trying to get his story.

Hasegawa and Kita entered the consulate, and other police trailed along. Smoke was coming from behind a door, and somebody asked if there was a fire. "No," Kita replied vaguely, "there is just something in there."

The police opened the door and found two men burning papers in a washtub on the floor. They stamped out the fire and managed to salvage one brown Manila envelope full of documents. The tour continued, and behind another door they found three or four men getting ready to burn five burlap bags of torn papers.

Hasegawa posted guards around the place, confined the staff to one room, arranged for the files to be turned over to the FBI and the Navy. He also asked Kita and

the other Japanese the same question that Reporter
Nakatsuka had found so fruitless: did they know there
was a Japanese attack on? No, they said solemnly, they
didn't know.

By now there was time for some of the formalities of
war. At 11:15, 72-year-old Governor Joseph E. Poindexter read his Proclamation of Emergency over KGU.
His voice trembled badly, but perhaps with good reason. One antiaircraft shell had already exploded in his
driveway; another pursued him to his office, bursting
in a corner of the Iolani Palace grounds. As the governor
wound up his address, a phone call came through from
the Army—get off the air; another attack was expected.
The Governor's aides complied with startling vigor—
seizing him the instant he finished, rushing him down
the stairs, into his car and away. The bewildered old
man thought he must have done something very wrong
on the broadcast and was under arrest.

In line with the Army's order, both KGU and KGMB
went off the air at 11:42. This was done, of course, to
prevent enemy planes from beaming in on either station
—undoubtedly a sound precaution, considering how
useful Commander Fuchida had found the local radio.
But the silence only added to the misery of the service
wives, huddled in their homes, lonely and afraid, longing for any news. Most of them kept their radios on
—listening for the occasional orders that still came over
the regular stations, or to the harrowing Fifth Column
rumors that poured out over the police radio.

Many of the wives were more than ready when formal
evacuation of the Hickam and Pearl Harbor areas began
at noon. The plan had been worked out long in advance
—buses and car pools would take everyone to the University of Hawaii, the various public schools, the YWCA;
from there the evacuees would eventually move in with
families in safe areas who had volunteered to take them.
Now the plan was under way—loud-speaker cars rolled
up and down the post streets, bellowing out instructions
to get ready.

At Hickam, Mrs. Arthur Fahrner struggled to load her

five children into the family car. But as fast as she packed them in, they would squirm out and run back to the house for some favorite toy. Finally she was ready, but just as she started off, ten-year-old Dan came running out—nearly left behind when he made a trip back for his swimming medal.

At Schofield, Major Virgil Miller's family faced a different problem. A Chinese GI had been sent to their house to tell them where to go, and the Millers weren't taking any chances. Fearing he was a Japanese soldier in American uniform, they made him shout his instructions through the locked front door.

Some didn't wait for formal evacuation. When the planes strafing Pearl City discouraged 11-year-old Don Morton from searching for his brother Jerry, their mother lost no time. She just scooped Don up in the family car and set off for the landing where the boys had been fishing. There was no traffic, but she kept honking the horn anyhow. It finally stuck, adding to the general din. Near the landing, Jerry emerged from the algarroba bushes and climbed aboard—a Marine corporal had pushed him to safety just before getting hit himself.

The boys' mother, Mrs. Thomas Croft, now turned the car around and headed for Honolulu. Huge explosions mushroomed up on their right. Thoroughly frightened, they stopped the car and ran into a cane field. There they sat for the next two hours . . . hands over their ears, heads between their knees. Whenever a plane flew by, Mrs. Croft would ask one of the boys to peek up and see if it was American. It never was.

Everyone had a different idea of safety. Mrs. Gerald Jacobs, another Pearl City Navy wife, stopped her car and stuck her head in a roadside bush—literally like an ostrich. Mrs. James Fischer stayed indoors, just as her husband told her to do. But for only so long. She suddenly put on her winter coat, ran out of Navy Housing Unit I, and began hitchhiking to Honolulu. A family friend saw her and gently led her back to shelter. Mrs. E. M. Eaton joined a group of friends who zigzagged madly down back roads to the Mormon church.

They took along the things they thought would come in handy. Mrs. Joseph Cote picked up a loaf of bread, a can of tuna, but no can opener. Mrs. Arthur Gardiner carried a blanket, a can of orange juice, a butcher knife, and *Pinocchio*. She and her two children then joined several other families in a small railroad ravine behind the junior officers' duplex quarters. *Pinocchio* proved a good idea, and the mothers took turns reading. Occasionally there were interruptions—cheers when a plane crashed, or an uneasy glance at some low-flying strafer— then back to the book again. As they read, they all did their best to keep a calm voice.

Once some Hawaiian-Japanese cane-field workers came running down the railroad track toward the little group. Everyone was sure the local Japanese had captured the island and this was the end. Mrs. Gardiner grabbed her butcher knife, ready to fight for her children's lives. But the field hands veered off and hid in the cane, equally terrified that they were going to be massacred by an aroused white population.

The local Japanese had heard rumors too. Early in the day the story spread that the Army planned to kill them all. Later this was modified—the Army would kill only the men, leave the women to starve.

There had already been some close calls. Five Japanese civilians had an especially narrow escape walking down a peaceful country road far from the fighting. They were spotted by Seaman George Cichon and several shipmates, who were bringing a truckload of ammunition from Lualualei Depot to Pearl Harbor. The driver stopped the truck, and one of the sailors wanted to shoot them all. At first the others more or less agreed, but suddenly some one said, "We are not beasts; these people had nothing to do with the attack." The men sheepishly got back in the truck and drove on. During the entire incident not a word was spoken by the five Japanese.

It was in this atmosphere that a young Japanese named Tadao Fuchikami, wearing a green shirt and khaki pants, chugged up to Fort Shafter on a two-cylinder Indian Scout motorcycle at 11:45 A.M.

Fuchikami was an RCA messenger, and this morning his day had started as usual. He punched in around 7:30, killed a little time, then picked up a batch of cables waiting for delivery. The cables had been put in pigeonholes, according to district, and Fuchikami just happened to take Kalihi, which included Fort Shafter. He thumbed through the envelopes to plan his best route—one of his first stops should be the doctor on Vineyard Street. The one for Fort Shafter would come later—there was nothing on the envelope that indicated priority; it just carried the two words "*Commanding General.*"

As he started off, he was already aware of the war. The operator had said something about planes dogfighting; he could see the antiaircraft burst over Pearl; he knew it was the Japanese. But war or no war, he still felt he had his regular job to do.

This morning it was slow going. The traffic was a nightmare. Then as he headed toward Shafter, he ran into a National Guard roadblock. They advised him to go home, told him they almost mistook him for a Japanese paratrooper. This was quite a jolt—Fuchikami hadn't realized how much his messenger's uniform resembled what the parachutists were supposed to be wearing. From now on he felt very conspicuous.

Next he hit a police roadblock on Middle Street. Only defense workers could get through. He rode his motorcycle on the sidewalk up to the barrier, showed the police his Shafter message, and they finally let him pass. When he got to Fort Shafter itself, he surprisingly had no trouble at all. A sentry waved him right on in. He drove straight to the message center and delivered the cable.

The message was decoded and delivered to the adjutant at 2:58 P.M. He saw that it reached General Short right away, who in turn sent a copy to Admiral Kimmel. It was a cable from General Marshall in Washington,

filed in the Army Signal Center for transmission via
Western Union at 12:01 (6:31 A.M., Hawaii time) and
received by Honolulu RCA at 7:33 A.M. just 22 minutes
before the attack. It said that the Japanese were pre-
senting an ultimatum at 1:00 P.M., Eastern Standard
Time (7:30 A.M. in Honolulu) and helpfully explained,
"Just what significance the hour set may have we do
not know, but be on the alert accordingly . . ."

Admiral Kimmel told the Army courier that it wasn't
of the slightest interest any more and threw it in the
waste basket.

He could have better used a message saying what the
Japanese were up to now. They had disappeared completely. No one seemed to have the slightest idea where
they had come from or where they had gone.

At first Kimmel thought they probably came from the
north. He had always felt there was more possibility of
an attack from the north than from the south. At 9:42
A.M. he even radioed Halsey on the *Enterprise* that there
was "some indication" of enemy forces to the northwest.

But soon all the information ran the other way. At
9:50 A.M. CINCPAC reported two enemy carriers 30
miles southwest of Barbers Point. Already maneuvering
in the area, the *Minneapolis* knew it wasn't so, tried to
scotch the report by radioing, "No carriers in sight."
The message came through, "Two carriers in sight."

At 12.58 A.M. four Japanese transports were reported
to the southwest . . . at 1:00 P.M. an enemy ship four
miles off Barbers Point. A bearing on a Japanese carrier,
which had briefly broken radio silence, could be read
as coming from either directly north or directly south.
The interpreter figuratively tossed a coin, called it directly south.

Recalling that two Japanese carriers had recently been
detected at Kwajalein, Admiral Halsey played a hunch
that fitted in nicely with the meager intelligence available—he began concentrating his search to the south and
southwest.

The ships emerging from Pearl Harbor did their best
to chase down the leads. When a message arrived

reporting the enemy off Barbers Point, Admiral Draemel hoisted the signal "concentrate and attack." There weren't many ships to "concentrate"—just the *St. Louis, Detroit, Phoenix,* and a dozen destroyers—but they all dashed bravely forward. They, of course, found nothing, and as they steamed on to join Halsey, they were themselves identified as the enemy by an *Enterprise* scouting plane. This generated more reports pointing to the southwest, some of which were relayed to Admiral Draemel. Without realizing it, his ships were at one point searching for themselves.

The air search was having no better luck. At first the only planes available were some old unarmed amphibians based on Ford Island. They belonged to Utility Squadron One, which performed chores like carrying mail, towing targets, and photographing exercises. Nothing else could fly, so they had to be used; but it wasn't an appealing assignment—even after rifles were provided for protection.

"I want three volunteers—you . . . you . . . and you," Chief G. R. Jacobs told three of the squadron's radiomen. Aviation Radioman Harry Mead soon found himself airborne in one of the planes. They had no luck, but they did establish that the Japanese weren't lying off Oahu. It made no difference; the rumors rolled on.

The Army couldn't get up any search planes in the early stages, but by mid-morning Major General Frederick Martin called Patwing 2 to put some bombers at the Navy's disposal. That was what he was meant to do under the Army-Navy plan for "cooperation." Nobody would give him a mission.

But General Martin heard somewhere that two carriers were south of Barbers Point, so he sent out four light bombers at 11:27 A.M. They found nothing. Then he sent some other planes a few miles to the north. They didn't find anything either. That afternoon he made one more try—this time at the Navy's request. He sent six B-17s to look for a carrier that was rumored to be 65 miles north of Oahu. They too found nothing.

On Ford Island, nine of the planes just in from the

Enterprise were still undamaged, and Ensign Dobson
rushed to get them in shape. Each one was loaded with
a 500-pound bomb, and tank trucks stood by to gas
them up.

The pilots waited at the command center, swapping
experiences and joyfully greeting late-comers who trickled in from forced landings all over the island. Lieutenant Dickinson arrived, having hitched one last ride—this
time in a launch from the Navy Yard. He was surprised
at the way men who had never been particularly close
now fell on one another's shoulders. One senior officer,
who had always seemed a crotchety martinet, threw an
arm around Dickinson and even produced a nickel, calling, "Somebody go and get this officer a cup of coffee
. . ." (It was great while it lasted, but Dickinson also
noted that within a couple of days relationships were
back to normal.)

By 12:10 the planes were ready, the pilots climbed in,
and Lieutenant Commander Halstead Hopping led them
on a flight that scouted a wide sector 200 miles to the
north. The right direction, but by now just a little too
late.

As they returned to Pearl late that afternoon, the sun
blazed unmercifully in Ensign Dobson's face. He was
dead tired, and it made him so very sleepy. He tried to
concentrate, but his mind kept drifting off. Could it be,
he wondered, that this day was just a dream . . . that
when he got back to Ford Island, he could go home to
his family after all?

As the search dragged on, the best clues lay untouched.
Major Truman Landon couldn't interest anybody in the
Japanese planes he saw flying north when he was bringing in his B-17. Lieutenant Patriarca had seen Japanese
planes flying north too, but he was so concerned about
alerting the *Enterprise* that he didn't think of anything
else. The Opana radar plot had quite a story to tell, but
when the Navy asked the Army radar people whether
they had any information on the Japanese flight in, nobody knew anything. And everyone forgot that radar not
only can track planes in but also track them out. Opana

carefully plotted the planes returning to the north—and the information center was manned by now—but in the excitement no one did anything with this data.

It made no difference to Commander Fuchida. The Japanese leader didn't even try to cover his tracks on the flight back to the carriers. There just wasn't enough gas for deception. As fast as the bombers finished their work, they rendezvoused with the fighters 20 miles northwest of Kaena Point, then flew back in groups. The fighters had no homing device and depended on the larger planes to guide them to the carriers.

Fuchida himself hung around a little while. He wanted to snap a few pictures, drop by all the bases, and get some idea of what was accomplished. The smoke interfered a good deal, but he felt sure four battleships were sunk and three others badly damaged. It was harder to tell about the airfields, but there were no planes up, so perhaps that was his answer.

As he headed back alone around eleven o'clock, a fighter streaked toward him, banking from side to side. A moment of tension—then he saw the rising sun emblem. One of the *Zuikaku's* fighters had been left behind. It occurred to Fuchida that there might be others too, so he went back to the rendezvous point for one last check. There he found a second fighter aimlessly circling about; it fell in behind, and the three planes wheeled off together toward the northwest—last of the visitors to depart.

At his end, Admiral Kusaka did his best to help. He moved the carriers to within 190 miles of Pearl Harbor. He wasn't meant to go closer than 200 miles, but he knew that even an extra five or ten miles might make a big difference to a plane short of gas or crippled by enemy gunfire. He wanted to give the fliers every possible break.

Now everything had been done, and Admiral Kusaka stood on the bridge of the *Akagi* anxiously scanning the southern horizon. It was just after 10:00 A.M. when he saw the first faint black dots—some flying in groups,

some in pairs, some alone. On the *Shokaku*, the first
plane Lieutenant Ebina saw was a single fighter skim-
ming the sea like a swallow, as it headed for the carrier.
It barely made the ship.

Gas was low . . . nerves were frayed . . . time was short.
In the rush, normal landing procedures were scrapped.
As fast as the planes came in, they were simply dragged
aside to allow enough room for another to land. Yet there
were few serious mishaps. As one fighter landed on the
Shokaku, the carrier took a sudden dip and the plane
toppled over. The pilot crawled out without a scratch.
Lieutenant Yano ran out of gas and had to ditch beside
the carrier—he and his crew were hauled aboard, none
the worse for their swim.

Some familiar faces were missing. Twenty-seven-year-
old Ippei Goto, who this morning had donned his ensign's
uniform for the first time, failed to get back to the *Kaga*.
Baseball-loving Lieutenant Fusata Iida didn't reach the
Soryu. Artistic Lieutenant Mimori Suzuki never made the
Akagi—he was the pilot who crashed into the *Curtiss*.
In all, 29 planes with 55 men were lost.

But 324 planes came safely home, while the deck
crews waved their forage caps. The men swarmed around
the pilots as they climbed from their cockpits. Congratu-
lations poured in from all sides. As Lieutenant Hashimoto
wearily made his way to his quarters on the *Hiryu*, everyone seemed to be asking what was it like . . . what did he
do . . . what did he see.

Now that it was all over, many of the pilots felt a
curious letdown. Some bragged for another chance because they missed their assigned targets. Others said
they were dissatisfied because they had only "near-
misses." Commander Amagai, flight deck officer of the
Hiryu, tried to cheer them up. He assured them that a
near-miss was often an effective blow. Then he had an
even brighter idea for lifting their spirits: "We're not
returning to Tokyo; now we're going to head for San
Francisco."

At the very least, they expected another crack at
Oahu. Even while Commander Amagai was cheering up

the pilots, he was rearming and refueling the planes for a new attack. When Lieutenant Hashimoto told his men they would probably be going back, he thought he detected a few pale faces; but, on the whole, everyone was enthusiastic. On the *Akagi*, the planes were being lined up for another take-off as Commander Fuchida landed at 1:00 P.M.—the last plane in.

When Fuchida reported to the bridge, a heated discussion was going on. It turned out another attack wasn't so certain after all. For a moment they postponed any decision, to hear Fuchida's account. After he finished, Admiral Nagumo announced somewhat ponderously, "We may then conclude that anticipated results have been achieved."

The statement had a touch of finality that showed the way the admiral's mind was working. He had always been against the operation, but had been overruled. So he had given it his very best and accomplished everything they asked of him. He had gotten away with it, but he certainly wasn't going to stretch his luck.

Commander Fuchida argued hard: there were still many attractive targets; there was virtually no defense left. Best of all, another raid might draw the carriers in. Then, if the Japanese returned by way of the Marshalls instead of going north, they might catch the carriers from behind. Somebody pointed out that this was impossible— the tankers had been sent north to meet the fleet and couldn't be redirected south in time. Fuchida wasn't at all deterred; well, they ought to attack Oahu again anyhow.

It was Admiral Kusaka who ended the discussion. Just before 1:30 P.M. the chief of staff turned to Nagumo and announced what he planned to do, subject to the commander's approval: "The attack is terminated. We are withdrawing."

"Please do," Nagumo replied.

In the home port at Kure, Admiral Yamamoto sensed it would happen. He sat impassively in the *Nagato's* operations room while the staff buzzed with anticipation. The first attack was such a success everyone agreed there should be a second. Only the admiral remained non-committal. He knew all too well the man in charge. Suddenly he muttered in almost a whisper: "Admiral Nagumo is going to withdraw."

Minutes later the news came through just as Yama-moto predicted. Far out in the Pacific the signal flags ran up on the *Akagi's* yardarm, ordering a change in course. At 1:30 P.M. the great fleet swung about and headed back home across the northern Pacific.

South of Oahu, Ensign Sakamaki was still trying. But despite all the vows he exchanged with Seaman Inagaki their midget sub was no nearer Pearl Harbor. A brief encounter with a reef had damaged one torpedo tube beyond repair. About noon they ran on another reef and smashed the other tube. They worked clear again, but now they had no weapon left.

"What are we going to do, sir?" asked Seaman Inagaki.

"We're going to plunge into an enemy battleship, pref-erably the *Pennsylvania*. We're going to crash against the ship and if we're still alive, we're going to kill as many as we can."

To Sakamaki's surprise, Inagaki bought the idea. He tightened his grip on the wheel and shouted, "Full speed ahead!" But it was no use. The afternoon turned into a jumbled series of frustrations. Sakamaki was dimly aware of trying and trying but just not getting anywhere. The sub wouldn't steer . . . the air pressure was more than 40 pounds . . . the hull reeked with the smell of bitter acid. He choked for air; his eyes were smarting; he was only half-conscious. Occasionally he could hear Inagaki sob-bing in the dark, and he was crying too.

"Let's make one more try," he gasped, but the next thing he knew he saw Diamond Head off to port. It was dusk and he had wandered a good ten miles from Pearl Harbor. He was beaten and he knew it. With his last strength he set his course for the rendezvous point off Lanai Island, where he was to meet the mother sub *I-24*. Then he passed out.

CHAPTER XI

"Chief, My Mother and Dad Gave Me This Sword"

SUNDAY AFTERNOON, Pearl Harbor was sure of only one thing—wherever the Japanese were, they would be back.

The *Pennsylvania*, still squatting in Drydock No. 1, trained her big 14-inch guns down the channel mouth. Fireman H. E. Emory of the *California* teamed up with an officer who had found an old Lewis machine gun. They made a swivel mount from the wheel of an overturned cart and established themselves on a mooring quay. On Ford Island, Seaman James Layman joined a working party filling and loading sandbags. He skinned his knuckles on the burlap, got blisters shoveling the sand; but the situation was desperate and he worked until it was too dark to see.

At the Navy Yard a Coxey's Army of servicemen, civilian yard workers, and 100 per cent amateurs struggled to get the undamaged ships in condition to fight. An officer of the *Pennsylvania* asked civilian yard worker Harry Danner to help find extra men to load ammunition. There were a number of yard hands around, but even on December 7 a vestige of protocol remained—the officer didn't feel he could give orders to a civilian. So the two men went around together, Danner serving as ambassador. They soon had enough volunteers, and a human chain was formed between three loaded whaleboats and the *Pennsylvania's* ammunition hoist. They transferred over a thousand bags of powder.

Danner next headed for the *Honolulu* to help get her engines reassembled. He had banged up a foot and thrown away his shoes, but he hobbled across the Navy

Yard as fast as he could with another worker. They might as well have been the Japanese invasion force. Trigger-happy sentries were now stopping anybody not in uniform, and it took a lot of persuading to get through. But the work was finished by 10:30 that night.

At the next pier other yard workers struggled to install the *San Francisco's* antiaircraft batteries. James Spagnola clambered around the guns, still sporting the golf shoes he wore when the attack began. It was a job that normally took two weeks, but this time it was done in one day.

Through all the pounding and hammering and the clatter of pneumatic drills, a juke box blared away at the pier canteen. Most of the time it played "I Don't Want to Set the World on Fire."

There was music on the *Maryland* too—her band tooted bravely on the quarter-deck while her gunners got ready for the next attack. The *Tennessee* was just as ready, but the rest of Battleship Row—once the core of the fleet's strength—was now out of the game.

The *Arizona* sprawled twisted and burning. A small boat alongside her fantail; Lieutenant K. S. Masterson climbed aboard and hauled down the torn, oil-stained colors still flying from her stern. He felt they should be saved as a war memento. Quartermaster Edward Vecera replaced the *West Virginia's* battle colors with a fresh flag borrowed from another ship. He asked an officer what to do with the dirty, ragged bunting just hauled down. The officer replied that normally all battle colors were sent to Annapolis, where they would be displayed in a glass case, but this time—well, maybe it would be better to burn them. Vecera carried out the suggestion.

On the *West Virginia's* quarter-deck a devoted band of officers still fought the fires that raged throughout the ship. Lieutenant Commander Doir Johnson looked at the melted porthole glass and thought of the limp watches painted by Salvador Dali. Against fire that hot, nothing could be done. The group was finally forced off about five o'clock. But men still lived on the *West Virginia.* Far below decks three sailors sat, hopelessly trapped in the pump room. They clung to life until the day before Christmas Eve.

It was a different story on the upturned *Oklahoma*. Little knots of men swarmed over her bottom—tracing the steady tapping that came from within . . . pounding back signals of encouragement . . . calling for more cutting equipment. Teams from the *Maryland*, the salvage ship *Widgeon*, the *Rigel*, the *Solace*, the Navy Yard, the *Oklahoma* herself worked at half a dozen different places along the huge hull.

The job wasn't just a matter of cutting a hole and pulling somebody out. The tapping echoed and reverberated through the hollow space along the keel until nobody could say where it really came from. The cutters had to make an educated guess and, once inside the hull, search out the source. They had to stumble back and forth through a dark, eerie, upside-down world . . . tapping and listening for answering taps . . . until they could pinpoint the right spot. Then more cutting to get finally through to the trapped men.

There were bitter disappointments. The first two men located were asphyxiated because the acetylene torch ate up all the oxygen. A call went out for pneumatic cutting equipment—slower but perhaps less dangerous. Julio DeCastro, a Navy Yard foreman and expert chipper, took out a crew of 21 yard hands, went to work with drills and air hammers. But a new danger arose— this slower cutting method let the trapped air escape faster than the hole could be made. As the air hissed out, the water would rise, threatening to drown the men before they could be freed. The cutters used rags, handkerchiefs, anything to keep the air from escaping too fast. They weren't always successful.

The teams lost all track of time. At one point the *Maryland* sent over some stew, and Fireman John Gobidas of the *Rigel* paused long enough to grab a bite. There were no spoons or plates; he just dipped his hands —foul with oil and muck—into the stew and spread it on some bread. He thought it tasted very good.

Inside the *Oklahoma* the trapped men waited. Eight

seamen buried in the steering engine room set up a curious democracy. Every move or decision affecting their
lives was decided by vote. Their first step was to pool
their clothing and their mattresses—the room was where
they always slept—and plug an air vent that spouted a
steady stream of water. Next, they investigated possible
routes of escape, but water gushed through every door
they tried, so they voted to sit back and wait. They found
some tools and banged the sides of the ship, but most
of the time they just sat. They had plenty of chance to
meditate, and 17-year-old Seaman Willard Beal thought
of all the mean things he had ever done to anyone.

Just forward, in the passageway off the handling room
of No. 4 turret, 30 other men were also waiting. They
sat in their shorts, covered with oil, with one flashlight
among them: The only hope seemed to lie in an escape
hatch that led to the top deck, which now, of course,
was straight down. Conceivably, a man might hold his
breath . . . pull himself 30 feet down the hatch . . .
cross the deck . . . and come up into the harbor outside
the ship. But it was a very long shot. Several tried and
came back, unable to do it. One succeeded—a nonswimmer, nonathlete from Brooklyn named Weisman.
He told the rescue crews where to look, and a cutting
team was organized.

The men in the handling room passageway had no
way of knowing this. They only knew that the air was
growing worse and the water was slowly rising as the
air was used up. By late afternoon there were just ten
men left, and Seaman Stephen Young bet money they
would suffocate before they drowned. His friend Seaman Wilber T. Hinsperger took up the bet.

They had by now lost all hope of ever getting out.
Still, no one cracked. Instead, they opened a door into
the "Lucky Bag" (the ship's lost and found locker) . . .
got out pea coats and mattresses . . . and lay down to
await the end.

More hours passed. Then suddenly—incredibly—they
heard distant banging and hammering echo down from
above. At first it would come and go; then it drew

closer. Young picked up a dog wrench and pounded back "SOS." The banging grew steadier until finally it was right outside. A voice yelled through the bulkhead, asking the men if they could stand a hole being drilled. Everyone shouted back yes, but it was a close thing. The air rushed out, the water surged up, and as the plate was twisted off, the men scrambled out just in time. Grinning Navy and civilian workers boosted them up through the ship's bottom; and they emerged into the cool, fresh air to find it was—Monday.

Rescuers rushed up with oranges and cigarettes, and a few minutes later Commander Jesse Kenworthy, the *Oklahoma's* executive officer, came by to see if they were all right. He had been on the ship's bottom directing rescue work ever since the attack. He would still be there at 5:30 Monday afternoon when Williard Beal emerged from the steering engine room; in fact, he wouldn't leave until the last of 32 survivors was pulled from the *Oklahoma's* hull some 36 hours after she rolled over into the Pearl Harbor mud.

But all this lay in the future. That Sunday afternoon the survivors were just starting to emerge. Three men were hauled out of a cofferdam, one of them clutching a basketball. He clung to it fiercely, wouldn't give it up even after reaching the *Maryland's* sick bay. Speculation ran wild—some said he had saved it as a reserve supply of oxygen . . . others that he planned to use it as a lifebuoy . . . others that he was just a typical basketball player. Ensign Charles Mandell heard that, while waiting for rescue, he had even shot a few baskets through a hole in the cofferdam beam.

Men were also trapped on the listing *California*. About three o'clock a rescue party cut into a compartment that was flooded with oil, hauled out two hospital corpsmen. They slumped on deck, looking like two bundles of sodden, oil-soaked rags. Pharmacist's Mate William Lynch walked by, calling the names of men still missing from his unit. One of the bundles suddenly popped up, crying "That's me!"

Other crew members waged a losing fight to keep the

California afloat. The tender *Swan* drew alongside, contributed some pumps, and Radioman Charles Michaels helped drag up mattresses in a futile effort to plug some of the leaks. It was hopeless. A diver from the salvage ship *Widgeon* reported a hole as big as a house. Someone asked him if a collision mat would help, and he gloomily replied, "I don't believe they make them that big."

Later more salvage experts turned up from the *Vestal*, but even their skill was not enough. Finally it was decided that the ship couldn't stay afloat but could be kept in an upright position with planned flooding. Gently the *California* settled to the bottom of the harbor.

The *Nevada* sat on the bottom too, and in the wreckage of the captain's quarters a sword lay twisted and burned behind a charred bureau. Later, when Captain Scanland found it there, he held it out in both his hands and turned to CPO Jack Haley, who happened to be standing nearby: "Chief, my Mother and Dad gave me this sword when I graduated from the Naval Academy many years ago."

Haley could sense all the captain's pent-up emotion and grief at being away from his ship during the attack. The chief understood perhaps better than most, for the *Nevada* meant everything to him too—she was his first and only ship, his home for the past 12 years. He couldn't hold back the tears.

Down in the *Nevada's* plotting room, Ensign Merdinger stubbornly stuck to his post. He knew from the water dripping into the room that the deck above was flooded. And he knew from the silent phones that few hands were left below decks. There was no longer any need for an information center; still he hated to leave. At three o'clock a rush of water through the seams of the door left no other choice. He phoned topside and was told to come on up. While the water poured in and swirled around the crew's feet, they carefully unplugged the phones, neatly coiled the extension lines, and hung them on their usual hooks.

But the casual approach had its limits. As the men

scrambled up the shaft to the conning tower, it occurred to Merdinger that normally some of them might have difficulty making the climb; this time there was no trouble at all.

On deck, preparations were being made for a last-ditch stand. Someone handed Marine Private Payton McDaniel a rifle and two rounds of ammunition. Slender rations, but McDaniel later discovered the rifle had no firing pin anyhow. A Marine detail was sent to the beach to dig emplacements for the World War I machine guns and BARs that had been salvaged. The basic defense plan—hold the ship as long as possible, then take to the hills.

At Hickam, Corporal John Sherwood and Master Sergeant Bonnie Neighbors were also preparing for a last stand. They dragged an old C-33 into the boondocks, dug a good position around it, and set up two machine guns. Private J. H. Thompson joined another man from the 50th Reconnaissance Squadron, who had established a machine-gun nest near the ruined Snake Ranch. The man had taken the trouble to stock it with beer and wine salvaged from the wreckage. Some of the bottles were broken, and the bugs had to be strained out, but this was a minor hardship. The two men cheerfully defended the position all afternoon.

"Help yourself" was also the rule at the officers' club. Everyone expected the Japanese that night, so the food and refreshments might as well be free. At base headquarters Colonel Cheney Bertholf, the post adjutant, carted out his files and burned them. Even Colonel Farthing, the base commander, was sure the Japanese planned to take over Hickam—that was why they didn't bomb the runways or control tower. Master Sergeant M. D. Mannion felt the place would fall so soon that he might as well pull out and go to Schofield. Up there he might at least be of some service in standing off the enemy.

Actually, Schofield was on the move. Most of the infantry and artillery were now at assigned defense positions around the island—the 98th Coast Artillery at

Wheeler . . . the 28th Infantry at Waikiki . . . the 27th
farther down the shore . . . other units along the north
coast, on the heights above Pearl, and at the bases on
the windward side.

As the long column of troops rolled into Kaneohe
around 2:30 P.M., Mess Attendant Walter Simmons had
only one thought: they had been run out of Schofield.
But he too was prepared for a final stand. He now
carried an old Springfield rifle and had bandoleers of
ammunition strung over his shoulder and around his
waist. He felt ready for anything and fancied that he
looked just a little like Pancho Villa.

The men shoveled out foxholes—Simmons dug his in
the unfinished bottom of the officers' swimming pool—
and set up machine guns all over the steep hill in the
center of the base. By sundown Kaneohe was prepared
for the next attack.

The island's scattered defenses were now being directed by General Short from Aliamanu Crater, three
miles west of Fort Shafter. The command post was
established in a deep ordnance storage tunnel—ideal for
holding out against the coming assault. The general had
moved in during the morning, trailed by the usual
retinue of staff and communications men.

Lieutenant Samuel Bradlyn was establishing the link
with Hickam, and as he set up his code equipment, he
watched General Short, General Martin, and other high-
ranking officers huddle together. They looked terribly
worried, and for the first time Bradlyn realized that
even generals were human beings who didn't always
know what to do and had to pace back and forth while
making decisions.

Of one thing they were certain—there had to be
martial law. General Short approached old Governor
Poindexter on this shortly after noon. The governor
dragged his feet—he thought it was probably necessary,
yet he hated to do it. He finally said he wanted to check
with the White House first, would give Short his answer
in an hour. He put through a call to the President at
12:40 P.M., and it didn't help when the operator—now

acting under the Navy censor—kept insisting, "What are you going to talk about?" The governor had been shoved aside already.

The President was properly soothing, agreed that martial law was all for the best. Then Short reappeared to press the point: for all he knew landing parties were on the way . . . the raid was probably the prelude to all-out attack . . . he couldn't afford to take chances. The governor finally signed the Proclamation, and martial law was announced at 4:25 P.M.

The civilians considered themselves in the front lines anyhow. Edgar Rice Burroughs, creator of *Tarzan,* joined a group of men digging slit trenches along the shore. Others rallied to the Territorial Guard, which was hastily built around the University of Hawaii ROTC unit. As the 2nd Battalion mobilized at Wahiawa, a sergeant drove up in a command car with some welcome news—the Army had sent him over from Schofield to help. He was a godsend: the unit had no equipment, and the sergeant knew how to get everything: blankets, mess gear, guns. He proved an ingenious, tireless worker and ultimately stayed with the outfit a whole month. Then one day he commandeered some whisky from a padlocked liquor store, and that proved his undoing. When the proprietor complained, it turned out the man was no sergeant at all—just a prisoner released from the Schofield stockade during the raid. He had immediately stolen a sergeant's uniform . . . then the command car . . . and had been stealing ever since, filling the home guards' desperate needs. He was a sort of military Robin Hood.

Nearly every organized group on Oahu staked out something to do. Boy Scouts fought fires, served coffee, ran messages. The American Legion turned out for patrol and sentry duty. One Legionnaire struggled into his 1917 uniform, had a dreadful time remembering how to wind his puttees and put on his insignia. He took it out on his wife, and she told him to leave her alone—go out and fight his old enemy, the Germans. The San Jose College football team, in town for a benefit game the following week end, signed up with the Police Department for guard duty. Seven of them joined the force, and Quarterback Paul Tognetti stayed on for good, ultimately going into the dairy business.

A local committee, called the Major Disaster Council, had spent months preparing for this kind of day; now their foresight was paying off. Forty-five trucks belonging to American Sanitary Laundry, New Fair Dairy, and other local companies sped off to Hickam as converted ambulances. Dr. Forrest Pinkerton dashed to the Hawaii Electric Company's refrigerator, collected the plasma stored there by the Chamber of Commerce's Blood Bank. He piled it in the back of his car, distributed it to various hospitals, then rushed on the air, appealing for more donors. Over 500 appeared within an hour, swamping Dr. John Devereux and his three assistants. They took the blood as fast as they could, ran out of containers, used sterilized Coca-Cola bottles.

All kinds of people went through the line. Navy wife Maureen Hayter was shocked when offered a swig of Old Grand-Dad afterward—it just didn't seem right. Another woman was a well-known prostitute. She couldn't give blood but wanted to do something. Dr. Devereux put her to work cleaning bottles and tubes. She turned out to be his most faithful volunteer.

Civilian doctors and nurses converged on the Army's Tripler Hospital. Among them went Dr. John J. Moorhead, a distinguished New York surgeon who happened to be in Honolulu delivering a series of lectures. Some 300 doctors had attended his first talk Thursday morning, half of them Army and Navy men. Dr. Moorhead had been an Army surgeon in World War I, loved the service, and took great pains to see they were invited. The service doctors accepted with enthusiasm—Dr. Moorhead was a world-famous specialist and, unlike almost everyone else, he could speak from actual battle experience.

On Friday night the doctor was slated to speak on "Back Injuries" but at the last minute the schedule was juggled and he spoke instead on "The Treatment of

Wounds." If the Program Committee had known the attack was coming, it couldn't have lined up a better subject.

Dr. Moorhead had Saturday off, but he was to speak on "Burns" at 9:00 A.M. Sunday. As he ate his breakfast, guns boomed in the distance. Walking through the hotel lobby, he heard that Pearl Harbor was under attack. He told Dr. Hill, who was driving him to the lecture, but the local doctor was unimpressed: "Oh, you hear all kinds of stories around this place."

They turned on the car radio and picked up the 8:40 bulletin. That convinced them and they dropped by Dr. Hill's house while he told his wife and children to take shelter. Then they drove on to the Mabel L. Smyth Auditorium so that Dr. Moorhead could give his talk. The two doctors were having the same trouble as everyone else making the lightning adjustment to war . . . realizing that it also affected their own day.

The lecture hall was almost empty—only 50 doctors instead of the usual 300, and no Army or Navy men. As Dr. Moorhead reached the platform shells began landing outside. He cheerily told the audience that the noise reminded him of Chateau-Thierry. Then he pointed out that this was Sunday, so he would give a sermon with an appropriate text: "Be ye also ready, for in the hour that ye know not . . ."

At this point Dr. Jesse Smith, a local physician, burst into the hall shouting that 12 surgeons were needed at Tripler right away. That did it—speaker and audience bolted from the room together.

Dr. Moorhead and his pickup team of civilian surgeons spent the next 11 hours operating with hardly any break. Once during the afternoon he dropped down to the mess hall for a bite, ran into Colonel Miller, the hospital commandant. The doctor suggested—perhaps a little wistfully—that maybe he should go on active duty. Miller said he would see what he could do, and a little later poked his head into the operating room: "You're in the Army now!" To Dr. Moorhead, this wonderful service was even more wonderful—no forms, questionnaires, or fingerprints; yet he had become a full colonel in two hours.

As he worked away, Colonel Moorhead displayed a mixture of competence and optimism that did wonders for the wounded. "Son," he told one boy, "you've been through a lot of hell, and you're going into some more. This foot has to come off. But there's been many a good pirate with only one leg!"

The wounded needed this kind of cheerfulness. Without it another boy who had lost a leg wanted only to die—he was sure his girl would no longer have him. Private Edward Oveka had a shattered leg too; and after he came out of ether, he was afraid to see if he still had his foot. He finally worked up his courage and took a look—it was still there.

Whatever their feelings, the men were incredibly quiet and uncomplaining. At Queens Hospital, one man lay riddled with shrapnel. When Dr. Forrest Pinkerton began explaining that he would have to delay treating the less serious wounds, the man calmly broke in, "Just do what you can, I know there are other people waiting."

Occasionally the mildest of disagreements would arise. At Hickam, Captain Carl Hoffman thought a drink might buck up a badly wounded major. He was telling someone to measure a shot when the major interrupted, "Don't tell him how much to put in the glass—fill it up." At the Navy Hospital, a seaman with a bad stomach wound wanted orange juice, but the doctor thought this would be fatal and ordered water instead. When the man objected, the doctor finally whispered to the nurse to get the juice—he would probably die anyway. "I heard you, Doctor," called the seaman, "and I still want orange juice." Perhaps due to this sort of determination, a week later the man was doing fine.

Everyone did his best to make the wounded comfortable. Morphine did its work too, and many drifted off to fitful sleep. Radioman Glenn Lane awoke long enough on the hospital ship *Solace* to see an attendant bending over him with some soup. The man was Filipino, and Lane started with fright—he was sure he had been captured by the Japanese.

A man didn't need narcotics to see himself in enemy hands. Dark, dreary thoughts ran through the minds of many still able to fight. Chief Peter Chang saw himself pulling a rickshaw. Fireman John Gobidas expected to be a corpse or a prisoner, but he prayed that Chief Metalsmith Burl W. Brookshire would somehow survive, to inspire others with the courage he had given the men on the *Rigel.* Electrician's Mate James Powers thought about those oriental brain tortures, then remembered he was a Texan and decided to make this another Alamo.

Actually, the only Japanese invasion of the Hawaiian Islands was by now well under way. It was just about church time when it all began on Niihau, westernmost island of the Hawaiian chain. Niihau was privately owned by the Robinson family, who operated the island mainly as a sheep and cattle ranch and lovingly preserved it as a pure Polynesian paradise—no visitors, no modern conveniences, no Western gadgets like guns, telephones, or radios. Once a week a boat came over from Kaui, 20 miles away, and left supplies at Kii Landing on the island's northern tip. There was no other communication with the outside world. In case of serious trouble, it was arranged that a signal fire would be built on a mountain in sight of Kaui. Otherwise, it was just assumed that everything was all right.

And this Sunday everything was all right, as the islanders flocked to the little church in Puuwai, about 15 miles down the west shore from Kii Landing. Puuwai was the only village on the island—a collection of small houses scattered among the rocks, cactus, and keawa trees. Everybody lived there except the Robinsons, who had a homestead at Kie Kie, two miles away.

But just as everyone was entering the church, two planes flew overhead. The islanders all noticed that one plane was sputtering and smoking; they all saw red circles under the wings. And even though they were

just ranch hands and cowboys, carefully protected from
the problems of the world, many of them sensed trouble
far more quickly than their sophisticated neighbors on
Oahu. Most recognized the Japanese insignia; some even
guessed an attack on Pearl Harbor.

About two o'clock one of the planes reappeared,
circling low over the pastures and hedges. The pilot
picked out a spot and bounced to a heavy landing. He
bumped over some rocks, through a fence, and stopped
near the house of Hawila Kaleohano.

There was trouble right away. Hawila ran up and
yanked open the canopy; the pilot reached for a pistol;
Hawila grabbed it first and pulled the aviator from the
plane. Then the pilot began searching inside his shirt;
Hawila tore it open and snatched out some papers and
a map.

By now the whole island was crowding around. The
villagers were shouting questions, and the pilot was
shaking his head, trying to show that he didn't understand English . . . he could only speak Japanese.

There was just one thing to do—send for Harada, one
of the two Japanese on Niihau. He was a 30-year-old
Nisei who had come to the island a year ago as a housekeeper, now worked as both the Robinsons' caretaker
and an assistant beekeeper. The head beekeeper was
the other Japanese, an old man named Sintani, who
had lived on Niihau for many years.

Even with Harada's help, no one got much out of the
pilot. He said he flew over from Honolulu; he denied
any raid; he was vague about the reason for his trip
and all those bullet holes in the plane. Finally the
islanders decided to hold him for Mr. Aylmer Robinson
himself, who was due in Monday on the weekly boat
from Kaui. He would know what to do.

Monday morning they escorted the pilot to Kii Landing and guarded him there all day. But the boat never
came.

Tuesday they tried again. Still no boat.

Wednesday and Thursday passed, and by now the
islanders were thoroughly alarmed. Harada came up

with a bright idea: wouldn't it help to move the pilot from Puuwai to his place at Kie Kie; this might calm down the village. Everyone agreed, and it was done.

By Friday it was high time for a signal fire. A group of men went off to build it, and everyone else settled down for another tense day of waiting. At Kie Kie a lone Hawaiian, named Haniki, watched the pilot. In the last day or so the Japanese had opened up a good deal. At first he admitted that he could read and write English, even if he couldn't speak it . . . later that there had indeed been a raid on Pearl Harbor. But, he said, he liked it here and hoped to settle down on Niihau after the war was over. He apparently wasn't such a bad fellow after all.

The pilot asked if he could see Harada, and Haniki took him over to the honey house. The two Japanese talked together for a few minutes, then all three men strolled into an adjoining storehouse, where the nets and hives were kept.

Haniki suddenly found himself facing two guns. Harada had stolen a revolver and shotgun from the Robinson house . . . hidden them in the storehouse until the right moment . . . and now the battle for Niihau was on.

The two Japanese locked up Haniki in the storehouse and dashed through the underbrush to the road. They held up a passing sulky, forcing out a Hawaiian woman and seven children. Then they jumped in, pointed the gun at a young girl on the horse, made her drive them to Puuwai as fast as she could. As they neared the village, they jumped off and raced for Hawila's house to get the pilot's papers. Hawila saw them coming and bolted for the fields.

Harada and the airman searched the house but found nothing. After an unsuccessful attempt to recruit Sintani, Niihau's other Japanese, the two men started searching through all the houses in the village. Again and again they shouted for Hawila, threatened to shoot everyone unless he was immediately produced. But this was an empty threat because almost all the villagers were now hiding in the fields. They did find an ancient woman, Mrs. Huluoulani, who stayed behind reading her Bible. She ignored their threats, and not knowing quite how to handle her, they left her.

They had a better idea anyhow. They stripped the Japanese plane of its machine guns and once again walked among the houses. This time they yelled that they would shoot up the whole place unless they found Hawila. As it grew dark, they began ransacking the homes in earnest. They ripped apart Hawila's house and finally discovered the pilot's pistol and map—but still no sign of his papers. They worked on through the night, turned the houses inside out, one after the other. Toward dawn on Saturday the thirteenth, they were back at Hawila's house, for one last search. Again no luck. So they burned the place down, hoping to destroy the papers too.

All this time, except for a brief period around 3:00 A.M., curious eyes peeked at the two Japanese from the bushes and weeds that grew in the rocky fields. The islanders had by no means accepted the capture of Puuwai, but after all, the Japanese had the only guns on Niihau. At a strategy meeting in the cactus grove behind the village it was decided to send the women and children to some caves in the hills, then return after dark and try to capture the two men. Somehow this plan fell through, but Beni Kanahali and another Hawaiian did manage to steal all the machine-gun ammunition, and that was a big step forward.

Meanwhile Hawila had hurried up the mountain to tell the men to get the signal fire going. But when they heard the news, they decided the fire wouldn't tell enough of the story. They must go themselves. So six of the men ran to Kii Landing, jumped in a whaleboat, rowed off for help.

After sixteen hours of steady rowing, they reached Kaui at three o'clock Saturday afternoon. They found Aylmer Robinson; he found the military authorities; and a detachment of soldiers, the six Hawaiians, and

Mr. Robinson himself were soon racing back to the rescue in the lighthouse tender *Kukui*.

Long before they got there the invasion had reached its climax. About 7:00 A.M. Beni Kanahali, having succeeded in stealing the ammunition during the night, tried his luck again. He sneaked back to the village to see what was going on. His wife came with him, and they both were promptly captured. There were the usual demands for Hawila, but Beni was now tired of the whole thing. He told Harada to take the gun away from the pilot before he hurt somebody. Harada said he couldn't, so Beni jumped the man himself. Then his wife piled in, then Harada on top of her, and for a few seconds the four of them scuffled about.

Harada pulled the woman away. She kicked and clawed as hard as she could. Beni yelled to leave her alone—or it would be Harada's turn next. The pilot jerked his arm free and shot Beni three times—groin, stomach, and upper leg.

According to legend, at this point Beni got mad. As a matter of fact, he was mad already. But he did now think he might die, and he decided to kill the pilot before he could hurt anyone else. With a great heave he picked the man up by his neck and one leg—he had often done it to a sheep—and smashed his head against a stone wall. Harada took one look, let Beni's wife go, pointed the shotgun at himself, and pulled the trigger.

CHAPTER XII

"We're Leaving Now—Explode Gloriously!"

IT WAS JUST SUNSET when Ensign Ed Jacoby trudged
ashore after losing the fight against the *West Virginia's*
fires. As he started toward the Ford Island BOQ for a
sandwich, a bugle sounded evening colors. He snapped
to attention, and the simple ceremony—taking place as
always, despite the day's disasters—reminded him that
the country lived on . . . that it had survived blows
in the past and could do so again.

Nurse Valera Vaubel stood at attention, too, as the
flag was lowered at the Navy Hospital. Then she joined
some others in a spontaneous cheer. At least this sundown she was still free.

But how much longer no one knew. Certainly not
Ensign Cleo Dobson, as he sat on the veranda of the
old BOQ, talking over the future with some of the
other *Enterprise* pilots. About all they could decide:
they were in a real shooting war and right on the front
line. Somebody suggested food, and that seemed a good
idea, for they had eaten nothing since leaving the *Enterprise* at 6.00 A.M. They raided the deserted kitchen and
found some steaks in the refrigerator. The salt and uten-
sils had all disappeared, but they cooked the steaks
anyhow on the big range and ate them sitting on the
veranda. It was dark now, but they could see well
enough by the flickering light of the flames on the
Arizona.

Farther down Battleship Row, acetylene torches flared
on the upturned hull of the *Oklahoma,* but the rest of
the harbor was dark. Within the blacked-out ships, men

had their first chance to rest . . . and worry. On the *Raleigh* everything had happened so fast during the day that Yeoman Charles Knapp didn't have a chance to be scared. But now he was off watch, and as he lay on a desk for a few minutes' rest, his mind flooded with questions. Would he ever see his mother and sister again, or watch a football game or love a girl or drink a beer or drive a car?

Certainly the outlook wasn't encouraging. Knapp heard that paratroopers were now dropping on Waikiki . . . that more landings were in progress on the north shore . . . and as if the Japanese weren't enough, that Germans were flying the planes. There was no doubt about it—one seaman swore that he had seen one of the captured pilots . . . a big, blond-headed Prussian . . . even heard him talking German.

On the gunboat *Sacramento,* word also spread that one of the pilots was blond, but he was apparently some kind of blond Japanese. Others spoke of huge six-footers, quite different from the Japanese everyone was used to.

Even more terrifying were the stories that the pilots were Hawaiian-born or American-educated. Seaman Frank Lewis of the *Dobbin* heard that the Japanese who crashed on the *Curtiss* was wearing a University of Oregon ring. At the Marine Barracks Private E. H. Robison heard that he was a University of Southern California man—Class of '37 or '39, people weren't quite sure which. At Fort Shafter, Lieutenant William Keogh heard that the pilots were wearing McKinley High School sweaters (they were all apparently lettermen). The cards seemed stacked against the defenders. The men at Fort Shafter could well believe the story that a Japanese admiral boasted he would dine at the Royal Hawaiian next Sunday.

And what was to stop him? Rumors spread that the ships at sea had also suffered. Quartermaster Handler of the *Helm* heard that the whole *Enterprise* task force was sunk; on the *Tangier,* Boatswain's Mate William Land heard that the *Lexington* was gone too. Not just the *Lexington* but the *Saratoga* as well, according to a story picked up by Signalman Walter Grabanski of the *California*.

Nor would there be any help from home, judging from another raft of rumors. The Panama Canal was bombed and blocked, someone told Chief Jack Haley of the *Nevada*, and this of course cut off the Atlantic Fleet. But worst of all, California itself was said to be under attack. On the *Helena* men heard that San Francisco was bombed . . . on the *Tennessee* that an invasion fleet lay off the city . . . on the *Rigel* that the city had been taken and a beachhead established. It might even be a two-prong attack, because word reached the *Pennsylvania* that a Japanese landing force had occupied Long Beach and was working its way toward Los Angeles.

True, there were a few encouraging reports. *California* seamen heard that the Russians had bombed Tokyo, and among the *West Virginia* men word spread that the Japanese had so little steel, they had filled some of the bombs with oyster shells. Perhaps the best news of all circulated among men from the *Oklahoma:* survivors of the attack would get 30 days' leave.

Also, the *Maryland* PA system announced that two Japanese carriers had been sunk, and a more lurid version of this story spread through the Navy Hospital: the *Pennsylvania* had captured two carriers and was towing them back to Pearl. But how could a man believe the good news when even a quick check showed the *Pennsylvania* still sitting in drydock?

About the best that could be believed was the report, spread on the *Nevada*, that the Japanese had landed on Oahu, but the Army was holding its own. The men on the ship were told to be doubly alert for any movement in the cane that ran down to the shore where the ship lay beached. No one remembered to tell them that the ship's own Marine detachment was patrolling the same area. As Private Payton McDaniel crunched through the cane, a man on the ship shouted he saw something move. A spotlight flicked on, and McDaniel froze, praying it wouldn't find him. Other Marines grasped the situation and passed word to the *Nevada* gunners to hold their fire. But it was a terrifying moment, for McDaniel knew that this was a night when men were inclined to fire and ask questions later.

At the sub base, one sentry fired so often at his relief that he ended up with the duty all night. In the Navy Yard, a fusillade of shots erased a small spotlight that was snapped on briefly by the men installing the *San Francisco's* antiaircraft batteries. Every time such shots were fired, they would set off other guns, until the whole harbor echoed with the shots of men who had no idea what they were shooting at. "You want to get in on this?" yelled a Marine sentry as Pfc. Billy Kerslake dozed off duty in the front seat of a sedan parked near Landing Charley. Kerslake nodded, reached his arm out the window, fired five pistol shots into the air, and fell back to sleep.

The firing quickly spread to nearby Hickam and added to the misery of the B-17 flight crews. It had been a tough day—first the long 14-hour trip from San Francisco . . . then getting the planes in shape . . . bivouacking out in the boondocks . . . fighting mosquitoes . . . trying to keep dry in the drizzle that began after dark . . . and now this. But the firing couldn't be ignored. During one outburst someone shouted, "The Japs are making a landing!" Tired men poured from their cots as the sky blazed with tracers. Sergeant Nick Kahlefent added to the din when he jumped out of bed on some thorns.

It was an equally sleepless night at Wheeler. Everybody had been evacuated from the barracks area, and no one found a very satisfactory alternative. Private Rae Drenner of the base fire department tossed and turned with 20 other men on the floor of the fire chief's living room. Every time shooting broke out, the men would dash off in their fire truck, dodging the hail of bullets aimed at them by jittery sentries. On the eastern edge of the field the 98th Coast Artillery let go a covering barrage . . . kept it up until the 97th at Schofield telephoned to complain that the shrapnel was ripping their tents.

Schofield got even when the 27th Infantry took pot shots at the 98th's guard detail. Two other Schofield units engaged in a pitched battle across a gully—it ended when one of the GIs, nicked by a ricochet, exploded into language which the other side knew could come from no Japanese. Down near the pack-train corral a sentry challenged three times (showing remarkable forbearance for this night), got no answer, and shot one of his own mules.

The guard at Aliamanu Command Post bagged a deer, and Mess Attendant Walter Simmons figures that in the fields around Kaneohe more mongooses died than on any other night in history. About 1:30 A.M. a small flare burst above Kaneohe—no one yet knows where it came from—and men all over the base began shooting at "parachutists." It made no difference that no one could see them or even hear a plane. A more tangible target was millionaire Chris Holmes' island in the middle of the bay. The story spread first that paratroopers had landed there; later it was only that the Japanese servants had revolted. In any case, a group of men chugged out in one of the few planes that could still taxi and sprayed the place with machine guns.

At Ewa a sentry saw a match flicker and almost shot his base commander, Lieutenant Colonel Larkin, who—against his own orders—was absent-mindedly lighting a cigarette.

As the shooting crackled all over Oahu, sooner or later someone was bound to get hurt. An elderly Japanese fisherman, Sutematsu Kida, his son Kiichi, and two others were killed by a patrol plane as their sampan passed Barbers Point, returning with the day's catch. They had gone out before the attack and probably never knew there was a war. In Pearl Harbor itself, a machine gun on the *California* accidentally cut down two *Utah* survivors while they stood on the deck of the *Argonne* during one of the false alarms.

Lieutenant (j.g.) Fritz Hebel sensed this kind of

thing might happen, as he led six *Enterprise* fighters toward Ford Island around 7:30 P.M. They had been searching for a Japanese carrier, arrived back over the *Enterprise* when it was too dark to land, were told to go on to Oahu. Now at last they were coming in.

Cautiously Hebel asked Ford Island for landing instructions. He was told to turn his lights on, "come on over the field and break up for landing." Down in the harbor, Marine Sergeant Joseph Fleck on the *New Orleans* heard the word passed to hold fire—friendly planes coming in. Ensign Leon Grabowski was told too at his 1.1 gun station on the *Maryland;* so was Radioman Fred Glaeser on Ford Island. So, probably, were others.

The planes moved in across the south channel and swung toward the mountains. Somewhere a BAR opened up . . . then two . . . then just about every ship in Pearl Harbor. Tracers criss-crossed the sky—30s . . . 50s . . . 1.1s . . . everything that could shoot. On Ford Island an officer desperately ran up and down the sandbags by Utility Squadron One's position: "Hold your fire! Hold your fire! Those are our planes!"

In the air, Lieutenant Hebel yelled over his radio: "My God, what's happened?" Ensign James Daniels dived for the floodlights at the southwest edge of the field, hoping to blind the gunners. The stunt worked and he swooped off toward Barbers Point. The others weren't as quick or lucky. Ensign Herb Menges plunged down out of control, crashing into a Pearl City tavern called the Palm Inn. Ensign Eric Allen fell near Pearl City too; he managed to bail out, but was riddled by gunfire as he floated down. Lieutenant Hebel tried to land his damaged plane at Wheeler, crashed, and was killed. Ensign Gayle Hermann spun his smashed plane 1200 feet down onto Ford Island, survived. Ensign D. R. Flynn bailed out over Barbers Point, was picked up alive days later by the Army.

Daniels hovered alone over Barbers Point. After about ten minutes the firing died down, and he blandly asked the tower for landing instructions. They were different this time—come in as low and as fast as possible, show no lights. Since he couldn't come in as a friend, he would have to try it like an enemy. He did and landed safely.

On the destroyer tender *Whitney,* crewman Waldo Rathman felt a good deal better: they really showed the Japanese this time. The gunnery was excellent, and it was a thrill to see those planes fall in flames. It made the drubbing of the morning seem a thing of the past.

Watching from her home near Makalapa, Navy wife Jeanne Gardiner couldn't judge the gunnery, but she prayed the antiaircraft fire would get the enemy. As Mrs. Mitta Townsend, another Navy wife, looked on from her home on the "Punchbowl," the moon emerged briefly, bathing Oahu in soft but revealing light. She prayed it would go behind a cloud.

Mrs. Joseph Galloway prayed too, pacing the floor at a friend's house in Honolulu. She had no idea what had happened since her husband left for his ship in the morning. Her portable radio blared occasional alerts about planes, but most of the time it was dead. In the background a distant station faded on and off with dance music from Salt Lake City.

In their desperate search for news other wives made the mistake of tuning in Japanese stations. Mrs. W. G. Beecher heard that her husband's destroyer *Flusser* had been sunk with the entire *Lexington* task force.

Mrs. Arthur Fahrner, wife of Hickam's mess supervisor, didn't need to fish for news. She knew all too well. Someone had told her of the bomb that hit the Hickam mess hall, said no one escaped alive. She took it for granted that Sergeant Fahrner died at his post, and now her job was to get the five children back to the mainland, into school, and find a way to support them.

The Fahrners had been evacuated to the University of Hawaii auditorium, and while the Red Cross performed miracles, there still weren't enough cots for the scores of families that sprawled on the floor. Sunday night Mrs. Fahrner and three other mothers formed a "hollow square" of adults and dumped their ten children in the middle. This at least kept them in one spot, but it still was a night of whimpering . . . of restless tossing . . . of endless trips to the bathroom over and around sleeping people.

Just when everything quieted down, some new disturbance would break out. One little girl lost a kitty with a bell around its neck. Soon it was hard to tell which caused the most commotion—the cat roaming and ringing its bell or the child calling and searching in the dark. The little girl had a way of turning up wherever the kitty had just left.

Slowly the hours dragged by. The children gradually dozed off, but the mothers were wide-eyed all night. Sometimes they talked together; other times they just lay quietly holding one another's hands, waiting for daylight.

The mothers were busier in the Navy storage tunnel at Red Hill, where other families were evacuated. Clouds of mosquitoes swarmed down the air vents, and the women spent most of the night shooing them off so their children could sleep. Then an unexpected crisis arose. One young mother forgot to bring any bottles for her month-old baby. Cups were tried, but of course the baby was too young. Someone suggested a sugar shaker, but the spout was too large. Finally Mrs. Alexander Rowell came up with the solution—she soaked a clean rag in milk and let the baby suck on it. That was what the pioneers did, she explained; she had read all about it in *Drums Along the Mohawk*.

Generous people opened up their homes to other evacuees. One Navy commander's wife at Waipahu took in 20 or 30 women and children, including Don and Jerry Morton and their mother, Mrs. Croft. Everyone made a point of being cheerful, but the rumors were frightening—it was said resistance was weak against the enemy advance from Kaneohe. Some of the mothers talked as though they were already prisoners, but Don and Jerry vowed to take to the hills and fight to the end.

Here and there a few families stubbornly refused to evacuate. Mrs. Arthur Gardiner had no great faith in the construction of the junior officers' duplex quarters near Makalapa, but it was home, and she wanted to be there when Lieutenant Gardiner returned. She pushed the dining room table against a wall, dragged four mattresses downstairs with the help of five-year-old Keith. She placed them strategically around the shelter and crawled in with Keith and two-year-old Susan. Keith was sick with worry and excitement but tried wonderfully to cooperate; Susan was in open rebellion and went along only when convinced it was part of a new game.

Mrs. Paul Spangler thought it might help to read to her four children as they sat in their blacked-out living room on Alewa Heights. So she rigged her coat over a floor lamp, gathered everybody around her, and picked up a book. Instantly a man was pounding on the door, shouting: "Put out that light!" She gave up and they all went to bed. Navy wife Lorraine Campbell dealt more successfully with the blackout at her home near Pearl Harbor—she turned off all the lights and put a Band-Aid on the radio dial.

Some blackout problems were insurmountable. As Allen Mau, a 12-year-old Hawaiian, tried to make cocoa for the evacuees at his home, he found he couldn't get the milk out of the refrigerator without turning on the automatic light inside. He could get his hand in all right, but not out with the milk bottle too. Finally he went ahead anyhow . . . and almost lost his arm when the whole family dived at the door to shut the light off.

In the darkness many turned their thoughts to the men who had rushed off in the morning. Days would pass before most of the families heard of them again. On Tuesday Mrs. Arthur Fahrner learned that a box of chocolate bars had mysteriously appeared at a friend's house—usually a sure sign that Sergeant Fahrner had been around. Yet she scarcely dared to hope. The following day she found out—the sergeant had been in the bakery getting bread when the Hickam mess hall was hit; he escaped without a scratch. On Wednesday Nurse Monica Conter still had no word of Lieutenant Benning, but she was doing her best to carry on. As she walked down the third-floor corridor of the Hickam Hospital, the elevator door opened and there he was in full combat uniform—looking even dirtier than any soldier she had seen in the movies.

It was Thursday morning when Mrs. Joseph Cote heard the chaplain call her name at the university auditorium. She slipped into the ladies' room and prayed for the strength to bear the bad news. When she emerged, the chaplain told her Chief Cote was fine. Later that day Mrs. W. G. Wallace was back on her civilian job at Pearl Harbor, trying not to look out the window at the charred ships that depressed her so. But a familiar shadow passed the window, and she instinctively looked up—it was her husband, Ensign Wallace, last seen Sunday morning. She threw herself across the desk, halfway through the window and into his arms. Then they slipped into the first-aid shack, where no one could see them, and cried.

It wasn't until Monday, December 14, that Don and Jerry Morton learned their stepfather had been killed on the seaplane ramp at Ford Island by one of the first bombs to fall.

But the waiting, the gnawing uncertainty, all lay ahead. This black Sunday night the families on Oahu had other worries. In the eerie darkness, Japanese seemed to lurk behind every bush. Betty and Margo Spangler, two teen-age sisters, normally slept out on the *lanai*, but this night they took over their mother's bed. Mrs. W. G. Beecher got her children to sleep, lay awake herself, listening uneasily as the palm trees brushed against the side of the house. Navy wife Reiba Wallace took in a frightened single girl who insisted she heard someone on the roof. Mrs. Wallace spied a rifle in the corner, promised to shoot both the girl and herself if the Japanese came in. This was somehow reassuring; the girl calmed down, and Mrs. Wallace kept it to herself that the gun wasn't loaded. Mrs. Patrick Gillis, a young Army wife, was sure she saw someone skulking outside her apartment house; so did the other five wives who had joined her. The police combed the grounds in vain.

About 4:00 A.M. another alarm went direct to Colonel Fielder in the intelligence office at Fort Shafter: Someone was signaling with a blue light up behind the base. Fielder grabbed a pistol, a helmet, and a sentry. Sure enough, a light was flashing up the mountain. He called for reinforcements, and the squad deployed through buffalo grass . . . crossed a stream . . . surrounded the area . . . and moved in. Two elderly farmers were milking a cow, using a blue light as instructed. A palm frond, swaying in the breeze, occasionally hid the light and made it look like secret code.

Colonel Fielder couldn't know it, but the danger was all over. Oahu was perfectly safe this gusty, squally night.

The Islands' 160,000 people of Japanese blood pulled no sabotage, probably no important espionage. Even Dr. Mori's phone call to Tokyo Friday night—when he talked so mysteriously of poinsettias, hibiscuses, and chrysanthemums—may have been above board. He always claimed it was just an atmosphere piece for the Tokyo newspaper *Yomiuri Shinbun*, and certainly the interview did appear in the paper the following morning—complete with reference to flowers. Actually, Consul General Kita didn't need outside intelligence help—he had more than 200 consular agents, and he himself could get a perfect view of the fleet any time he chose to take a ten-minute drive.

Nor was there any danger from the great Japanese task force north of Oahu. Admiral Nagumo's ships were 500 miles away . . . pounding silently home . . . steaming through heavy mist, slightly south of their outbound course. The crews were strangely quiet. Down in the *Akagi's* engine room, Commander Tanbo's men didn't even take a ceremonial drink of *sake*. He later learned this was typical—the men whooped it up only over the small, insignificant victories, the big ones always left them sober and reflective.

The Japanese submarines south of Oahu were no

threat either. Most of them had lapsed into the role of observers. Commander Katsuji Watanabe casually studied Pearl Harbor from the conning tower of the *I-69*, lying several miles off shore. He watched the flames still licking the *Arizona* and at 9:01 P.M. noted a heavy explosion aboard her. This respite was welcome, for the commander had spent a hard day dodging destroyers. Some of them probably thought they had sunk him, for Watanabe was a master at deception. He would pump out made-to-order oil slicks; and as final, conclusive evidence of his destruction, he liked to jettison Japanese sandals into the sea.

Lieutenant Hashimoto aboard the *I-24* reflected on the change one day had made in the shoreline. The twinkling lights were all gone; Oahu was now just a gloomy shadow. The *I-24* turned east and hurried off for her rendezvous with Ensign Sakamaki's midget. The whole Special Attack Unit was to reassemble at a point seven miles southwest of Lanai, and one by one the mother subs arrived. All night long they waited, riding gently up and down in the ocean swell within easy sight of each other. No midgets ever appeared.

On the *I-24* it was discovered that Sakamaki never expected to come back. His belongings were neatly rolled up; his farewell note (with the fingernail and lock of hair) lay ready to be mailed. There were complete instructions what to do, including some yen for the postage.

But Sakamaki was not dead. After his collapse at dusk, the midget cruised lazily eastward by itself. At some point he must have recovered long enough to surface and open the hatch. In any case, when he finally came to around midnight, he noticed first the moonlight, then a soothing breeze that filtered down from above. He poked his head out the hatch and gulped the cool night air.

Seaman Inagaki woke up and also took a few deep breaths. But he was still groggy and soon fell back to sleep. Sakamaki stayed awake, drinking in the night, letting the sub go where it wanted. The sea wasn't rough, but an occasional wave washed his face. Stars twinkled through the drifting clouds, and moonlight danced off the water. He began having dangerous thoughts for a

man on a suicide mission: he got to thinking it was good
to be alive.

About dawn the motor stopped, and the midget just
drifted. As the light grew brighter, Sakamaki saw a small
island to the left. He decided it was Lanai—a remarkable
display of faith in the sub's ability to steer itself. Actually,
the boat had drifted far off course, rounded the eastern
end of Oahu, and was now heading northwest along the
windward side of the island.

Sakamaki shook Inagaki awake and pointed out the
land—they might still be in time for the rendezvous. He
ordered full speed ahead. The sub started and stopped
. . . started and stopped again. White smoke poured from
the batteries; they were just about shot. Sakamaki waited
a few minutes (like a man attempting to start a car on a
low battery) and tried again. Nothing happened. Once
more. The motor caught, and the midget bolted ahead.
Almost instantly there was another jolt . . . a frightful
scraping . . . a shuddering stop. They had run her onto a
reef again.

This time they were stuck for good. There was nothing
to do but scuttle the sub. It carried explosives for just this
emergency, and Sakamaki quickly lit the fuse. For a few
seconds he and Inagaki watched it sputter, to make sure
it didn't go out. Then they scrambled up the hatch.

They climbed out on the cigar-shaped hull, wearing
only G-string and loincloth. The moon was sinking in the
west, a new day lighting up the eastern sky. Around
them the surf foamed and pounded. About 200 yards
ahead they could just make out a dark, empty beach.
Sakamaki had a final pang of conscience—shouldn't he
stay with the midget . . . was this the way of a naval
officer? Then he thought, why not try to live; he was not
a weapon but a human being. He bade the sub good-by,
almost as though it were a person: "We're leaving now—
explode gloriously."

He dived into the sea about 6:40 A.M.—his watch,
which he had loyally kept on Tokyo time, stopped at
2:10. The water was colder than he expected, the waves
higher than they looked. They spun him helplessly

about as he struck out for shore. Inagaki had jumped with him but was nowhere to be seen. Sakamaki hailed him, and a voice called back, "Sir, I'm over here." Sakamaki finally spied a head bobbing up and down in the combers. He yelled a few words of encouragement, but no one knows whether Inagaki heard. His drowned body later washed up on the beach.

As Sakamaki struggled through the surf, he realized that the charge had not gone off in the sub. Five . . . ten minutes passed. The hideous truth dawned—on this too he had failed. He wanted to swim back but just couldn't make it. He had lost all his strength. He no longer swam at all. He just swirled about—coughing, swallowing, spitting up salt water. He was utterly helpless. Everything went blank.

When he came to, he was lying on the beach near Bellows Field, apparently cast up on the sand by a breaker. He glanced up into the curious eyes of an American soldier standing beside him. Sergeant David M. Akui was on guard, packing a pistol at his hip. The war that was just beginning for so many men had just ended for Prisoner of War Kazuo Sakamaki.

At this moment it was 12:20 P.M. in Washington, D.C., and ten highly polished black limousines were just entering the Capitol grounds. The first was convoyed by three huge touring cars, nicknamed *Leviathan, Queen Mary,* and *Normandie.* These were filled with Secret Service men guarding President Franklin D. Roosevelt, who was on his way to ask Congress to declare war on the Japanese Empire.

The cars stopped at the south entrance of the Capitol, and the President got out, assisted by his son Jimmy. Roosevelt wore his familiar Navy cape, Jimmy the uniform of a Marine captain. Applause rippled from a crowd that stood behind sawhorse barricades in the pale noonday sun. The President paused, smiled, and waved back. It was not his campaign wave—this was no time for that—but it wasn't funeral either. He seemed trying to strike a balance between gravity and optimism.

The Presidential party moved into the Capitol, and the crowd lapsed back into silence. Here and there little knots clustered about the portable radios which the more enterprising remembered to bring. All were facing the Capitol, although they couldn't possibly see what was going on inside. They seemed to feel that by studying the building itself, a little history might somehow rub off onto them.

Like the President, the people were neither boisterous nor depressed. They had seen movies of the cheering multitudes that are supposed to gather outside chancelleries whenever war is declared, but they didn't feel that way at all. Occasionally someone made an awkward, halfhearted attempt to follow the script. "Gee," said a teen-age girl, clinging to a bespectacled, rather unbelligerent-looking sailor, "ain't there some way a woman can get into this thing?"

It was almost painful, yet it was typical. Like the men at Pearl, who kept linking their experiences to football and the movies, the people had nothing better to go by. A nation brought up on peace was going to war and didn't know how.

Ever since the news broke early Sunday afternoon, they had groped none too successfully for the right note to strike. "Happy Landings!" cried a man who phoned a Detroit paper for confirmation—and the editor detected the tone of false gaiety. "Gotta whip those Japs!" a Kansas City newsboy chanted self-consciously as he passed out extras. And at Herbert's Drive-Inn Bar in the San Fernando Valley, a customer pulled one of a thousand forced, flat jokes: "You guys with Japanese gardeners—how do you feel now?"

Along with the awkwardness went a naïveté which must have seemed strange to the more sophisticated warring nations of the world. The Vassar faculty passed a resolution formally offering its "special training" to the service of the country. A Washington cab driver phoned the White House, offering to carry any government worker to his job free—a proposal likely to astonish any official who did time in Washington during the ensuing years. Members of the Pilgrim Congregational Church in St. Louis debated whether to bomb Tokyo, decided not to—"we're a people of higher ideals." A man in Atlanta wired Secretary of Navy Frank Knox to hold Japanese envoy Kurusu until all Navy officers on Wake were released, and ex-Ambassador Joseph Davies to Russia seriously discussed the possibilities of using Vladivostok as a base.

But most people didn't worry about bases; they were sure the United States could defeat Japan with absurd ease. The country at large still regarded the Japanese as ineffectual little brown men who were good at imitating Occidentals but couldn't do much on their own. "I didn't think the Japs had the nerve," said Sergeant Robert McCallum when interviewed on a Louisville street corner. As reports spread of disquietingly heavy damage at Pearl Harbor, many agreed with Professor Roland G. Usher, a German authority and head of the History Department at Washington University in St. Louis—Hitler's *Luftwaffe* may have helped the Japanese out.

But rising above the awkwardness, the naïveté, and the overconfidence ran one surging emotion—fury. The day might come when formal declarations of war would seem old-fashioned, when the surprise move would yet become a stock weapon in any country's arsenal, but not yet. In December, 1941, Americans expected an enemy to announce its intentions before it fought, and Japan's move—coming while her envoys were still negotiating in Washington—outraged the people far beyond the concept of any worldly-wise policymaker in Tokyo.

Later, Americans would argue bitterly about Pearl Harbor—they would even hurl dark charges of incompetence and conspiracy at one another—but on this day there was no argument whatsoever.

Young Senator Cabot Lodge of Massachusetts had been an ardent "neutralist" (just a month earlier he had voted against allowing U. S. merchant ships to enter Allied ports), but right after he learned of Pearl Harbor from a filling-station attendant, he was on the air . . . urging all Americans, no matter how isolationist they

might have been, to unite against the attack. Senator
Arthur Vandenberg of Michigan, leader of the isolationist
bloc, had heard the news in his bedroom, where he was
pasting up clippings about his long, hard fight against
U. S. involvement in the war. He immediately phoned
the White House, assuring President Roosevelt that whatever their differences, he would support the President
in his answer to Japan.

It was the same with the press. The isolationist, rabidly
anti-Roosevelt Los Angeles *Times* bannered its lead edi-
torial, "Death Sentence of a Mad Dog." Some papers tried
to prod isolationist leaders into controversial statements,
but none were coming. Senator Burton Wheeler of Mon-
tana, for instance, snapped back, "The only thing now is
to do our best to lick hell out of them."

And the sooner the better. There was an overwhelming
urge to get going, even though no one knew where the
road might lead. At Fort Sam Houston, Texas, Brigadier
General Dwight D. Eisenhower got the word as he tried
to catch up on his sleep after weeks of long, tough field
maneuvers. He was dead tired, had left orders not to be
disturbed, but the phone rang and his wife heard him
say, "Yes? . . . When? . . . I'll be right down." As he rushed
off to duty, he told Mrs. Eisenhower the news, said he
was going to headquarters, and added that he had no
idea when he would be back.

The Capitol swelled with the same spirit of angry unity
and urgency as the Senators filed into the House Chamber to hear the President's war message. Democratic
leader Alben Barkley arrived arm in arm with GOP
leader Charles McNary; Democrat Elmer Thomas of
Oklahoma linked arms with the old isolationist Senator
Hiram Johnson of California.

Next the Supreme Court marched in, wearing their
black robes, and then the members of the Cabinet. Down
front sat the top military leaders, General Marshall and
Admiral Stark. Further back, five Congressmen held
children in their laps, lending the curious touch of a family gathering. In the gallery Mrs. Roosevelt, wearing
black with a silver fox fur, peeked from behind a girder

—she had one of the worst seats in the House. Not far away sat an important link with the past—Mrs. Woodrow Wilson.

At 12:29 P.M. President Roosevelt entered, still on Jimmy's arm. There was applause . . . a brief introduction by Speaker Sam Rayburn . . . and the President, dressed in formal morning attire, stood alone at the rostrum. He opened a black looseleaf notebook—the sort a child uses at school—and the Chamber gave him a resounding ovation. For the first time in nine years Republicans joined in, and Roosevelt seemed to sense the electric anger that swept the country, as he grasped the rostrum and began:

> Yesterday, December 7, 1941—a date which will live in infamy—the United States of America was suddenly and deliberately attacked. . . .

The speech was over in six minutes and war voted in less than an hour, but the real job was done in the first ten seconds. "Infamy" was the note that struck home, the word that welded the country together until the war was won.

Facts About the Attack

Most Americans caught in the Japanese attack on Oahu went through successive stages of shock, fear, and anger—a poor climate indeed for pinning down exactly what happened. And even about the basic statistics it's dangerous to be dogmatic. There are different ways of counting things; should, for instance, an obsolete airplane that is out of commission anyhow be counted as "destroyed by the enemy"? Keeping these cautions in mind, here are the answers to some basic questions that are bound to arise:

How many ships were in Pearl Harbor? Best answer seems to be 96. Most maps show 90 ships, but omit the *Ontario, Condor, Crossbill, Cockatoo, Pyro,* and the old *Baltimore.*

What was U.S. air strength? Some 394 planes, according to Congressional investigation, but many were obsolete or being repaired. Available aircraft: Army—93 fighters, 35 bombers, 11 observation; Navy—15 fighters, 61 patrol planes, 36 scout planes, 45 miscellaneous.

How big was the Japanese Striking Force? There were 31 ships—six carriers, two battleships, two heavy cruisers, one light cruiser, nine destroyers, three submarines, eight tankers. Air strength—432 planes used as follows: 39 for combat air patrol, 40 for reserve, 353 for the raid.

What was the strength of the Japanese Advance Expeditionary Force? Probably 28 submarines—11 with small planes, five with the famous midget subs. (The Congressional investigation set the figure at 20, but this is too low, according to the Japanese.)

When did various events occur? Most reliable sources agree the raid began about 7:55 A.M., ended shortly before 10 o'clock. At Pearl and Hickam few noticed the five neat phases spelled out in the CINCPAC Official Report. To the men it was a continuing battle flaring up and down in intensity, with a 15-minute lull around eight-thirty. The most stunning single moment—the *Arizona* blowing up—seems to have taken place about 8:10. Some eyewitnesses feel that the explosion came at the very start of the attack, yet this couldn't be so, judging from the experiences of the five *Arizona* survivors who were located.

In fixing the time for various events, this book depends on both official records and the memory of eyewitnesses. Neither source is infallible. Logs and reports were sometimes worked up long after the event, and in the excitement of battle a fighting man could lose all track of time.

The time range at the top of each left-hand page is intended only as a rough guide. Some incidents necessarily start before or continue beyond the period indicated.

What were the American casualties? Navy—2008 killed, 710 wounded, according to the Navy Bureau of Medicine. Marines—109 killed, 69 wounded, according to Corps Headquarters. Army—218 killed, 364 wounded, according to Adjutant General's figures. Civilian—68 killed, 35 wounded, according to the University of Hawaii War Records Depository. Of the 2403 killed, nearly half were lost when the *Arizona* blew up.

What was the damage? At Pearl Harbor 18 ships were sunk or seriously damaged. Lost: battleships *Arizona* and *Oklahoma*, target ship *Utah*, destroyers *Cassin* and *Downes*. Sunk or beached but later salvaged: battleships *West Virginia*, *California*, and *Nevada*; mine layer *Oglala*. Damaged: battleships *Tennessee*, *Maryland*, and *Pennsylvania*; cruisers *Helena*, *Honolulu*, and *Raleigh*; destroyer *Shaw*; seaplane tender *Curtiss*; repair ship *Vestal*.

At the airfields 188 planes were destroyed—96 Army and 92 Navy. An additional 128 Army and 31 Navy planes were damaged. Hardest-hit airfields were Kaneohe and Ewa. Of the 82 planes caught at these two fields, only one was in shape to fly at the end of the raid.

During the attack there were about 40 explosions in the city of Honolulu—all, except one, the result of U. S. antiaircraft fire. These explosions did about 500,000 dollars' worth of damage.

What were the Japanese losses? Tokyo sources agree that the Striking Force lost only 29 planes—nine fighters, 15 dive bombers, and five torpedo planes. In addition, the Advance Expeditionary Force lost one large submarine and all five midgets. Personnel lost: 55 airmen, nine crewmen on the midget subs, plus an unknown number on the large submarine.

Acknowledgments

"Uniforms meant nothing," recalls Chief Albert Molter, reflecting on Pearl Harbor. Others agree that it was a day when rank was forgotten, when all that counted was the good idea, when people wanted only to pitch in together.

They have shown the same spirit in contributing to this book. Admirals, sailors, generals, privates, ordinary civilians—some 577 participants—have unselfishly joined forces to help me piece together this picture of that famous Sunday.

Some of these people are still in Oahu, and sitting down with them on that balmy, tranquil island conveys best of all what a shock the attack must have been. You feel it when Brigadier General Kendall Fielder painstakingly reviews that last peacetime evening with General Short . . . when James B. Mann describes seeing the first planes in the early sunlight above Haleiwa . . . when Webley Edwards explains how he desperately tried to make his radio audience believe the news . . . when Tadao Fuchikami tells of his motorcycle ride with the famous message from General Marshall to General Short.

As they tell their stories, nothing seems to be too much trouble. Vivid impressions still linger—Richard Kimball delving into old registration books at the Halekulani Hotel; George Walters rooting through his papers on Drydock No. 1; Dr. Robert Faus wading through dusty files on the emergency ambulance service. And there was the evening Master Sergeant McMurtrie dug out the letter which explained better than a dozen investigations how little grasp anyone had of radar at the time. Six weeks before Pearl Harbor, McMurtrie (then a private) had been shifted from radar work to KP, and he joyfully wrote home, "In the kitchen you can take pride in what you're doing."

Sometimes nothing short of a personally conducted tour would explain a point, and I want to thank Master Sergeant Francis Clossen for showing me around Wheeler; Technical

Sergeant Billy Kerslake for guiding me through Kaneohe; Mrs. Anne Powlison for a tour of the Kailua area; Colonel Robert G. Fergusson for going over the old Coast Artillery setup; and Mrs. Paul Young for re-enacting her harrowing morning in the family laundry at Wahiawa. The Army, Navy, and Air Force public information offices, of course, paved the way at Pearl, Hickam, Schofield, and Fort Shafter; and though I must have stretched their patience to the breaking point, I never found any limit to their help.

Many of the participants are now far from Hawaii, but they were no less willing to take time out and talk about Pearl Harbor—sometimes under circumstances that must have been trying, to say the least. Lieutenant General Truman Landon was on the verge of leaving for Latin America, but he seemed to have all the time in the world as he recalled the B-17 flight from California. Rear Admiral William Burford was cornered on the golf course near San Diego, but was as amiable as if he had just broken par, while he described how the *Monaghan* rammed the midget sub. And I'll never know what lunch plans Admiral Halsey sacrificed to sit with me instead, relating the story of the *Enterprise* planes.

Some of these people gradually evolved into my "experts" on certain localities . . . and found themselves more ruthlessly imposed upon than ever. These unsung heroes included Commander Victor Delano on Battleship Row . . . Edmond Jacoby on Ford Island . . . Master Sergeant John Sherwood on Hickam . . . Master Sergeant Francis Clossen on Wheeler . . . Chief Walter Simmons on Kaneohe . . . Chief Charles Leahey on Pearl Harbor.

Others I depended on greatly for their specialized knowledge on certain points: Vice Admiral Walter Anderson for background on fleet organization; Dr. John Moorhead for the medical side of the story; Admiral Charles M. Cooke for incidents on the flooding of Drydock No. 1; Admiral Claude Bloch for information on the midget submarine penetration of the harbor. I especially appreciate the time Joseph Lockard and Joseph McDonald spent, helping on the riddle of the Opana radar contact.

Often eyewitnesses not only gave me their time but lent me personal papers to fill out the story. Among them: Lieutenant Colonel George Bicknell, Brigadier General Kendall Fielder, Rear Admiral William Furlong, Rear Admiral Peyton Harrison, Rear Admiral S. S. Isquith, and Captain William

Outerbridge. Invaluable diaries were contributed by Commander J. G. Daniels, Thomas Lombardi, and Henry Sachs. Mrs. Hubert K. Reese also made available the diary of her gallant son Lieutenant Hubert K. Reese, Jr., who was lost on convoy duty in 1943.

Most of the Japanese participants were later killed in the war, but fifteen were located and contributed firsthand accounts. Their task was not easy, but they tackled it with vigor and frankness, and the result is a vital part of the story. I am extremely grateful to Takahisa Amagai, Dr. Sukao Ebina, Dr. Tadataka Endo, Shigeru Fujii, Mochitsura Hashimoto, Toshio Hashimoto, Lieutenant Colonel Masanobu Ibusuki, Kazuyoshi Kochi, Vice Admiral Ryunosuke Kusaka, Kazuo Sakamaki, Yoshio Shiga, Shin-Ichi Shimizu, Suguru Suzuki, Yoshibumi Tanbo, and Hoichiro Tsukamoto.

Where eyewitnesses were not available, and in some cases to supplement their accounts, I have relied on a mountain of written material. The 40 volumes of the U. S. Congressional investigation are full of nuggets. The War Records Depository of the University of Hawaii has much data, including a priceless collection of school children's themes. The Honolulu Harbor Master's records have essential facts on wind, weather, and shipping. The Honolulu Board of Water Supply has the best information on damage to the city.

The Honolulu papers had lively coverage, and I'm indebted to Editors Ray Coll of the *Advertiser* and Riley Allen of the *Star-Bulletin* for letting me rummage through their files. Special thanks go to Managing Editor Thurston Twigg-Smith of the *Advertiser* for digging out material on Niihau.

Numerous books contain valuable information on the attack. *The Rising Sun in the Pacific* by Samuel E. Morison (Little, Brown, 1948) and *Battle Report: Pearl Harbor to Coral Sea* by Walter Karig and Welbourne Kelley (Farrar & Rinehart, 1944) have detailed over-all accounts. Blake Clark's *Remember Pearl Harbor* (Harper, 1942) preserves many colorful incidents. The civilian side is thoroughly covered by Gwenfread Allen's *Hawaii's War Years* (University of Hawaii Press, 1945). On the question of responsibility, *Admiral Kimmel's Story* by the Admiral himself (Henry Regnery, 1955), *The Final Secret of Pearl Harbor* by Rear Admiral Robert A. Theobald (Devin-Adair, 1954), and Walter Millis' fascinating *This Is Pearl* (William Morrow, 1947) should all be read by anyone trying to understand this knotty problem. Lieutenant Clarence Dickinson's *Flying Guns* (Scribner's,

1942) and Eugene Burns' *Then There Was One* (Harcourt, Brace, 1944) both touch on the story of the *Enterprise* planes.

Various aspects of the Japanese side are covered in *Midway* by Mitsuo Fuchida (U. S. Naval Institute, 1955); *Sunk* by Mochitsura Hashimoto (Cassell & Company, 1954); *I Attacked Pearl Harbor* by Kazuo Sakamaki (Association Press, 1949); *Zero!* by Masatake Okumiya and Jira Horikoshi with Martin Caidin (Dutton, 1956).

Additional information can be found in many magazine articles that have been written on the subject. To name a few of the best: Robert Ward's account of Japanese planning in the December, 1951, issue of the *United States Naval Institute Proceedings;* Captain Fuchida's own story of leading the air attack in the September, 1952, issue of the same magazine; Barry Fox's touching reminiscences of a housewife's feelings in the January, 1943, issue of *Harper's.*

A more personal kind of help has come from every side. Vice Admiral John F. Shafroth graciously arranged off-the-record interviews with various key figures. Richard MacMillan and Adney Smith gave indispensable guidance in Honolulu. Captain Ralph Parker generously shared his deep understanding of Navy life. Eugene Burns, Russell Starr, and Captain Joe Taussig offered invaluable leads. Lieutenant (j.g.) Herbert E. Hetu and Chief William J. Miller proved that they could locate anybody who had ever been in the Navy. Lieutenant Commander Herb Gimpel worked miracles in getting pictures on a moment's notice. Rear Admiral and Mrs. Hall Mayfield helped in more ways than I could ever list.

In pulling the story together, *Life* magazine supplied wonderful research assistance, and in this connection I am especially indebted to Charles Osborne of the *Life* staff. Roger Pineau, Malcolm Boyd, and Harold Daw contributed other valuable research. Miss Florence Cassedy joined that brave band of typists who have faced my handwriting, and my mother performed as valiantly as ever on the index.

But all these contributions, great as they are, would not be enough without the 464 eyewitness accounts written especially for my use by the people listed on the following pages. These are the heart of the matter, for while no one person is necessarily infallible, the consensus of several hundred is very likely to approach the truth. Like the Armed Services and the individuals mentioned in this Acknowledgment section, these people share no responsibility for my thoughts and conclusions, no blame for my errors or inadequacies, but all the credit for whatever new understanding may emerge from this story of December 7, 1941.

List of Contributors

Each name is followed by the vantage point from which the account was written. Where supplied, the present rank of those still on active duty is also included.

Charles H. Abrams, Pearl Harbor

Edwin W. Adams, Wheeler Field

Carp. Harry R. Adams, *Vestal*

FPC Wayne Lax Adams, *Vestal*

Donald B. Addington, *Phoenix*

CPO Enrique S. M. Aflague, *Minneapolis*

E. H. Akins, Wheeler

Donald B. Alexander, Kaneohe NAS

Bruce G. Allen, B-17 flight

Frank Allo, Hickam Field

Walter C. Anderson, *Nevada*

V. Adm. Walter S. Anderson, USN (Ret.), *Maryland*

Carroll T. Andrews, Wheeler

John V. Armstrong, *Oklahoma*

Terrance J. Armstrong, *Oklahoma*

Thomas E. Armstrong, *Oklahoma*

Kenneth Atwell, Hickam

Marlin G. Ayotte, Pearl Harbor

Charles O. Backstrom, Hickam

M/Sgt. John W. Baker, Tripler General Hospital

Woodrow Baily, *Tennessee*

Robert W. Ballou, Kaneohe NAS

QMC Willard A. Beal, *Oklahoma*

Cdr. John R. Beardall, *Raleigh*

Earnest T. Bedell, *Shaw*

Mrs. Monica Conter Benning, Hickam hosp.

Robert S. Benton, *West Virginia*

Charles E. Bergdoll, B-17 flight

Joseph Berry, *Helena*

S 1/c Ben Bill, Navy housing

HMC V. G. Biskup, Naval Hosp.

H. E. Blagg, *Maryland*

Maj. Gen. Gordon A. Blake, USAF, Hickam

QMC John D. Blanken, *San Francisco*

Stanley J. Blazenski, Naval Mobile Hosp. No. 2

Alec C. Boatman, *Tennessee*

Erwin J. Bohenstiel, Ford Island

Charles M. Bohnstadt, *Sacramento*

Nicholas T. Bongo, Hickam

P. E. Bos, Ford Island

C. E. Boudreau, Navy Receiving Station

S. F. Bowen, *Tennessee*

Maj. Samuel Bradlyn, USAF, Hickam

Albert E. Brawley, B-17 flight

Samuel Lester Brayfield, *New Orleans*

Brainard J. Brewer, construction work near Schofield

Chester L. Brighton, *Helena*

Donald W. Brown, *West Virginia*

E. F. Brown, Pearl Harbor

K. R. Brown, *Tucker*

W. M. Brown, PT boats

Clarence Bruhl, Submarine Base

Norman C. Brunelle, Pearl Harbor

Wilfred J. Brunet, *Honolulu*

Lester T. Buckley, Schofield

Mrs. Mary Buethe, Navy housing

R. Adm. J. W. Bunkley, USN (Ret.), *California*

R. Adm. William P. Burford, USN (Ret.), *Monaghan*

Joseph John Burke, *Patterson*

J. P. Burkholder, *Tennessee*

Martin T. Burns, *Phoenix*

J. W. Burton, Ford Island

Max E. Butterfield, Hickam

PNC Edward P. Campbell, *Tennessee*

Mrs. Lorraine Campbell, Navy housing

CWO W. M. Canavan, *St. Louis*

Chief Gunner Ralph A. Carl, Jr., *Tennessee*

Kenneth D. Carlson, *Selfridge*

Brig. Gen. Richard H. Carmichael, USAF, B-17 flight

Richard M. Carse, Schofield

Peter A. Chang, Submarine Base

S. B. Chatfield, *Wright*

Donald C. Christensen, *Phoenix*

George A. Cichon, *California*

Erwin F. Cihak, B-17 flight

Fred R. Claesson, Ft. Kamehameha

Henry B. Clark, Jr., *Cockatoo*

Peter M. Clause, Schofield

M/Sgt. William M. Cleveland, Hickam

E. J. Clifton, *Sumner*

Chandler Cobb, Pearl Harbor

Leslie Coe, *Nevada*

Charles Coleman, *St. Louis*

TEC Durrell E. Conner, *California*

A. J. Corizzo, *Bagley*

Mrs. Aletha Cote, Hickam housing

Felder Crawford, *Maryland*

Edward G. Creighton, *Monaghan*

Capt. Mark Creighton, USAF, Hickam

John Crockett, Navy Yard

George V. Cruise, *Helena*

Carlos J. Cunningham, Ford Island

Charles R. Cunningham, *Jarvis*

Carl E. Currey, *Maryland*

PNC L. L. Curry, Jr., *Oklahoma*

Mrs. Iva Daniels, Navy housing

Cdr. J. G. Daniels, *Enterprise* flight

Henry R. Danner, Drydock No. 1

Sydney A. Davis, Hickam

William H. Deas, *Castor*

Cdr. Victor Delano, *West Virginia*

W. E. Dellegar, *Oglala*

George E. Denning, Schofield

Thomas A. Denton, 1010 dock

Fred L. Dickey, Wheeler

Cdr. Cleo J. Dobson, *Enterprise* flight

James W. Dollar, *Phoenix*

Ambrose A. Domagall, *Ward*

Thomas J. Donahue, *Monaghan*

George A. Dorfmeister, *Detroit*

Raeburn D. Drenner, Wheeler

Ivan C. DuBois, Hickam

James Duncan, civilian plane

Y. Dupre, *Dobbin*

Mrs. Rhea Dupre, Navy housing

M/Sgt. J. H. Dykema, Hickam

Albert A. Dysert, *Helena*

Douglas A. Eaker, Submarine Base

Mrs. F. M. Earle, Navy First Aid Sta.

R. Adm. A. R. Early, USN (Ret.), Pearl Harbor

Mrs. E. M. Eaton, Navy housing

Charles P. Eckhert, Hickam

AD1 George W. Edmondson, Ford Island

Leonard T. Egan, Wheeler

Wilfred Eller, Naval Mobile Hosp. Unit

Fred R. Elliott, *West Virginia*

BTC H. E. Emory, *California*

Walter F. England, Oiler *Y.O.44*

EN1 Charles W. Etter, *Blue*

G. Taylor Evans, Jr., *California*

Mrs. Florence E. Fahrner, Hickam housing

Maurice Featherman, *West Virginia*

MMC William R. Felsing, *Pennsylvania*

Ernest L. Finney, *Nevada*

Mrs. Joseph G. Fischer, Navy housing

John P. Fisher, Ft. Shafter

Joseph W. Fleck, *New Orleans*

Don Flickinger, Wheeler

Charles A. Flood, *Helena*

Brig. Gen. William J. Flood, USAF (Ret.), Wheeler

Charles L. Flynn, *Pruitt*

Jack F. Foeppel, *Raleigh*

Mrs. Claire Fonderhide, Hickam housing

James L. Forbis, *Arizona*

Frank G. Forgione, *Oglala*

Cdr. Howell M. Forgy, USN (Ret.), *New Orleans*

Roy Foster, Schofield

Cdr. Vance Fowler, *West Virginia*

W. R. Frazee, *Argonne*

Dr. Arthur F. Fritchen, Naval Hosp.

Arthur W. Fusco, Wheeler

John M. Gallagher, *Solace*

Capt. Wilmer E. Gallaher, *Enterprise* flight

Mrs. Joseph Gallaway, Navy housing

RMC R. L. Gamble, *Tennessee*

LeRoy V. Gamman, Ft. Shafter

Mrs. Jeanne D. Gardiner, Makalapa housing

Carey L. Garnett, *Nevada*

BM1 Thomas Garzione, *Vestal*

L. George Geiger, Hickam

Antonio Gentile, Jr., Hickam

M/Sgt. J. D. Gentry, *Pennsylvania*

Alvin Gerth, *Pennsylvania*

Fiore Gigliotti, *St. Louis*

Roy W. Gillette, Ft. Shafter

Mrs. Alice N. Gillis, Honolulu

David Wynne Gilmartin, *Utah*

ATC Frederick W. Glaeser, Ford Island

John M. Gobidas, *Rigel, Oklahoma* rescue

Daucy B. Goza, Ford Island

John D. Grabanski, *California*

Cdr. Leon Grabowski, Naval Hosp.

C. A. Grana, *California*

Capt. Lawrence C. Grannis, USN (Ret.), *Antares*

Tony J. Gregory, Schofield

MUC C. S. Griffin, *Nevada*

Edward J. Gronkowski, Hickam

A. M. Gustchen, *Honolulu*

Glenn W. Haag, *Argonne*

Robert Paul Hagen, PT boats

Ralph B. Haines, motor launch

George H. Haitle, *Maryland*

Francis L. Haley, *Nevada*

Joe Hallet, *Tautog*

Maj. Robert W. Halliday, Hickam

George W. Halterman, Hickam

LCDR Frank S. Handler, *Helm*

Joseph Patrick Hanley, *Rigel*

G. S. Hardon, *Monaghan*

Verdet Windford Harpin, *New Orleans*

Joseph C. Harsch, Waikiki

C. J. Harrold, Honolulu, Ft. Shafter

Fred C. Hart, Submarine Base

Alfred B. Hauft, Ft. Shafter

CMC Gilbert J. Hawkins, *Sacramento*

Harry Haws, *Montgomery*

Dr. Will Hayes, Waikiki, Hickam, Pearl Harbor

Mrs. Maurine K. Hayter, Alewa Heights

Maj. Gen. Leonard D. Heaton, Schofield hosp.

BMC K. V. Hendon, *Nevada*

John E. Henry, Hickam

Roy Henry, *Honolulu*

Thomas A. Henry, *Bagley*

Maurice J. Herman, Schofield

John E. Hewitt, *Widgeon*

Robert L. Hey, Hickam

Robert F. Hilbish, Schofield

Ralph F. Hinkle, Navy Yard

Carl Hoffman, Hickam

William Hole, *Medusa*

M/Sgt. John K. Hollwedel, Honolulu, Hickam

Mrs. John K. Hollwedel, Honolulu

Henry H. Homitz, Hickam

Otto Honegger, *Honolulu*

LCDR R. L. Hooton, *West Virginia*

James C. Hornberger, Jr., Ft. Shafter

Alfred D. Horne, Jr., *Pelias*

Wilbur K. Hunt, Hickam

Joseph S. Hydrusko, *Solace, Oklahoma* rescue

William T. Ingram, *Oklahoma*

R. Adm. S. S. Isquith, USN (Ret.), *Utah*

C. H. Jackson, Submarine Base

LCDR Gerald M. Jacobs, Pearl City, Ford Island

Edmond M. Jacoby, *West Virginia*

1st Lt. Haile H. Jaekel, USAF, *Salt Lake City*

John Jaskowski, Hickam

BM/1 James H. Jensen, USCG, *West Virginia*

Glenn A. Jewell, *Ontario*

CWO R. E. Johnsen, *Rigel*

Doir C. Johnson, *West Virginia*

H. G. Johnson, Schofield

James Albert Jones, motor launch

Mrs. Imogen Jones, Wahiawa

BMC R. E. Jones, *Pennsylvania*

M/Sgt. Nicholas H. Kahlefent USAF, B-17 flight

Capt. J. B. Karstein, USAF, Hickam

Warren G. Kearns, Kaneohe NAS

Lt. Col. Bernard T. Kelly, USMC, *Helena*

Maj. William T. Keogh, Ft. Shafter

Francis X. Kiefer, *Helena*

Richard L. Kile, *Avocet*

Cdr. David L. G. King, *Helena*

Howard E. King, Hickam

Lewis A. Kirk, *Honolulu*

Oliver A. Kirkeby, *Tennessee*

Charles W. Knapp, *Raleigh*

Joseph F. Kneeland, *Helena*

Richard P. Knights, *Oklahoma*

Wilbur F. Kohnle, *St. Louis*

EMC Jan Kolodziej, *Oklahoma*

James Korthe, Navy housing

Mrs. James Korthe, Navy housing

George C. Kovak, Maui, Hickam

Arnold E. Krause, *New Orleans*

Kenneth Krepps, Wheeler

Peter A. La Fata, *Swan*

James C. Lagerman, Ford Island

Mrs. Bess Lalumendier, Wheeler

William D. Land, *Tangier*

Lt. Gen. Truman H. Landon, USAF, B-17 flight

John Landreth, *Nevada*

Col. Frank H. Lane, USAF, Hickam hosp.

Glenn Harvey Lane, *Arizona*

Ansell C. LaPage, *Blue*

Lt. Gen. Claude C. Larkin, USMC (Ret.), Ewa Field

C. J. Lawrence, *Phoenix*

Howard L. Lawson, Schofield

ATC James S. Layman, Ford Island

EMC W. R. Leckemby, *Shaw*

Vance B. Leneave, *Medusa*

Charles A. Leonard, Schofield

Frank A. Lewis, *Dobbin*

Cdr. Julien E. Lindstrom, *St. Louis*

GMC Robert E. Linnartz, *Nevada*

William C. Long, *Honolulu*

Russell A. Lott, *Arizona*

Charles Lowe, *Maryland*

Jack C. Lower, Navy Yard

Jack J. Luscher, *Detroit*

William A. L. Lynch, *California*

James W. McAdams, Wheeler

William E. McCarthy, Jr., Ft. Shafter

TMC Eugene N. McClarty, *Downes*

Malcolm J. McCleary, *Oklahoma*

J. E. McColgan, Ford Island

Dr. H. P. McCrimmon, Kaneohe NAS

Mrs. A. C. McCullaugh, Navy housing

W. Payton McDaniel, *Nevada*

James H. McDonough, Honolulu

R. Adm. John M. McIsaac, USN (Ret.), *MacDonough*

Lt. Oden L. McMillan, USN, *Nevada*

Robert L. McMurray, *St. Louis*

Kenneth Magee, Hickam

Fleet Chaplain William A. Maguire, Pearl Harbor

Cdr. Everett A. Malcolm, *Arizona*

TDC Cecil S. Malmin, Kaneohe NAS

TDC Thomas S. Malmin, Ford Island

LeRoy G. Maltby, Kaneohe NAS

Guido J. Mambretti, Hickam

Charles Mandell, *Maryland*

Aloysius J. Manuszewski, Schofield

Vern L. Marcum, Schofield

Donald J. Marman, *Honolulu*

Orion C. May, *San Francisco*

Mrs. Hall Mayfield, Makalapa housing

ALC Harry R. Mead, Ford Island

Stanley Meldrum, Schofield

Cdr. Charles J. Merdinger, *Nevada*

Kenneth M. Merrill, Hickam

Mrs. Annette E. Merritt, Honolulu

Joseph C. Messier, *Helena*

Charles J. Michaels, Jr., *Swan*

Harvey H. Milhorn, *Arizona*

Edward Miller, Submarine Base

Russell F. Miller, *Maryland*

Walter Miller, Jr., tug in Pearl Harbor

JOC William J. Miller, *Castor*

Albert J. Miskuf, *Helena*

Albert H. Molter, Ford Island

M. G. Montessoro, *Castor*

Joseph T. Moore, Hickam

Rev. F. E. Morgan, Pearl Harbor

L. A. Morley, *Honolulu*

Shirl P. Morrill, *Pennsylvania*

ADC Russell C. Morse, Ford Island

Lt. (j.g.) Don Morton, Pearl City

George Murphy, Jr., *Oklahoma*

John A. Murphy, *Vestal*

Howard E. Myers, *St. Louis*

Charlie Ross Naylor, *Breese*

George L. Newton, Jr., B-17 flight

Joseph F. Nickson, *San Francisco*

R. N. Nilssen, Kanehoe NAS

Raymond B. Nolde, *Ward*

Quentin P. Norcutt, *St. Louis*

J. Harold North, *Maryland*

John R. Nugent, Schofield

Burdette E. Odekirk, *Maryland*

Robert A. Oborne, Jr., Ford Island

Edward F. J. O'Brion, *Arizona*

Carroll J. Oliver, *Pennsylvania*

Persifor S. Oliver, *Bagley*

Edward M. Oveka, Hickam

BMC Allen S. Owens, *Nevada*

John E. Parrott, *San Francisco*

Gilbert R. Patten, *Nevada*

Maj. Earl S. Patton, USAF, deep-sea fishing

GMC L. R. Peacock, *Enterprise* patrol boat

Capt. Carl A. Peterson, USN, *California*

Robert J. Peth, Ford Island

Emmett Pethoud, Jr., Hickam

R. Adm. John S. Phillips, USN (Ret.), *Neosho*

John F. Plassio, Wheeler

ADC Henry Popko, Kaneohe NAS

James H. Power, Jr., *Pennsylvania*

William Power, *West Virginia*

ADC William N. Powers, *Neosho*

Louis A. Puckett, Navy Yard

Charles T. Putnam, Navy tug

CPO Harand N. Quisdorf, Ford Island

Stanley H. Rabe, harbor craft

James G. Raines, *Curtiss*

M/Sgt. Walter T. Raisner, USAF, Schofield

Lt. Col. R. L. Ramsay, USAF, B-17 flight

R. Adm. Logan C. Ramsey, USN (Ret.), Ford Island

Weldon V. Rash, *St. Louis*

Waldo H. Rathman, *Whitney*

Lt. Col. Ernest L. Reid, USAF, B-17 flight

Glenn Homer Robinson, *Oklahoma*

Joseph H. Robinson, *Mac-Donough*

Robert J. Robinson, Ft. Shafter

E. H. Robison, Pearl Harbor Marine Barracks

Don E. Rodenberger, *Oglala*

Jack Rogo, Ford Island

F. A. Rogue, *San Francisco*

John J. Romanczyk, *Vestal*

Mrs. Alexander Rowell, Pearl City, Red Hill

Raymond G. Roy, *Selfridge*

Vernon C. Rubenking, Wheeler

Millard J. Rucoi, *Pennsylvania*

George J. Sallet, *Bagley*

W. V. Samples, Honolulu, Navy Yard

Brig. Gen. LaVerne G. Saunders, USAF, Hickam

HMC T. A. Sawyer, *Solace*

Albert F. Sandall, *Oklahoma*

George Santella, *Allen*

Cdr. D. S. Schroeder, Pearl Harbor

Walter H. Schuh, *Maryland*

Raymond Senecal, Schofield

Marion T. Shepherd, Hickam

M/Sgt. John P. Sherwood, Hickam

Bert F. Shipley, Hickam

Thomas F. Shook, Jr., *Phoenix*

Carl W. Shrader, Wheeler

Capt. W. B. Sieglaff, USN, *Tautog*

R. Adm. R. B. Simons, USN (Ret.), *Raleigh*

CPO Walter Simmons, Kaneohe NAS

Eldon E. Smart, Pearl Harbor

Capt. Billie J. Smith, USAF, Hickam

YNC George B. Smith, *Oklahoma*

Gordon F. Smith, Wheeler

CWO Hugh W. Smith, Jr., Navy Receiving Sta.

Joseph W. Smith, *Dale*

Ray C. Smith, *Vestal*

Robert W. Snyder, *Detroit*

Frederick Sommer, Schofield

James A. Spagnola, Navy Yard

Capt. Paul E. Spangler, USN, Naval Hosp.

Mrs. Paul E. Spangler, Alewa Heights

Mrs. Jackie Bennett Sprague, Hickam housing

Leonard M. Stagich, *Montgomery*

Arnold J. Stengtein, *Nevada*

Mrs. Barry Fox Stevens, Kaneohe Bay

Virgil A. Stewart, Hickam

John G. Stirnemann, *Solace*

Frank P. Stock, *Vestal*

Capt. Herald F. Stout, USN, *Montgomery*

Anthony Sudano, Pearl Harbor

Douglas Sugate, *Medusa*

Charles A. Super, *Mac-Donough*

John Swanson, Submarine Base

Capt. H. E. Swinney, USAF, Hickam

Cdr. William P. Tanner, PBY patrol

Homer R. Taylor, B-17 flight

Hoyle A. Taylor, *San Francisco*

William E. Taylor, *Phelps*

Gordon E. Tengwall, *Oklahoma*

R Adm. William R. Terrell, USN (Ret.), *Tucker*

R. Adm. Francis J. Thomas, USNR (Ret.), *Nevada*

J. H. Thompson, Hickam

Luther Thompson, Hickam

Mrs. Margrett S. Timmons, Waikiki

E. A. Titsworth, Hickam

A. M. Townsend, *St. Louis*

Mrs. A. M. Townsend, Honolulu

CTC Earle K. Van Buskirk, Ford Island

BMGC Elmer A. Vandenberg, *Solace*

JOC H. C. Varner, *Rigel*

LCDR Valera C. Vaubel, Naval Hosp.

QMC Edward M. Vecera, *West Virginia*

Mrs. Robert B. Vokac, Schofield housing

R. A. Wadsworth, *Vestal*

Mrs. Ellison Wallace, Tripler

Cdr. W. G. Wallace, St. Louis

Mrs. W. G. Wallace, Honolulu

Maj. Leo G. Wears, USMC, *Oklahoma*

Harold R. Webb, *Nevada*

Paul J. Weisenberger, *Helena*

Mrs. Elizabeth S. White, Honolulu

EN1 Robert W. White, *Ontario*

QMC Robert J. Whited, *Antares*

Ralph E. Wiley, Hickam hosp.

Frank B. Wilkes, *Tangier*

Warren S. Wilkinson, Hickam

Donald R. Williams, *Argonne*

Robert D. Williams, Wheeler

John W. Wilson, Hickam

V. Adm. L. J. Wiltse, USN (Ret.), *Detroit*

Blaine K. Wolff, *Narwhal*

Henry T. Wray, *Argonne*

Charles A. Yokom, PT boats

Stephen B. Young, *Oklahoma*

Adolph J. Zlabis, *Vestal*

INDEX

235

THIS
VIOLENT CENTURY

Bantam War Books Tell the Story
of Military Conflicts Throughout the World

1 9 1 8

April 21   Baron Manfred von Richthofen's career comes to an end. *A History of the Luftwaffe* by John Killen.

1 9 1 9

Jan. 1   More than a thousand Soviet troops attack American soldiers entrenched around the village of Nijni Gora in northern Russia. *The Ignorant Armies.*

1 9 2 7

Oct. 18   HMS *L 4*, a British submarine under the command of Lt. Frederick J. C. Halahan, R.N., rescues the crew and passengers of the SS *Irene* from Chinese river pirates. *Submarine Warriors* by Edwyn Gray.

1932

Dec. 26   Chesty Puller drives off sandinista "bandits" who are attacking his train just outside El Sauce, Nicaragua. *Marine! The Life of Chesty Puller* by Burke Davis.

1937

April 10   German bombers attack the Spanish town of Guernica. It is the town's market day and 1,600 civilians die. *Full Circle* by Air Vice Marshal J. E. Johnson.

Aug. 17   Having missed their fighter escort, eleven out of twelve Japanese carrier-based attack bombers are shot down over Hangchow by defending Chinese fighter planes. *The Ragged, Rugged Warriors* by Martin Caidin.

1939

Sept. 14   The author, a young British aviator, is called to active duty. It is going to be a very long war. *Tale of a Guinea Pig* by Geoffrey Page.

1940

April 7   HMS *Sealion* in the middle of the German invasion fleet on its way to Norway watches the ships sail past. Rules of engagement prevent an attack. *Submarine Commander* by Ben Bryant.

May 10   The Phony War is over. German troops invade Belgium and Holland. *Churchill and His Generals* by Barrie Pitt.

Sept. 15   The critical day in the Battle of Britain. The Luftwaffe is beaten back from her daylight skies and Stanford Tuck, one of Britain's greatest air aces, shoots down a German Me 100. *Fly for Your Life* by Larry Forrester.

Nov. 11   British Swordfish torpedo bombers attack the Italian fleet anchored in the harbor of Taranto. *To War in a String Bag* by Charles Lamb.

<u>1 9 4 1</u>

March 15   A hunter killer group commanded by Captain Donald MacIntyre sinks a U-99 and captures its captain, submarine ace Otto Kretschmer. *U-Boat Killer* by Donald MacIntyre.

April 16   Egyptian liner *Zamzam* sunk in South Atlantic by German surface raiders. *The German Raider Atlantis*, Rogge & Frank.

May 24   "I turned around to look for *Hood* and stared and stared and stared. It was clear to the horizon and *Hood* was no longer there. She'd had a crew of nearly fifteen hundred. Three of them survived." *Heart of Oak* by Tristan Jones.

May 27   German battleship *Bismarck* sunk. HMS *Hood* is avenged. *Pursuit* by Ludovic Kennedy.

July 4   The 10th Gurkhas with the 2nd Bn. of the 4th in reserve attack Vichy French and Syrian troops defending Deir-es-Zor, Syria. *The Road Past Mandalay* by John Masters.

Aug. 9   Douglas Bader loses a leg as his fighter plane is shot down over France. Fortunately it was one of his two artificial ones. *Reach for the Sky* by Paul Brickhill.

Oct. 31   U.S. destroyer *Rubin James* sunk by German submarine. *Tin Cans* by Theodore Roscoe.

Nov. 22   Major Robert Crisp fights his "Honey" tank against Rommel's panzers at Sidi-Rezegh in the North African desert. *Brazen Chariots* by Donald Crisp.

Dec. 7   Japanese carrier-based aircraft attack the U.S. fleet at Pearl Harbor. *Day of Infamy* by Walter Lord.

Dec. 24   The gallant defenders of Wake Island are overwhelmed by a Japanese amphibious landing force. *The Story of Wake Island* by Brig. Gen. James P. S. Devereux.

Dec. 27   British and Norwegian commandos attack the German garrison at Vaagso, Norway. *The Vaagso Raid* by Joseph H. Devins, Jr.

1942

Jan. 27   Lt. Commander Joe Grenfiel, commanding USS *Gudgeon*, sinks the Japanese submarine *I-173* near Midway Island. *Combat Patrol* by Clay Blair, Jr.

Feb. 8   From the embattled fortress of Corregidor the submarine USS *Trout* loads two tons of gold bars and 18 tons of silver pesos for transport to Pearl Harbor. *Pig Boats* by Theodore Roscoe.

Feb. 11   Three German capital ships are making a run from the French port of Brest up the English Channel toward a safe haven in Germany. *Breakout!* by John Deane Potter.

March 6   Operation Nordpol commences with the capture of a British radio operator in Holland by Abwehr personnel. The problem now is to turn the agent so that he sends false messages to England. *London Calling North Pole* by H. J. Giskes.

May 8   British commandos blast their way into St. Nazaire harbor so as to destroy the Normandy dock. *The Greatest Raid of All* by C. E. Lucas Phillips.

June 1   Captain Frederic John Walker, R.N., in *Starling,* with *Wild Goose* and *Kite* in support as a hunter killer group stalk Captain Poser's *U-202*. This German submarine is hidden 800 feet below them in the depths of the Atlantic. *Escort Commander* by T. Robertson.

June 4   Nazi General Reinhard Heydrich dies of wounds received on May 27 when his car was bombed by Czech OSS agents. His side had neglected to develop penicillin. *Seven Men at Daybreak* by **Alan Burgess.**

June 16   Sub. Lt. C. L. Page captured and then executed by the Japanese. He'd stayed behind as a coastwatcher to radio intelligence reports on Japanese troop and naval movements from the Tabar Islands to Australia. *The Coast Watchers* by **Eric A. Feldt.**

June 21   Rommel captures the British North African fortress of Tobruk. *With Rommel in the Desert* by **H. W. Schmidt.**

June 27   Russian submarine *K-21* fires a spread of four torpedoes at the German battleship *Tirpitz*. *Russian Submarines in Arctic Waters* by I. Kolyshkin.

July 27   Special Air Service jeeps destroy Rommel's precious Ju 52 transport planes at Sidi Haneish airfield in North Africa. *Stirling's Desert Raiders* by **Virginia Cowles.**

Aug. 7   U.S. marines land on Guadalcanal. *The Battle for Guadalcanal* by **Samuel B. Griffith II.**

Aug. 8   Wounded and nearly blind, Japanese ace Saburo Sakai nurses a shattered Zero fighter over five hundred miles of ocean after attacking the Americans on Guadalcanal. *Samurai* by **Sakai and Roger Pineau.**

Aug. 9   British bombers lay mines in the Channel to block the *Prince Eugen* from the Atlantic. *Enemy Coast Ahead* by **Guy Gibson.**

Aug. 15   The American tanker *Ohio* finally docks at the besieged island of Malta in the Mediterranean. *Red Duster, White Ensign* by Ian Cameron.

Sept. 13   Over the North African desert, German ace Hans-Joachim, "The Star of Africa," with 158 victories, dies as he fails to successfully exit his burning Me 109. *Horrido!* by Raymond F. Toliver and Trevor J. Constable.

Sept. 17   Admiral Donetz secretly orders his U-boat commanders not to attempt to assist or reach the survivors of their attacks. *The Laconia Affair* by Leonce Peillard.

Oct. 4   British motor torpedo boats in battle action against German convoys off the Dutch coast. *Night Action* by Peter Dickens.

Dec. 11   British commandos who had paddled their fold-a-boats through sixty miles of German-occupied territory mine and sink several large German merchant ships tied up in the French harbor of Bordeaux. *Cockleshell Heroes* by Lucas-Phillips.

---

1 9 4 3

Jan. 31   General Von Paulus surrenders the German 6th Army at Stalingrad. *Enemy at the Gates* by Walter Craig.

Feb. 7   Commander Howard W. Gilmore, wounded on the bridge of the USS *Growler,* gives the order, "Take her down." He dies but his ship survives. *Sink 'Em All* by Charles A. Lockwood.

Feb. 26   British agent Yeo-Thomas, "The White Rabbit," parachutes behind German lines into occupied France. *The White Rabbit* by Bruce Marshall.

Feb. 28   Norwegian commandos sabotage the heavy-water plant at Vemork, Norway. *Assault in Norway* by Thomas Gallagher.

March 30   Upon landing in Norway, his unit is destroyed by the Germans and this Norwegian commando, Jan Baalsrud, embarks on an incredible journey of survival. *We Die Alone* by Horwith.

May 12   The German Afrika Korps in Tunisia surrenders. One unit, the 164th Light Afrika Division, fights on until the following day. *The Foxes of the Desert* by Paul Carell.

May 16   Lt. Machorton returns to Imphal from the jungles of Burma. Wounded, he had been left to die. *The Hundred Days of Lt. Machorton* by Machorton and Henry Maule.

May 17   Guy Gibson and Squadron 617 destroy the Moehne and Eder dams. *The Dam Busters* by Paul Brickhill.

May 30   Although American troops have secured the island of Attu in the Aleutians, individual Japanese defenders still lurk in the surrounding hills. *The Thousand Miles War* by Brian Garfield.

July 8   Rudel's cannon-firing Stuka takes part in the biggest tank battle of World War II, Kursk, Russia. *Stuka Pilot* by Hans Ulrich Rudel.

July 11   Allied troops invade Sicily. *One More Hill* by Franklyn A. Johnson.

July 11   General George Patton is very much there too. *War As I Knew It* by George S. Patton.

July 27   The German city of Hamburg is consumed by a firestorm. *The Night Hamburg Died* by Martin Caidin.

Aug. 17   British bombers attack the German doomsday missile development base at Peenemünde. *V-2* by Walter Dornberger.

Sept. 9   Fresh from his triumphs in North Africa, Popski along with his jeeps is landed in Teranto harbor by the USS *Boise* so that his private army can commence its invasion of Italy. *Popski's Private Army* by Lt. Col. Peniakoff.

Sept. 12   Colonel Skorzeny rescues Mussolini. *Commando Extraordinary* by Charles Foley.

Sept. 14   Russ Carter parachutes into Paestum, which is just south of the Salerno beachhead. *Those Devils in Baggy Pants* by Russ Carter.

Oct. 11   Running on the surface in La Pérouse Strait, one of America's greatest submarines fails to survive an attack by Japanese aircraft. *Wahoo: The Patrols of America's Most Famous World War II Submarine* by Rear Admiral Richard H. O'Kane (Ret.).

Oct. 14   The Schweinfurt Ball Bearing works were the target. Sixty B-17s failed to return from it. *Black Thursday* by Martin Caidin.

Oct. 29   Three British POWs escape from Stalag-Luft III. *The Wooden Horse* by Eric Williams.

Nov. 2   American destroyers in battle action against the navy of Imperial Japan at the Battle of Empress Augusta Bay. *Admiral Arleigh (31 Knot) Burke* by Ken Jones and Hubert Kelley.

Nov. 5   Donald R. Burgett wins his paratrooper wings. *As Eagles Screamed* by Donald R. Burgett.

Nov. 13   The Japanese battleship *Hiei* goes to the bottom, sunk by marine and navy airmen. *The Cactus Air Force* by Thomas G. Miller, Jr.

Nov. 20   American marines land on the Japanese island of Tarawa. *Tarawa* by Robert Sherrod.

Dec. 2   Bari, Italy. German bombers sink twenty Allied merchant ships, and a deadly, secret cargo is released. *Disaster at Bari* by Glen Infield.

1944

Jan. 3   "Pappy," after chalking up 25 victories gets shot down over Rabaul. *Baa, Baa, Black Sheep* by Gregory "Pappy" Boyington.

Feb. 1 American and Filipino guerrillas launch an offensive against the Japanese. *American Guerrilla in the Philippines* by Ira Wolfert.

Feb. 22 Heinz Knoke shoots down a B-17 Flying Fortress over his home town of Hameln, Germany. *I Flew for the Führer* by Heinz Knoke.

March 5 Brig. Tom Churchill takes command on the island of Vis in the Adriatic Sea. *Commando Force 133* by Bill Strutton.

March 18 Chindit units battle hand to hand with the Japanese invaders of Burma. *Fighting Mad* by "Mad" Mike Calvert.

March 20 USS *Angler* surfaces off Panay Island in the Japanese-occupied Philippines to rescue 58 refugees. *Guerrilla Submarines* by Ed Dissette.

April 13 Over Hamburg, Germany, an FW 190 becomes the author's 25th aerial victory. *Thunderbolt* by Robert S. Johnson, with Martin Caidin.

June 6 In the first minutes of this day the green light goes on in a C-47 flying over the Cherbourg peninsula. *As Eagles Screamed* by Donald R. Burgett. *D-Day* by David Howarth

June 9 Normandy beachhead. Keith Douglas KIA near Tilly-sur-Seulles. *Alamein to Zem Zem* by Keith Douglas.

June 22 An American pilot uses a 1,000-pound bomb to cure a long-standing rat problem in his old barracks now occupied by the Japanese. *Into the Teeth of the Tiger* by Donald S. Lopez.

June 24 Marine General "Howlin' Mad" Smith relieves Major General Ralph Smith from command of the 27th Infantry Division on the island of Saipan. *Coral and Brass* by General Holland "Howling Mad" Smith.

June 25 German ace Robert Spreckels shoots down British ace J.R.D. Braham in air combat over Denmark. *Night Fighter by J.R.D. Braham.*

June 26 The French port of Cherbourg falls to Allied invasion forces. *Invasion: They're Coming!* **by Paul Carell.**

June 29 An SS squadron in Russia on the Mogilev-Minsk road is shooting German officers found to be moving toward the rear without proper written orders. *The Black March* **by Peter Neumann.**

July 18 The city of St. Lô is finally secured. *The Clay Pigeons of St. Lô* **by Grover S. Johns, Jr.**

Aug. 15 Operation "Anvil," the Allied landing in the South of France. "The best invasion I ever attended." *Up Front* **by Bill Mauldin.**

Sept. 15 A young marine goes ashore on Peleliu Island which was one of the most bitterly contested of the Pacific island landings. *Helmet for My Pillow* **by Robert Leckie.**

Sept. 17 Disguised as a slave laborer, British Sgt. Charles Coward, a prisoner of war in Germany, has just spent the night in hell, locked inside the Auschwitz concentration camp. He now knows the secret of the camp and has vowed to tell it to the world. *The Password Is Courage* **by John Castle.**

Oct. 3 A young infantry captain enters Germany. It is 11:15 A.M. and the war in Europe is a long way from being over. *Company Commander* **by Charles MacDonald.**

Oct. 25 Lt. Seki successfully crashes his plane into the USS *St. Lô* (CVE-63) and sends this escort carrier to the bottom. *The Divine Wind* **by Roger Pineau.**

Having attacked a Japanese convoy with unbelievable ferocity, *Tang* fires a final misfunctioning torpedo which turns back and sinks this famous submarine. *Clear the Bridge* **by Richard O'Kane.**

Nov. 26   If you have ever wondered where some of our best writers are. Flying a P-51 on an escort mission over Hanover, Germany, Bert Stiles is KIA. *Serenade to the Big Bird* by Bert Stiles.

1 9 4 5

Jan. 4   The 761st Tank Bn. attacks the town of Tillet. It is just to the west of Bastogne. *Hit Hard* by David J. Williams.

Feb. 3   Convoy JW-64 sails north from England on its way to Russia. *A Bloody War, 1939–45* by Hal Lawrence.

Feb. 23   U.S. marines raise the American flag on the peak of Mt. Suribachi. *Iwo Jima* by Richard Newcomb.

Feb. 28   Company K attacks the town of Hardt just to the west of Düsseldorf, Germany. *The Men of Company "K"* by Leinbaugh and Campbell.

March 15   Bob Clark, Clostermann's No. 4, flying a Hawker Tempest, shoots down an Me 262 piloted by Walter Nowotney, one of the Luftwaffe's greatest aces. *The Big Show* by Pierre Clostermann.

April 1   The Japanese island of Okinawa is invaded. *Okinawa: Typhoon of Steel* by Belote and Belote.

April 16   A German steamship with 7,000 evacuees aboard is sunk outside of Hela, Prussia, by a Russian submarine. There are 170 survivors. *Defeat in the East* by J. Thorwald.

April 26   Adolph Galand leads a flight of Me 262 jet fighters in one of the last air battles of the European war. *The First and the Last* by Adolph Galand.

April 29   General Patton climbs down from one of his tanks to liberate the American POW camp of Mooseburg in Germany. *Prisoner of War* by Kenneth W. Simmons.

April 30   British "Crocodile" flame-throwing tanks take up positions outside the German town of Oldenburg. *Flame Thrower* by Andrew Wilson.

May 3   American armor overruns Jagvelband 44 at Salzburg-Maxglan, Germany, and the war is over for this squadron of futuristic German fighters. *Rocket Fighter* by Mano Ziegler.

May 8   German ace Erich Hartman chalks up his 352nd and final aerial victory. *Horrido!* by Raymond F. Toliver and Trevor J. Constable.

May 8   On a leave train bound for the South of France, the author learns that the war in Europe, at long last, is officially over. *To Hell and Back* by Audie Murphy.

June 2   The USS *Tinosa* recovers the crew of a ditched B-29 just south of the Japanese island of Kyushu. *Sink 'Em All* by Charles A. Lockwood.

June 21   The Japanese commander on Okinawa, General Ushijima, commits suicide. *Marine at War* by Russell Davis.

    The U.S. high command declares Okinawa to be secured. *With the Old Breed* by Eugene B. Sledge (April 1991).

June 22   With her last two torpedoes, and just before heading home, USS *Crevalle* sinks a Japanese destroyer. *Hellcats of the Sea* by Lockwood and Adamson.

July 25   U.S. carrier aircraft raids Japan's Kure naval base, destroying or damaging most of what was left of the Imperial fleet. *Combat Command* by Frederick C. Sherman.

July 30   Japanese submarine *I-58* sinks the USS *Indianapolis*. *Abandon Ship!* by Richard E. Newcomb.

Aug. 17   A German U-boat commander surrenders to the Argentinian navy only to be accused of having brought Hitler to Antarctica. *U-Boat 977* by Heinz Schaeffer.

Sept. 2   General Wainwright, recently released from a Japanese POW camp, is present on the deck of the USS *Missouri* as the Japanese formally surrender. *General Wainwright's Story* **by General Jonathan M. Wainwright. Edited by Robert Considine.**

Sept. 11   After three and a half years of imprisonment, Australian soldiers and American sailors liberate the Kuching prison camp in North Borneo. *Three Came Home* **by Agnes Newton Keith.**

1 9 5 0

June 25   The North Korean army moves south and the world is once more at war. *This Kind of War* **by T. R. Fehrenbach.**

Dec. 10   Their breakthrough is now completed, and the marines who fought their way down from the Chosin Reservoir are finally in the clear. *The March to Glory* **by Robert Leckie.**

1 9 5 1

April 22   In the Battle of Solma-Ri, waves of Chinese infantry engulf the British Gloucester regiment. The survivors fight their way out to the south. *Now Thrives the Armourers* **by Robert O. Holles.**

1 9 5 5

Jan. 4   On the Foum-Toub-Arris road four men are ambushed and burnt to death in their jeep by Algerian rebel forces. *The War in Algeria* **by Pierre Leulliette.**

1956

Oct. 10 Dedean Kimathi, the most wanted Mau Mau terrorist, is taken by four Kikuyu tribal policemen. *Manhunt in Kenya* by Sir Philip Goodhart and Ian Henderson.

1958

April 5 A 28-year-old police constable accepts the surrender of Hor Lung, the last of the top level Chinese Communist leaders at large in Malaya. *The War of the Running Dogs* by Noel Barber.

1963

June 11 A Buddhist monk burns himself to death on a street corner in Saigon. *The New Face of War* by Malcolm Browne.

1964

Nov. 24 Belgian Paras and the Lima One Flying Column of mercenaries save the lives of a thousand hostages in the Congo. *Save the Hostages* by David Reed.

1965

May 15 *SR-71,* the legendary recon U.S. aircraft, sets an 80,000-foot Mach 3.12 record. Twenty-five years later the *New York Times,* on February 24, 1990, reports that the air force will retire it. *Air War Vietnam* by Frank Harvey.

June 17   Navy Phantoms shoot down the first MiGs to be destroyed over Vietnam. *The Story of Air Fighting* by J. E. Johnson.

Dec. 18   Air cavalrymen are going into a hot landing zone at Ben Khe, Vietnam. *Year of the Horse—Vietnam* by Col. Kenneth D. Mertel.

1 9 6 6

Jan. 17   A B-52 collides with its KC-135 tanker and a hydrogen bomb is lost. *One of Our H-Bombs Is Missing!* by Flora Lewis.

Oct. 13   A navy flyer's wife receives a telegram listing her husband as MIA. His plane was seen to explode over enemy-occupied territory. No parachute was observed and no radio distress calls were received. *Touring Nam* by Greenburg and Norton.

1 9 6 7

Sept. 15   The Brown Water Navy's Force 117 goes into battle along the Rach Ba Rai against the 263rd Vietcong Main Force Bn. *Seven Firefights in Vietnam* by John A. Cash, John Albright, and Allan W. Sandstrum.

1 9 6 8

Jan. 29   The Tet offensive starts and a marine doctor has no clue as to what the next two days will bring. *12, 20 & 5, a Doctor's Year in Vietnam* by John A. Parrish, M.D.

Feb. 25   Khe Sanh. A marine patrol is ambushed. One third of it returns to the perimeter. *Welcome to Vietnam, Macho Man* by Ernest Spencer.

July 3   A long year starts for an American soldier who has just landed in Vietnam. *One Soldier* by John Shook.

Nov. 15   Near Binh Tri village a scout dog finds a Vietcong mine. Casualties: dead 1 dog, 1 PRU, 12 others wounded. *The Advisor* by John L. Cook.

1 9 7 0

Oct. 10   There is a patrol just outside the village of Truong Lam, and the word is "Incoming!" *Platoon Leader* by James R. McDonough.

1 9 7 2

April 1   An EB-66 meets a SAM 2 just south of the DMZ and the co-pilot punches out at 30,000 feet. *Bat-21* by William C. Anderson.